# The Samplist

## Francis Ellen

*Ronak Publishing*

Published by Ronak Publishing

A CIP catalogue record for this book is available from the British Library

ISBN: 0-9548031-0-8

Printed and bound in Great Britain

Ronak Publishing
PO Box 16814
Glasgow G12 0ZB
Scotland, UK

http://www.ronak-publishing.com
admin@ronak-publishing.com

Typeset by Gravvo, Glasgow. Cover design by Farzeen

*Ronak*
*Publishing*

*For my mother*
*For my wife*
*For my son*

To Nat & Dave, and Robert Sinclair, and to my father

Special thanks:

Pat Shove
Yo Tomita
Tom Hopkins & Amy Jones

# ONE

TWO poe-faced girls carrying miniature executive briefcases squeezed past Alex as he watched Skuggs fight the revolving doors for possession of the giant papoose strapped to his back. Straining forward, his head poking out of his parka, it never occurred to Skuggs to do anything but pull as hard as he could until he and his tuba popped out onto the street.

"Stuck again Skuggs? You know, you're really going to have to take up piccolo," said Alex.

There were two virtuosos at the Academy and Skuggs was one of them. His mastery went far beyond the trouser-flapping oompahs normally associated with the instrument. He could float a melody over a bass line with such precision he sounded like two people playing, and the power of his lower register would embarrass the soundman at a Motorhead concert.

He unplugged himself. "Ah need gas."

Skuggs had somehow got the idea that his intake of beer was related to his ability to play the tuba. He believed he needed the fizzy stuff in beer: the carbon dioxide, the bubbles, the gas. He thought that every blast, every puff, every delicate wisp of moistened air that left his body was energized by this wonder-fuel.

"Jar?"

"Skuggs, it's nine-thirty in the morning."

He tightened the straps of his tuba case, gave Alex a slap on the back then chugged off to wait for the pubs to open.

Skuggs was Alex's flatmate. He never paid rent, but then he hardly used the flat. Where he spent his nights when he wasn't crashed on Alex's couch was anybody's guess, but Alex liked him; more than that, he respected his intelligence. As big as a bear with crazy, piercing eyes always peering out of the hood of his oversized parka, most people thought Skuggs strange. He was strange all right, but Alex knew that his talent for the tuba was not an isolated aberration. Whatever it was that powered his musical gifts sometimes spilled over into the rest of life—not often, but enough for Alex to realize that Skuggs might come in handy when some deep thinking was required.

In a previous life Alex himself was considered a deep thinker, but that was in a previous life. In this life he was a pianist and, judging by his grades, he was not much of a pianist either.

Alex fought his way into the Academy against a stream of oncoming traffic. It was exam day. Every room, every available space, would be filled with musicians filled with nervous energy.

The foyer was throbbing in a dissonant cacophony of excited anticipation. Frantic stories of last minute fine-tuning and double shifts of intensive practice rang round the marble walls like frightened melodies in a Stockhausen chamber work. Alex looked for a safe route to the staircase, which was no more than thirty feet away but on the other side of the seething overspill from the overcrowded practice rooms. A panic-stricken girl sawed scales on air-violin. Five young men, sporting identically barbered beards, huddled together blowing fartily into mouthpieces. A trumpeter buzzed up and down while a little figure beside him rapped out make-believe timpani rolls. A large youth stood next to Alex, eyes closed, miming a trombone cadenza.

Alex spotted the blond with the breasts.

A searing pain shot through his eye. "Terribly sorry. I'm terribly sorry," said the large youth who'd missed a low note on virtual-trombone and smacked Alex upside his head.

"Go to a practice room and do that, fucking lunatic!"

"I said I was sorry. There *are* no practice rooms. Exam day. There's no need to swear."

Alex made his way, gingerly, through the mêlée, avoiding low blows from cellists, and onto the stairs. I need to pee, he thought.

Two spunky trumpeteers had claimed the washroom and were blaring out Flight of the Bumblebee in syncopated canon. Alex jammed his hands over his ears and wondered how he was going to relieve himself without suffering inner-ear damage. The decibel level tailed off as one of the trumpeters blew breathily into his trumpet while pressing a little key at the far end of the instrument's plumbing. A spinning wad of saliva shot out of the little hole exposed by the open key and pirouetted downwards before splattering onto Alex's shoe.

"Cheers," said Alex.

"No problem," replied the trumpeter before launching back into the Bumblebee.

"Hi girls! It's only me," he announced as he flung open the ladies washroom door. Three of the four cubicles were open, each occupied by a girl playing cello. The girl in the first cubicle stopped to watch him grab a tissue and clean his shoe.

"Practicing some novel bowing angles I see," said Alex.

"Is there a man in here?" came a voice from the locked cubicle.

"Bloody practice rooms," said the girl in the first cubicle. "It's always the bloody same. If you don't get in here by eight you have to practice in the shitehouse."

"You couldn't give a minute could you?"

"Sure, I've a counterpoint tutorial in five minutes." She loosened her bow.

"There is a man in here. Get out you pervert!" warbled the locked cubicle.

"It's okay," he shouted, "just two minutes! I have to hand in a semen sample to the bursar's office. Just you go right ahead and finish your…" he made a face, pinched his nose, and fanned the air, "composition." The girls in the open cubicles laughed.

"Get out! Get out! I'm going to report you," cried the locked cubicle.

"Go ahead. My name is Martin Watson, third-year guitar."

"You'd better be careful Alex," said the girl from the first cubicle, sotto voce, as she packed away her cello. "McNabb wants your arse."

Alex was not a fitness fanatic. It was five regular floors up before you even got to the door leading to the staircase that led to the trombone room. No one used the trombone room except her. That's where she'd be. That's where she always was. Even on exam day it was unlikely that any intrepid tromboner would venture seven floors to the trombone room where they would have to contend with her while in a state of mild oxygen starvation. It was her territory. She *owned* the trombone room. He stopped on the sixth floor to catch his breath and have a quick smoke.

Something resembling Tchaikovsky's Violin Concerto cut through the air as he approached. He stared, mesmerized, through the small window cut in the door. Her face, contorted in nervous tension, matched the landscape of harmonic clams leaping boldly from her instrument. She battled on despite an avalanche of errors. It made him love her even more. He burst into the room, arms open, in expectation of giant hugs.

"Here I am!"

She didn't miss a beat. A muscle in her neck bulged. Her top lip curled. The movement of her bowing arm became more mechanical. Her tone deteriorated. Beads of sweat glistened on her forehead. But on she went. She was a performing machine. Nothing, but nothing, could stop her once she got started. Alex sat at the Steinway and doodled some Beethoven. "Why don't you take all your clothes off and let me ogle you?" he offered.

On she went. Her red nylon sweater betrayed the movement of her breasts in proud counterpoint to the accuracy of her playing.

She had a body men kill for and women covet. She had a high rib cage with ample breasts sitting firmly above a tiny waist that flared out generously to form a derriere that black girls would brag about. Her small belly was proportionately justified to the curve of her perfect thighs, which were now locked together in sympathetic harmony with her tension. She had a classic, hourglass figure—not unlike the instrument she was torturing so mercilessly.

Do people look like their instruments the way they look like their dogs? Alex wondered. But then she really didn't look like a violin. She looked more like a viola—not quite as chubby or rounded as a cello, not as petite and fragile as a violin.

She stopped playing and, with her violin still under her chin, flicked through the manuscript in front of her. "You know," he said, "I can help you with your problem. And you could help me with mine."

She dropped some manuscript onto the music stand and charged into Bach's great Chaconne.

# Two

 Elliot got his guitar out, dropped some soiled manuscript onto the music stand and sat down to wait for Peter, the guitar professor, to arrive with Andre Boskov from the Royal Northern College. He fingered the large Band-Aid he'd slapped on his forehead after giving the bust of Beethoven on the third-floor landing a Glasgow Kiss. It wasn't the first time that Elliot had engaged in violent behaviour towards the busts of great composers dotted around the Academy. Elliot felt that Beethoven needed a stiff kicking, regardless of whether he was deaf or not. He hated Beethoven's bouffant.

Elliot was a Chinese Liverpudlian who went to music college to avoid working. He spoke no Chinese whatever but was fluent in Scouse. He took up guitar while he was on the dole and had secured a scholarship to study at the Academy after practicing almost without pause for fifteen months. Elliot was the Academy's other virtuoso but, unlike Skuggs, who was denied proper acknowledgement for playing an instrument of low status, Elliot's skills were shrouded in attitude problems. Peter was taking heat from the faculty on this point, and Elliot's attacks on the busts had been noticed.

Peter entered with a small, thin man, his face hidden by thick-rimmed glasses, wild matted hair and a beard that started just under the eyes. Elliot was immediately offended by Boskov's hair.

"Elliot, this is Andre Boskov—you've met. He's going to observe today, okay?"

Elliot fingered his Band-Aid.

"So," Boskov stroked his beard, "what's on the menu today then?"

"Elliot's been working on a Bach cello suite. His own arrangement."

"Excellent. Bach before brunch. Tell me," Boskov leant over to examine Elliot's hand-written manuscript, "how do you see Bach?"

"I don't."

"Elliot," Peter sighed. "Not today please."

Elliot's face lit up. "I see Bach as the epicenter of the great swirling vortex of the Baroque."

Peter nodded in encouragement.

"The painting, the architecture, the politics, the cultural upheaval, all were given voice by Bach. He is the soul of an epoch of man." Elliot smiled broadly.

"Interesting," said Boskov.

"Another Kraut git," said Elliot. Before Peter could throw him a look he continued, "Krautgit, the eighteenth-century Swedish mathematician, likened Bach's great fugues to a sonic realization of the most complex of mathematical theorems. But with a spark of the eternal woven within…" Elliot pointed a finger to the sky.

"Let's hear some shall we?" Peter interrupted.

"The piece," Boskov said. "How do you see the piece?"

Elliot's expression changed. The contempt for Boskov's haircut evaporated as he studied the page and internally modelled the sounds Bach had written for the cello hundreds of years before. Music consumed Elliot. His love of Bach was true. "There's no directions. No expression marks in Bach's manuscripts, so I look on the written music as bare bones."

"Play!" Boskov ordered.

Elliot didn't hear him. He was already deep inside the music. Deep inside Bach. Inside his head. Inside his soul. When he played Bach, he played *for* Bach. He'd never told anyone, but sometimes he thought he *was* Bach.

He closed his eyes, placed his right-hand thumb on the sixth string, which he'd tuned down a tone to the D above the C of the original work. Almost in trance, he played.

It was effortless, powerful, beautiful. The fingertips of his left hand never strayed more than a hair's breadth from the frets. His right hand was an extension of his very being. After the first few arpeggios he lifted his head and smiled the smile that first attracted Peter to his playing. He smiled the smile that signalled he was somewhere else. Somewhere better. Somewhere where his anger didn't live.

Alex figured this might be his last chance. McNabb wanted rid of him. He thought maybe if he showed him what he could do, really do, then McNabb might get off his back and let him graduate. The small practice room was a mass of cables with three keyboards and a computer sitting dead in the middle. He'd set up the nearfield monitors beautifully the day before, then decided to add a subwoofer, which sat in the corner—no need to worry about directional placement for the lower frequencies. Perhaps, he thought, if McNabb doesn't like his music, at least he'll enjoy actually feeling Debussy through the seat of his pants? Anything was worth a try.

The door swung open and McNabb entered carrying a clipboard. He looked around the room, shook his head then left. A moment later he entered again.

"Alex Stone, third-year piano?"

"Yes."

"Well, thank god for that. I thought I'd gone through a rip in the universe and ended up in NASA mission control," he quipped.

Alex offered a weak smile. McNabb studied his clipboard and snapped his fingers. "Let me see it."

"See what?"

"The music. Let me see the music."

"What music?"

"It says here, third-year keyboard technique exam. Your arrangement?" He leant over and sniffed the qwerty keyboard. "What's this?"

"It's a keyboard."

"I see. Waiting for your secretary, eh?" He checked his clipboard again. "It says here, Debussy." He snapped his fingers, enjoying the power. "Come on boy, the manuscript."

"I'm twenty-eight years old. I'm not a boy," he choked, "I don't have a manuscript." He wished now that he had Elliot's balls. If he spoke to Elliot like that he would rip his throat out. What the hell was he doing here anyway, listening to this little man? Jumping to heel when he could have been running his own department by now, maybe even his own company? Alex was filled with self-loathing for not standing up for himself, but he wanted the degree. At least that was his excuse. McNabb couldn't help himself. He was just doing what little men do.

"I want to see the work. Your arrangement?"

"It's in my head. And on floppy disk." Alex held up a floppy disk.

"Floppy? Floppy? I won't have it. I simply will not have it. If the powers that be allow this," he gave a magician's wave over the electronics, "then I accept. I accept. But we have standards to maintain. I am here to ascertain pedagogical facility. Technique! Technique!"

"But it's a bit silly, no?"

"I beg your pardon?"

"Technique. A technique exam. I mean it's not like you can separate technique from everything else is it? I mean it's not like a musician is an apple, an orange, and a banana, and you can isolate the banana and study it, is it?"

"Banana?" Ready to burst a blood vessel, McNabb rushed out of the room.

I'm fucked, thought Alex.

Elliot strummed the final chord with a great flourish. He sat in concentration until the last few harmonics died away then pulled a face and fingered his Band-Aid.

"What do you think?" Boskov asked.

Elliot was puzzled. "Of me playing? What do *I* think of me playing?"

"Mm."

"It was alright."

"You really thought that?"

Elliot tried to remember how he had played. He wasn't used to judging his playing in retrospect. He was used to listening, analysing, correcting, planning, while he was actually playing, but the only way he could hear it after the fact was by running it through his head again, like a tape recorder. He thought for a few seconds then, "Apart from a few minor technical errors, it was sublime."

"Sublime! You thought it was sublime?"

"Elliot's given to overstatement," offered Peter.

"Mm. What you were saying earlier about treating the music of Bach as bones upon which you base your interpretation. What if one... drops a few bones?"

Elliot gave Boskov the same look he'd given Beethoven before he stuck the head on him. "Do you want a punch in the mouth?"

"Elliot, calm down," said Peter.

"Okay, so I dropped a few *bones* because I kept getting mental images of a man with a bird's nest growing around his ugly yap and I cocked-up a couple of bits."

"Easy Elliot," said Peter.

"Bones?" He thrust the guitar at Boskov. "Here! You play it! Let's hear the sound of a Brontosaurus falling down in the British Museum."

"This is too much Peter. He's violent."

"Just go away and leave me alone." He pawed his Band-Aid. "I hate playing for people like you. I didn't invite you to listen. You took it upon yourself to comment. Ooh, me bleedn head."

Boskov moved smartly to the door. "I'll see you later Peter."

"You've got to stop this," said Peter.

"What?"

"This temper. I can't keep covering for you. That was Andre Boskov. *The* Andre Boskov. The man who could take you on as a post-grad. He can launch your career for god's sake. Do you want a punch in the mouth?"

"He asked for it. Pretentious, egotistical, no-talent hairy fuck."

"There you go again!"

"I don't want to go to his college. *He's* going to teach *me*? Has the man no shame? Why's he even here? The fucker's heard me before, he knows I'm brilliant."

"Why must you be so bloody arrogant? You have an immense talent. But it's not enough. Boskov's on just about every guitar competition panel in the world for god's sake. You know that, you're always pointing it out to me."

"Cheating bastards. How can there be corruption in music? I go in for a competition. Play like a god. And his students, who sound like they're throwing rusty nails at an orange box, they win!"

"Listen to yourself!"

"And they're all bleedn crap. My old granny can play better than that lot."

"Stop it! Stop it! Why? Why?"

"Stop what?"

"You really don't know do you?"

"Know what?"

"You just compared your playing to that of a god."

"Did I?"

"Yes. Not Williams, Bream, Segovia. That would be mere... egomania."

"So?"

"It doesn't endear you to people. People like humility... You can make it you know."

"If I kiss Boskov's arse?"

"That's right. That's the deal. He doesn't help people who want to punch him in the mouth. He helps people who kiss his arse. So the next time you see him, you'd better pucker up those lips and smooch. I'm offski. Think about it."

Alex poked his head round the door. "Hi guys, got any spare guitar strings?"

"What for?" asked Peter.

"I want to hang myself and I want it to be messy. Anyone for tea?"

# THREE

The cafeteria was full. Alex and Elliot had got almost to the front of the line when Elliot turned to the girl standing behind him. "What did you say?" He said it as if he were about to start his third fight of the day. The girl was stunned. "I heard you. I heard you." He went nose-to-nose. "You called me a yellow nigger." She was speechless. "If you were a guy, I'd punch yer fucking lights out!"

A young man with the girl intervened. "Hey, that's enough. You're frightening her."

"When I talk to you, I'll throw you a bun," said Elliot, still staring holes in the girl.

"Elliot. Sit down. You're insane. Sit down," Alex said. Elliot stared at the girl some more then sat down, planting his guitar case beside him. Alex leant toward the couple. "He's had a bad day."

"We all have bad days," said the young man, "but we don't…"

"Hey pal," said Alex, leaning over until he could whisper the words right into his ear. "Why don't I go over there and tell him you called him a chink? That really makes him crazy." The young man looked over at Elliot, who was still scowling, and decided to order lunch.

Alex spent the next five minutes trying to convince Elliot that he might be the only person in the world who could even conceive of the phrase he had accused the girl of using. Alex knew the girl had said nothing, but he also knew that arguing with Elliot was a waste of time.

Martin Watson arrived and slapped a stack of papers onto the table. "I don't believe it," he said, and waited for a reaction. Elliot and Alex didn't react. Martin was a guitarist who practiced twelve hours a day but it never seemed to make the slightest dent in his mediocre musical abilities. He always practiced in front of a full-length mirror, convinced that if his hand positions looked like John Williams' hand positions then surely the music would follow. In winter he wore a single heavy woollen mitten on his right hand to protect his precious fingernails. In summer he wore a heavy woollen mitten on his right hand to protect the same fingernails that had been protected by the same mitten all winter. He was balding but quite handsome with broad shoulders that tapered to a lean waist. His physical attributes meant he could have infrequent sex with desperate girls and thus convince himself that he was not gay.

"I really don't believe it!" he said, this time adding weight to the complaint with an exaggerated waggle of his head. Martin's head waggled a lot when he spoke, unconsciously layering a suggestion of arrogance onto almost every sentence he uttered. Elliot took sport in inducing Martin's involuntary head movements, and believed there were speed, ferocity and duration records that he was always trying to better.

"I've just been to the bursar's office," Martin said. "Someone reported me for using the ladies toilets."

"It serves you right," said Alex.

"I didn't do it!" he protested. "I'm innocent!"

"The ladies toilets are much nicer," said Alex. "Carpets. Thick toilet paper. Little waste bins. Ladies toilets are always better. Cleaner. A proper environment to take a dump."

Martin leapt up. "It was you! You did it. I know you did. And you gave them my name!"

"No one would do something as puerile as that," said Alex. "It's just a mix-up. Forget it."

"Why were you in the ladies toilets?" Elliot asked.

"I wasn't. I just said. Are you deaf?" Martin's head was bouncing around like a plastic dog in the back of a car doing ninety. Elliot raised his eyebrows in acknowledgement of a serious attempt on the ferocity record.

Allan, another guitar player and self-professed born-again Christian, arrived.

"I saw you rehearsing for your latest porno film yesterday. You're such a show off," Alex said.

"I have no idea what you're talking about," said Allan.

Alex made some snakelike hand movements. "The dexterous hand of the would-be maestrissimo probes the moustachioed harp player," he said, laughing.

"She hasn't got a moustache," Allan was tripping over his words. "You're making this up. He's making this up everyone. Don't listen to him. Were you staring into my practice room again?"

"See that guy over there," said Elliot. "The tall one that looks like an oboe? He's a guitarist. First year. Do you know what he does? He cuts off his big toenail and sticks it on his thumb. It's disgusting. Look, he's showing it to that hairy Boskov bastard. Christ, he's worse than Martin with his rubber glove in the shower."

Martin must have been giving Elliot a piece of his mind, in his mind, because his head looked ready to dislocate itself from his shoulders. Elliot didn't notice that new records were being smashed. "Look!" he said. "He's pointing to his foot." The guy that looked like an oboe was offering Boskov his right hand for examination and pointing to his foot.

"He's proud of it," said Elliot. "The guy's got a fucking toenail on his thumb. One of those big, brown three-dimensional ones that grow until they encase your whole body." Elliot looked straight at Martin. "The kind your granny used to have."

"My granny didn't have three dimensional toenails," Martin found himself saying before realizing it.

"What's this?" asked Elliot, picking up some manuscript from the stack of papers in front of Martin.

"You wouldn't like it," said Martin.

"Christ, it looks hard," said Elliot, flicking through the music. "Fuck me, look at those time signatures, these'll give you a fucking brain haemorrhage."

Alex peered at the music and pulled a face. Every measure on the stave was bristling with hundreds of little cartoon ants with clubfeet. Each line was filled with annotations and directions; it was more of a thousand tiny Rorschach tests than a musical score.

"Please." Martin gestured that he wanted the manuscript back.

"I'm just looking, for fuck's sake," said Elliot. "Christ, the harmony's a nightmare. It sounds like Skuggs's stomach after ten pints of Guinness."

"You can't hear that harmony," challenged Martin, wagglefree. "It's too complex. It's impossible to hear just by reading."

"Christ, I wish it was," said Elliot. "It's giving me a nervous breakdown. It's a load of shite." He threw the manuscript onto the table and concentrated on Boskov and the tall guy that looked like an oboe.

"You should show it to Boskov," he said. "This is music to be discussed. It's of the mind. Normal people like me can't understand complex stuff like this. It's beyond my intellectual capacity to understand the subtle nuances, the allusions, the little musical jokes."

"It was Mr. Boskov who gave this to me actually," said Martin. "I'm playing in his masterclass. He's giving a masterclass, and I'm in it."

"Masterclass?" said Elliot. "Christ, it's the myopic leading the blind. Here, hold this." He grabbed the music again before Martin could get to it, opened it and thrust it into Alex's hands. He took his guitar out of its case and started to play. Long bass notes with exaggerated vibrato followed by zipping scales then some crashing chords that attracted curious onlookers from the tables around them. Alex tried to follow the music so that he could prepare to turn the pages, but it was upside down, the music really was too complex, and he was lost. Elliot didn't seem to mind at all. Darting the odd glance at the music then charging into another outrageously atonal passage then stealing another look as if drinking in great draughts of tones then spewing them out staccato, legato, rasgueado.

Boskov was attracted by Elliot's bold performance. Elliot gestured subtly to Alex for a page turn. He duly obliged. Boskov stood, fingering his beard. Martin noticed Boskov's interest, folded his arms, pursed his lips and began an almost imperceptible head movement just behind the beat, although it was probably stretching it to say there was a beat at all. The music was shifting its tonal centre and changing signature constantly. As Boskov moved away Elliot played more and more quietly until finally, sitting dead still, he waited until Boskov had left the room—and a few onlookers started to applaud prematurely—then he crashed a chord and giggled. There was a ripple of light applause around the room.

Elliot leapt up and took a deep bow. "You like that?" he said, taking the music and throwing it onto the table.

"As a matter of fact I do," Martin replied. "Perhaps if you worked harder you'd gain the intellectual rigour required to understand modern music." Martin grabbed the music and left in a huff.

Elliot beamed a broad smile. "I wasn't playing his music. I just made that up. Load of shite, eh? Hey Allan, how about a game of chess tonight?"

"Chess is so boring," said Alex.

"Humphrey Bogart used to be a chess hustler. That's me," said Elliot pointing at himself. "Humphrey Bogart meets Segovia's wildest dreams with the looks and body of Bruce Lee."

"Right Elliot," said Allan.

"I'm telling you man. For a Chinaman, I'm Conan the Barbarian." He flexed his biceps.

"Who's the best at chess between you two?" asked Alex.

"He's a patzer," said Elliot. "He's never won a game against me. I could beat him blindfold on twenty-five boards simultaneously."

"Right Elliot," said Allan.

"All right, tonight, I'll play you blindfold. I'll rip out your jugular."

Skuggs arrived, panting. "Where's your tuba?" asked Alex. Skuggs gave a look like a cartoon cat just discovered its tail was on fire, and ran off. "He's left his tuba on the bus again," said Alex. "The drivers have a sweepstake on whose bus he'll leave his tuba. They make him play show tunes before they give it back."

"By Christ though, Skuggs can play," said Elliot.

"Are you serious?" said Allan.

"Haven't you heard him? He's fucking brilliant. A virtuoso. A magician."

"Yes. But… It's only a tuba," said Allan.

"Only a tuba!" screamed Elliot. "What the fuck does that mean? You're a fucking tubaist! It's a lesser instrument on the

Darwinian scale of musical instrument importance? It's like you're saying, 'Big deal, so what?'"

"I am," said Allan, chuffed that he pushed Elliot's buttons.

"You wouldn't if he were a string player or a pianist, or a percussionist. Though you wouldn't know the difference anyway unless you were told. You've got no rhythm."

Allan turned to Alex. "Do you have people like him in the piano department? Always putting everyone down and thinking he's some kind of genius?"

"I am a genius," said Elliot.

"In your own mind," said Allan.

"Of course."

"Why do think you're so wonderful?"

"Why do you ask?"

"Why do you always answer a question with a question?" asked Allan, smugly.

"Why you orrways question ansah with question?" said Elliot, straightening his back and nodding.

"See!" said Allan. "He's always doing this Buddha crap."

Elliot gave a compassionate smile. "I *am* the Buddha… don't you think?"

# Four

Principal Todd told his secretary he was not to be disturbed under any circumstances. He locked the door to his office and closed the blinds. Soon he was standing in front of the full-length mirror admiring himself in his new dress. His new red dress, and his new patent leather stilettos. That the dress suited him was not in doubt. He looked best in slinky and he'd wanted some patent leather shoes for the longest time. He felt super sexy with his new stockings and suspenders hidden beneath the just-above-the-knee hemline, but he couldn't help wondering how he'd look if he shaved his beard off.

With gestures more feline than feminine he picked up a small watering can and proceeded to tend to the many plants adorning the inner sanctum of his office.

"Principal Todd!"

The voice blaring over the intercom knocked him off balance. Half of the water in his little can flew out, spilling onto some papers on his desk. He lost his balance, put too much pressure on the fragile heels he was wearing and toppled over, landing hard on his behind.

"Principal Todd!" came the voice, louder. Then his secretary's voice, "Mr. McNabb. Mr. McNabb. Please. I told you,

Principal Todd will not be disturbed. I'm sorry sir. I'm sorry. He grabbed the intercom. I couldn't stop him."

Principal Todd looked down at his feet, fearing the worst. The heel had come clean off the left shoe and the right shoe was scuffed and creased. He had a ladder running the length of his stockings.

Outside the Principal's office McNabb was wrestling over the intercom with Todd's secretary Mrs. Gibb, who was not one to be trifled with. She picked up a letter opener and lunged at McNabb's hand. He tried to get away but the knife caught him, opening a tiny cut on the side of his pinkie. "McNabb, if you don't get away from me I'll stab you in the heart!" she said, exhilarated and surprised at her reaction to McNabb's bullying.

"There's no need for that. I just want to see him," said McNabb, his courage waning heavily at the sight of his own blood. "I'm bleeding," he said, examining the microscopic wound. He took out a paper hankie and wrapped his pinkie.

Principal Todd kicked off his shoes, stood up and gathered himself. After a few deep breaths he was ready to answer. "Thank you Mrs. Gibb. Really, thank you. Please ask Mr. McNabb to wait."

Mrs. Gibb gave McNabb the evil eye. She pointed at a seat with the knife. McNabb sat, meekly.

Principal Todd made McNabb wait for a full hour before seeing him. That McNabb had interrupted his private time was bad enough, but destroying his new red shoes was unforgivable. Whatever it was that McNabb wanted, Todd promised himself to make sure he wouldn't get it. His dress was packed safely away under lock and key now and it would be a full twenty-three hours before he could be free again. It wasn't, he felt, much to ask; to don a few comfortable clothes in private, to water his plants and contemplate life, it wasn't much to ask. But Todd was sure that McNabb knew something was going on.

I know something's going on, thought McNabb as he entered the room that should have been his. He shot quick glances around the room, trying to memorize the placement of every object in sight. Just a clue, just a sign, something, there must be something.

McNabb erroneously believed Principal Todd to be homosexual. McNabb wished it were a hundred years ago when homosexuality was considered deviant behaviour, a mental disease that would render Todd unfit to lead the country's premiere music college. Then he'd show him; he'd kick his poofy arse onto the street. The Academy was full of woofters already, it simply wasn't right that the bloody principal should be in the shirt-lifters club as well.

Todd knew that McNabb thought he was homosexual. Most people thought he was homosexual. For as long as he could remember, Todd had liked to dress in women's clothing; he had no idea why, and he'd long since given up caring about the why. As a child he was a sissy. As a teenager he was singled out as a Nancy boy. As a student he'd fended off numerous advances from male lecturers and too many clergymen. Now, in his early fifties, married to a woman he loved deeply, Todd still had the strong urge to dress up in women's clothing. But he wasn't homosexual. He had never been attracted to men. He hadn't told his wife about his urges because he didn't want to break her heart. Who could believe that such a thing could mean nothing, nothing at all? In a country where the national dress, for men, is a skirt, Todd wasn't allowed to wear a dress. If he wore a tartan skirt with a silly little pouch dangling in front, and a puny knife stuck in his sock he'd be considered manly. If he wore the whole highland regalia without any underpants, as do many men in Scotland, he'd be considered as macho as Popeye. But if the skirt's not plaid, you're a weirdo.

"I want Alex Stone expelled!" McNabb blurted. "He was rude. He was insolent. He has no talent to speak of. Are we really going to allow him to fool us with those… flashing lights?"

"Alex Stone?" asked Todd, perfectly aware of who he was.

"Alex Stone. Third-year piano."

Todd shook his head.

"The one with the computers," continued McNabb, "He's a bloody…"

"Yes, young Mr. Stone, of course," said Todd.

"Well?"

"Well what?"

"I want him expelled."

"On what grounds?"

"I just bloody said."

"If you wish to continue this conversation you'll speak with a civil tongue." This is the way it always was with McNabb. Todd had been brought in over McNabb's head and McNabb hated him for it.

"He's incompetent. Untalented. Rude. I've just come from a technique exam and he wanted to play his music on a computer for god's sake. And he made obscene references to a banana."

"Banana?" Todd tried not to laugh.

"He used the word floppy and the word banana in sentences not a million miles apart and I'm not stupid. I've been teaching long enough to know when a student thinks he's being funny."

"So, you're saying that he said you had a… floppy banana?"

"No. He didn't say anything outright. It was his attitude."

"A floppy banana?" Todd was starting to enjoy himself.

"What do you intend to do?"

"Mr. Stone came to us as a mature student, after a successful career in computers."

"But this isn't a computer laboratory!" McNabb interrupted.

"I'm aware of that. If I might finish?" Todd was deliberately emphasizing what he knew McNabb would perceive as his femininity. If this man could ruin his new shoes then Todd could at least pump his blood pressure a few notches in retaliation. "I was given to understand that he was a rather gifted programmer. He worked in the defence industry. Did you know that?"

"No."

"Well, he earned enough money to pay his own fees. I thought that someone with his intellect and drive deserved a chance. I don't know what he was doing in the defence industry but he wanted out. He wanted to study music. I thought he might be a valuable addition to the student body."

"He's rude and arrogant."

"He's never been rude to me. And as for arrogance, do we not ask our students to perform in front of hundreds of people? Is that not what we're training them for? A little self-belief goes a long way in music."

"He has no talent!"

"Did I not just finish explaining that he has talent in abundance?"

"In computers? What have computers got to do with music?"

"Times are changing Mr. McNabb. We must change with them. My gut feeling is that Mr. Stone has a lot to offer."

"This is outrageous."

"Oh, not really, I think you're taking it all a bit too seriously. It's only music. They're only young people studying music you know."

"So I'm to accept his flashing lights in lieu of technique?"

"You can do what you like. He won't be expelled as long as I'm principal. Close the door on your way out and, this is very important so I want you to listen carefully; never, on any account, interrupt my private time again or there will be hell to pay. Good day," he smiled.

Bloody poofter, thought McNabb.

# FIVE

Alex hated Elliot's flat. From the outside it looked promising, but it was a pit. To a tourist, Cecil Street would seem quite smart; wide for a West End street and lined with the odd tree on each side. The location was pretty good also: close to shops, the underground, in an area loaded with pubs and plenty of bus stops, Cecil Street had all the qualities a student might wish for. But Elliot's flat was typical of what was on offer once inside the façade. The rents were cheap but not cheap enough. Elliot shared the house with twelve other tenants and he shared the filthiest bathroom in the Western hemisphere with six of those tenants. But, black with the grime of years of neglected use, freezing, unlit and as frightening as any bathroom could be, it was a paragon of palatial elegance compared to the downstairs toilet, which Elliot shared with the other six people in the house. The toilet had actually been reclaimed from the room of a tenant who now lived in a space the size of an average kitchen table. Alex tried to avoid using the toilet at Elliot's place but these things are sometimes unavoidable. The tenant who lived in the toilet flat had a taste for whores and as the wall that defined the membrane between his flat and the toilet proper was made of painted corn flakes boxes, taking a dump there was an existential experience. Crapping two inches from someone who was busy heaving into a bargain-basement whore was not an experience Alex enjoyed very much. Elliot, on the other hand, took great delight in living in such bohemian surroundings.

Elliot's flat was a flat for the same reason that the man living in the toilet lived in a room rather than a toilet. Elliot's room had one of the landlord's corn flakes box interior design jobs which defined and separated the living room and the bedroom, making the filthy hole he lived in a flat rather than a mere room with some breakfast cereal packaging disguised as a dividing wall. Elliot was not much of a one for housework either. The carpet was a colourless germ factory and, to Alex's horror, it was always wet. There was a large ceramic sink in the corner of the room that Alex would piss into when Elliot left to visit the man in the toilet downstairs. He felt guilty about this until Elliot would return with fresh stories of the adventures of the man who lived in the toilet downstairs.

Alex had a tape he wanted Elliot to listen to. He'd put a lot of work into the tape and he felt that Elliot's opinion was worth suffering one evening of Elliot's house of horrors.

Allan, the fundamentalist Christian who believed in Adam and Eve, the virgin birth, the resurrection, and that the Pope was the anti-Christ, also conveniently believed that unwinding properly after a hard day at the Academy required the intake of large amounts of hash. By the time Alex arrived, the place was reeking of reefer made with Allan's favourite, Afghani-Black.

The chess match was already in full swing. There were two chessboards set up in-between Elliot and Allan. Elliot was sat in a large recliner facing the window, with his back to the chessboards. He was wearing a football sock tied around his head as a blindfold. Indian takeaway cartons overflowing with cigarette butts and roaches stubbed into penicillin-spotted leftovers were dotted around the room. Alex patted the couch to make sure there were no surprises in wait, and sat down next to Allan.

"I don't see why I have to actually *wear* a blindfold," said Elliot. "I've never washed this sock."

"Jeezis guys, he's really playing blindfold?" asked Alex.

"On two boards simultaneously," said Elliot. "I would've done twenty-two but I've only got two sets."

"Knight to king's knight four," said Allan, staring at the back of Elliot's head. Without touching any of the pieces, he lit a joint then leant back, spreading himself on the couch.

Elliot was deep in thought.

"Toke?" said Allan handing Alex the joint.

A gleeful smile broke across Elliot's face. "It won't work Allan."

"What?"

"I'm sitting here bursting blood vessels. Every cell in me brain glowing like a fucking laser, and you're trying to take the piss out of me. My brother would've smashed your face in for that."

"What's up?" asked Alex.

"He pretended to play a piece onto a square that's already occupied by another piece. He's trying to confuse me."

"I resign," said Allan, tipping over both his kings.

"Why?" asked Elliot.

"Because I have a lost position."

"How do you know?" Elliot laughed.

"It's obvious, no matter what I do, you checkmate me."

"Yes, on both boards, but how do you know?"

"You can see the position as well as I can."

"Better," said Elliot, rubbing his eyes under the football sock. "I created it. So show me how I was going to checkmate you. Show me the moves."

"Look," said Allan, becoming agitated. "I've had it with chess for tonight. I don't want to argue about it. If it means so much to you, you win, okay?"

"With white I've got forced mate in eight, but knowing you, you'll fuck-up before that. With black it's unclear but a bloodbath nevertheless."

"Yeah, Elliot. You're the best. It's a bloodbath. If you say so." Allan took a deep draw on the joint then left the room.

Elliot took off the sock, turned his chair around, picked up his guitar, which always he kept close at hand, and started to play quietly while studying the chessboards. "I love chess," he said. "It's incorruptible. It's where logic meets art. There's these games from the old days, they're called classics. It's usually the Duke of Some-Fucking-Where playing against a master. And the master sacrifices bleedn everything. And the Duke's got all his pieces and he thinks he's gonna beat the bastard. So the master says, 'It looks like you've done me this time you jammy bastard.' And the Duke says, 'Let's double the stake?' And the master checkmates the Duke with his last two pieces. That's what it's like playing Allan."

Elliot added a coda to his story by way of a few bars of baroque on guitar. "I am a chess master you know."

"Eh?"

"I'm a chess master. A real one like." Elliot was looking at his hands, half for the notes and half in embarrassment at his confession. "I've got an official rating, like. At least I used to have."

"Honestly?"

"Do you think any bum off the street can play blindfold on two boards simultaneously?"

"I suppose not. I just thought you were good. You know, better than Allan."

"Better than Allan? For fuck's sake." Elliot switched quietly into a Barrios waltz. "But I haven't played in years really. I got pissed off with it. I was in this competition and I had this position. I was in shock. I'd fucked up. I'd played a Mora-Smith gambit. I didn't know at the time that it was such a dodgy opening. I was just a kid like, and the opening was so aggressive, I loved it. I was playing against this git with a pipe, a fucking mathematics professor. They're usually easy to beat. Especially if you're a kid cause they get a red face, and they think too much. But there were theoretical flaws in the opening that I didn't know about at the time. But what happened was that I found the saving line. I sacrificed two pieces and forced a draw. It was the best game I'd ever played. It was a fucking work of art. It should've been published. But those bastards that ran the competition, they gave the brilliancy prize to a dickhead who'd won his game against a fucking carnival of blunders. So I told them like." Elliot's playing seemed almost disconnected from his consciousness. Alex was hypnotized by his ability to play so beautifully while so deeply involved in some long-gone memory. "I said, 'Are you serious? That's a loada shite. You're just too thick to see it.' So I thought, fuck em, and I gave up."

"You gave up because they didn't give you a prize?"

"Well, that and my old man. I like my old man but he was always pissed out of his head and coming down to the competitions and shouting and bawling and that. It was a laugh when I was really young but it gets old when you get older. And now it's the same with music. I think I might leave college."

"But you'll get your degree in a few months." Alex could hardly believe what he was hearing. Here was Elliot, gifted, supported by his teacher, the real possibility of a concert career in front of him, and he wanted to throw it all away. "You want to throw it all away?" he blurted.

"If I don't, I'll end up killing someone. I hate them, I do."

"Who?"

"Those bastards that teach at the Academy. Peter's okay, but he's still an arselicker. He doesn't give you a hard time, but he doesn't stick up for you either. I've had enough of it. Even when you do a concert, it's like the whole audience has had its brain removed. They have to be told what's good and what's bad. They're all scared to have their own opinions, so if you don't have a bunch of people telling them that you're good then you're gonna end up playing for three people and a dog at the local church hall for the rest of your life. Recording killed classical music. Who the fuck wants to listen to me when they can buy a record of Bream or Williams? And how many guitar concerts do you think the average person goes to in a lifetime? I'm sick of it."

"Look, just sleep on it, eh? Give it some time."

"Hey, don't tell Allan I'm a chess master. Let the bastard suffer for his insolence. I think I'll stay up. I want to analyse this position." Elliot stopped playing. He began rearranging the chess pieces in front of him.

Alex took a tape out of his pocket. "Elliot will you do me a favour and give this a listen?"

"What is it?"

"Just give it a listen and tell me what you think."

Allan was in better spirits when he returned from his expedition to the downstairs toilet. He rolled another joint. Alex's need to return to his own flat, his own comfortable, clean bed ebbed away with each puff on Allan's creation.

When Alex opened his eyes it was past ten in the morning. He lit a cigarette to kill the taste in his mouth. Elliot was asleep in the recliner. Allan appeared from behind the cornflakes wall after spending the night in Elliot's bedroom. "Wakey, wakey!" he cried.

Elliot woke and looked at his watch. "Fuck, I've got a concert today." He rubbed his eyes and checked his watch again. "Fuck."

"Well, you'd better get a bend on," said Allan.

"It started five minutes ago," said Elliot. "I was supposed to play at this school. They'll all be sitting there right now waiting for me to start. Hee-hee."

"Did someone rub a donkey's arse on my tongue last night?" asked Alex.

"That's the dope," said Allan. "Good stuff, eh?"

"I thought you were a Christian? How come it's okay to smoke all that dope but you're not allowed to lie with your neighbour's wife unless she's a harp player with a moustache?" asked Alex.

"Dope takes me closer to Christ," said Allan. "She hasn't got a moustache."

"Well, I've got to get closer to a toothbrush in a hurry."

# Six

When Alex got into the street the sun was shining and the cool breeze felt so good he decided to walk to his flat, which wasn't more than a couple of miles away.

Alex liked Glasgow. He especially liked the people. Just walking around the city made him feel good. He walked all the way home. After showering and two bowls of Rice Crispies he was ready to work. The tape he'd given Elliot was just a first draft, a flavour of what he knew he could achieve, given the right tools.

Alex had amassed a lot of equipment. He had three samplers. He had a software sampler he'd written himself. He had FM synthesizers, analog synthesizers, physical modelling synthesizers, software subtractive synthesizers and some vintage analog synths. He had four keyboard controllers, ribbon controllers, breath controllers, digital delays and reverbs, two digital mixing boards, some high quality nearfield monitors, and he had a beautiful collection of microphones, his pride and joy.

He'd collected most of his stuff while he was still a programmer. He was very well paid writing routines in assembly and machine code for satellite defence systems. The thing he liked most about the job was the money, it allowed him to do what most single men like to do; buy toys.

He used to laugh when people asked him what he did for a living and he'd say he wasn't sure. He had signed the Official Secrets Act, which meant if he opened his mouth about the wrong things to the wrong people then the government would throw him into the Tower of London or somewhere, but the truth was that he really didn't know what he was doing most of the time. Like most things associated with any bureaucracy, software development for the government was a big, stupid, expensive, badly managed affair, where all of the people involved are at least partly in the dark. This meant that he'd write routines much of the time without knowing exactly what they were for or what they did; it also meant that software development was painfully slow and very exacting. In the real world where people write software to sell to the public, they work in interactive teams where ideas can be freely exchanged before the software is hoisted onto the public long before it works properly. Commercial software companies use customers to find the bugs. The customers become the beta testers, and they pay for the privilege. Where Alex worked there was no possibility of mass testing to iron out flaws. Nobody wants a satellite to start firing lasers out of turn, so the software has to be robust before it's put to use. Alex was a pretty good programmer before he worked in defence but by the time he left his job he could write bug-free code that would compile first time; a completely useless skill. The problem was he was starting to realize that the job had changed the way he thought. It had changed the way he saw things, changed his perceptions, changed his character. He didn't mind sitting in front of a computer screen for fourteen hours a day, although in truth he mostly sat at a desk and programmed with pencil and paper, or pen and paper if he wanted to show off. He didn't think about what most people might describe as the ethics of what he was doing. He cared not a jot if some of his software was used to zap an enemy goatherd or two. But after spending most of his life telling computers what to do, he realized he was losing his ability to relate to normal people. People, that is, who have little or no understanding of the inner workings of universal machines, or computers.

The other reason he had to leave software development was that he never got to meet any girls.

Four years ago the thought of going in to work to translate pseudo-code into low-level commands for advanced controls had suddenly become suffocating. What was once an exciting intellectual challenge had become first easy, then boring. There was simply no end to it. He no longer stayed at work until midnight every night. He wanted a life. More and more he would leave work early to make time for music. He had always loved music, but the obsession for pure software was waning and music was taking its place.

His parents had forced him into piano lessons as a child. At the time he hated them for it, preferring instead to play computer games. By the time they agreed he could forego the agonies of formal piano lessons he was writing his own computer games. These skills were easily translatable into highly paid programming work. There was no need for university; writing code was enough for employers to bid for his skills. When he first approached the Academy he thought he could use the computer as his instrument. Principal Todd had been kind about it. He was interested in the concept of the computer as a musical instrument but there were simply no resources. How would they judge it? Who would teach it?

Todd said he could study there if he got his piano chops up to scratch. Alex thanked his parents a million times for forcing piano down his throat as a youngster. He practiced every day until his fingers hurt and he finally got accepted as a piano student.

He soon realized though, that he would never come close to the abilities of his contemporaries; kids who'd taken piano seriously all their lives. Some had practiced three to four hours a day from the age of five or six.

It was frustrating that he got no credit for the work he was doing with computer music, but worse that he was perceived as a mediocre talent. It was worse still that McNabb was trying to sabotage his dreams of graduation.

McNabb had no idea of the craft that went into his work. McNabb had no idea of the level he was working at. McNabb thought that using a computer was simply cheating; like taping it and playing it back. He had no idea. Alex had spent the last three years creating some of the most complete sets of waveform samples of Steinway pianos in existence. He'd spent thousands of hours digitally recording every note on the keyboard at every conceivable velocity using microphone setups discovered through endless sessions of trial and error. He'd sampled almost every piano in the Academy, and there were a lot of pianos in the Academy. He'd built a virtual piano from the thousands of samples he'd stored away; a hybrid of what he thought were the most beautiful, balanced, sonorous tones, the most advantageous ambiances, the clearest tunings. His virtual piano contained snapshots of over forty pianos recorded under varying conditions. It was so huge that he couldn't load his piano onto his three samplers; and his homegrown software sampler, which could handle the bulk, simply wasn't fast enough to process the music he wanted to create. He had to load his piano onto his samplers piece by piece; sometimes just a single note played twenty or thirty different ways. Sometimes he loaded his samplers without any notes; just pedal sounds or partial harmonics, even the odd knocking sound or fluffed note to add authenticity. He would delve into the digitally recorded waveforms themselves, writing little routines to stretch a frequency or filter a decay.

# The Samplist

When he played music, it meant sculpting every note, every nuance. Every attack was hand drawn, every rhythm controlled down to a level that chemists might describe as molecular. Like the programs he wrote that used low-level frequencies to detect incoming anti-missile missiles; nothing could be left to chance. Computers have to be told everything. Playing a virtual piano inside a virtual space is hard because of the way sound behaves. Sound evolves through time. A human piano player can think in musical phrases. In computer terms, Alex thought of musical phrases as similar to the pseudo-code that he used to translate; very high-level descriptions. Human piano players transmit high-level descriptions of the music into the piano through their hands in real time. Alex had to paint each note, each hiatus into phrases the way an artist might use colour in his paintings. Two notes were never the same. There were phrases within phrases within phrases; like the nested loops in software programs. There was silence intertwined with sympathetic harmonics or with other silences. Raw waveforms were his basic materials, the tonal pigments he'd mix in his imagination. Software was his palette. His programming skills were his brushes, his hands, his gestures. His canvass was time. His canvass was human perception. It was a constant battle against the tyranny of perfection. Nothing could be left to chance.

Dumb luck had given Alex perfect pitch; the ability to distinguish sounds the way most of us can distinguish colours. Lots of students at the Academy had perfect pitch but most used it to whine about out-of-tune performances or to memorize telephone numbers. Musicians with perfect pitch seldom explore its power. To Alex, every note was a birth and death, every sound an evolving spectrum of discrete frequencies. Every performance was a negentropic sculpture, a kind of sonic calculus describing a relationship between time and human perception.

Alex could hear the universe in a tone.

McNabb dismissed it all as flashing lights and fraud.

He sat in front of one of his weighted keyboards. It wasn't switched on or plugged in. He practiced silent scales for an hour or so before he left for the Academy.

McNabb sat behind his desk puffing on an empty pipe. "Why do you want to leave?" he asked. Elliot had been called in to McNabb's office to explain why he had failed to turn up for the morning's concert at a nearby school. Elliot decided he couldn't be arsed explaining himself. The sucking noise McNabb was making with his pipe had convinced Elliot it was time to leave the Academy. He'd just informed McNabb of his decision.

"I love music," Elliot answered.

"Why do you want to leave?" McNabb asked again.

"I've had it with show business."

"Serious music is not show business."

"Yes it is, it's just crap show business. And there's no such thing as serious music anyway. Serious people call it serious music then tell the rest of us that's what it's called."

McNabb sucked some air through his pipe, which was now audibly filling with saliva.

"Mozart spoke to me in a dream last night," said Elliot. "He said he wouldn't have shat on this place if he'd been alive today. He said you were all a bunch of wankers, and he told me to leave."

"Really?"

"You did ask."

There was a knock on the door. Peter entered, gasping for breath. "Excuse me for the intrusion. This is my student. I just heard…"

"Our business is finished here," said McNabb.

"No," said Peter. "You see. Elliot has been going through a very emotional period lately. He's really extremely gifted. But very highly strung. He probably swore at you? He does that when he's nervous. It's a condition."

"It's documented in many medical journals from the late nineteenth century." Elliot smiled broadly. "When they really knew a condition when they saw one. I'm off. Cheerio." He jumped up, grabbed his guitar case, gave Peter a quick wink and left the room.

"May I?" asked Peter, gesturing to a seat.

McNabb nodded. "You must think a lot of that young man. He's quite mad, isn't he?"

"I think he is, yes, but he's a wonderful musician."

"I've heard him."

"It's a game we play."

"Game?"

"He threatens to leave. I offer him money to stay, and he stays."

"You give him money? But he has a scholarship."

"It's not much. You should see where he lives."

"He missed an engagement this morning."

"He didn't have the bus fare. He was embarrassed."

"I see."

"Then it's okay?"

"He is an exceptional talent."

# Seven

Friday. On Fridays Alex would take time off to join Skuggs for a jaunt into oblivion. Alex couldn't face spending any more time at the Academy than he had to. After checking his equipment was safe and intact, he locked the practice room door and headed for the pub around the corner. He would hire a van on Monday to lug it all back to his flat.

"Jim," said Alex, by way of a hello to the huge bouncer who populated the doors of the Haven public house of a Friday night.

"Okay Alex."

Alex had become friendly with Jim following a choral concert. Friendly might be too strong a word though, when you're dealing with someone who's willing to give up a Friday night for little more than the chance to break a few heads. Jim broke heads on a regular basis, and Alex was happy to be on good terms with him. After the choral concert, which Alex had been press-ganged into, Jim had stopped him at the door. Alex was wearing formal dress: dinner suit and black tie. Jim had assumed that Alex was the new bouncer hired to replace him. When Jim found out that Alex had been singing in a concert and was wearing a bouncer's uniform for reasons a million miles from Jim's fear of unemployment, Jim had offered all that he had, "Anyone gives you any trouble, just see me."

Jim had already made good on his promise on more than one occasion. Glasgow pubs are an unnerving blend of camaraderie and violence. The friendliness shown by total strangers toward each other in Glasgow pubs is genuine and offered freely. The violence, which appears usually in the hour before last bell, is just as genuine and strongly correlated to both the amount of alcohol consumed, and inversely to the degree of good spirits previously offered.

Elliot was already sitting with a couple of pints in front of him when Alex arrived.

"Where's Skuggs?" asked Alex. He downed half of his beer in a single draught.

"I saw McNabb today," Elliot said. "I told him Mozart called him a wanker."

"Did you listen to the tape?"

"Yeah."

"Well?"

"It was nice. Chopin."

"And?"

"Chopin. Chopin and Chopin. The same piece twice."

"And?"

"Was there something else on it?"

A raucous scene started at the door as a troop of young men in cheap suits entered, shouting obscenities at each other. It was Friday night; Alex wasn't the only one who needed to get out of the real world for a while. The local offices would be emptying tired workers into the streets and bars for the next few hours. Jim followed them to the bar to give them one of his friendly chats.

"No," said Alex. He waited for Elliot to get it. "And?"

"Do you want a full critique? You know, swirling arpeggios engulfed in a sea of tranquil resonance?"

"No, no, didn't you get it? One of them was digital. I played one on a piano and I programmed the other. Didn't you notice the difference?"

"No."

"They both sounded real? Like a real performance?" Elliot's lack of interest didn't faze Alex. Elliot was painfully honest, if he'd detected anything in the tape that could be ridiculed, he'd be busting a gut for sure. "I knew it would work. I knew it. I knew it."

Some girls had joined the noisy crew at the bar and were adding a shrill overtone to the merriment. Jim watched them closely. One of the men had somehow squeezed a condom over his closely shaven head until it was clinging to his face below the nose. He was blowing up the reluctant balloon with great forty-a-day wheezes. He heightened the effect of his unlikely party piece by pretending to pump a jack with his foot on each snort. His comedic talents were sending the girls in his company into virtual hysteria.

"Knew what would work?" asked Elliot.

"Look, stay on at the Academy, for a while, will you?"

"Okay."

"Okay?" Alex was surprised. Elliot had seemed so sure last night that he had to leave.

"Sure. Why not?"

"I thought it was killing you. Eating you up?"

"I feel better now that I've talked to McNabb. Anyway, Peter stuck up for me. I left and he pleaded with McNabb to give me another chance. Said I wasn't in complete control of me mental faculties and all that. Then he gave me a wad of cash to stay until the finals are over."

Martin arrived and started to make his way to their table.

"Listen. Listen." Alex was hardly able to contain himself. "Listen, I've been working on some ideas. I want your opinion."

Martin plumped himself down beside them.

"Your honest opinion," Alex continued.

"Me honest opinion," said Elliot staring at Martin. "All right, I think Martin is the ugliest guy at the Academy."

"Very funny," said Martin.

Skuggs appeared holding three pints of Guinness. His tuba case was swaying from side to side, banging into people as he made his way to the table. He concentrated all his energies on retaining every ounce of fluid in his beers. When he had safely landed the beers on the table he lowered his tuba to the floor.

"Gas!" he exclaimed. "Seen the geezer with the Johnny on top?" He pointed at the ad hoc floorshow. "That's talent." He lifted a pint and jammed its contents into himself in a split second. It looked more like eating than drinking, like he had taken a bite from the glass. He lifted the second beer and ate half of it in a single chomp. He paused, as if struck by a thought, then manufactured a huge belch and said, "A condom man. Is it possible? Do you think it's a special one? I'd like to be able to do something like that."

Alex took out a small tape player and shoved in a tape. The pub was filling up quickly. The jukebox would soon be switched on and the night's conversation at an end. The hell with it, he thought. The place was noisy but his tape player was pretty high quality, also the beer, the atmosphere, and Elliot's positive reaction to his efforts had already made him giddy enough to ask the barman to play his tape. He thought better of that; classical music on a Friday night could incite a riot. He'd stick with his little tape player.

"Here guys, do me a favour. Listen to this. I'll get a round in." He planted the tape player in the middle of the table and headed for the bar. The place was getting packed. As he waited for the barman to get to him he watched the guy with the condom on his head, who was now running out of puff.

"He's gonna make it. He's gonna make it," said one of the man's friends to Alex.

"And they say that chess is the biggest waste of intelligence outside of an advertising agency." Alex was hardly thinking when he said it.

"You trying to be smart?" asked the condom guy's friend.

"Eh?" This was the way it was in Glasgow pubs on Friday nights. Maybe this is the way it is in pubs on Friday nights everywhere? Alex knew what was coming. They were bored with the condom blowing. They were drunk. They were full of piss and vinegar. Condom Man needed an out before he passed out and his pal just looked plain nasty.

"George. This guy's laughing at you," Condom Man's pal said to the guy who had spent the last ten minutes trying so hard to get big laughs from the population of the bar, he'd almost blacked out.

George peeled off the condom. His efforts had left a deep red welt running around his bald head at zero degrees latitude. He pushed his face right up to Alex's. "You laughing at me? You laughing at me?" There was a hush around the bar as the rest of the drinkers divined that the time for merriment had been prematurely curtailed and violence was afoot. The only sound was the distant tinkle of Alex's Chopin.

"It's one of those poofters from the music academy round the corner," said George's friend. "Got your tutu with you then? Do a wee dance for the boys then?" He did a wee dance himself, drawing a nervous titter from one of the duller girls in his pack.

Alex knew the next move in this particular little dance was George smashing his head into Alex's face. If Alex moved back too quickly, George would react. If Alex stood his ground, George would react.

Alex thought, fuck it. "Oh, you've all gathered round to make fun of me," he said. "Poor me. About to get the piss taken out of me by Low-Brain-Cell-Count and his brother, Gummo." George and his pal were stunned, which gave Alex a chance to move away slightly, at least to avoid the dreaded Glasgow Kiss. "I knew I'd seen you somewhere before," he said, pointing at George. "It was when I saw you in that hat. The pink one you were wearing a minute ago... You're my penis aren't you?"

George wasn't impressed.

"You are!" said Alex. "No? Well, by Christ, you're the spitting image. I wondered what the hell my penis was doing in a pub with a bunch of strangers blowing up a flunky on his head instead of sitting in my pants where he belongs."

George threw a hard drunken punch. Alex tried to move straight backwards to avoid the relatively slow blow that was incoming from eleven o' clock, but people had crowded in so tightly to watch the sport that he backed into someone before gaining enough distance to fully outrun George's haymaker.

There was a horrible squelch. All went black. His face went numb. There were screams. There was a distant thud on the back of his head as it cracked into a seat; the person who had got in the way of his weaving from the punch had conveniently moved away far enough after contact so that Alex might at least fall down and crack his head without impediment.

"Look at his nose, ugh," he heard one of the girls saying. The Chopin played on like a far off music box in a cheap spaghetti western.

"Ah'll fuckeen killum. Ah'll fuckeen killum," George blasted.

Everything was black. He wasn't sure if his eyes were open or not. There were violent crashing sounds, more screaming, then Jim, "Right, you're out." There was light; he wasn't blind. It was fuzzy, but that was Jim dragging George and his nasty little friend out on their arses. A couple of people helped him up, assuring him that his nose wasn't 'that bad'. As it turned out it wasn't that bad. He felt the tender spot on the back of his head but there was no blood. His nose had already stopped bleeding.

"Okay Alex?" shouted Jim rubbing his hands together after a job well done. "Jim!" said Jim to the barman. "Jukebox!"

"Canny get it workin," replied the barman. "Geeza minute?"

Alex went to the gents to stuff a couple of wads of toilet paper up each nostril and check the rate of expansion of both his nose and the lump on his head. When he got back to the table he resisted the urge to ask how his nose looked.

"Nice one," said Skuggs.

"Thanks for helping me out guys," said Alex.

"I suppose I'll have to get the round in," said Elliot.

"Jim took care of you," said Skuggs. "If he hadn't taken that beer bottle off that guy, you would have really been in a mess."

"He was going to hit me with a bottle?" he asked, suddenly aware of the danger he had been in.

"That Jim's fast for a big guy, no?" said Skuggs.

"Did you listen to the tape?" Alex asked.

"What tape?" asked Skuggs.

"For fuck's sake guys."

"Oh, the tape. The tape. Yeah, right," said Skuggs.

Alex gave them all a venomous stare and rewound the tape. By the time Elliot returned with the drinks—another three pints of Guinness for Skuggs, the commotion had thrown his schedule and he had to catch up—they'd all listened to the tape under Alex's close supervision.

"One of those performances was done on a computer," said Alex.

"Really? That's amazing," said Skuggs, finally showing some interest.

"To be honest, it was pretty obvious," piped Martin.

"Was it?" asked Alex, Elliot and Skuggs almost simultaneously.

"You were a programmer before you came here right?" said Martin. "And McNabb is always complaining about your computers and synthesizers. Your flashing lights? So when I heard the tape it was obvious that one of them was artificial."

The word artificial used in reference to his music usually bent Alex out of shape. Maybe Martin was being deliberately rude, maybe not? Either way, this is what he wanted. He'd asked for opinions and he was getting them. Even Martin, professional practicer and sometime sycophant could be trusted to hold to his guns when it came to musical tastes. Alex had their attention, albeit at the cost of a sore face. Perhaps he shouldn't get defensive, just sit back and listen?

"But you worked that out by deductive reasoning," said Elliot, "not because you can actually hear it."

"No, the reasoning simply backs up what I heard. It's obvious."

"You're a fucking liar," said Elliot. "How would you know anyway, you're tone bleedn deaf."

"You could really hear the difference?" asked Alex. He knew that if he let Elliot walk all over Martin then it would end up in a stupid argument. He needed information, not another brawl.

"It's obvious I'm afraid." Martin's head was getting into gear. "Why? Is there some point to all this? Apart from proving

that natural instruments are infinitely superior to electronic facsimiles." Like McNabb, Martin completely misunderstood the
whole issue, but Alex bit his tongue.

"Which one? Which one was the computer?" asked
Skuggs.

"Ah, he's got a fifty-fifty chance of guessing right anyway,"
said Elliot.

"It's obvious," said Martin, "the second one."

They all awaited Alex's response. He hung his head then
drained the dregs in his glass. "He's right," said Alex.

"I know it," said Martin. "The second one sounded completely dead."

"It didn't," said Elliot. "It sounded different but it didn't
sound inferior."

"There were no upper partials in it," said Martin.

"Upper partials?" Skuggs laughed. "What the fuck are
upper partials?"

Martin meant to enjoy his victory. "The sympathetic vibra-
tions that are set-off when playing piano are too complicated to
model artificially."

"He's right," said Alex. "Thanks Martin, for your input."
Alex had heard enough.

"You're welcome. What time is it? I've got a date tonight."

"Is she ugly?" asked Skuggs.

"Of course," Elliot answered for Martin.

"I only shag ugly girls," said Skuggs. "They appreciate you
more."

"Phillipa and I are going to an evening of early music," said
Martin. "Phillipa plays the sackbut."

Elliot and Skuggs burst out laughing. "And the pink oboe,"
said Elliot starting to double up.

"And the blue-veined flute," added Skuggs.

Alex kept a grip on himself. "Thanks Martin."

"Anytime," said Martin. He gathered his things and left. Skuggs and Elliot giggled like schoolgirls as Elliot waggled his head about.

"Man, is he full of shit or what? He was dead wrong," said Alex.

"I knew the fucker was bullshitting," said Elliot.

"I need more gas," came Skuggs's mantra.

"I knew you couldn't tell the difference. I knew it," said Alex.

"You can't," said Elliot. "My ears are precision instruments, and Skuggs's got perfect pitch."

On cue, Skuggs belched.

"That was middle C," he said. "I can fart D double flat if you like. The arse lends itself to flat keys rather than sharp."

"The well-tempered sphincter," said Elliot.

"Apart from when I've had a vindaloo."

"Plays aleatoric tunes then," said Elliot, hardly able to speak. "I heard it play some Smith-Brindle last Friday."

"The triple tonguing was a buggar," said Skuggs.

The jukebox started blaring. Elliot and Skuggs tried to gather a straight face but kept jiggling around in-between drinking.

Alex had two pieces of toilet paper hanging from a swollen nose, and a lumpy head. Elliot was still wearing the Band-Aid from his attack on Beethoven. Skuggs was filling up with gas. The jukebox was painfully loud. The bar was jumping. Alex had to shout at the top of his voice so that Elliot and Skuggs, who were no more than three feet away, could hear. "I've signed up for Professor Ingles' electronic music class."

"She'll fill you in man. You're a guy. She hates guys," shouted Skuggs.

"She's ordered a bunch of new equipment. Good stuff. I can use it."

Elliot screamed his two pence worth, "Only if you cut your dick off! And you'll have to listen to her compositions!"

They drank the rest of the night, without speaking, until the barman threw them out. They walked home in a drunken stupor, passing other drunks without acknowledgement. After loading up with Indian take-away, Elliot staggered back to his pit, and Alex and Skuggs went back to Alex's place where Alex did his best to convince Skuggs that he really would throw him out if he didn't stop farting. Skuggs fell asleep on the sofa and unconsciously continued his flatulent symphony. Alex collapsed onto his bed and woke up the next day in pain from the beating and the beer.

# EIGHT

He was deep in thought when the phone rang, almost sending him out of his chair. Skuggs was lying half on, half off the couch, still wearing his heavy parka. Alex had been at his desk for four hours already, he never slept properly after he drank. Skuggs slept like a baby whether he drank or not. Alex had expected him to sound like a jumbo jet on take-off when he slept but he never did; he literally slept like a baby, making tiny, silent snorts. This small miracle was tempered by his flatulatory pronouncements. All that gas had to go somewhere when he wasn't blowing it into his tuba. Alex had all the windows open but it hardly made a dent in Skuggs's inventory.

"Party tonight?" It was Elliot, calling from a box, his pit didn't have an inside telephone. There was a strange noise in the background.

"Muso party?" asked Alex. "They're wakes man. They just sit around all night listening to Mahler. Am I invited?"

"You? Why would anyone invite a boring bastard like you? I'm invited. Allan's invited. Shut the fuck up Allan!" It was Allan making the noise in the background, it sounded like he was singing. "But you can come along."

The last thing in the world Alex needed right now was a muso party. He wasn't invited either. Alex had hardly been to a decent party in his life. He was starting to think that fun at parties was a myth created by television and movies and co-workers who had to believe their weekends hadn't really been a complete bust.

"No. Not me," said Alex. "I have to work tonight."

"You're blond'll be there." Allan was singing happily in the background but Alex couldn't make it out.

"What?"

"Your blond's going. Why d'you think Allan's so chuffed? He reckons he's gonna get big laughs watching you fall on your ass."

"You guys want to come round here before we go?"

Skuggs slept most of the day. It took more than an hour of browbeating before Alex finally convinced him to take a shower. By the time Elliot and Allan arrived Skuggs was unusually squeaky clean. Allan rolled a few joints while Skuggs blasted some borrowed Mozart on his tuba. Suitably mellowed, they headed to the pub; even muso parties didn't get in gear until after closing time. Alex hardly drank. Elliot spent most of the evening quizzing Allan as to why bunny rabbits were barred from heaven. When they were ready to go, they bought a dozen cans of Guinness, joined up with a few other groups from the Academy who'd been in the same pub, then spent the next hour arguing about where the party was, and the fastest way to get there. When they arrived at the party, Alex was heartened by the absence of Mahler on the stereo. There wasn't any music playing at all but, to Skuggs's great delight, the kitchen table was stacked with booze. He opened a party-size can of lager and poured it into a punch bowl he'd foraged from under the sink.

"This'll do me," he said, stroking the bowl jealously.

Alex checked around the place, but there was no sign of the blond. One room was locked; he assumed that it was where the occupants of the flat had stashed their valuables. He decided to hang around in the kitchen for a while before heading home. Someone put on a Gary Glitter record. The party had started in earnest. He wondered how these people ever got to be music students in the first place with their Gary Glitter records.

Elliot came running up to him, spilling red wine out of a little plastic cup. "She's here," he said. "She's here. She's in that room. She's fucking practicing." Allan was in tow, making exaggerated gyrations with his eyebrows. "You want to get yourself in there for a duet," he said.

"Her name's Laura," said Elliot. "She's Spanish." Alex felt dizzy. "She's only been here three months, but her English is okay."

"Spanish?" said Allan. "Ah, that explains the breasts."

Alex had never thought of her as a person with a name, just a body. It was as if she had suddenly stepped out of some mythical world. He'd gotten so used to visiting her, sharing his thoughts, his moods. In a moment he realized that his visits had been more than mere lechery, beyond stalking; he'd talked to her like she was his psychiatrist, his confidant, his silent friend.

"Come on!" shouted Elliot as he and Allan bustled him toward the locked room. A girl appeared from the room and closed the door carefully behind her. "This is Sheila," said Elliot. "She told me about Laura. And she's gonna have sex with me later." Sheila gave Elliot a smart whack on the head.

"So, you're the one?" she said. At this, the blood drained from his face. Was this just an elaborate joke? What was going on?

"I think she likes you," she said. "A lot."

Alex was having trouble breathing.

"Look at him," cried Elliot. "He's shiting himself." Elliot put his ear to the door. "She's still practicing!" Elliot was in ecstasy at this. Allan joined him. They jammed their ears to the door and giggled like schoolgirls. Sheila took both their ears and peeled them off the door.

"Well?" she shooed him closer to the door. "In ye go." She opened the door and pushed him in. He stumbled. It was dark. Was this a joke? He heard the door lock behind him.

"Is this a joke?" he said, worried that his friends were playing a cruel prank, and praying they were not.

There she was, a curvaceous vision in the faint light of a bedside reading lamp. Her breasts, her breasts, her breasts. These breasts were once in a lifetime deals. Most men never in their lives get close to such perfection. These were the breasts that women in California thought they were going to have when they paid for the implants. These were the breasts that inspired the poets.

She stopped playing and carefully packed her violin into its case.

"Ola Alex." She smiled. He tried not to pass out.

"Come," she said. "You and I will make love I think, Senior Alex."

Make love? Alex had never made love before. Making love was what they did in movies. Since arriving at music college he'd humped, banged, shagged, fornicated, and he'd once administered a sound beefing to a horny cellist following a particularly dull choir practice, but he'd never made love before.

She had to be taking the piss. Any minute Elliot and Allan would burst into the room to settle wagers and take notes to fuel months of cruel banter. He backed up against the locked door and dug in his heels. Laura was immediately distressed.

"You do not like me?"

"Like you? Yes, I like you. I'm crazy about you," he stammered. "Look, you're not taking the piss are you?" He wanted to slit his throat as soon as he said it.

"Taking piss? I don't know. You come to my room everyday. You talk and talk and talk." She moved slowly toward him. "I try to practice and you talk and talk and talk. I play Bach, you talk. I play Paganini, you talk. Now, no talk."

He wasn't imagining it, her voice; it was astonishing. It wasn't just her accent, which would have driven him wild anyway; her voice was lilting, pure; as musical as her violin playing was stilted. She came close, her breasts brushed against him in time with her breathing. Each gossamer touch sent a mild electric shock through his body. He actually tingled. He'd never tingled before. And a beautiful girl wanted to make love to him. Make love!

This was real. It was really happening. His dreams were coming true. Her face. He had to touch her face. He brushed his hand against her cheek. She kissed the backs of his fingers. He'd spent so much time obsessing over her body, her perfect body, he'd never taken the time to drink in the loveliness of her eyes, her mouth; it was so voluptuous.

"Your mouth," he said, kissing her softly. "It's so voluptuous."

"What is voluptuous?" she whispered. She moved away and whipped off her sweater then unhooked her bra.

"Oh, my God," he said. "I believe, oh lord, I believe."

She giggled, took off her shoes, took off her jeans, and wriggled out of her panties. There was a burning in his chest he'd never felt before. He'd never seen anything so attractive in his life. She was all he had imagined and a million times more, a trillion times more. He was engulfed by her. She was a sonata made physical. And she was blond, really blond.

"How can I go on after this?" he said, taking off his shirt. "Any other state of being than this state will be torment. You've doomed me to eternal pain. If I ever have to leave this room I will kill myself."

"Then we will stay here."

"But people will want their coats," he said, pushing coats off the bed and onto the floor.

"My violin?" She made sure the instrument beside her was safe from his frantic sweeping of the bed covers.

The next ten minutes were a timeless dream of absolute joy.

He was torn out of bliss at a loud knocking sound.

"Go away!" she shouted.

Alex knew he couldn't go on for another second. This was no time for running code through his head; his usual strategy when over-excitement threatened to curtail his fun.

"I can't go on," he said. "If you move a centimeter, it's over." She straddled him. He was sure he would explode.

"You must think of something else," she said. "A sweet diversion."

She reached over him, opened her violin case and took out the instrument. His taut libido loosened with every twist on the bow. As she put the violin to her neck a flash of what he was in for assured him that tonight could last a long time after all. He relaxed to watch the performance, no longer at the edge of his sexual tether.

She played a Bach gavotte, music that was subtle and rhythmic and exacting. From the first note it was apparent that things had changed. Her playing was light and confident. Her hips made little circles in time with Bach's pocket masterpiece. He felt the blood rush back into his groin. It was perfectly in tune; music so exposed she should have been hacking and sawing by now. But no, it was perfect. She was possessed.

Every muscle in his body was already straining when she started to push the tempo. She attacked the gavotte as if it were a Paganini show tune. She ground her hips deep into him, round and round and round, faster and faster, her bow flying off the strings.

Outside the room a little group had formed. Elliot, Allan and Skuggs all had their ears planted against the door.

"Un-fucking-believable! She's still practicing!" said Elliot. Skuggs's mouth was hanging open, his punch bowl spilling lager onto the floor.

"Poor bastard," said Allan.

"I don't know," said Skuggs. "Is there a CD player in that room?" he asked the crowd around him. No one seemed to know.

She locked her legs under his; they were both lifted from the bed by the power of her performance. His body arched wildly as he approached his finale. She went on; crescendo, ac-celerando, faster and faster, her hips moving this way, that way, in great round circles then clipped little bounces. Alex hit a frenzied climax.

"NnnnngAaaargh!" He finished. She hadn't. His back, lev-itated by ecstasy, flopped onto the bed. She raced through the music at an impossible speed. Bow hair snapping, her own hair flying. Alex was straining every muscle in his body but now it was to hold on, to hold on until she finished. He fought the withdrawal impulse with every fibre of his being, he would not surrender. She held her arms out wide. Violin in one hand, bow in the other, her body jerked involuntarily, she shivered, then again, and again. She hugged herself, smiling. Both of them glistened and slipped against each other

"She sounds pretty good," said Skuggs. "Was that Alex shouting?"

They both lay, panting heavily, exhilarated. He felt he was floating above the bed. He ran his hand across her forehead, her face, her neck, her breasts, my God those breasts. She laughed. "My violin," she said, carefully placing the instrument and bow in the case.

There was more knocking.

"I never play like that before," she said.

"Me neither."

"I never feel like that before, never, never." She kissed his lips, then his forehead. "I love you Alex."

"You love me? You love me?"

"Yes, I love you."

"I love you," he said. And he meant it. It was that simple. No harps or cupid's arrows, no chocolates or flowers or jewellery, no weekend in Paris, no strolls in the park, no screaming arguments. No doubt.

"Come, we go to the party." She bunched her hair. She held an elastic band in her teeth and fixed her hair the way she fixed it every day.

"Just one moment," he said. "In case I get hit by a bus later, one moment." He stared at her the way he'd stared at her almost every day for the last three months. But it was different. She was naked. My God, she was naked. But that wasn't all. He was different. Everything was different.

"You like to look at me I think?"

"Yes. Yes, I do. I'll never have sex again. I've just had all the sex I was ever going to have. All packed into tonight."

She pinched him. "Make love, not sex."

"I'll never wash my winkie again. You should never rosin that bow again."

She covered her mouth to laugh. "You make me laugh. You are a dirty boy, I think."

"I am," he said. "I am a dirty boy."

They dressed quickly. She put on some lipstick. She didn't wear make-up, just lipstick; that was all she needed.

"How do I look?" she asked.

"You mean, do you look as if you just… made love?"

She nodded.

"You're beautiful," he said, cupping her face in his hands. And when we step out there, everybody's going to be too busy wondering why you're with a geek like me to think about whether we shagged or not."

"Made love. I don't like this shag." She kissed him.

"Do you have a key?"

Laura rapped loudly on the door, "Sheila! Sheila!"

Sheila stood with her arms folded, waiting for Alex's friends to get out of the way. When the way was clear she opened the door and the couple stepped out. Everything seemed normal. He'd almost expected a fanfare, all the partygoers lined up on both sides applauding. Sheila gave Laura a knowing smile.

"Was that you playing?" asked Skuggs, spilling his beer all over the place. "Or was it a record?"

"Easy Skuggs. Down boy," said Alex. Laura was unnerved by Skuggs's attentions. Alex put a protective arm around her.

Alex had a dopey smile on his face that refused to quit. The music was loud, Gary Glitter had been banished in favour of Miles Davis. Being close to her was enough for him. She stayed close to him. She seemed comfortable. He felt comfortable.

Elliot cornered Sheila. "You know what they say about Chinamen?" he said.

"Huh?"

"You know; that they're small down there. Well, it's true."

"Is it?" Sheila tried to make some room between her and Elliot.

"They've got tiny little tadgers."

"Have they?"

58

"Except for me," he said. "I'm hung like a bull."

"I'm happy for you," she said, pushing him to a safe distance.

When the party was over Alex tried to persuade Laura to come back to his flat but she would have none of it. She shared a flat with Sheila and had to be up sharpish to continue her mammoth practice schedule. Walking home from the party it was the usual Saturday night in Glasgow: drunks singing out of tune, half-eaten fish suppers and empty beer cans littering the street, people peeing in doorways and others shouting for Hughie before splashing a final exclamation point into the gutter, but all of it was a distant backdrop to the music in Alex's head. Skuggs had blabbered all the way back but Alex heard nothing but the gavotte going round and round and round. He hadn't known a few hours before that his life had been so empty. He was a computer geek but he'd had a few relationships, and his sexual activity had picked up tremendously at music college. Nothing had prepared him for this though. Not only had he told her he loved her, he knew it to be true. It was so natural, so normal to love her. When people told him in the past that they were in love he'd interpreted it as a kind of mental aberration, perhaps a neurochemical imbalance or some kind of auto–suggestive mechanism? It had simply never occurred to him that there could be an emotion so tangible it felt like a physical force. He'd felt lust many, many times and he'd expressed his lust as often as fate or good fortune would allow. He lusted after Laura for three months, but then that wasn't Laura, that was her body, that was before she spoke, when she was a mannequin, a projection, an object. The girl he'd lusted after in the trombone room simply didn't exist, she'd never existed, she was his creation. Now he felt Laura creating him, and he wanted to be created by her.

# NINE

Monday morning. Alex resisted the urge to head straight for the trombone room. He had a class scheduled with Professor Ingles, the electronic music teacher. Ingles was known as the electronics teacher but Alex was the first student ever to sign-up for her class. Mostly, she spent her time composing.

Ingles's electronic workshop was a techno DJ's wet dream. Wall-to-wall vintage synthesizers made the place look like a pre-WWII telephone exchange. No techno musician was ever going to get near Ingles' lab though; this gear was strictly for experimental composition. Alex had never heard a piece of experimental music that rose above caterwauling. Experimental music was serious music, it was as serious as music could get; it had to be serious and it had to be listened to seriously by serious people otherwise someone might get the mistaken idea that it was crap.

Alex wasn't there for the music; he was there for the gear. For some reason or other, rich people liked to donate money to the Academy. Usually, this money was spent on grand pianos. The Academy was, as they say in the financial markets, long on grand pianos. There was hardly a space that didn't have at least one grand piano squashed into it. Even the trombone room had a grand piano, a very nice grand piano at that, and Alex had sampled it many times in the wee small hours of the morning when the chances of stealing a clean waveform were highest.

Someone very eccentric must have croaked because instead of leaving money to be ploughed into more pianos, they left it to the discretion of Professor Ingles.

Ingles seemed happy to see him. He'd hardly sat down when she started drawing sine and square and sawtooth waves on the blackboard with scrapey chalk strokes that made his hair stand on end.

She was a short woman in her mid-forties with close-cropped hair. Her constant uniform was a man's three-piece suit designed when her synthesizers were high technology.

Ingles was a puritanical feminist; willies were monstrosities, evolutionary aberrations, the very thought of which sent her to the nth degree of aggravation. What's more, all the wrong people had them. Anyone in possession of such a vile object was a sworn enemy, and anyone without one had to do exactly what she said or she'd reluctantly have to write them off as mindless inadequates. Alex was on his guard.

She switched on a reel-to-reel tape. It was like being tossed into the world's noisiest construction site where half of the workers were watching a horror movie in 3D surround. This was the experimental music that coughed up a couple of grand here and the odd committee-driven award there. She had obviously spent a lot of work getting the timing right because he couldn't stop himself jumping out of his chair every time the wall of sound, built mostly from shrill voices whispering in Latin, was split open by a blood-curdling scream. This was the auditory equivalent of the Spanish Inquisition; had he known any secrets he'd be spilling his guts all over the place. He grit his teeth and tried to affect a pose of deep interest seasoned with a little amusement. If he blew the gaff here he might never get his paws on all the equipment he imagined would soon take the place of her noisy telephone exchange. As the last exaggerated whisper was mercifully disappearing she switched off the tape.

"So," she said, twirling the chalk expertly between her fingers, "the only non-abstract quality is the structure. I used a kind of arch-like motif, rather like some of Bartok's better efforts."

Better efforts? he thought. Alex wasn't a big fan of Bartok but he would have sold his soul for some Bartok during Ingles' sonic atrocity. Of course, it's rumoured that Bartok had a dick and therefore his music had to be flawed, despite its eminent plagiarisability. She seemed like she wanted a reaction. This was his chance.

"It's very radical," he said. "But you'd better be careful, it's dangerous to play music so overtly political in this place."

"You saw that?" She seemed genuinely surprised.

"The politics of gender have never been applied to the actual totality of sound before." He kept close scrutiny at all times, one slip and she'd see him for the shallow carpetbagger his desire for better equipment had made him. "People have used lyrics of course, but I'm sure you're breaking new ground here."

This was a revelation to Ingles. A man who understood her music? A male with a brain? "You know," she said, "for a man you surprise me." She hopped up onto her desk and let her legs swing back and forth with the glee of a four-year old. For a moment, the part of her schizophrenic DNA sequencing she tried so hard to submerge came bubbling to the fore. She looked quite girlie. Alex felt almost sorry he hadn't meant a word of it.

But he was in, and he knew it. He decided to go a little deeper. "A man can be more than testosterone. I try to keep in touch with my feminine side." He was glad that Elliot and Skuggs couldn't hear him. They'd be scheduling him on blind dates with Martin by now. "For me it's... it's the well from which creativity springs." There was joy written all over her. This was working better than he'd hoped. He'd thought he might have to attend her classes for weeks before cracking her. Maybe he wouldn't have to listen to any more of her compositions if he played his hand correctly?

"That new gear," he said. "When does it arrive?"

"Any day now."

He was beyond suspicion, a soul mate, a pal, a fellow traveller on the road between art and gender.

"Can I have a look at the manuals when they arrive?"

"Oh, I have some of them." After rooting around in her storeroom she appeared carrying a stack of books and pamphlets. She plumped them down on her desk. "They were sent in advance. It's pretty complicated literature." He felt a flash of anger. Literature? Why hadn't she consulted him anyway? So what if he was only a student? She had drawn basic waveforms all over the blackboard as if it meant something. So what? If she'd consulted him perhaps she might have bought gear worth using.

Of course, he hadn't checked the manuals yet. He was transfixed, unable to bring himself to touch them. He was frightened. What if it was a useless bunch of crap? Something just dandy for a John Cage impersonation, something perfect for writing bullshit program notes suggesting the music actually had some cultural significance—a tune being too much to ask.

"What's wrong?" Ingles sensed his trepidation. She picked up a manual and flicked through it. "Don't know much about computers," she said, throwing the manual back onto the pile. "Better mug up, I think." She took the tape reel off the machine and packed it into a hard white box then placed it carefully on a shelf among the hundreds of other white boxes containing her life's work. "You know something about computers, yes?"

"Yes." His curiosity overcame his fear. He checked the covers of the first four or five manuals. "Yes, I do."

There was some crap, well it wasn't crap exactly, it was pretty good stuff but useless to him: Kurtzweil, Roland, Yamaha synthesizers. She had really pushed the boat out; this stuff wasn't cheap. There were some languages, Cmusic, C++, now it was getting more interesting. She'd never use this stuff in a million years. This was great, he could help her set up her synths, he could show her all the wild and crazy sounds she'd get from her new digital acquisitions, he'd show her how well the sounds complemented her analog synths, he'd give her some blarney about cold, but easily controlled, digital sounds and about the warm but difficult to tame analog sounds, how the technology defined the character of the sounds and how she could incorporate it into her art. Thank God, he thought when he found evidence of gargantuan storage capacity, parallel processors, digital signal processors, some extremely high quality reverbs and delays, and plenty of mixing capabilities. This'll do nicely, this'll do, he thought, trying to hide his excitement. If he could steer her away from the computer and sampling equipment and toward the synths, he'd be quids in.

"Perhaps you could give me a few pointers?"

Yeah honey, he thought, how about writing code twelve hours a day for ten years, then you might actually be able to use this stuff? But what did he care? She was being gracious and he was wondering why he was on the verge of being thrown out of an institution that had a professor of electronic music who had no students and spent all her time proving that the Emperor's New Clothes wasn't a myth.

"I'd be honoured," he said. "Truly."

"Yes. Why not? This equipment makes us one of the best resourced music labs in the world you know."

"I know."

"Yes. Yes, the consultant was quite clear about that."

"Consultant?"

"We hired a consultant to help us define our needs."

"You paid someone to tell you what to buy?" He cleared his throat. "Good idea," he added, before his intonation gave him up. This equipment could speed up his work five, maybe tenfold.

Alex had spent too long with Ingles. No time to go see Laura. He had a tutorial he'd prepared for. He hated tutorials worst of all. There were three in his group, including himself. There was little Graham who had perfect pitch and a sharp tongue but zero social skills to temper his talents. Like most of the students at the Academy, Graham was an obsessive. He was twenty-years old but he looked nine. He sailed through practical exams and Alex had it on good authority that he was a pretty hot timpani player. Alex could tell if a timp player was bashing his drum out of time, but that was it, he had no idea what else it was that timp players did. Graham's pals in the percussion department had told Alex that Graham was a shoo-in for an orchestral job but he was having difficulty on his course because he couldn't sight read very well. He couldn't sight read very well because he learned timpani by playing along with records in his bedroom. He knew almost the whole classical repertoire by heart, which seemed quite a feat to Alex, but their tutor was unimpressed.

The other student in the group was a singer named Sally. Sally was a big girl, which Alex took as a sign that she might have a real chance of making it in opera. The Academy did turn out quite a few successful opera singers and Alex couldn't help but correlate the size of a singer to her chances of making it. After all, whoever heard of a skinny opera singer?

Poor Sally got the worst of it in tutorials. She had a lovely voice but that was it. The outside world would probably assume that having a lovely voice was just about all one would need to become a singer. But music colleges insist on something they call 'musicianship': whatever it is that you can't do well. In Alex's case, it was playing piano. In Graham's case it was reading on sight. In Sally's case it was everything except singing. Sally couldn't read, she could hardly tell a minor from a major, she hadn't picked up any music theory to speak of in two-and-a-half years of painful tutorials.

Their tutor, a certain Mr. Liddell, was a failed pianist with a degree in musicology. Liddell's sole aim was to make the study of music as dreary and, in Sally's case, terrifying as humanly possible.

Every week, at the end of a tutorial, Liddell would give them a melody line. They would take it home and write a four- or five-part harmony for the line. Liddell insisted that the harmony be written in ink to ensure maximal misuse of time. They'd bring their harmonizations in every week, and every week Liddell would point out why every single note they had written was wrong. His pet hates were consecutive fifths, exposed octaves, and doubled thirds. He'd smash the piano with his full body weight every time he got to the offending passages, "Listen! Listen!" he'd bark. "Listen how muddy that is!"

Alex and Sally and Graham had no idea what 'muddy' meant, nor why it was supposed to sound bad. Alex didn't have time to do Liddell's harmonization this week, so he'd copied out last week's, with all of Liddell's corrections—Liddell always re-wrote everything; there was never a time when any of them had ever produced anything acceptable. When Alex handed over his work to be criticized—expecting Liddell to either twig that he'd written it himself the week before, or to build a shrine to Alex for finally writing harmony without fifths or octaves or doubled thirds—Liddell went crazy.

"Bloody rubbish!"

"But there's no fifths, no doubled thirds."

"What's this suspension for?" He clanged the keys like he was hammering nails.

"If you hit anything like that it would sound bad," said Alex in defence of Liddell's harmonization.

"All right. All right. How's this?" Liddell sat poker-straight. He closed his eyes, rested his hands delicately on the keys, took a deep breath, exhaled slowly, then dropped his fingers into the keys with such tenderness that Graham missed the irony.

"Sounds good to me," said Graham.

"Have you no ear?" he raged. Sally jumped.

"I've got perfect pitch," said Graham. Graham knew Liddell didn't have perfect pitch.

"You people! You think that matters?"

"It matters to you," said Graham. Sally clutched her notebook to her bosom. If Liddell tore into Alex so savagely he would surely explode when he saw her octave-laden effort.

Liddell was transmitting so much vitriol at little Graham, his eyes were fit to pop right out. Graham, of course, cared not a jot. All Graham cared about was symphonic music and his timpani.

"What's this chord?" Liddell shouted at no one in particular. He brought his hands down onto the keyboard like he was trying to break it into pieces.

"Are you talking to me?" Graham asked, quite matter-of-factly. Sally's eyes were welling up, it was always bad but this tutorial was shaping up terribly. What, in God's name, would he do when he got to her?

"Yes," said Liddell. "I'm talking to you."

"It's a second inversion D sharp major," said Graham.

Liddell slammed the piano lid shut. "E flat! E flat! Haven't you learned anything?"

"Same thing," said Graham, looking bored.

"It's not the bloody same thing. Perfect pitch? This is what perfect pitch does for you. You can't tell the difference between a D sharp and an E flat?"

"That's because there is no difference, see!" Graham lifted the piano lid and played a D sharp. "This is D sharp," he said. "Now observe how my fingers stay on the same notes and play E flat." He repeated the chord.

"It's the key you fool. It's in a different key, therefore it's a different chord."

"No it's not. Would you like me to demonstrate again? If, however, you were to ask a string player to play a D sharp and an E flat, you'd probably get two different notes. This is a piano. They're the same."

Alex thought he'd better intervene before Liddell killed him. Graham was no more than five feet tall. He was twenty-years old but he hadn't started shaving yet. On occasions when he had to walk home late at night, he used a little flashlight his mother had given him. The police had picked him up once and driven him home: he looked so young they thought he was lying about his age. But Graham was as unyielding as a little five-foot bar of tempered steel. He was fearless.

"If we could get back to my harmony?" Alex said. He knew Graham was going to like what he had a mind to do, and it might cheer Sally up as well. "Do you think we could get this sorted out and leave the E flat for now? What did I do wrong next?" he asked. This question had almost become a mantra in Liddell's class. Liddell enjoyed the question; it reminded him that he was in charge. Alex handed him his harmony and Liddell went into mumble-mode while he re-wrote the whole exercise in red ink.

When he had finished, he handed it back to Alex and said, "Study this, you might learn something, although I doubt it."

"I think I've learned a lot today," Alex said. He turned back a couple of pages and held it up for Graham and Sally to see then he showed it to Liddell. "This is what you wrote last week. It's in red ink. Every note. In red. Written by you. Apparently, what I'd written was rubbish so you put me straight." He flicked a couple of pages forward, he held it up for Graham and Sally to see, "I copied everything you wrote last week. I brought it in, and you say it's rubbish. All of it, every note." Graham was loving this. Sally was puzzled.

"How dare you," said Liddell to Alex.

"How dare you," said Graham to Liddell. "You should be ashamed of yourself. I have an important concert tonight. I need to rehearse, and I'm sure Alex and Sally have better things to do." Graham got up and left.

"Come on Sally. Let's go," said Alex, taking Sally's hand. "We'll be here next week, Mr. Liddell. It would be great if you could try a little kindness for a change."

On his way to the trombone room, Alex stopped, as usual, to set up a base camp and collect himself before the final ascent. When he had regained full control of his cardiovascular system he lit a cigarette. He could hear her running through some scales. He'd enjoyed giving Liddell one up the arse; the little shit deserved it. Later, he would have to pick up the van and lug his stuff back to the flat but now he would see Laura. He stubbed out his cigarette and popped a mint into his mouth.

It was almost a conditional response; when he got to her room he peered in. She started in on Bach's great Chaconne. He watched for a second, wondering whether he should wait until she'd finished the piece. He'd spent three months watching her, wanting her. He'd spent three months talking to her, quite unselfconsciously, like she was his best friend. She knew everything about him. He'd told her all his hopes, his dreams, his petty gripes. From now on he would learn what she wanted, who she was, why on earth she wanted him. He decided he wouldn't charge into the room, it was time to pretend he was a mature adult.

He opened the door slowly, but not too slowly; he had always blustered his way into the place making a great show of his entrance, if he snuck in too stealthily now, it might give her a fright. This time he would enter like a normal person and sit quietly until the music was over.

When he stepped into the room she threw her arms out wide. "Alex!" With her violin in one hand and the bow in the other she rushed to him and hugged him tightly.

They kissed.

"My God," he said, "you stopped in the middle of a tune. You really, really like me."

"Sit down silly."

He pulled up two chairs. He told her about Liddell, explaining every detail like a small boy telling his mother about his day at school.

"I do not like Mr. Liddell. He is a very bad teacher, I think. I think there are many bad teachers in this place, and not too many good ones."

"McNabb's the worst. He wants to throw me out."

"I know. You tell me many times."

"Sorry." He had forgotten that he'd told her just about everything that had ever happened in his life. Somehow, she'd taken it all in despite the language, the accent, and the violin playing. She took his hand.

"Do not apologize. I am here. I am with you."

"You know everything about me," he said. "I want to know you."

"You know me. But I want you to know something about me. It is very important."

"Yes?" he said, with a little trepidation. "You haven't had a sex change? You're not a murderer? You're not married?" At this, he suddenly took fright. "You're not married?"

She gave him a stiff punch in the arm. "Listen," she said. "The other night. That is not my habit, okay?"

"Okay."

"No, it's not okay."

"It's not?"

"Listen! I haven't been with… I'm not interested in boys."

"Me neither."

She gave him another dead arm. "All my life, since I have three-years, I play violin. No boys. Boys are trouble."

"You've had boyfriends before?"

"I have one boyfriend before. But he say he was more important to my music."

"So his arse was out the window?"

"His what?"

"You got rid of him?"

"Yes."

"And you're telling me the same thing. Music comes first, yes?"

She had been sitting with her violin and bow on her lap, unconsciously tapping the fingerboard from time to time. She got up and put her violin away and locked the case. She sat down on his lap and rested her arms on his shoulders.

"No," she said. "Do you understand?"

"Look," he said. "I don't understand anything anymore. I'll never get in the way of your music, or anything else you want."

"Do you understand?" she asked again.

"Yes. Yes. I understand," he said, and squeezed her tightly. They sat in silence for moment, then he added, "When you sit on my lap like this it gives me a boner… Do you know what a boner is?"

"Yes." She lifted an eyebrow and gave a little wiggle. "I understand."

There was a loud crash. Laura jumped. The door opened slowly. It was Skuggs. He was fighting for breath.

"What's up?" asked Alex, concerned that something very bad had taken place. Skuggs stood, barely, with his hands on his thighs gasping for air.

"Sit down," said Alex. He led him to a chair as Laura left the room. Skuggs sat with his head between his legs. He lifted his head up. His face was beetroot red. His eyes were almost the same shade and filled with tears. Laura came back with some water and offered it to Skuggs. He made a pained face that contained an implied thanks but his need for oxygen was greater.

"What's up Skuggs? What happened?" asked Alex with a growing sense of dread.

"I didn't know it was this far," he panted. "I got halfway… Couldn't decide what to do… I knew you'd be here… Christ." He sipped some water.

"What's up Skuggs?"

Skuggs sipped some more water, then took out a grey handkerchief that was probably supposed to be white and blew his nose. "Ran outa drinking vouchers. Got a fiver?"

"Christ Skuggs! I almost shat myself. That's it? You came all the way up here for a loan?"

"I fell outside. I think I've skinned my knees."

Alex got his wallet out. "Here, here's a tenner. Beat it."

"Okay. Cheers mate." Skuggs gave Laura a little wave. She waved back. Skuggs left.

"I think your friend is a little crazy."

"He's a lot crazy. Come back to the flat. I'll make you my famous chili?"

"I want to hear your music. You talk about your… sample?"

He nodded.

"Your computer? All the time. I want to hear."

"Let me run and get Skuggs before he hits the pub. I have to get my gear back to the flat. Then we can pick up some stuff from the supermarket. I'll cook then I'll let you hear some stuff. Okay?"

He ran out to catch Skuggs, who was sitting three steps down the staircase with his trouser legs rolled up, checking his knees.

"Skuggs, I've got a job for you."

# TEN

It took them three hours to ferry his equipment back to the flat. Skuggs bitched for the duration, but the promise of twenty non-returnable drinking vouchers plus a free nosebag full of chili was enough to keep him on the job. Alex deliberately took as much time as he could at the supermarket, checking every expiry date, criticizing E numbers and points of origin to ensure that Skuggs would be ravenously hungry by the time the food was prepared. Alex didn't want Skuggs around tonight but he didn't want to ask him to bugger off out of it either. If Skuggs were kept waiting long enough he would wolf his food down and rush to the local gas station to make up for lost time.

"I thought he was going to eat the plate," said Laura after watching Skuggs devour a mountainous plate of food in the time it took her to sip some water, spread a napkin on her lap, and break bread. Skuggs had already left by the time they were both seated.

"It wasn't a pretty sight but he's a healthy, growing boy."

"Mm. This is good."

"Don't sound so surprised. It's perfect bachelor fare. I usually make a cauldron of the stuff. You should try it on the sixth or seventh day, after it's matured."

"Cauldron?"

"Big pot."

"It's good. You can cook."

"Only this I'm afraid." He could hardly contain himself at the thought of Laura actually showing interest in his music. No one had ever shown any interest in his music. He knew she was probably just being polite but he'd been working for years on his own with no one to share his failures and his triumphs, he was bursting to talk about it.

"You really want to hear my music?"

"Of course."

"Will you stay here tonight?"

"Not if Skuggs is here."

"He won't be," he said, already planning how he would pitchfork Skuggs out of the door if he had to. Although, somehow he knew that Skuggs wouldn't be back tonight. For all his eccentricities, Skuggs was sympathetic to the needs of others, when had a mind to be.

"He won't be," he confirmed as he pointed the remote at his sound system. "What do you want to listen to? Classical, Romantic, Baroque, Rococo, Renaissance, Jazz, Rock, Techno, Trance, New Age, African, Cuban?"

"Anything. I like all music."

"You like rap? Massed pipe bands? All rap sounds the same to me and pipe bands are like someone captured fifty cats in a sack then taped the sound of them getting clubbed to death."

"You are Scottish. You no like pipes?"

"I like the Pibroch; solo pipe playing, it's very beautiful, evocative, but massed bands are too loud. It's painful."

"Put anything on. Put Pibroch on."

Listening to the haunting wail of the Pibroch, he wondered whether the deepest sounds of a culture really reflect the character of the people. Laura was Spanish. Spain was famous for Flamenco. Flamenco was sexy, like her. Flamenco was fiery, like her, it was hot and sultry; it was spontaneous and brilliant and full of life. The Pibroch was a dirge, it was cold and precise and exacting, it was austere and insistent, like a chill wind on a dark highland night. The Pibroch had beauty, but it was a difficult, demanding beauty. Flamenco had a gravitational force that drew the listener. The Pibroch demanded too much of the listener. They both sat in silence, sipping wine. Alex, inwardly kicking himself for trying to impress her with his eclectic record collection and Laura, too embarrassed to suggest changing the music; after all, this was pure Scottish music, he might take offence.

"This is spooky. Fancy some Flamenco?" he said when the drones had started to eat into his soul.

"Yes please," she replied, her open-mindedness cured for the present.

"The Pibroch is an acquired taste, like whisky."

After some Flamenco and a little more wine, the freeze that the Pibroch had threatened had passed.

"Tell me about your music," she said.

"Well, I've developed a new sampling technique. The lower register of the piano starts at around twenty-seven and a half hertz and the highest fundamental is over four kilohertz. The most difficult part is the harmonics. The lowest fundamental is around 25 decibels below its strongest harmonic, and the higher harmonics go above ten thousand hertz. Nyquist's theorem states that a sampling rate where every sample contains at least two cycles should be enough, psychoacoustically, but I don't think that's true. Nyquist is just the start, the birthplace."

Laura was nodding along with the sound of his voice, following his intonation. Alex had never spoken to anyone about his sampling before. Everything he knew about the piano was tripping over everything he knew about sampling and both were racing with everything he knew about computers to see the light of day.

He began to pace furtively as he talked. The rhythm of a Bulerias filling the room only made him more animated.

"Then you have the mechanical noises. You can't ignore them. A recording engineer will tear his eyes out trying to eliminate them from a piano recording but you can't. You just can't. So, if you don't account for them in the final performance then it'll sound fake. It won't be conscious, of course, but the listener will know something's wrong. They're around two hundred to a thousand hertz so they're not hard to deal with from a sampling point of view, but you have to treat them differently across the range of the music. You have to scale them according to the reality of the music, more on the higher register and subtler in the lower and middle registers. Then you get to the core problems."

He was no longer even aware he had an audience. Totally immersed in his thoughts, making pained faces when he got to points in his logic where his ideas might be stretched, where he wasn't quite sure if he had the problems licked or not.

"You see, because of Nyquist's theorem, CDs are recorded at forty-four to forty-eight kilohertz, usually at sixteen-bit resolution. And it's not enough! It's just not enough!" He gave her a start at this realization.

"But if you increase the frequency, say double it, and if you increase the resolution, and bear in mind that each bit carries more information than all of the previous bits added together so thirty-two bits isn't double sixteen. Seventeen is double sixteen, and eighteen is double seventeen. So suddenly you have a gargantuan difference in resolution. And that creates new problems. You've suddenly correlated the aliasing problems to a deeper resolution. You can fix them with filters, but who the hell wants to fart around with filters?" He shook his head. She shook her head.

"Also, because of the higher frequency and resolution, now you need huge storage capacity and faster processing." He held his hands in front of his face as if holding a crystal ball. He looked into it deeply. Laura looked into it. He held it between them, and turned it in his hands.

"But I've solved it. I've found the answer. It's simple really, at least in computational terms." She looked at him through the invisible ball of answers he held before her.

"Non-linear sampling frequencies. It's simple. I use a pseudo-random number generator to vary the sample rates above forty kilohertz so that the cycle is constantly varied. And!" he exclaimed with an emphasizing finger. "I can grab huge samples using less memory. It's simple. The artefacts disappear. It just becomes a matter of recording the right samples with the right microphones from the right angles at the right distance, then adding the right combinations of sympathetic harmonics and mechanical noises. And! The best part! I include a few mistakes. Nothing much, just a couple of brushes against wrong keys at the limits of the performance. No one's perfect." He suddenly came out of his trance. "Are they?"

Laura cleared her throat, sipped some wine then cleared her throat again and said "But..." She put her wine on the table, clasped her hands together, cleared her throat again, "But... what is a sample?"

It was as if someone had stabbed him in the gut with a knife dripping in some fast-acting poison that induced intense embarrassment. "Oh, God... I'm sorry. I'm sorry. What a moron... Not you, me," he added quickly. "I'm sorry."

"It's okay." She smiled.

"I'll start again. Not the whole thing. I'll explain." They sat on the sofa. He took both her hands in his. Her hands were small. Her skin was smooth, warm; it felt good, sitting there with his Spanish girlfriend, holding hands. He thought for a moment then, "A tape recorder. You know what a tape recorder is?" He felt himself being thrown back into software development class. The trouble with software is that whatever is easy to understand about it is boring. Then it immediately moves from easy and boring straight into frightening inscrutability. There's no middle. It's either too easy or too difficult.

"A sample is a recording," he continued. "Like a tape recording, except, it's digital. I record onto a hard disk or into RAM or ROM or onto a CD instead of onto a tape, but it's the same thing exactly, just a different medium." Would she understand medium? he thought. This is difficult, her English is good but this is hard enough when it's your first language. "It's a recording of one note. I sit at the piano and I play one note, say, a middle C. Then I record every other note, very carefully, until I've recorded every note on the piano. So, at the end I have eighty-eight notes, all the notes on the piano recorded. Now all those notes are on my computer, my sampler. I can hook up a keyboard to it and then I can play those notes as if it was a piano."

"I understand." She squeezed his hand to show he was on the right track.

"The problem is that they were all recorded with the same velocity. The partials are wrong, there's hardly any sympathetic harmonics and what there are is wrong." He could see he was losing her. "I'll show you. I'll let you hear it." He led her to his computer and sat her down in front of it. He pulled up another chair for himself. He clicked the mouse a few times and soon had his demonstration prepared.

"Those samples, those single note recordings? Here they are. This is how it sounds if you just sample the notes then play them back on a computer." It was Chopin, his third prelude in G major. It sounded lifeless. Stilted and artificial, the left-hand part ran up and down the arpeggios mechanically. All the notes were still there, all the notes exactly as Chopin had written them but without a shred of humanity.

"That sounds bad," she said after he had switched it off prematurely.

"Well, that's what people think I'm doing. That's what McNabb thinks I'm doing when I tell him that's its all sampled, that it's all done on a computer. He thinks it's just defining the notes. Like writing the score on a computer screen. It's too much for his pea-brain to comprehend.

"Listen to this. This is a performance I created that's supposed to sound like me playing. It's not the greatest playing in the world but what I was trying to do was to prove that I can invest the music with what we'd normally describe as an interpretation. I'm using a lot more samples here. Thousands. Different velocities, varied attacks, harmonics, pedals sounds. I even created some harmonics based on some of the chord shapes. He clicked the mouse and Chopin's third prelude in G major appeared again, but this time the melody danced lightly over a singing bass.

"This is good," she said almost immediately.

"Like my Chili, eh?"

"I love Chopin. You play very well."

"But I didn't actually play this," he said as he clicked the mouse and the music stopped. "I played this. This is a recording of me playing a regular piano." Another click of the mouse and the Chopin appeared again.

She listened for a few seconds. "But it sounds the same to me. It's good."

"That's it," he said, trying to contain himself. "That's the point. The first one I did totally from my samples, sitting here at the computer. I didn't touch a piano key."

"But," she said with a pained look. "What's the point? You play very well. Why use a computer?"

"Because of this." He clicked the mouse. This was music that deserved Elliot's mock critique: 'Swirling arpeggios engulfed in a sea of tranquil resonance,' he'd said. Her mouth dropped open. Alex knew that this is what Chopin meant when he wrote the piece. He'd spent months just trying to figure out how fast a piano could be played. His interpretation was at the very limits of what is mechanically possible on a piano. Any faster and the keys simply wouldn't return in time for the next note. Nothing was played on the beat, every note at least a few milliseconds away from the pulse, sometimes pushing the beat, sometimes reining it in. He'd sampled a complete set of partials just for this piece. The sympathetic harmonics accompanying every combination of notes were there. He'd recorded from hundreds of different positions, using cardoid and hypercardoid microphones, large and small diaphragm microphones, pressure zone and contact microphones. He'd recorded from every conceivable angle and position. He could tweak the ambience but generally he had recorded in an appropriate environment: acoustics were everything. When you record a piano, you also record the space in which the piano exists. There was no way to know what would sound best until he'd tried it, there was no manual to follow, no rules to confide in or break. It was all trial and error. Sampling was a black art and he was its master.

Not only could nobody, in his opinion, possibly guess that this music wasn't played on piano, it sounded like Chopin himself had been raised from the grave to play it, the fireworks in the left hand providing an emotional counterpoint to the simple harmonic narrative in the right. He did cheat slightly, but only in his choice of music. There were no interminably long bass notes to deal with here, no endless harmonics evolving and setting off other notes that in turn would set off others still. Nothing was looped. No matter how well it was executed, the most sensitive ear would always detect a loop. Loops were a workaround, a trick, and not that clever a trick either. If you had to extend a note you could just slice off a bit from the middle and stick it onto the back of it. It wasn't difficult to do and it saved lots of precious memory. But loops were useless to him.

The music finished, he gently lifted her chin up to close her mouth.

"Maravilloso," she said, quite absently.

"I think Chopin would have loved that. But I can hardly go dig him up to get the proof."

"It is so beautiful."

"You're the only person that's heard it. When I get hold of Ingles' new equipment I think I can improve it. There's a couple of spaces in the harmonics that I could fill, and a couple of places that could do with some more space. What's most interesting is that you can't just speed it up. Every new performance, every new tempo has to be approached from scratch, otherwise it sounds fake. I think this is at the limits of what a human might be capable of."

She gave him a look of disbelief.

"Well, we didn't get to hear Chopin or Liszt. You never know. Listen to the music they wrote. This is certainly where they were headed. It's too much to say that they might have used computers if they'd been available, but look at their scores; or Beethoven, crammed with directions, like they were trying to bash what they wanted into the performer's skull. They killed themselves to try to get their meaning across." He let out a huge sigh. "But because I can't do this with my fingers, like a proper pianist, it gets treated like worthless shit. This is my interpretation of the music. The computer is my instrument. I've worked just as hard as any pianist to develop my technique."

"Can you do it with a violin?" she asked.

He sat in thought for a few seconds then, "With a violin you haven't got the problem of the sounds evolving toward infinity, like piano, and you have a fundamental at the core of every note. That would make it easier. But everything else would be much more difficult. You'd need an infinite number of samples to create a general instrument, like this. The variety of attack in string instruments is too complex." He rubbed his chin, deep in thought. "But it might be possible to create source-specific instruments." She looked puzzled. "Like, if we wanted to play a piece of Bach, if we knew the piece we wanted we could probably keep the number of samples down by analysing it phrase by phrase. It might be possible. I've been working on building a violin in pure software, but it's so hard. I don't think I can do it. It's a shame, because if you could build a violin in software then, in principle, you could build a better violin than a Stradivarius. Really. There's no reason why not. But I don't think I can, unfortunately."

"But you could play the Chaconne?"

"Sure," he caught himself quickly. "Well, maybe. There's a lot of double-stops in that tune. I'm not sure what the phasing problems would be, or the phrasing problems come to that. But if we got a good enough instrument, with a lot, and I mean a lot of patience, we could probably have a stab at it. We could build Paganini!" He made a crazy face. He drew make-believe lines across her forehead with his fingers. "Vee could use dee criminal brain or zee normal brain. Vee could raise Paganini from zee dead! Zee great maestro among us once more; El Diablo! Zee Devil himself!" He tickled her ribs. She giggled as she tried to fight him off.

"Tonight vee make zee love without Senior Violin, no?" he said before he kissed her. Those breasts, he thought. Those breasts. Then his mind went blank.

Todd held on to his wife's hand until it was so cold he knew she wasn't there anymore. He didn't cry. He felt nothing. He picked up a bottle of pills from the bedside table, the same pills he had crushed so carefully a few hours ago and given to his wife. He wanted to follow her now. What was life without her? They had no children. He had no family. He was alone. For the first time in twenty-five years he was alone. He longed to lie down beside her.

But his wife had been clever. The moment she had persuaded him to help her leave life with a little dignity, although in truth it was the cancer that had persuaded him in the end, she made him promise that he would 'be brave', that he would go on with his life, his career, his music.

A year ago the cancer came, it crept into her throat for no reason at all. She didn't smoke, she hardly drank, she ate well and lived a healthy life, but still it came for her. After six months of terror and anger and tears it showed itself. Then the fight. For five months she fought, and Todd watched her fight. They both wanted to believe. The doctors charmed them with rescue fantasies, but it was little more than medieval torture. Zapped with rays until her lovely hair was straw. Filled with drugs that made her so sick she begged for death. And worst of all, they reached in to where the cancer was and stretched until there was room for it to grow.

His friend was gone.

They had started as friends, as kindred spirits. They shared their love of music first then they shared their love. It was simple, idyllic. He graduated, they married, their love sustained, their friendship deepened.

He folded her arms across her chest then pulled the sheet up over her face, not quite knowing why. He thought about calling someone but he didn't know who to call.

She had suffered too long. Finally, she had raged silently at her doctors, at him, at the world. She made him take her home to die. She was in terrible pain right up to the end and he knew it was his fault. He had been too selfish. He used moral arguments against assisted suicide, but he simply couldn't bear the thought of losing her. Of course, she forgave him. She absolved him of all of his sins in a reversal of catholic doctrine.

There would have to be an autopsy. They would find the cause of death but this was, thankfully, a society where a blind eye is turned to genuine euthanasia.

Alex spent most of the night in a deep, blissful sleep dreaming deep, blissful dreams. He mostly enjoyed dreaming. His dreams usually flitted randomly between sex, music and mathematics with the three often fusing in an orgy of lusty equations or filthy whole-tone scales performing libidinous acts that would be decried as abominations across most cultures. He never analysed his dreams and never tried to remember them. He never ever tried to figure how a resonance could feel so erotic, or how a woman's body could solve logic problems he'd fought with for weeks. He'd never woken from a dream with any great insights or ready-made solutions, but he'd often woken with the knowledge that a problem somewhere had been solved and that the day would reveal what the problem and the solution were. He never analysed it because he didn't want to lose it. He especially didn't want to stop waking-up with a boner fit to explode; a sure sign that either a revelation was afoot or he hadn't had sex in a long time.

But today his dreams had become disturbing.

The naked bagpipe-playing ballerina that had just convinced him to give the Pibroch a second chance, changed abruptly into an elderly J. S. Bach who was drawing a violin bow across his pronounced belly. The bow was metal; it was sharp, more like a scimitar than a bow. The sound was dreadful and it was cutting great slices of flesh from Bach's belly. Alex became aware he was dreaming when Bach floated toward him wearing a mindless smile below dead, staring eyes. The Chaconne. It was the Chaconne. But it was really bad. Why was Bach doing that to his own music?

Alex tried to wake himself up but he couldn't move. He rolled from side to side; his strategy on the rare occasions when his dreams took a bad turn and he was trapped inside one of them. This is a dream, this is a dream, he told himself. Bach's face faded but Alex was immersed in the black liquid that floated near the surface of his dream world. It was like some dark, sweet potion that would send him back down if he gave in to it. He had to get to the surface. He had to resist for just a moment and then he'd be free. He held his breath and fought the urge to give himself over to sleep. He'd been here before. If he gave in now Bach would come back, and God knows what else he'd bring with him. He could still hear the bloody Chaconne, and it was getting louder.

He opened his eyes. Bach's face was there, right in the room, hovering above him. He braced himself. He knew it was a dream. His dreams had followed him into real life often enough that he knew even this horrible nightmare would fade in a few seconds. He just had to stay awake. If he allowed himself to fall back into the dream it would be much worse. Just as his dreams of jolly debauchery had stepped into his world on a few happy mornings, these horrific images could follow. But he knew it was a dream. He knew that Bach's larded face and stupid wig would soon slip back into his subconscious where they belonged.

Bach's face faded again. This time he knew it was gone. He stared at the ceiling. The music was still there, even louder. He scrunched up his eyes. He shook his head. He poked his fingers deep into his ears and dug around until they popped.

Still the Chaconne sounded.

He sat bolt upright, gripped with fear.

Laura sat at the foot of the bed, naked. She half turned to acknowledge his entrance into the waking world. She offered a strained smile, cocked her head slightly and jammed the violin harder into her neck, dragging the bow heavily across uncooperative strings.

"Morning!" she barked with such a gargantuan effort of concentration it almost broke his heart. If violinists are presented with a pause in the music they can fart the odd word. The Chaconne offers three or four such platforms where the performer can gather herself before plunging into even greater levels of technical difficulty. Laura had forsaken such an opportunity to greet Alex, and he melted.

He stared at his beautiful conundrum and wondered if it would be like this every day. He checked the time. It was six in the morning. Surely a posse of neighbours would crash into the room any minute and string them both up by the thumbs? Maybe a few passing alley cats would throw trash at the window to shut up the racket? If Skuggs came back and saw this it might send him into a catatonic state. The simultaneous presence of a vision of pure beauty creating such an aural atrocity would be like the meeting of matter and anti-matter to Skuggs. He was a sensitive boy and such a deluge could induce an infinite feedback loop.

Alex decided he would hate himself later, and feel guilty after she got to the end of the piece.

He shuffled along the bed toward her. Like most musicians, Alex had a natural power to concentrate, to unconsciously focus so deeply that anything outside the object of his attention became invisible. He didn't want to hear the music so the music was gone. He was deaf. All he could see was her hair; a thousand shades that differentiate the real blonds from the counterfeits. He couldn't resist the urge to touch it. He unconsciously swept a few strands from her shoulder. His fingers brushed lightly against her neck.

Her curt, stilted arm movements gave way to a relaxed power that became manifest in sound as he kissed her neck. The Chaconne rose like an island of beauty from a dark, dissonant sea. Ah, he thought, deciding where next to plant his lips, now that's the Chaconne.

He drew back in amazement. The sounds he was hearing were real, they were coming from her violin, they weren't in his head. She played on; unaware of the quantum leap her playing had taken.

This is what Skuggs was rambling about, he thought. After the party Skuggs had recited a drunken monologue all the way back to Alex's flat. He tried to remember what Skuggs had said but all he could see was Skuggs standing in the middle of George Square swinging a fish supper around, and shouting "She's brilliant! She's Fucking brilliant. And those tits! Yer a jammy bastard!"

Her shoulders tensed almost imperceptibly, the angle of her bowing arm became a little more acute. The round, deep timbres morphed into shrillness.

Alex placed his hand on her naked hip. My God, he could feel it. He could actually feel her change. It wasn't just muscles relaxing or her breathing achieving regularity, he could feel something more. Her body moved *into* the music. The music was free again. Bach was alive again.

He pulled his hand away. In a few seconds the tension was back. A touch could send her from self-conscious hacking to profound virtuosity?

Then he remembered the sex. Or at least he remembered the part with the violin. So immersed was he in his own ecstasy he'd failed to notice that she hadn't just played well during sex, she hadn't just played brilliantly; it was beyond brilliance. Did he miss that or forget it? He planted his hand on her back. Again, Bach appeared inside the music. He took his hand away and Bach took flight, leaving a cold facsimile; a nervous music student biting off a lot more than she could chew.

Alex wasn't someone who got nervous easily but this was starting to frighten him. He'd found the perfect woman, the perfect partner. But this was weirdness verging on the supernatural. He'd allowed himself to be swept up by the whole experience. Perhaps reality was going to have its say after all? Maybe his Laura was crazy Laura, or possessed Laura; like some old black and white movie where she'd use him to conjure her spirits, to catalyze her talents, and he'd become her cipher, pandering to her every whim, and chomping on bluebottles?

He shivered. He was sweating but he felt cold. She was closing-in on the finish line. Alex decided to try one last experiment. He knelt behind her and placed his hands on her shoulders, then slid them slowly down over her breasts while pressing himself against her. The warmth of her body was comfortable, familiar, but he tried to stay detached, to observe, to listen and observe.

Sure enough, he thought, there's a correlation between the extent of the contact and the quality of the playing. But it's a sliding scale. There are diminishing returns. She improves tremendously when I touch her, but the more I touch her...

Laura played a final double stop.

"Your thing it digs in my back," she said playfully.

He clean forgot what he was thinking about. "Put your fiddle away," he said. "I need a good hard shag."

She kissed him. "I have to practice my darling please, just another hour."

"Okay, okay. Then let me rephrase. I need a good hard shag. Bring your fiddle."

She was still giggling uncontrollably as he pulled her onto him.

When they had both showered and dressed it was still only eight o' clock in the morning. Alex fixed some coffee and toast and found out that he couldn't make coffee properly. Laura assured him that she'd get a proper coffee maker and teach him how to do it right.

After she had finished her toast but before she had a chance to resume her practice Alex piped, "Look, what's going on?"

"Huh?"

"With the music and the sex, what's the deal?"

"Huh?"

He could see it in her face. She was being genuine. She had no idea what he was talking about.

"Laura, every time we have sex you turn into Itzhak Perlman. Well, not to look at, thank God."

"Huh?"

"When I touch you, the music changes. You must be aware of it? Even the slightest touch brings it on."

"You do not want me to play when we make love? You no like?"

"On the contrary. It's beyond anything I ever dreamed sex could be. It's my two favourite things all rolled up into one bumper pack. I'm not complaining, I'm asking, what's the deal? What's going on? How come your playing is so crap normally and so wonderful when we have sexual contact?"

Like most things he said, it just rolled right out of his mouth without a nanosecond of reflection. He didn't even realize he'd said anything wrong until her face crumpled and the tears came.

He instinctively fell to his knees and begged like a dog, "I'm sorry, I'm sorry."

"It is crap."

"No, no. It's not. I didn't mean that. That's not what I meant."

"You have a great technique, but it is hidden in tension," she said between heart-ripping sniffles.

"Huh?"

"That is what my teachers say. It is crap. It's crap. It's crap. I am a freak." Alex retrieved a box of paper tissues from the kitchen and handed her one. She blew into it. "I work so hard."

"I know."

"I practice all the time."

"I know." Sensing that he was in the clear for his thoughtless gaff he asked the question that was vexing him, "This is what happened with your boyfriend in Spain?"

She completely ignored his attempt to probe into her previous relationship. "I am a freak. I am crap."

Alex couldn't help smiling inside every time she said 'crap'. She obviously had no idea what it meant apart from something not good. She started to cry uncontrollably. He held her as she expelled her sorrow. By the time she had built a little mountain of moist tissues in front of her and her eyes had puffed up enough to inspire any good corner man to throw in the towel, Alex had worked out that telling her the truth was the best strategy.

He lifted her head so that he could look straight into the watery slits that her eyes had become. "I'm so sorry to have been so crass, so thoughtless and hurtful. I didn't mean to hurt you. But I did." He kissed both her eyes. The strong salty taste only reminded him further that he had cut deeply into her with his offhand remark and that he'd better get this one right or she might just cut him loose. "Understand this," he said. "All the work. The pain. The endless hours of practice. It's worked. It's there, in you. You can play like a god. It's magnificent. It's wonderful, beautiful. It's natural and vibrant and vital, and you can do it. You can."

She held both her arms up in the air and half shrugged the way only Latin women can when they want to show a world of feeling behind a single word. "So?"

"So you should be grateful."

She cocked an eyebrow in warning but Alex pressed on.

"Most people in this world never get to experience what you can do. Even people who play violin or some other instrument, most never reach those heights. I never played like that in my life and I never will."

"Yes, Alex. Please, when I play with the London Symphony Orchestra you can give me good hard shags during the cadenzas? What a career?"

He tried not to laugh and wondered if she really knew how he was warping her vocabulary. But it was so cute the way she said things with her Spanish accent that he found it impossible to truly empathize with her. He wanted to rip her clothes off. He wanted to take back everything he'd said. Maybe they could have gone on happily for years if he'd kept his trap shut? The truth, the truth. If he just stuck to the truth it would work out fine. He dismissed his random sexual thoughts, but his train of thought disappeared with them.

"Laura, you're missing the point. If you can play like that then you can play like that. All you have to do is..." At this he realized that he had no idea what he was talking about. Her face was ravenous for the solution he was about to share with her. "Keep having filthy sex with me and playing violin during it until you don't have to anymore." She was perplexed by his blunt suggestion, but he'd learnt from old jazzmen that if you play a wrong note then the best thing to do is to go right on playing that note as if you really meant it.

The more he thought about having sex with Laura the more it sounded to him that he'd hit on the right solution.

Surely if he loved her, and if he told the truth, then whatever he said couldn't be wrong? Again, he turned to jazz to inspire him to convince his Laura, his true love. If a jazzman plays a particularly effective lick, he should always go back to it, examine it, explore it, expand it, milk it.

"We shouldn't take the music for granted," he said, sensing that his strategy might be perceived as somewhat selfish if he failed to conjure a justification. "Let's forget about bringing your talent into your everyday routine and make sure first that the talent is here to stay. Acknowledge it, welcome it, bask in it. Talent can be fickle. Let your talent learn to trust you, and learn that it won't leave you first. Don't try to browbeat it into submission. Let it be." He could see he was getting through. "And if it doesn't work we can make recordings and I can filter out the squelchy sounds in the mix."

She smiled. It was enough. She blew her nose.

"Does it really sound that good?" she asked. "I think that I hear the music I think I play in my head."

He had no idea what that meant but she seemed happier. "Just carry on. Go in and practice as usual."

"Do you think I should see a psychiatrist?" she asked.

"Psychiatrist? I'm your man!" came a voice from the box room. The door opened and Skuggs stood, in his parka with the hood up. Laura buried her face into her hands.

"Skuggs! Have you been here all night?"

"Dunno."

"Have you heard what we've been saying?"

"I had nowhere to go. Got kicked outa everywhere. I sneaked back in and hid in the cupboard."

"Box room."

"Feels like a fucking cupboard," he said, rubbing his neck. "I didn't hear shit. Only that yer bird needs a psychiatrist."

"Her name's Laura."

"I know. I'm a pretty good psychiatrist, Laura. What seems to be the problem?" Skuggs sat down, crossed his legs, pulled back the hood of his parka then grabbed the last piece of cold toast from her plate. "Really," he continued. "Maybe I can help?"

Alex grabbed Skuggs's arm. "Yes, you can help. Let's go. Laura, just shut the door behind you. Skuggs and I are off. Skuggs get your tuba!" Skuggs gave a start then rushed around the small apartment, passing his tuba twice before he found it. Alex helped him strap the case onto his back, all the while watching to make sure she was okay. She gave them both a little wave goodbye as he pushed Skuggs out of the door in front of him. "You're paying my bus fare today," he shouted at Skuggs. "And you're buying me lunch. For your cheek."

# ELEVEN

"How's it goin Skuggs?" said the bus driver as Skuggs planted enough money into the little slot to cover the tickets. Skuggs crammed his tuba into the luggage rack without serious injury to any of the other passengers. They plumped themselves down on one of the long seats opposite two schoolboys. Skuggs stuck out his tongue at them then took out a newspaper and held it right up to his face. One of the boys whispered something to the other then pointed at Skuggs. Skuggs was scanning the passengers through two peepholes cut in the newspaper. On another day Alex might have been embarrassed but today he didn't care.

The bus stopped to let an old man and woman on. They were both stinking drunk and rocked back and forth grabbing on to each other and any nearby passengers before the bus had even pulled back into traffic. They sat down in the seat in front of a pretty redhead who stared out of the window in a vain effort to make herself invisible. The man fell asleep on contact with the seat while the woman squinted at the passengers. She had long unkempt hair and a waterlogged face, and if she had any teeth it wasn't obvious from the way her chin met her nose.

She took a few swigs from a bottle wrapped in a brown paper bag then leant toward the redhead.

"Ahm Aggie, how jidoo Freckles?" She sprayed the words onto the redhead from close range. She pointed at the old man sleeping beside her. "That's no my man," she said. "That's just some old shite I married forty years ago."

The redhead kept her eyes trained on a spot somewhere outside.

"Hey! I'm talking to you, Carrotheed! Is that a beamer?"

The girl's face heated up.

A moist ripping sound appeared around Aggie's lower regions. "Was that you Ginger?"

The two schoolboys started to break up at this. One of the nose-laughing boys produced a long string of mucus, which hung dangerously from his nose while the other pinched his own nose in self-defence.

Skuggs threw down his paper. "A torso-length pendulum bogey!" he shouted, pointing at the elongated snot like it was one of the great wonders of the world.

Alex grabbed Skuggs's arm. "Our stop," he said, dragging him off the bus. As the bus pulled away the driver gave them a salute.

"My tuba, I've left it on the bus!" screamed Skuggs. He loped after the bus, catching up with it fifty yards or so down the road after it stopped at traffic lights.

"That's about eighty quid you just cost me," said the driver as Skuggs rescued his instrument.

"Sorry Eric," said Skuggs.

Choral practice. Everyone had to be there according to Mc-Nabb's dictate. The make-up of the choir was simple; everyone who wasn't in the orchestra was in the choir. During early run-throughs, where the orchestral part was played on piano, even members of the orchestra were required to augment the choir.

McNabb believed that this experience would help the orchestra more deeply understand the music when they came to play their own parts. Most members of the orchestra would have loved to kill McNabb for this alone.

Today the torture was heightened by the premature presence of choristers from the Scottish National Orchestra's brigade of semi-professional singers. These people were serious. Where a student might mumble his way through rehearsals and perhaps give it some welly on the night of the performance, the SNO choristers were paid expenses to take it all very seriously. That meant they gave it Pavarotti right from the first runthrough.

The SNO chorus didn't usually appear this early in the schedule. Normally they'd trot-in a couple of rehearsals away from the concert and McNabb would use them to show-up the students. More odiously, the opera students who'd been singing the solo parts would suddenly be relegated to the chorus as the semi-pros strutted their stuff. The fact that this was a music college escaped McNabb when it came time for the major choral concerts. Hell, his public were watching. The local newspaper critics would be there. No need to take chances on students when the semi-pros were available.

McNabb felt he was a gifted and much under-appreciated conductor and the yearly choral concerts were his chance to display his talents. Alex had no idea whether McNabb was a good conductor or not. He couldn't tell a guy waving his arms about from a conductor. He didn't play an orchestral instrument and guessed you'd have to actually be in an orchestra before you could tell the difference. He'd quizzed Skuggs about it a few times but Skuggs maintained that all conductors were 'pish' and that orchestras would be much better off without them.

The only students who might have given a damn about the choral concerts were the singers, if they'd been allowed to sing solo. The pianists would rather be playing piano. The string section would rather be practicing their chamber and solo works. The woodwinds would rather be fiddling with reeds and twiddling with mouthpieces. The percussionists would rather be socking their drums, and the brass players would rather be in the pub. Skuggs would rather be in the pub drunk and Alex would rather have pins stuck in his eyes than sing in the choir. But the punishment for absence far outweighed the crime. McNabb had failed post-grads for missing rehearsals.

With five minutes to go the auditorium was already ninety-percent filled, and the place was smelling-up nicely. The SNO chorus had arrived early, en masse, and were already seated, which gave students beyond first-year a chance to grab seats strategically placed as far from the serious shouting as possible. Alex and Skuggs took a position near the back of the hall where they might get through the next two hours with a bit of mime and some conspicuous page turning.

"Did you hear anything last night?" Alex asked Skuggs. The thought that Skuggs had heard him and Laura was making him feel sick.

Skuggs raised both eyebrows a few times.

"For fuck's sake Skuggs," he pled, checking around him to make sure no one could hear. "Tell me the truth. This is important to me. I really like her."

Skuggs kept gyrating his eyebrows up and down and up and down as if performing facial aerobics. Alex grabbed Skuggs's ear and twisted it sharply. Skuggs was at least twice the size of Alex and could probably have broken him in two if he'd a mind to, but Alex was furious.

"Okay, okay, okay, let go, let go, let go."

Alex twisted it harder.

"I didn't hear a thing. You were asleep when I got back. I went into the cupboard and crashed. Honest. Honest."

Alex let go of the ear that was now red and thick. Skuggs rubbed it; his eyes were watering profusely.

Alex felt guilty. "I'm sorry I hurt your ear but you asked for it."

"Want a sandwich?" Skuggs reached into his pocket, pulled out a horrific-looking Spam sandwich and stuffed it greedily into his mouth.

"No thanks, where the hell do you get this stuff? Who eats Spam? What is this, World War Two?"

"I like Spam. It's great," he said, displaying the contents of his mouth with every syllable.

"This year!" boomed McNabb from the stage as a few late-comers crept in and frantically searched for seats. "This year, we're going to attempt some Britten."

"I like Britten," said Skuggs.

"So I've asked our SNO friends to attend all the rehearsals in the hope that we might not embarrass ourselves," McNabb continued.

"Did you know he was a poof?" said Alex.

"No way man. I like Britten. His orchestrations are great."

There was a commotion behind them as one of the SNO choristers took a seat. "Christ," Alex said under his breath, "We've got one behind us."

Skuggs turned to the man who'd just sat down, "Hey Jim, was Benjamin Britten a poof?"

The man cleared his throat. "Eh, well. Yes, I think he was a homosexual. Yes."

"Told you," said Alex.

"The Britten is extremely difficult," McNabb shouted. "But if we work hard we can master it, I believe."

The place was already too hot. There were far too many people in the hall and although most of the windows were open there was no evidence of any wind, but experience told him that before the session was over there would be wind aplenty, manufactured inside the hall, and much of it by his crimson-eared companion; if that Spam sandwich was anything to go by.

"I can't sing this," said Skuggs fumbling with a filthy score that was caked in stains and almost falling to pieces in his hands. "Written by a poofter. I used to like this guy." Skuggs thumbed through a few pages as McNabb discussed some of the finer points of his plans with his accompanist. "What the fuck is this?" he said, far too loudly. He started to read from the score, "For I will consider my cat Jeoffry. For he is the servant of the living God... For I am possessed of a cat, surpassing in beauty, from whom I take occasion to bless Almighty God... For the Mouse is a creature of great personal valour. For the Mouse is of an hospitable disposition."

The man behind them cleared his throat, "Em, it's Christopher Smart."

"Eh?"

"Christopher Smart. An eighteenth-century poet."

"It's shite!" Skuggs shouted. Alex buried his face in his hands to laugh. McNabb made a mental note of the general direction of Skuggs's pronouncement. He couldn't quite gauge who was causing the rumpus in the back of the hall but he could see that he'd have to make an example of someone before the day was out if he was to succeed with the Britten.

"Members of the orchestra will be delighted to hear that they will not be needed for the Britten," McNabb announced to a wave of groans. "Rejoice in the Lamb is performed to an organ accompaniment." He tapped his little baton on the lectern in front of him. "Let's see how far we can get, shall we?'

The next half hour was as dismal as Alex might have feared. The guy behind them made it impossible to hear themselves even if they'd wanted to join in the throng. It was so hot that Skuggs actually unzipped his parka.

"I'm melting," said Skuggs. He lifted his leg up and farted unselfconsciously. The music, that was roaring around them, stopped abruptly but Skuggs was in full flight. His perfect B flat rose three semitones then hung melodiously in the silence of the expanding odour that accompanied his flatulatory gaff. He finished the fart with a rising portamento then a little trill an octave above the main theme. Skuggs may have had perfect sphincter control but this performance was pure chance music. He seemed surprised at the accusatory stares surrounding him.

"Spamfart," he said, by way of explanation.

McNabb strained to see who it was that had interrupted his rehearsal. His face went quickly from red to a strange violet colour. "Boy!" he screamed. The few people that had seen the humour in Skuggs's defence stopped laughing. Skuggs was a rabbit caught in the headlights. The colour drained from his face in an instant.

"Stand up! Now! Stand up!"

Skuggs shot up.

"Not you, moron. You! You, behind him!" Skuggs sat down, eyes as wide as saucers.

"Stand up!"

Alex turned to the SNO guy. "He means you, mate."

The SNO guy stood up, his mouth hanging open in disbelief.

"From bar 68," said McNabb, tapping his little stick; sure that he would embarrass his victim.

"This is a rather difficult passage, I'm sure we'd all appreciate it if you could sight sing it for us."

The SNO guy shrugged and belted it out from bar 68 right to the end of the page, and waited for McNabb to apologize.

The auditorium doors crashed open. A woman in a red cocktail dress and three-inch stiletto heels marched up onto the stage.

"Nice legs," said Skuggs. "Red stilettos. Mm... Red stilettos." A murmur swept through the auditorium as the identity of the woman became clear. It was the principal. Principal Todd was up there on the stage dressed for a date with William Holden.

"Skuggs, it's the principal, it's Todd. He's lost his marbles."

"He hasn't even shaved his beard off," Skuggs observed. "He's not bad though. Nice legs."

The woman in the red dress walked straight past McNabb to the piano. After a moment's discussion a bewildered accompanist got up to let Todd sit. Todd thumbed through a few pages of the score in front of him while McNabb and the accompanist whispered furiously. The accompanist left the auditorium which was, by now, humming with gossip and theory.

He's had a breakdown.

It's a joke. He's making a joke.

He's a tranny.

No, he's a crosser.

It's a Wendy Carlos job.

He was such a nice man.

Alex suspected that all of it was probably true. He liked Todd. Todd was a nice man but it looked as if Todd had turned into a nice woman when no one was looking.

McNabb was ready to burst with joy at this gift from heaven but he was careful not to show it. He'd sent Edna, the accompanist, out to get 'help'. McNabb calculated a series of possible outcomes; all of which ended up with him in charge and the shirt lifter out on his arse, where he belonged.

The scene was too much for some of the more sensitive members of the student body; first one then another girl started sobbing. Soon, there was a nose–blowing fiesta. A few students left; some with hankies on faces, others simply fleeing the scene to grab up the best practice rooms while everyone else gawped at the show.

Alex and Skuggs wished now that they'd sat up front for the best views. This was just fun for Skuggs but Alex, although a little slower off the mark than McNabb, began to realize that Todd's actions would have serious repercussions for him. He was sure he could detect a smirk on McNabb's face. McNabb was vice principal; he would have to step in to fill the gap that would surely appear as soon as they dragged Todd off that stage.

First one, then another, then a whole bevy of staff appeared. They all rushed onto the stage as if ready to tackle some imaginary fire, but the sight of Todd sitting confidently at the piano seemed to sap their will. They all ended up in a whispering huddle at the edge of the stage.

Skuggs absently produced another Spam sandwich but before he could get a bite it was torn out of his hands by neighbours who'd suffered one Spamfart too many.

Before the onstage huddle had managed to agree on an appropriate play, Todd slammed the piano lid. The huddle jumped as one.

"I'm wearing a dress!"

"No shit!" someone shouted. Everyone who wasn't onstage laughed. Todd smiled. Maybe he wasn't crazy after all?

"My wife died last night."

The laughing stopped. The sound of Todd's heels clattered around the hall as he walked to the front of the stage.

He patted his dress down and collected himself.

"But I'm not mad." He turned to the huddle. "Strange as it may seem. Difficult as it may be to comprehend. I am in complete control."

No you're not sister, thought McNabb. This was delicious. He'd played a thousand scenarios where he wrested power from this pervert. He knew he was a pervert. He knew it and now everyone knew. But he'd never imagined anything as sweet as this. No need to scheme. No need to fight. She was handing it over to him on a silver platter.

"You are my only family now," Todd said to his audience. "I do not need sympathy. I make no excuses nor do I ask forgiveness. I ask only for understanding. I am the same person today as I was yesterday. I am not alone. I have you. I have music."

Yes, yes, thought McNabb, go on, build the scaffold high you arse-bandit.

Alex knew swift action was called for. He jumped to his feet and started to applaud. Skuggs had no idea why Alex thought Todd's speech was so inspiring, but he gave a loud wolf whistle and joined in the ovation. After a few seconds four, then five then ten students were standing, applauding.

Maybe if McNabb hadn't acted, the whole auditorium might have given Todd the lift he needed, the support he craved. But McNabb waved the audience down until only Alex and Skuggs were standing. McNabb pointed to the door.

"You are all excused," he said. "Please leave in an orderly fashion. Mr. Todd needs our understanding."

Todd was too confused, too tired to fight back. He hadn't come to the Academy dressed like this to fight. He wasn't trying to make a statement. He just wanted to go on. To find a way to go on. The students loved him. Every time he'd given a concert they'd always reacted more than warmly. They'd always demanded encore after encore. He knew they loved him. He'd played this out in his head all night long. He would be himself. They would see that it was still him, still the same man. He could hardly comprehend their reaction. He had frightened them. They were young. It was too much for them.

As the students filed quietly past Todd, most couldn't look at him. The principal in a dress? It was too surreal, too painful. The few that stole a glance saw his tears. Todd had gone off his trolley for everyone to see. McNabb stood stoically with his hand on Todd's shoulder, the way real men touch each other when emotions surface.

There would be a staff meeting where McNabb would plead Todd's case against the reluctant acceptance that this kind of behaviour simply wouldn't wash. There would follow swiftly a meeting of governors where everyone would agree that Todd's bereavement had sent him over the edge. He might not be summarily dismissed but he'd at least be put on an indefinite sabbatical, from which it was unlikely he'd return. McNabb would assume Todd's duties and by autumn term he'd be a shoo-in for a permanent placement. The universe was at last starting to make sense to McNabb. Everything was gravitating to its rightful place.

Alex felt a deep vacuum where his stomach had been. Todd was his only defence against expulsion, and now Todd had gone. McNabb would have him out within the week and there was no way he could plead his case. The staff would be too worried about their own positions to come to his defence. The governors were a bunch of old farts who'd certainly agree that he was a mediocre talent doing the wrong course.

Alex made straight for the electronic music lab and set about getting the new equipment online. He had a week, maybe two before the axe would fall. He wasn't sure why he knew he had to get something done with the new equipment. Perhaps another tape, or maybe a new set of waveform samples that he could play with when he came home from the job he'd have to get after he was thrown out? But still he felt an over-powering and largely unconscious imperative driving him.

He worked feverishly through the evening and most of the night. He was familiar enough with the basic functions of most of the equipment that he could set it up without referring to the dense manuals that accompanied such gear. The samplers were easy enough. They were heavy the way high quality electronic equipment feels heavy: sturdy, expensive, and full of promise. He resisted the urge to play with them. He stacked the gear as logically as he could, given his frantic state. The computers were a pain; the monitors were almost too heavy and, even though they were state of the art, each system had to have its software installed individually. There was no need yet for a network that might have made the installation a bit easier. The synths were really just a matter of finding the right space. Hooking everything up through the mixing board and a rack of effects was time consuming but mainly routine. He'd test it all tomorrow.

# TWELVE

When Ingles woke him his face was mottled with impressions of the trimpots he'd been slavering over.

"This is wonderful! Well done. Well done." She was beside herself. For days she'd poked around in boxes, inducing terror every time she opened a manual. She really wasn't sure whether she could set the gear up at all, and had been considering calling her consultant to see if he couldn't send someone round to do it for her. Ingles was used to working with vintage analog synthesizers, recording her compositions straight to tape. She knew her synths inside out. She could hear a sound in her head and almost immediately build that sound, but all this digital equipment was a different world.

Alex had saved the day.

She handed him a tissue. It took him a minute before he knew what it was for. She hummed and fiddled with the samplers while he wiped down the mixing desk. Every time she got an LCD to light up or a CD tray to offer itself she gave a happy little squeal and clapped her hands. Alex was groggy but amazed at her unselfconscious display of rampant femininity. He was beginning to wonder why he had always perceived her as butch.

"You know," she said, pressing buttons in time to a tune in her head. "If I hadn't seen that leakage escaping out of your mouth a minute ago I'd probably give you a big kiss."

Alex folded the tissue to find a clean patch and wiped his mouth. "So, it's okay then?"

"It's marvellous. Does it all work?"

"I haven't tested it all yet. There's always a few teething problems but it should be okay. I can tweak it all later."

"Tweak it all! I like that. Tweak it." She tweaked his nose and giggled. "I think you and I are going to get along just fine."

"I think I'm going to get kicked out."

She was lost for words. She had finally found a soul mate, someone who liked her music and was technical to boot. Surely he was mistaken? She pulled up a chair.

"You know about Todd? Principal Todd?"

"Oh, dear. What must you think of me? It's dreadful. So tragic."

"Yes it is. But his new fashion sense is probably going to get him flung out. No?"

Maybe Ingles had some insider info on cross dressing to cheer him up? Maybe they wouldn't throw Todd out? There had to be a certain level of tolerance. Todd was an artist, and artists tend to do strange things sometimes.

"I'm sure they'll throw him out," she said, stomping on his last forlorn hope. "He's a good friend you know. I knew his wife. I've never seen a couple so close. They were very lucky." After a moment's reflection she stuck her thumb in the lapels of her jacket. "Look at me! Isn't this cross dressing?"

Alex was thrown by her candour.

"Well? Have you ever seen me in a dress? A skirt? Twin set and pearls?"

Alex wasn't sure whether he should answer. He'd insinuated himself into her confidence, he didn't want to spoil it by liking her and thus opening his gob to spill out some insignificant truth.

"I'm a cross dresser myself."

He tried to clear his mind. There was no telling how she might react if he agreed with her. He did his best to maintain an air of interest.

"I'm a dyke!"

Alex knew she was a dyke. Everybody knew she was a dyke. But she was his first dyke. Telling him that she was a dyke must have meant something to her but he had no idea what. He hoped that it meant she trusted him. If she trusted him then at least he could use her lab until he got his arse kicked out of the place. It certainly didn't sound as if she had any plans at all for fighting Todd's corner. Todd had become Typhoid Mary; anyone who took his part might go down with him.

"I'm a dyke!" she repeated, as if about to burst into a song from a corny Broadway musical. Perhaps he was meant to react in some way but still he hung on to his silence. He was no expert on dykes, but one thing he did know was that no one was allowed to use the word 'dyke' except dykes. They had reclaimed the word and wore it as a badge of honour.

"There, I've said it. I've come out to someone. To a male."

"I am a male." It slipped out before he could stop it. Luckily, she was more interested in her confession than his idiotic response.

"I've come out to a male. Someone at my place of work is aware of my sexual orientation."

Everyone at her place of work was aware of her sexual orientation. Everything about her screamed her sexual orientation. She bashed about the Academy in her daft three-piece suit and clunky brogues like a pantomime cousin. Her music always had gender references in the titles. Her program notes always harped on feminist hobbyhorses. She appeared at evening functions always with women, most of them either bull- or diesel-dykes (according to Skuggs). Nobody had ever reported seeing her with beautiful women. This was one of the great philosophical conundrums that Skuggs liked to formulate lengthy expositions upon: How come dykes always end up with women that look like men?

"Am I shocking you?"

"Er…"

"A woman can dress like a man with impunity. But if a man dresses like a woman, all hell breaks loose. If Steven were a big bruiser they'd put it down to his current mental state. He'd be given a second chance. But he's rather delicate. You know, feminine. So it's interpreted as confirmation of deeper problems."

Alex rubbed his chin and wondered how he was going to get her back to the point of all this; he was about to get kicked out and what was she going to do about it?

"It is thought-provoking isn't it?"

"Mm."

There was a knock at the door and Laura appeared. Alex was happy to see her but Ingles seemed even happier.

"This is Laura. My friend."

"I see. Hello Laura. You have a wonderful man here." She took Laura's hand to shake it but ended up stroking it and staring into her eyes.

"Alex, she's so beautiful. Quite stunning."

He couldn't help feeling a wave of pride. So what if they did kick him out? He had Laura. He could get a job programming. They could get married.

Get married? Get married? What was happening to him? Only crazy people got married. But he could see that Ingles was in her spell, just as he had been, just as he was.

"Thank you." Laura was used to compliments and handled them easily. "Skooggs said you might be here," she said, deliciously mispronouncing his name.

"He's been here all night. He set up my lab. He's my hero."

This couldn't be bad. Ingles was giving him a good press.

"Yes, I think Alex is full of surprises." Laura seemed happy to hear Ingles' review.

Two females were bumming him up. This had never happened to him before. He felt good. People liked him. He liked himself. Maybe he was a good guy after all?

Ingles left, but before Alex had a chance to jump on Laura, she sat him down.

"I saw it."

"Todd?"

"What are you going to do?"

"I've no idea. I suppose I can go back to programming." He watched for a reaction. Maybe she'd like the idea? He could bring in bags of cash and she could have niños. Why not? They could live happily...

"Estas loco?"

"Eh?"

"Are you crazy? Do I have to slap you?"

"Eh?"

"You will let this beat you? What are you doing here? What is the point?"

He couldn't work up an answer. But she waited. She folded her arms to let him know that he'd better answer, but he just sat there feeling sorry for himself.

"You sit there. Feel sorry for yourself all day. But I want an answer. What is the point?" She emphasized her point; stabbing him sharply in the shoulder with her forefinger; a forefinger that had been built up with thousands of hours of violin practice, it was the Arnold Schwarzanegger of forefingers, it felt like a little tungsten rod drilling into his body. She poked at him again as he was still reeling from the first onslaught. "Well?"

"Shit, that hurts. Take it easy. Really, that's sore."

"Pobre Alex," she said in a voice women usually reserve for toddlers. She poked him again, so hard this time that his chair went flying backwards. It was all he could do to stop from toppling right over.

"What's got into you?" he said, kneading his shoulder.

"What's got into me? What's got into me?" she said with the air of someone desperately trying to contain the decibel quotient of her rage. She stamped her foot hard into the ground.

"Laura," she said, parroting what she obviously felt was him at his simpering worst, "Why your playing is so crap?"

"That's not what I said," he pleaded. "I'm sorry. I didn't…"

"Do not apologize! Never apologize to me for telling truth." Alex felt like a cornered rat. He had no idea what he was supposed to say. "Tell the truth about you!"

"What truth?" If there was an answer that might satisfy her, he was at least a million miles away from it. She started to walk around him slowly, like she was about to interrogate a prisoner. His eyes followed her cautiously. He could live without another poke in the shoulder.

"This!"

"What? What this?"

"This! Your toys. All your little toys. Your tapes. Your samples. Your computers." She put her face right up to his. He covered up his shoulders with both hands as if covering a pair of imaginary breasts. "What is it for? What is the point?"

"I don't know what you mean?"

"Alex, don't to make me scream." She took some deep breaths that seemed to calm her. "You gave up many things, too much money to study here. Why?"

"Well, I love music. I had to study music."

"And?"

"And I wanted to see how far I could take it."

"How far have you take it?"

"Taken it."

"What were you going to do when you left here, when you get the degree?"

"I don't know. I never thought about it."

"Well, think about it now. What good are your tapes? Who cares? Who wants your tapes?" She touched a nerve with this.

"Who wants my tapes? Nobody. That's who wants my tapes."

"How do you know?"

"How do I know? Because it's all I ever hear in this place. I'm a cheat. I'm a fraud. It's easy. I'm not really playing it."

"This is in your head. It is not real."

"McNabb…"

"Shut up with McNabb! Have you tried? Have you sent your music to anyone?"

"No."

"Why not?"

"I don't know."

"Well, you better know."

"Look, no one wants to hear classical music played on a computer. Rappers can sample music, techno geeks, DJs, hip-hoppers, experimental avante-garde–complete-load-of-shiters can sample music and they can all get away with it, they can all be accepted. But no one wants to hear classical music played on a computer."

She gave him a stiff poke in the shoulder that rocked him back in his chair. "How do you know?" She waited for his answer. He shrugged. She left the room, slamming the door behind her.

He could hardly work out what hurt him more; her over-developed forefinger all but poking holes through his flesh or her accusing barbs poking holes through his weak argument.

She was right. He was so completely immersed in his own little world where he could convince himself that he was some kind of undiscovered genius. He was safe inside his inconsequential battle with a mental pygmy like McNabb. He didn't have to go to a traditional music college. He could have gone to a modern, trendy establishment where his computer music might have been welcomed, where his programming skills alone might have inspired awe in a non-technical faculty. He knew now why he had decided to study at the Academy. It was his own elevated opinion of his talents that had urged him to study there. He remembered now. She had made him remember. He remembered how he had been convinced that he would become the world's first computer virtuoso. He didn't want to go to a college where every whim, every effort on the part of the student was lauded and encouraged as a creative act, he wanted to go somewhere where he had to fight to survive, where his programming skills would be so far outside their experience that they might as well be invisible. Where virtuosity was just the start. Where talent was simply a first step. He wanted to compete on the same level as people who had studied music since they were children. Laura made him realize that McNabb was the reason he had come to the Academy. McNabb was the test, the only test worth his view of his own abilities, and he was failing it.

He pinched the bridge of his nose, not quite knowing why. He started to cry. He hadn't cried since he was a child. He couldn't remember the last time he had cried. He wasn't even sure how to do it properly. It just kind of overwhelmed him. It wasn't that he was about to be thrown out of college. It wasn't that his girlfriend had made it known that she knew him better than he knew himself, and that he wasn't as cool a guy as he secretly liked to think he was. He cried because he felt completely helpless. Laura had opened something inside him, something that had changed him. He had enjoyed a taste of the delights offered by this new emotional vent. Now he was plunging into an abyss of self-doubt. He crept into a corner, rolled himself into a tight ball and cried.

# THIRTEEN

 **Elliot** was well-pissed when Peter told him he'd have to play in Boskov's masterclass; Boskov had insisted. Elliot figured that Boskov planned to embarrass him in public. He'd seen it all before; audiences at these affairs were not there to hear the students play, they were there to see how famous teachers plied their trade. No matter how well the student played, he was little more than an audio-visual aid the star of the show could bend to his every whim. If an experienced concert artist wanted to help a group of students he could do it in private.

Public lessons weren't necessarily a bad thing, he'd seen some pretty good ones, but there was an altogether different breed of 'master' out there and Boskov was one of them. He produced a lot of fine guitarists but more because he cherry-picked the best after their talents had blossomed than as a result of anything he taught them. Elliot knew that Boskov wanted him as a post-graduate student—even though he'd threatened to punch him in the chops.

By the time he got to the green room, the masterclass had started. Peter didn't look pleased but that might have been because Anne, a third-year guitarist who'd transferred from a school in Paris, was sobbing into his shoulder. Elliot knew at once what had happened, but offered Peter his standard litany of excuses as he unpacked his guitar.

"Sorry I'm late. I slept in. I fell down a manhole. The dog ate me homework. Me granny passed away. I've gorra terrible urinary infection and I couldn't be arsed... What's up with her?"

"Boskov said her playing was," Peter stopped himself, he wasn't sure whether it would set Anne's water works off again, plus he felt like such a plonker saying it. And he was worried about providing Elliot with any more excuses to act crazy.

"Well, what did he say?"

"He said her playing was too decadent."

"Too decadent! Too decadent!" screamed Elliot. The green room was right next to the auditorium stage. His voice echoed round the hall. Boskov, who was onstage between victims, strained to see who it was making all the commotion.

"Jeezis Elliot, take it easy eh?" pleaded Peter.

"Too decadent! He's too fucking hairy!"

Peter hung his head and blamed himself. He liked Elliot. Elliot was easily the most talented student he'd ever taught. If Elliot went on to forge a career for himself, some of the credit would go to him. If he became known as the teacher of a concert guitarist then other students would want to study with him.

"Look Anne," said Elliot tenderly, "your playing is lovely. Don't listen to that bastard. I like your playing." This seemed to satisfy her. Elliot was in a different league from the rest of the students and he wasn't known for telling lies when it came to music. Elliot finally noticed Martin sitting in the corner, as pale as a ghost, clutching his guitar to himself and mumbling quietly.

"What's up with you? You look like you're about to shite yourself."

A ripple of light applause from the auditorium signalled that Boskov was ready for the next student.

"Right Martin," said Peter rubbing his hands together. "You're up next."

Martin was rooted to the spot, holding on to his guitar like it was his favourite teddy bear.

"I'll get him for you Anne. Has anybody got a knife?" said Elliot. He scanned the room for a suitable weapon, then poked around behind a chair. "This'll do." He held up a soupspoon. Peter tried to make a grab for him but he was off before he could extricate himself from Anne.

Elliot slowed his pace as the audience came into view. It wasn't such a bad crowd for a guitar masterclass. There must have been sixty people in the audience. Masterclasses, like lunchtime concerts, were free and open to the general public. Elliot couldn't recognize any students in the audience.

Boskov was sitting with his legs crossed and his hands made a little basket in his lap. There was no guitar to be seen.

"Mmm… Elliot's going to play some Bach for us today," said Boskov, to polite applause.

"I received some manuscript in the post this morning from a young Czech composer," Elliot shouted. "Mr. Boskov is particularly famed for his interpretation of the avant-garde. I was hoping he might give me a few pointers."

A light round of applause seemed to put Boskov in the mood.

"The manuscript?" Boskov managed to ask the question like a seventeenth-century aristocrat.

"The manuscript!" shouted Elliot. "I dropped the manuscript in a puddle on the way here." He held up an explanatory digit. "But not before I had committed it to memory." He sat.

"I really need to…"

Elliot clattered his footstool this way and that until Boskov raised his voice to the unreal level Elliot favoured. "I really need to see the music. How can I critique what I cannot see?"

"Mr. Boskov can use his ears," shouted Elliot, by now comfortable with the footstool, but fighting to tune his guitar. Elliot's stage manner was more Neanderthal than raw. Most classical guitarists develop a method to tune their instruments quietly. The trip from the green room to centre stage can play havoc with nylon strings. Elliot liked to 'tune it from scratch' when he got onstage. This meant turning the machine heads while thumping a note until the sound dropped an octave or so, then thumping it all the way back up. He did this for all six strings then he pulled on each string fiercely. "Getting the lead out," he shouted.

Boskov didn't care what Elliot played. As long he the little shit didn't embarrass him. Elliot was the best prospect he'd ever heard. If he was a little eccentric, then no matter; all the easier to market him.

The audience hardly noticed the journey from tuning the guitar to playing the guitar. One minute he was yanking the strings this way and that, the next he was pulling them that way and this, but the line between tuning and the actual music was completely invisible, and Elliot had crossed over it into the world of modern music.

The spoon, still in his right hand, thumping against the guitar's body then scraping, like chalk on a blackboard, against the lower metallic strings, Elliot swung his head around, pursed his lips and leant over so far until he would surely fall off the chair, but then leant back, breathing deeply. He tried to work up a good sweat. A sweaty performer meant some deep music was going on... somewhere.

Not sure whether they were still watching him tune the thing or if some hyper-modern music was already in flow, the audience gave Elliot the silent respect that classical music audiences always offer.

Elliot loved to improvise, and with a few pints in him could do a passable impression of everyone from Django Reinhardt to BB King (or at least, he thought so) but most of all, he loved to play 'kid-on' modern music to people too embarrassed to complain.

Boskov stared upwards so that the audience might think he was solving some great musical equation as he listened to Elliot's scraping and bashing about.

Elliot had had enough; he crashed an atonal chord then, with a flick of the wrist, the spoon shot past Boskov's head and smacked noisily into the wall. Boskov was still in his trance; unaware that only Elliot's bad aim had saved him a trip to the emergency room.

Elliot leapt up and bowed deeply. The light applause woke Boskov. Elliot sat for a moment, then dove into the Prelude from Bach's Fourth Lute Suite. Now it was Elliot's turn to go into trance. Boskov's feigned seriousness cracked as he watched Elliot tear into the music. It was a grand fusion of fire and wind. Great runs chasing circular motifs layered on shimmering chords powered by an incessant pulse; the heart of all of Bach is the pulse. Elliot had proof that Bach was about emotion. Proof that all of the gesticulation, the theorization, the heady, trumped-up theories and intellectualisations, the self-evident complexity and the glimpses of the future were secondary. It was a simple truth to Elliot. If Bach wasn't God then what was the point of a god? Elliot could feel the pulse of Bach as easily as the rest of us feel our own hearts beating. It was beyond tempo or signature or beat, it was an unfolding, a revelation; the human soul laid bare in sound. Elliot understood. He made audiences understand. His performance transcended his instrument.

Alex woke in a Zen-like state. The labours of constructing Ingles' lab and the discovery that the great love of his life saw through him, read him like a book, pushed his buttons and had his number, had induced a deep slumber and had somehow purged his mind of all conscious thought. He proceeded to put the finishing touches to the new setup, flitting here and there, testing software, linking connections, finalizing the design. Ingles would see a logically designed studio, because he'd explain to her that that's what it was. But he designed it with his own work in mind. The actual thought, the conscious thought, the idea, hadn't yet occurred to him, but somewhere it had already happened. It had all led to this. It would all make sense to him as soon as his mind started to function normally again, if indeed it ever had functioned normally in the first place.

He surveyed his creation proudly. A neat row of huge monitors; perfect for the musician who has to work with lots of applications open simultaneously, now properly networked. In his pique over the fact that Ingles had used an outside contractor rather than himself, whom he felt, was the most apt choice for such work, he'd neglected to fully examine the specifications of the computers now before him. They were a work of art; great bulky grey metal boxes, anathema to anyone with even a shred of the aesthete within them, but perfectly functional; easy to open and fiddle with, easy to fill with peripherals and to interconnect with their clones. Perfect. But more than that, the unnamed consultant had chosen terrific motherboards, sturdy, robust, with plenty of potential. He'd installed the fastest processors and incredibly expensive digital signal processing boards into each machine. Ingles wouldn't even know these things existed, and even if she did, it might take months to explain their true value to her. The hard disks were blisteringly fast and gargantuan, with the largest cache memories he'd ever seen, and likewise the volatile memory was copiously huge and quick. In a year or so it would look like an average system, in three years it would look out of date, almost quaint. In five years people would laugh at it; a relic, a joke, people would probably ask how on earth one could even work with such a system. But for now it was perfect. Before he came to the Academy but after the music bug had bitten him he would dream about turning all of the supercomputers at the department of defence over to his music. He'd do great redundant calculations to work out what he might be able to do given free rein on such a system. Of course it never happened, never could happen, but in this room he had more than that. He had everything he needed, including the will—supplied by Laura—to do what he was about to find out he had to do.

Elliot knew the audience had no idea what they'd just witnessed. They had enjoyed it. They'd enjoyed it the way they might have enjoyed a journeyman guitar player on a summer evening in some little bar on the Costa del Sol. It was appreciated the way bumpkins might have appreciated Hamlet when Shakespeare toured sixteenth-century Middle England. They enjoyed it, but would have enjoyed a dancing bear or a fire-eater or a juggler as much or more. Elliot always felt he was competing with all of music history as well as the audience. It was always a fight for him. Each performance was a battle to break through, to enlighten, to reveal the mind of the composer in spite of the audience. Guitar was his instrument, his handicap, his weapon, his open wound. Violinists, singers, pianists; all of them have access to an instrument that can clobber the audience over the head; they can commit the form of grievous audible harm so envied by Elliot. A violinist can sway this way and that to tell the audience that something wonderful might be happening; give them a clue then go in for the kill. A violinist can bounce and scrape and lunge at the strings, using the bow to direct or misdirect the attention like a vaudeville magician. A violinist can vibrato before sounding the note—glimpsing the future, carving the shape of the sound to be. The pianist sits at the controls of a great mechanical tank of an instrument; its very presence informs of its depth. From brooding anguish to intimate insight to sparkling fairy dust the piano delivers its message past all of the defences of even the dullest audience. The harmonic possibilities of the instrument allow great walls of sound to hang in the air, waiting for newborn tones to join them where they greet each other in temporal metamorphosis. Where the violin journeys through the sonic ether into controlled infinity, the piano's tonal caravan unfolds with a fatalistic determination too complex to predict. The life of the sounds and the silence and the space that breathes them easily envelope and defeat the audience. The singer has a still more powerful arsenal. The unique resonating cavities of the human form contain and create sound before releasing it into the world. The singer holds absolute domain over thought made manifest. Without mechanical contraption making undue calls on the intellect, the birth of sound is purely biological, the shaping of music an artefact of the fusion of mind and body.

Elliot made bow after bow, great overblown gesticulations that might inform the audience of their good fortune. The audience might have thought that Elliot believed himself to be onstage at a great concert hall in front of cheering thousands. A few of them checked their watches as others gathered belongings and some folded the single-page program for safekeeping. One or two matched Elliot's stamina until the palms of their hands glowed red.

When Elliot first arrived at music college, his professor had sought to mould his unkempt talents. Elliot had never even heard another classical guitarist play. He literally thought he was the world's first classical guitarist. He bought a cheap nylon strung guitar, went to the library and borrowed some music and a few simple pedagogical titles to show him where the notes were and what they were called. Then he simply played. He practiced all day long and half the night seven days a week, only pausing to wolf down a tin of soup or a bowl of cornflakes. Mundane duties, such as shopping, or signing on the dole, or bathing, became massive obstacles that would creep into his concentration during the endless scale exercises he had devised to properly train and tame his fingers. Elliot would laugh out loud when Peter asked him to crescendo here, decrescendo there, to observe fermatas and sforzandos, to emphasize the counterpoint or lean on leading notes. Elliot liked Peter but knew that he didn't understand music. Elliot knew how to play every piece of music he attempted. He didn't know why this was, but he knew it was so. Elliot had been playing the guitar roughly a third below concert tone; he had no idea that musicians used a standardized tuning. When Peter gave him a tuning fork he finally found out what middle C sounded like.

The first few days after arriving back at his bed-sit with the second-hand, and badly beaten up, nylon strung guitar were like learning to breathe. In a few weeks he could sight-read almost anything put in front of him. He could read bass and alto clefs on sight. Classical guitar mostly is written in the treble clef but the guitar sounds an octave below the written notation. Elliot had borrowed symphonic music and made extraordinary stabs at reading whole scores on sight. He had no idea that people didn't do this. His talent was formed the way the talent of an athlete in the African bush might have been formed—without reference to any standard or norm.

Elliot could sympathize with the plight of Beethoven, who filled his scores with directions so that dumbo musicians might understand, but felt that Bach was correct in making the assumption that the music would explain itself without editorial.

Elliot would infuriate Peter when he held that the composer had mistakenly asked for a crescendo when none was required, or when the composer would direct him to play forte when pianissimo was clearly what he must have meant. He created a litany of excuses for the poor composers who had misinterpreted their own compositions. That he lived in his own world was obvious to anyone who spent any time at all discussing music with him. That he lived in a world where all of music seemed somehow revealed to him was less obvious. Peter had come to suspect that what seemed like arrogance bordering on madness might indeed be a revelation or gift beyond his understanding. Either way, their lessons had become more of a musicological dig than a guitar tutorial. There never was a single occasion where Elliot acquiesced to Peter's directions. At first, Peter would rage at him; his anger fired, in part, by his envy of Elliot's certainty more than his skill, though he was constantly staggered by the way Elliot melted technical problems: the more difficult they became, the more ease with which he handled them, and by the knowledge that he was a less than redundant partner in Elliot's musical development. Although Elliot still had a penchant for finding the most infuriating statements, the boldest, baldest justifications, Peter found himself, more and more, asking Elliot how he knew the music went this way rather than that, or why he approached a passage from a given direction. But most of all, he found himself giving in to the music, drinking in the truth that Elliot revealed so selflessly when he played.

Elliot mustered his dirtiest look for Boskov. He concentrated all of the disgust he felt, the anger, the frustration, the painful denial of the violence he believed so apt, and tried to beam it into Boskov's brain, then he walked slowly offstage, like a warrior after bloody battle.

"Take no prisoners?" said Peter as Elliot entered the green room.

"No fuckeen prisoners," answered Elliot.

Peter and Elliot both looked at Martin who was muttering to himself as he fingered the Bach he had worked on so diligently.

"You're up Shakey," said Elliot. Martin jumped, grabbed his footstool and headed to the stage. His legs turned to jelly when he saw the twenty or so people still spotted around the auditorium. Boskov gestured to the chair beside him. Martin sat then fought to open his footstool to the correct position without dropping the guitar balanced on his lap. He gave every appearance of suffering from late-stage Alzheimer's; his hands shook uncontrollably from the stage fright that had gripped him for a week and had now erupted to its conclusion; his head shook uncontrollably from whatever it was that made his head shake. When he eventually sorted his footstool, but not his head—which was gathering pace—and twiddled with the tuning, he gave Boskov a strange undead grin. He had practiced this a hundred times in his bedroom; he was prepared.

"I'm going to play some Bach!" he declared quite confidently and, for a fleeting moment, the possibility existed that he might. "But I broke a nail last night and this is an extremely taxing piece so please bear with me."

"For fuck's sake," said Elliot, peering from behind the green room curtain. "Here we go with the excuses."

"It is very taxing indeed," helped Boskov. "The previous work we heard was essentially a transcription of some violin music. This is a transcription of some Lute music, this increases the technical problems substantially." To the audience, Boskov was lending a hand, being the master he reported himself to be in the little photocopied programs now strewn around the room or marking the spot on a seat for an absent audience member. This was a much more comfortable place for Boskov, this was where he reigned. The words had hardly left Boskov's lips when Martin prematurely ejaculated into the music. He got through eight bars before the tension in his hands drove the music into a ditch. "False start," he mumbled to himself before diving straight back in. This time he managed a couple of bars before spluttering to a halt.

"Mmm, this is something we guitarists have to live with," said Boskov. "Our instrument is so exposed, so fragile. We must work here on relaxation. We will get to the music in good time." First one, then another member of the audience made to leave, wearing embarrassed expressions. The rest were trapped. Such sparse audiences have nowhere to hide, exposed almost as much as the performer, the rest knew that only one or two could escape with good grace.

Martin's undead smile returned, his face glowed beetroot throughout the ten-minute exposition Boskov delivered on breathing exercises. All the while Martin could think of nothing but the fear of trying to play with that broken nail causing so much trouble. Boskov made him suck gulps of air then expel them slowly. He made him bend right over his guitar until he almost tipped off his chair. He made him lean back until he thought his head would drop off. Then he implored him to breath the silence before the music, to incorporate the anticipation of the music into his performance. The tension in his hands left him. He breathed the silence before the music; he incorporated the anticipation into the music.

Then he played less than a bar before breaking down again.

Alex dragged every manual, every document he could find stashed in Ingles' cupboard and built a little skyscraper that reached up to his waist. Most people would be daunted at the mere sight of such a huge technical library, but to a self-taught software developer and musician it was a pure delight. He

skimmed a few titles then tossed them to the floor. The lack of
sleep, the toil of setting up the studio, the inner turmoil that
Laura had planted and nurtured to a tearful flowering at the
speed of emotion lifted him to the higher plane, his refuge, a
place where his mind could soar. The state that might be per-
mitted just before one falls asleep or, as in his case today, after
tears have washed away self-consciousness was somewhere with
which he was familiar. He could still think and feel like any
other human being, but it was all somehow far away, controlled;
observed rather than experienced. This was the landscape
where he could find simple answers to complex problems,
where his most complete realizations of musical works could
live without his own physiology limiting and twisting them into
weak caricatures. It was once, for him, a place of pure logic,
where the input required no understanding beyond a few self-
referencing rules that defined each problem as a universe unto
itself. He had known joy in this world, where he could liquefy
code, melt it into a philosophical caramel, then splash around
melding one strand into another; he could construct and de-
construct great baffling architectures here as easily as a child
might build a sand castle. It was like playing with infinity. After
he turned to music he became aware that there is an infinity of
infinities and he'd known just one. When the music came he
thought emotion had come with it; now he knew better. When
he first surveyed this world he didn't see anything like the to-
pology that had come with music. That had been a magnificent
enlightenment, expanding his vision, painting colour onto a
beautiful austerity, but he knew now that always he had been an
observer, an object in the world but not of it. Now he was one
with this strange benevolent autism, able to see it as well as be
seen by it. Now it seemed so precious, such a gift that he might
offend if he used it to apply problems from the real world. Now
this was a place simply for play.

Noticing that the manuals he'd tossed down had formed a pattern on the floor, he grabbed handfuls of documents from his dwindling skyscraper and arranged them around him until he stood at the centre of a semi-circle, the manuals arranged in rows and ranks, waiting for the slightest gesture from the conductor's podium, on which he now stood.

The concept of conducting had always embarrassed Alex. Do conductors actually do something, or are they just waving their arms about? Were the musicians really paying attention? Would they really surrender the creative urge to the will of one individual for the betterment of the music? Do orchestras respond to conductors the way Bugs Bunny would have us believe? There never was a single occasion where Alex had been able to detect a relationship between the baton and the beat.  Much as he respected Skuggs's terse conclusions on such matters, he'd conducted his own observations and found little evidence to support the elevated status of the conductor. It seemed to him that all of the work was done in rehearsal. All of the decisions jotted on manuscript with little pencils; each local territory in the musical landscape drawn and measured well in advance of all the jumping about. The movement of the baton was mostly incomprehensible, no two conductors shared the same gestural lexicon; it was hard to resist the conclusion that most conductors were little more than penguin-suited go-go dancers, strutting their stuff on tiny podiums to gawping bumpkins. The difference between great conductors—real conductors—and the rest, was the difference between a chess grandmaster and the local checkers champion.

Alex had never witnessed it but he knew that real conductors could perform huge symphonic works from memory, they could isolate the quietest line, carve the most delicate shapes in real time from a dense orchestral texture. Still, Alex thought, it had to be a fight to actualise the ideal performance, the sound that existed deep within a conductor's ambition; the faith be-yond the hope.

Computers have no soul. Computers have no integrity. Computers have no intellect, no intelligence, no emotions, no creative impulse, no desire or ambition. Computers comply, they obey without question or dissent; they add nothing of their own and leave no trace of themselves. Computers don't grow silly beards or have affairs and they can't get drunk during inter-mission; they don't fidget or bitch or fart or cough, they never split their lips' or suffer hangnails or haemorrhoids and they ar-rive at the flick of a switch. To the strong-willed conductor, computers might define the perfect orchestral player.

Alex dreamed of the perfect orchestra; each player with unique, self-similar algorithms, responding within parameters loose enough to fake sentience but tight enough to forge un-derstanding.

He tapped an imaginary lectern with an imaginary baton to draw the attention of his imaginary orchestra. He brought the strings in with a jealous detaché to announce Beethoven's Ero-ica.

The door swung open so hard it bounced off the wall.

"What the fuck are you doing?"

Ripped from his fantasy, Alex's face reddened.

"Eh? What's all this?" Elliot picked up a second violinist and a couple of members of the cello section. He read a few ti-tles. "'Bleedn Advanced Assembly Programming for Dickhead Maniacs.' This is an orchestra, isn't it? You're playing an orches-tra in your head. You've lost your mind man. Get a grip for fuck's sake."

"Beat it," Alex grabbed the manuals back and arranged them in their proper sections. "Leave me alone. I can't be ar-sed."

"Don't you want to come watch Martin humiliating him-self? You've missed the best bits but Boskov is a merciless bas-tard, he'll probably keep at it for another hour or two."

"Look Elliot," Alex leant right into Elliot's face. He tried to find the exact words that might send Elliot on his way, "Piss… off."

"So, what were you playing anyway? Beethoven? You piano players are so predictable. I hate that bastard."

"Stravinsky."

"Liar. It was Beethoven."

"It was Beethoven. Now please, beat it. Leave me alone." Alex had already given up. Elliot was impervious to the desires or needs of others. He was a most complete demonstration of self-containment. Nothing anyone ever said about anything made a blind bit of difference to him. He made up his mind instantly and absolutely on anything and everything, regardless of the state of his knowledge.

"Can you do it?" asked Elliot.

"What?"

"An orchestra? Can you pull off a whole orchestra? On your computers?"

"No."

"Why not?'

"Cause I can't. It's too hard. There's too many… Christ Elliot. No."

"But the piano sounds good. You'd fool anyone with that." Elliot sat in a swivel chair and spun around.

"I don't want to fool anyone. I want them to take me seriously."

"Why?"

"Because I do."

"Good reason," said Elliot. Each time he spun around to a keyboard he typed some imaginary sentences.

"What's wrong with wanting to be taken seriously?" asked Alex. He started to clear up the manuals, sure that his conducting was over.

"What's wrong with fooling people?" Elliot was getting dizzy but wouldn't give up on the spinning.

"People listen to you play and they're in awe. They take you seriously. You can get away with bloody murder in this place cause you can play."

"But it doesn't matter a toss anywhere else, does it? Anywhere else I'm just a chink with greasy hair."

"Buy some shampoo then… and don't start all that oppressed shit. I can't be arsed. Really, buy some shampoo."

"You just don't get it do you?" Elliot stopped spinning and held on to the chair in case he keeled over. "You're so obsessed about being taken seriously. You're so jealous of everyone else. You don't see what you've got. You think people take me seriously so my life is complete because that's what's missing from your life."

"Okay Elliot, what's missing from your life then?"

"Almost everything. Apart from my virtuosic talents, my two-hundred IQ and my good looks, my life is a black hole of despair."

"You don't believe in IQs, and you're an ugly bastard."

"I don't believe intelligence can be measured. I'm just using two hundred as a relative term so that people such as yourself can understand what I'm on about."

"Such as myself?"

"Don't worry. At least I can communicate with you."

Alex could hardly decide whether to get offended or break a keyboard over Elliot's greasy nut. "I'm so lonely," continued Elliot. His semi-permanent smile broke into a kind of pout. Maybe it was a smirk? Alex wasn't sure; he was so used to Elliot's smile. He looked like a different person without a smile welded onto his face. "It's so lonely in here."

"In here?"

Elliot pointed to his head, then took the opportunity to give it a scratch. "You guys think I'm just farting around when I brag about myself."

"No, we don't. We know you're serious."

"But I'm not serious. I am just farting about. But that doesn't make it not so."

Alex couldn't feel sorry for Elliot. That would be ridiculous, insane. Anyway, he had himself to feel sorry for. "You're telling me, the guy with banana hands and no future, that not only is it hard being regarded as a natural virtuoso, it's even harder because it's true? Elliot, if I had a machine that could suck out your talent and implant it in me and leave you as a vegetable, I'd have you strung up and powered on by now."

"But you do."

"Elliot, let me say it again. Please, leave me alone. Your life is hard? Tough shit. I don't care."

"Well, do it then. Turn on the machine. It won't turn me into a veggie though."

"But that would be the best bit," said Alex, with enough venom to surprise himself. Elliot was a good pal; he'd never done his genius act on Alex before. Alex wasn't used to people perceiving him as stupid. Untalented? Yes. Immature? Yes, but not stupid. The inscrutable nature of low-level software development usually elicited awe. He knew that most of it was down to hard graft. He knew that what appears to the uninitiated as indecipherable hieroglyphs give themselves up to anyone willing to work twelve to sixteen hours a day for a couple of years. It was as if Elliot was trying to dismantle his last bastion of self-worth.

"Go on. Do it," said Elliot.

Alex tried to imagine what it must be like to be Elliot. How deep were his gifts? Elliot never displayed any kind of effort at all. He played anything on sight like it was an old friend.

If the music was physically impossible to play on guitar—if there were too many notes in a chord, or they were unreachable, or outside the range of the instrument, he'd arrange it. He arranged music in real time. He solved layer upon layer of musical problems with as much effort as the rest of us use to add a couple of single-digit numbers. The harder the problem, the more impossible the task, the more relaxed and entertained he became. Put a symphonic score in front of him and he'd play as if privy to some private joke. Then he'd remember it. He remembered everything he ever played.

It was sickening. Alex was jealous. "You have a photographic memory?"

"No."

"But you remember everything? Everything you ever played, you can remember it?"

"Yup."

"So you have a photographic memory?"

"Nope."

Alex sighed. Elliot had come to torture him.

"It's like the IQ thing," said Elliot, sensing that Alex needed some help. "Photographic is what people call it who haven't got it. It looks like a photograph from the outside but it's got time and depth too. What you see from the outside is like a little slice of it; like looking through a window on the other side of a long room but even then, the window only gives you a snapshot, a photograph, stuck in time."

"You are such a lucky bastard then. That's what you're saying? You never have to try. It's all revealed by default? No effort, no thought, just knowledge?"

"I think it's what comes before thought. I think it's what normally turns into thought. When it becomes thought then it's more like the photograph that everyone thinks you have in your head. But it's so lonely. You've no idea how it feels to fly around in here with no one to talk to but dead composers."

*In here?* Elliot was hardly introspective at the best of times. Maybe he was doing a bit of bluebottle munching himself? Alex still couldn't feel compassion for someone who had everything, someone who could openly call him stupid, and be right—the really sharp barb—would have to get crazier than this to earn whatever it was he was after.

"So when you talk to normal people. People like me. You're slumming? You're killing yourself to find ways to communicate with a lesser species?"

"Will you hate me if I say yes?" The pain in Elliot's voice, the smile, replaced by an expression that hardly knew itself, told Alex that Elliot wasn't trying to hurt him. He really was trying to communicate from a higher plane. At least that's how Elliot saw the world, must have seen the world. The power that gave life to his music condemned him to isolation.

"So, when you talk to us mere mortals you're really shouting at us from the other side of that wee window?"

"Kinda," answered Elliot from far away. "I miss things. I make a joke of it, but I miss things. I don't know why. It's like I can see into peoples' souls, but I don't care. No, maybe sometimes I want to care, but I don't feel. I can see it all but I can't feel it, not real life. When I play, it's like I'm tracing emotions; I draw little pencil lines with me guitar around the human soul. It's a trick."

"I have no idea what the fuck you're on about. If you're gonna slum it down here with the boneheads, you'd better be prepared to get a bit dirtier cause you sound like some wanker poet. Make sense." The bitterness of discovering his limitations, or rather, being instructed on his limitations, hardened into defiance. Elliot may have been reaching out, but he did it like he was picking a fight. Alex was angry and didn't hide it.

Elliot stroked his lower lip with his forefinger; the way he did when presented with a new manuscript, but he wasn't about to devour this problem the way he'd devour mere music. After a long rumination that would normally see him leaping into Bach or Barrios or ripping into some unsuspecting victim with sledge hammer wit wrapped in chirpy Liverpudlianisms, he said, "It's not enough. It's just not enough."

"Aren't you geniuses all supposed to go for a walk in the sea?" said Alex. "You know, it's all so hard being a superior being that you just have to go swim with the fishes?"

Elliot didn't hear him. "When I found music. When I really heard it for the first time. I knew there had to be people like me out there. They were speaking to me. It didn't matter how I lived. It didn't matter that I never had any money. It didn't matter that they thought I was a moron at school cause I failed all me exams. When I heard Chopin it was like a river running through me. Bach flew me through cathedrals. Britten made grief an auditory sensation."

"But he was a woofter, don't forget," Alex grinned. Elliot didn't.

"I thought I was communicating with them all. But I wasn't. They were communicating with me. It's like being in a prison cell and everyone shouts at you all day, but no matter how much you scream back at them, they don't hear you. It's like watching their shadows on the wall. You can imagine they're real, but in the end you know it's just an echo. I'm sick to death of it all," he said to himself.

"Man, you're a broken record."

"You look at me and all you see is what you haven't got."

Alex booted a few computers. There wasn't much point in wasting the whole day listening to Elliot bleating about his lot.

"I don't want a fight Elliot. I'm a hack, Okay. Leave me to it."

"Why won't you understand? I'm not talking about you."

"Really?"

"I'm no threat. That's me."

Alex loaded some files into an editor he'd written years before. "How about this Elliot? How's your programming skills?" He typed without looking up then pointed at the screen. Wee problem here Elliot. Perhaps you could help me? Whadya say? Do you think this routine gives me enough control of the attack envelope or should I leave well alone? I mean, I have all the natural envelopes anyway, and I've used filters to ramp the velocities between them, but I'm not sure whether the wave files can stand on their own or whether I should fanny around with them. And this case function call is a bitch; it's just not efficient. Do you think I should re-write it? Maybe you could help me squeeze a couple of nanoseconds from the streaming routine?"

Elliot wondered whether to keep on trying.

"Of course, if I sit you down here for a few minutes, your big, huge, wobbly brain will just absorb me and my computers. You'll find all my cheats and shortcuts. You'll…"

"Let me help you," said Elliot.

"Eh?" Alex suddenly realized that perhaps Elliot could do all that. Perhaps he could learn everything Alex knew in a few hours?

"I can help you with your music."

"You think you can learn to program in…"

"Don't be a moron… sorry. I can help you with the performance. The interpretation."

"I'm doing okay thanks."

"You are. The Chopin was nice. But it was wrong."

"Christ Elliot. I'm beginning to see why you have to smile all the time. It's to offset smashes in the face."

"That's right." Elliot pulled himself out of the funk. What did he expect from Alex anyway? It wasn't Alex's fault.

Elliot reached over to tap the keyboard. A drop of blood smeared a key. Elliot examined the little red crescents his nails had made in the palm of his hand. Alex grabbed Elliot's hand; the crescents were surrounded by closely bunched rows of little white scars.

Alex felt suddenly powerless and ashamed.

"Sometimes I get a little tense," he said. He took out a hankie and clutched it hard. "You get to hump a goddess, I get this. Lets have a go at that Chopin and see if we can't figure out what the fuck he meant, eh?"

Alex had thought the remaining problems with his Chopin were purely technological, that he'd nailed the performance well enough. The trick, he thought, was to play it fast enough to blind the listener without blowing the gaff that the performer wasn't human. Elliot insisted from the start that it required two pianos—an idea that Alex felt would immediately tie a tag to it saying 'counterfeit', but he let Elliot mould the whole performance in any way he wanted. What was the worst that could happen? Maybe he'd end up with a few gigabytes of useless space, maybe he could salvage something from Elliot's approach? Elliot decided that the left hand arpeggios needed a soft pedal and the right hand needed a sustain pedal. "This is what old Freddykins meant," he said after every suggestion was compiled and run. Alex built a new piano for each hand; the left with layer upon layer of progressively stronger velocities which didn't even venture halfway into a typical grand's dynamic range, in the right he crammed as many pedal-down layers as he could. The sustain pedal was a bitch—each layer needed so much information—but he had the processing power right in this room to go way beyond anything he'd tried before. He built a piano uniquely designed for this piece according to Elliot's design. There were huge gaps in the instrument; if it were human it would have looked like a guy with one half of his head swollen out of proportion and his left front teeth missing. It was useless for anything but this particular little piece of Chopin. Alex added some resonant harmonics—all of which made Elliot shake his head. He added some noise, a little background hiss, some foot movement, some pedal creaks, a little breathing. Elliot wasn't happy with the harmonics. Alex assured him that he'd record some more, and include a little room ambience from each harmony and the transition between the harmonies, and he'd record a unique set of release samples to model the aftermath of each note. Elliot insisted on mistakes; not great blunders; that would defeat the purpose of the exercise but fleeting, almost imperceptible errors, a finger hanging too long on a note, a lot (Alex suspected too many) of wayward velocities. Elliot was convinced that the best approach was to phrase it by looking down at the detail through successively enveloping phrases. The finest resolution Elliot was interested in was the beat. Elliot didn't want to hear about actual time. The beat is nebulous, it spreads and smears and dilates and contracts, it shifts shape, changes form and character, it pumps the blood and regulates temper. Alex had to take care of everything inside the beat. Elliot had no interest in how Alex produced what he wanted and quickly went from huff to ecstasy and back again as Alex fought to make the music do Elliot's bidding. Elliot's demands went from the beat through a hierarchy of phrases—that he decided existed, whether or not they might—through the music itself then spilled into the virtual room where the piano played. He considered the effect relative humidity might have on the sound, the number of people in the audience (Alex inserted a couple of muffled throat clearings and a restrained cough at the start to give the feeling of immediacy; of life) and the sound absorption their presence would cause. He considered the room reflections —what novel harmonic structures would evolve according to the physics of the room and the variously dense objects within—and questioned Alex's original microphone placements.

Alex made it clear that microphone placement was already decided. He wasn't privy to Chopin's innermost thoughts the way Elliot claimed he was but he'd spent thousands of hours experimenting with different microphones and microphone placements. He had to produce a recording that sounded authentic, that sounded authentically recorded within a given space; that was all. He had to make the sound wet enough to suggest distance but dry enough to inject immediacy. Maybe he could have done better? He never was satisfied, but this would have to do, his whole library was based on the placements now recorded. Changing now would mean starting from scratch.

"Start from scratch then," said Elliot. "Look, you want to produce the greatest performance. You want perfection. You want people to come in their pants. You want them to think you're a genius."

"I just want to hear how good it can be. Do you have any idea how long it took me to build this library? If I go back to the beginning it might not turn out as good, it might be worse."

"But it might be better. Worth taking a chance, no?"

"But there are diminishing returns," Elliot didn't get it. Alex had to make him understand what he was asking. "You're asking for a new basic sound. It won't necessarily be better, just different… maybe even if it's better then only five or six percent."

"Five or six percent's not to be sniffed at," said Elliot. "Imagine living five percent longer or having five percent more

sex or having the quality of an orgasm improved by five percent."

"When did you ever have sex?" asked Alex.

"I've had plenty of orgasms," he said holding up his hand.
"Anyway, no need for cheek. I don't want to waste my time
giving everything I've got to have it diminished by your sloth."

Alex pictured the mountain that Elliot egged him to climb.
He had a list of new techniques he wanted to try that had
grown as he came closer to the music he worked to realize.
Maybe it was time to get to work? "Yer a fuckin bastard Elliot."

"I most certainly am. This'll be a fitting legacy."

"Eh?" Alex hardly heard him. His mind rushed with possibilities.

"I'm snookered. Fancy a curry?" asked Elliot.

They headed to the pub to pick up Skuggs. Going for a
curry without Skuggs was a crime against humanity—or so
Skuggs said.

# FOURTEEN

Today's lecture was supposed to be on Messiaen's bird-song. Alex prepared himself for a weather balloon full of dode-caphonic gas smelling up the room. Messiaen was one of McNabb's babies. He'd met him once, or so he claimed, at some posh do. This fleeting personal knowledge gave him dibs on everything Messiaenic. But McNabb was busy; too busy to bother with the sycophantic spew that passed for one of his lectures. Geoff Baker appeared, looking a little worse for wear. Geoff was a gem of a teacher; quite out of character with the timbre of the Academy he was known to preach that music was fun.

Geoff planted some papers onto the lectern. He was pretty well stewed. He had a hard time standing straight. Geoff was almost always drunk but, like professional drunk drivers, it seldom interfered with his ability to get the job done.

"Birds do it better," he said. "End of lecture." He staggered stage right and flopped into a chair as if the lecture had drained every ounce of energy he could muster.

"This is a disgrace," came Martin's warble from the back of the hall. The whole audience turned to witness Martin thrust an accusing finger into the air. "You sir, are drunk," he said, like he'd just sprung out of a Dickensian drawing room.

"You're right there," said Geoff.

"I will report you sir."

"Sit the fuck down shakey," shouted Elliot.

"Perhaps for once the savant can keep his mouth closed?" said Martin. It was plain that he'd prepared the retort in advance. Elliot wasn't too popular, his talent elicited jealousy. He'd made a lot of enemies, and a few sniggered at Martin's challenge.

Elliot stood up. "He studied at the conservatoire. Whilst serving as the organist at La Trinité," he gave a little wave with the accent. "He studied with Dukas, Emmanuel and Dupré. His first published work, in 1929, showed he was developing his own modal system using augmented triads and tritons. He later explored unfolding arithmetical systems, Greek metrical rhythms and veered somewhat into serialism. One day he was walking through the park when he heard a bird singing and thought to himself, 'by Christ that's a load of shite. If that bird had any sense he'd arrange that tune for piano and orchestra. What the fuck do birds know about orchestration anyway?'"

One or two people applauded but the majority in the room had heard it all, or a variation thereof, before.

"You are disgusting," said Martin. "Who do you think you are?"

Elliot's smile left him.

"You missed the oriental rhythms. He used oriental rhythms," said Martin.

"No, he didn't, he thought he used oriental rhythms. He got them wrong, but nobody ever noticed. Sitting around in cafes and art galleries, wanking on about the idea of the music instead of the sound. Another example of what happens when the explanation of the music supplants the music itself. Maybe the music is great? But why bother with listening when it's all decided? Better to build a cathedral around the justification."

The thing that got Martin more than Elliot's barbs or his talents, or his constant use of redundant expletives, was that when Elliot set about a trashing he sounded like a philistine, but he always knew the theory, the historical background, as if he secretly studied for such occasions.

A globule of soaking paper thumped against Elliot's forehead, and stuck dripping into his eye. Martin had friends. The hall burst into laughter. Saliva running down his face, Elliot waited for the laughter to abate, but it kept on going. A few people left but there were still almost a hundred people in the room and most of them kept on laughing.

"Buncha twats," said Elliot. He peeled the paper off his forehead and left.

"I'm starting a petition to get that man removed!" said Martin pointing at Geoff, who was half asleep. "Who's with me?" he cried.

Alex went after Elliot. He bumped into Skuggs. They searched the Academy then the pub.

"He must have gone back to his pit," said Skuggs. "Should we go see him d'you think? Fuck, they really hate the wee man."

"They're just scared. They come here, they're the best in their school, or the best in their orchestra or region, or whatever. Then they get here and they meet fuckers like you and Elliot and they get pissed off. Doesn't matter how hard they work. They can't get close to you guys. Elliot won't give them a break so they hate him. If he was nice about it instead of being so superior they'd get to like him."

"But that was outa order," said Skuggs.

"It was a public execution. They wanted blood. He gave them their chance."

"How d'you fancy we fill-in the queer?"

"Queer?"

"Martin."

"He's his own punishment, man. Let's find Elliot before he tops himself. He's been acting really strange, well, stranger than usual."

When Martin arrived back at the lecture theatre with McNabb, Geoff was sprawled across his chair, snoring loudly. He was covered in spitballs. Martin's first attempt at rabble rousing had been a success. McNabb looked as regretful as a dog. "Thank you Mr. Watson," he said. "I can take it from here. I think Mr. Baker needs help. I'm sorry the student body had to see this."

"He's not fit to teach," said Martin, "he's a disgrace."

"That's enough Mr. Watson. Run along now."

McNabb stood silently, to make sure nobody was around. "Prick," he said. He circled around the pitiful heap on the chair. "Mr. Popular? Well, cheeky chappie. You're out. You can go borrow a dress and join Todd down at the docks for all I care." McNabb kicked Geoff's leg. Geoff carried on snoring. He kicked him again but Geoff was too drunk to give McNabb any pleasure. McNabb kicked again but missed Geoff's leg and crunched his toes into the leg of the chair. He hopped around unable to breath then toppled over.

Martin saw it all. He'd snuck back into the lecture theatre and hid in the back row. He could feel the adrenaline pumping through his system. A dull pain in his crotch grabbed his attention. He fiddled around in his underpants to try to give his erection a little breathing room. He watched McNabb hobble up the stairs and out, then he went hunting for Phillipa.

Elliot could hear them shouting but he didn't have the energy to go all the way downstairs and open the door.

They banged on the door until their knuckles were raw, then sat down to have a breather. Alex lit a cigarette. Skuggs produced a Kit-Kat from one of the many pockets on his parka.

"You know mate," said Alex, smoke pouring from his nose, "things are changing. Bad things are afoot."

Skuggs munched the whole Kit-Kat in a oner and fished around in his pockets until he found another. "Got a sweetie shop in there?" said Alex, "can I have one."

"Finished man," said Skuggs stuffing the chocolate into his mouth.

"Shitebag liar."

"So, what do you two losers want?" Elliot stood at the door. His face was puffy; he'd been crying but didn't own a mirror where he could check such things.

"Been greetin man?" said Skuggs. Elliot was a little surprised that Skuggs had twigged instantly but he couldn't be bothered. He walked up the stairs. They followed, giving each other little glances. Elliot actually crying was quite scary.

"Things are strange," said Alex under his breath.

"Got any drugs?" asked Elliot as he pummelled his front door with his shoulder—the only way to get it open.

"Allan's the junkie," said Skuggs. "Want me to go phone him? I can grab some chips when I'm out. Elliot gave a cursory nod. "Salt and vinegar?" shouted Skuggs as he ran away.

Elliot didn't speak. He just sat staring at the chessboard in front of him, guitar in his hands, playing almost unconsciously. Alex didn't want to push anything. He wasn't much of an agony aunt. When Elliot came to him for help he was so immersed in his own problems he'd probably made it worse. He'd recently taken to bawling his eyes out himself. All this emotional stuff was new to him. He felt lost. He sat back to listen to the sublime sounds Elliot produced from his instrument. The music drew him in until he closed his eyes and forgot where he was or why he was there.

The music stopped.

"Well, Keemosavee, what are we going to do with it?" asked Elliot.

"Uh?"

"Our bloody music. The Chopin?"

"It'll take ages man. You want all those samples re-recorded. Then there's…"

"Forget that. It's good enough."

"Good enough for what?"

Elliot carefully placed his guitar in its case. "Good enough to make money."

"Make money? How?"

"How do you normally make money from music?"

Alex had no idea what he was talking about but had no appetite for his guessing games.

"I'm sick to death with the lot of them. Bunch of sheep," said Elliot. "Why don't we make them pay?"

Alex bit his lip.

"If I play me cards right. If I kiss the right arses at the right times in the right order. If I go study with Boskov and listen to his drivel for three years and I tell everybody I owe it all to him, then I get to play twice a month in a freezing church to a couple of old grannies and a few guitar students. If I enter every major competition in the world, and win them, which I won't, then I can play at the local town hall for thirty people. I can make a record and sell a thousand copies—if I'm lucky."

"It's better than working for a living, no?" Alex cursed himself for taking the bait.

"Not much better."

McNabb was unassailable. Even as a senior lecturer he'd managed one or two a year. As principal his batting average was bound to improve. He pored over the instrumental lesson schedule—the throbbing in his foot only a minor inconvenience—he circled a few names then commanded Mrs. Gibb to bring him the records of three students.

Nobody hated McNabb more than Mrs. Gibb. She would have resigned in a second if she really believed she'd have to serve him from now on. She knew full well what he was up to but believed he was simply engaging in fantasy. There had been rumours. She was close to the students, and students talked, but nothing was ever confirmed. Such a grievous breach of trust seemed too much to Mrs. Gibb.

McNabb could have found the records on his own, but why bother? In more than twenty years as an educator nobody had ever taken him to task on such matters. He never hurt anyone. Why, if young girls found him attractive, what could he do about it? They were old enough to make choices.

McNabb had no idea what they looked like. How they looked didn't matter anyway. All that mattered was their grades, their attitude, their ambition. The first two students had good grades. His charm might still work but there was no point in creating difficulties for oneself. Something borderline was what he was after and Laura had all the credentials. She was failing everything. Her teachers had given her a wide berth, maybe too wide? Her dedication and hard work had saved her but it was clear that results were not forthcoming. McNabb decided that this student needed a little special attention, and if that should lead to something more, as it often did, then so be it.

He closed her file and sat back to imagine how she might look. This was all part of the process. First, the imagining, then the meeting, then the help, the bending over backwards to help, then, if it followed its natural course, she'd see him, a powerful man, a good man. He'd never do anything she didn't want, never. He wasn't a monster, after all.

Skuggs arrived back at Elliot's pit carrying a single bag of freezing, soggy chips and a heartfelt plea that he had no choice but to devour the other two bags while waiting for Allan to pick up his phone. Alex used Skuggs's guilt to make him turn out his pockets. Elliot and Alex ate the four Kit-Kats he'd stashed and left the third bag of chips to its fate.

Allan arrived shortly after Skuggs and produced a chocolate-sized lump of dope and a speech making it clear that it had to be paid for. Allan was excited that they'd invited him round for nothing more than a smoking session and wondered whether he might use the evening to lead the whole heathen bunch of them into the bosom of Christ.

"None of yer fucking religion tonight Allan," said Elliot holding the dope up to the light like a precious stone as if he could check the quality by looking through it. "Get rollin."

"Can I try your guitar?" asked Allan as he passed a beautifully rolled joint to Elliot.

Elliot lit up, inhaled deeply then had a coughing fit. He grabbed some air and inhaled again, this time holding the smoke in long enough to feel the heat in his lungs before coughing it up again.

"Eh?" asked Allan, always desperate for an audience.

"Okay," said Elliot, but any Dowland and you're out on yer arse."

Allan grabbed the guitar greedily. "I've been working on some Granados," he said and started to play almost inaudibly. Alex was struck by the difference between Allan and Elliot's playing. Allan sounded apologetic where Elliot would soar. Allan's playing couldn't drown out the sound of Skuggs stuffing the chips into himself.

"Shite, eh?" said Elliot, as if reading Alex's mind. "So did you work it out yet?"

Alex had worked it out. It was dumb. It wouldn't work, it couldn't work, but he had no choice. McNabb was certain to kick him out. Laura was certain to give him a body swerve if he didn't do something. He had nothing to lose.

"Let's discuss it," he motioned at Skuggs and Allan, "later."

"Allan can't hear us," said Elliot. "He can't play and think at the same time. And Skuggs doesn't give a damn."

"Damn about what?" asked Skuggs, a chip dropped out of his mouth. He grabbed it before it hit the floor and popped it back into his mouth.

"I need more music," said Alex.

"How about some Giuliani?" asked Allan.

"Thought you said he couldn't hear?" said Alex.

"What do you reckon you need? How long'll it take?" Elliot asked. "Yeah, Giuliani, go on." Allan pitter-pattered into a little tune.

"Dunno, full pelt, coupla weeks," answered Alex, already scanning the music in his mind. "Maybe some standards, you know, Beethoven's Pathetique, some Bach, maybe Brahms? Just enough to whet the appetite, no point in overcooking it."

"So, what do you think?" asked Allan. He stole a glance away from the fingerboard.

"Shite Allan, shite."

"Not you Buddha, him?"

"Sounds nice," said Alex. "Lovely."

Allan stopped playing. "You're taking the piss, aren't you? You think it's shit as well, don't you?"

"Nah, can't hear it Allan, too quiet. Can't you play louder?"

"Louder? Are you serious? That's ninety percent of guitar playing," said Elliot. "That's what's hard. He can play louder but he can't control it. His hands'll seize up after a few bars. Christ, you pianists have such an easy time of it. You just sit there and lean harder and the sound comes out. Lucky bastards. Mind you, I reckon the harp's harder. All those fuckin pedals. French horn's a killer as well, I suppose."

Allan's spliff was starting to hit home. Elliot stared into space. "What about poor old Skuggs here? Fucking tuba. Waste of time."

"Certainly is," Skuggs confirmed. "But I'm the best. I'll never go short of work. Always have enough for my drinking vouchers. That's all that matters."

"Don't you ever crave stardom?" asked Alex. "Don't you ever imagine yourself getting standing ovations? Sluts chasing you down to administer blowjobs and other wanton sexual acts?"

"I do okay," replied Skuggs.

"But man, if you were a pianist you could get away with a little cravat even, and nobody would call you gay."

"Pianist?" said Skuggs. "Waste of time. They let them dream at college but nobody makes a living playing piano, there's always some ninety-year old bastard who was great when he was twenty, and he gets everything going. Pianist? Fuckin end up teachin bairns to sing My Grandfather's Cock. Poor fuckers. They're all livin in a dream world. They think my tuba's funny. I make great farty noises and they get a laugh. They put on a face and sweat and that when they're playin, and everybody leaps outa their seats when they're finished, but that's it man. As soon as they leave here they're completely buggered. They're just kids. No fuckin idea at all. Whoa, chipfart!"

He lifted a leg to help it on its way.

"E, G, B, D flat," Skuggs offered. "First inversion C seven flattened ninth ya bastard. I'm fuckin Charlie Parker on the sphincter. Try doin that on a Joanna."

"I never tire of listening to a master," said Elliot, laughing. "Where's the root?"

"Fuck the root. One of these days I'll make a thirteenth," said Skuggs when he was sure he'd finished. "The whole thing's a con man. Out of five hundred students maybe two or three a year end up playing for a living, the rest teach or do something else. Pianists? Man, you see wee Japs… sorry Elliot." Skuggs interrupted himself.

"See what I have to put up with?" said Elliot. "He's too thick even to get being a racist right. I'm Chinese, fart boy."

"You know what I mean. Like they're five and better than anybody at this college. But every year they make a big deal outa some poor bastard. They give him a medal and he thinks maybe he can make it. No chance man. No fucking chance. Solo pianists, if they haven't made it by the time they're twelve they're snookered." Skuggs sucked on the joint like a rank amateur. "Look at poor Allan." Allan was oblivious; he plinked on. "He's not even as good as Elliot."

"Not even?" cried Elliot.

"But there he is dreaming away. Maybe one day he'll wake up and he won't be shite." Allan pulled a face. Skuggs went on. "See! Conditional reflex! Nice one Elliot. There's about three guitarists in the world that make a living and about twenty pianists. But there's plenty of tuba players pumping away all over the shop. I mean *really* making a living; not teaching or fannying around in wine bars or buskin like a bum. Nobody's ever gonna think I'm cool like a conductor or a pianist, and I might not get a permanent orchestral job, but I'll work. And I won't have to teach, thank Christ. If you've no made it by the time you get here, you're no gonny."

"What about Elliot? Everybody says he's gonna make it."

"He's an exception. Started late. Lucky he doesn't need a lot to live on though, cause he won't make a fortune... unless he gets shagged up the arse by the right guy."

"How will I know if I meet the right guy?" sniggered Elliot.

"You'll know him when you see him. Sad thing is that you chumps think I'm joking."

"I know you're not joking," said Elliot. "But I'll never make it anyway, even if I get burgled by the right guy."

"How so?" asked Skuggs.

"Can't be bothered. Hate playing for people. People are a pain in the arse. Why don't they go and learn how to play themselves instead of bothering me? Look at Allan, he's giving it a go. I wouldn't mind if they just came round here one at a time and listened while I played, but having to get to a concert hall and it's freezing cold and you have to talk shite with them afterwards, then you have to get the bus or the train home."

"You could buy a car," said Alex.

"Hate cars."

"I love playing for people," piped Allan. He'd finished his tune but nobody noticed.

"Yeah, we gathered that," said Elliot.

"You're just selfish," said Allan. "You have a God–given gift. You should share it, like I do."

"Fuck. I wondered how long we could go without hearing about Jesus and his poxy Dad. Am I blaspheming?"

"You can't blaspheme. You don't believe," said Allan.

"Good," said Elliot. "Cause I've got a bone to pick with God. I want to know why he made me perfect but denied women with big breasts the ability to see it."

"What've you got against small-breasted women?" asked Skuggs.

"Them as well," said Elliot.

Alex said, "But guys, even if you don't make it, even if you have to teach, we get to play music for three or four years. Most people have to work in shitey offices with bosses they want to kill."

Skuggs explained, "But by the time you finish here and get into one of those shitey jobs, the fuckers who're there now are in charge and they want you to suffer for getting to play music for three years. And if they've gone bald in the meantime and you've got hair then you're destroyed. They'll wear you down, suck out your soul cause they hate you. And they should hate you, cause you just ran around in a tutu while they had to work for a living. You've got a chance if you go bungey jumping with them though. These types like to bungey jump."

"You're all so negative," said Allan. He placed Elliot's guitar carefully in its case and started to roll another. "Who cares whether you 'make it' or not?" He made little quotes in the air with his fingers to signify his distaste for the phrase. "Music is God's voice. His gift. You think you're playing to people; you're not, you're reminding people of the eternal in us."

"You're all schizos you religious types. Fucking headcases. If Christ came back tomorrow you'd be the first up the ladder nailing the poor bastard."

"That's ridiculous," said Allan.

"They said I was schizophrenic when I was a kid. Cause I heard voices."

"You heard voices? What voices?" asked Skuggs.

"Chess players. Dead chess players."

"Spooky," said Skuggs.

"But I didn't imagine it. They used to come when I was playing; explain strategies and that. Good stuff. How about some Dowland?" said Elliot.

"What have you got against Dowland?" asked Allan. "It's so beautiful."

"Not when you play it," said Elliot. "Dowland's okay, a bit poofy but it's okay."

"I find renaissance music depressing," said Skuggs. "When I hear it I always think of the horrible life that most people suffered, especially the poor people; which was just about everybody except a couple that got to hear the music and look at the paintings and that. And have you ever seen the dances man?"

"But the renaissance gave scum like us a chance to live didn't it? I mean we all had to live on pigshit and chickenlips before that didn't we? But rich geezers wanted art and the high life so talented fuckers got a chance to earn cash by entertaining them," said Elliot.

"They still got treated like shite though," said Skuggs. Look at Bach. He wrote music sixteen hours a day 'cept when he slipped his wife one every year."

"Bach wrote to the glory of God," said Allan.

"Bach is God," said Elliot. "You're a music student for fuck's sake, you should know that."

"Wonder if his wife was ugly," said Skuggs.

"He was, for sure," said Elliot. "Anyway, what's the deal with you and your bird? When ya getting married?"

"She's pissed at me right now cause I'm a wimp," replied Alex.

"No offence man, but she is fuckin gorgeous," said Skuggs.

"She's not bad," said Allan.

"Not bad?" said Elliot. "This from a man who has sex with Fidel Castro's hairy sister."

"She's a wonderful harp player," said Allan.

"I never thought I could end up with anyone as beautiful," said Alex.

"So you've ended up with her then. It's a done deal?" said Elliot. "But she's a crap violinist, so you've no need to get jealous Allan."

"She's not you know," said Alex, "but you're not gonna believe this." He stopped himself.

"What?" asked Elliot.

"Nah, forget it. She's not that bad a violinist. She just practices too hard; makes her tense."

"Then you've got to relax her laddie," Skuggs winked.

Did Skuggs know? Alex inhaled deeply on the sodden roach and held in the smoke for as long as he could then let it out slowly. The tension in his chest melted. What did it matter if Skuggs knew? He was no blabbermouth. It wasn't that he could keep a secret, or he could be trusted more than anyone else, it was more that he didn't care about anyone's business outside of the guilty excitement of knowing. He took pleasure in the business of others but only the way a housewife might watch an afternoon chat show to pass the time. Skuggs saw himself as a student of human nature. He liked to keep things simple.

Skuggs was eight-years old when his father took him to a band practice. His father was a miner in a Scottish colliery who played a mean euphonium. Skuggs immediately fell in love with the tuba. It was so huge; he wanted to climb inside to see how it worked. He begged his father to get him a tuba. His father let him take some 'tuba lessons' on his euphonium, telling him that the euphonium was really a miniature tuba. In the months that followed, his father had to pry the instrument away from him to get to rehearsals. In the way that only children—and unbalanced adults—can manage, Skuggs gave his life over to his obsession. He had no problems at all reaching notes in the higher register, but he spent most of his time trying to extend the lower range of the instrument. He tried to convert the euphonium into a tuba. After three years playing tuba on euphonium, his father produced a slightly banged up tuba for Skuggs. He was playing in his father's colliery band by then, and already its star. The band wouldn't let him drink until he was fifteen. It wasn't just the music for Skuggs. The whole experience of rehearsing new material, then a couple of bottles before heading home gave him purpose, a meaning that went beyond the apparent banality of playing and drinking and going home. On competition days it was onto the bus—sometimes he'd help load the crates onto the bus—a few pints after, then back onto the bus to empty the crates; didn't matter how they did in the competition. It was always the same on the way home, beer and piss stops then into bed. Skuggs loved it. He knew this was what he wanted to do for the rest of his life. When his father explained that everyone else in the band had to work forty hours a week a mile underground, and that perhaps Skuggs should reconsider, he turned his attention to classical music. The technical training in the colliery band stood him in good stead. By the time he got to college, he was miles ahead of his fellow students—and most of the lecturers—which gave him more time to ferret around for work. Skuggs didn't believe in practicing; what was the point of playing in your bedroom when you could do it in front of people for money? In band he'd always been sober before and during competitions, but orchestras didn't have big bruising miners to break your nose for you if you got drunk before a performance. Skuggs found the transition from après concert libation to pre- and during-indulgence, both smooth and balanced; it just somehow seemed right. And right now he was considering adding some of Allan's whacky-baccy to the mix.

Skuggs handed the joint to Alex.

"Jeezis Skuggs, did you drop this in a puddle? Allan, can you roll one for me? I don't want to share with slaver boy here, or any of you lot, you're all filthy bacteria-infested germ buckets."

"Okay," Allan answered, and set to work. He carefully emptied a whole pack of Rizlas into four little piles. He folded three papers from each pile, licked the edge of each then tore off a strip. He discarded the torn strips then licked the gum of a paper and stuck another to it. He attached a third paper to the two. "I don't like too much paper," he said. He repeated the tearings and the lickings until he'd made four piles of pristine casings. The others watched in awe.

"Where does a man of God such as yourself learn such things?" asked Elliot.

Allan fished around in his pocket until he found a little plastic pot, the kind that 35mm films come in. He emptied half a pack of cigarettes onto the table. Again, with the nimble technique born of experience he licked the side of each, ripped a strip off then emptied the contents into his little plastic pot. He held the lump of black, pliable dope over the pot, flicked his Zippo and heated it. He closed the Zippo and scraped crumbs of hash into the tobacco. He did this four or five times. The others stared in amazement at Allan's skill. No one talked in case they disturbed a master at work. He gave them a start when he put the lid of the pot on and shook the whole thing like he was backing Tito Fuentes. When the shaking was done he filled the eight skins with his concoction.

"May as well stock up," he said.

He ripped the cigarette packet apart and tore eight perfectly matched strips of card. "This is the hard part," he said, acknowledging his audience. "Wish you guys were as attentive when I'm playing guitar." He rolled each joint with a precision and care lacking in his guitar playing, but nobody wanted to mention it; at least not until he was finished.

"There," he said, holding up one of his creations. "Not too tight, not too loose, like a perfect chuff on a summer's night."

"Ugh. Thanks for the image." Skuggs made a face.

"Two each," said Allan. "That should keep us going for a while. You can all roll your own next time."

"Are you sure you're religious?" asked Alex. "I mean, in a non-Rastafarian kind of way?"

Alex puffed on. He was new to Allan's heavy dope smoking regime. The truth was that he didn't really feel much happening. Maybe he expected too much? Some of the guys at work used to do a lot of smoking but Alex had always turned down their kind offers to get involved. At heart, he was a bit dubious about drugs.

"I don't feel anything," he said.

"You do," said Allan. "What d'you expect, pink elephants? It's only dope, it's a herb, it's not like a proper drug."

"Got any proper drugs?" asked Elliot. "Mind you, this feels all right to me. It's nice."

# FIFTEEN

"Your playing's getting worse."

It was true. She knew it was true.

"I thought we were getting somewhere but the past couple of weeks, it's all gone." Plowright was a good teacher, better than most, he was right and she knew it, she felt it.

"I work so hard."

"You work too hard."

"What to do?"

"Stop working so hard. Take a break. Stop worrying."

"I am crazy, I think."

"Well, you're in good company in this place then. Don't worry, you're not going to fail. We'll get you through this."

"I'm not worried about failing exams, but my music, where is it?"

"Just take it easy. Go on get out," he smiled. "Go on, go shopping, get drunk. It's not the end of the world."

"It is the end of my world. Music is more than exams…"

Plowright had heard all this before. "Am I your teacher? Well, you have to trust me. I'm ordering you not to play for two weeks. I don't want you to even touch that instrument. Do you hear me?" He tried to sound forceful but instead made her smile. "I'm serious, no violin for two weeks."

She started to pack her violin away while Plowright left wearing a deep frown and harbouring a hope that he'd seemed stern. In truth, he was worried; her playing was falling apart and he felt a little ashamed. It wasn't uncommon for students to enter the Academy with talent and exchange it for a little psychosis. He didn't know what to do and he was worried that he might make matters worse.

It wasn't supposed to be like this. She had talent. She knew it. She'd played violin from the age of three. She couldn't even remember her first lessons. It was as natural as breathing. There was never a time in her life without music. Music was everything, or had been everything until she met Alex. She was so different from Alex, they were two pieces of a puzzle. He was analytical and needy and self-conscious. She was sensitive and sure, she spent little time wallowing in the kind of reflection that Alex believed necessary to create music. He wanted to dissect everything, to pore over, to peek inside and examine and pull apart, to build and rebuild until the music matched some blueprint, an ideal, inside his head. She had never questioned music or her ability to realize music. It was simple; she played. That was all. The violin might have been a part of her; a detachable organ to channel her inner voice, her emotions. She had never questioned it, never thought about it, it was always there, defining her. She was a violinist, a musician, an artist, there never was a question to be answered, never a suspicion to allay.

But now she suspected the worst, that her talent, which she could never have imagined could be separate from the rest of her being, was deserting her, disappearing, vanishing like a photograph fading in the sun. But she couldn't hear it. So powerful was her innate ability to forge what Alex might describe as 'musical models' in her 'mind's ear' that those models superimposed themselves thoroughly onto the reality that was her playing and somehow masked the actual sound. She no longer had a reliable musical feedback mechanism. The very thing that took her abilities, her music, into a more precious and rarefied domain—the unselfconscious realization of musical thought—had separated itself from the physical means of production; it was like being a footballer who had lost his timing, miskicking and fluffing his passes, but unable to see that the passes were firing wildly off in all directions. It was as if she were selectively deaf, no, it was as if she had contracted musical dyslexia, unable to divine the gap between the music she thought she was producing and the music actually produced; she felt it but she couldn't hear it.

The single-mindedness, the strength of mind and character, that had once been an ally in her musical development now worked against her like a cancer. She *suspected* her playing sounded bad but she couldn't hear it at all. Her answer to every and all problems related to violin in the past had been to redouble her efforts, to work harder, to fight through it (whatever *it* might have been) but it seemed that the harder she worked, the more she felt something was wrong. She had hoped her teacher would dismiss her worries as simply that; worries, but he had confirmed that her playing was deteriorating, and she had no way of knowing to what extent.

McNabb saw Plowright leave and took his chance. He slipped into the room and gave her a start.

"Spot check!" He rubbed his hands together. Laura raised an eyebrow and put her hand on her hip with a shrug.

"I am not in the mood. Please."

"This isn't a joke young lady." He sat down. "The teaching is too lax in this place. I'm going to change all that. I'm going to make this place the best in the country."

"Mister McNabb, this is the only music college in the country."

"We'll start with a few scales shall we?"

Laura couldn't believe this was happening. "My teacher say no violin for two weeks."

"I say some scales please." He looked at his watch. "I'm a busy man. Why did he tell you no violin?"

"Because my playing has gone. Kaput!" She flung her arms up. Her breasts bounced. McNabb was hypnotized. This was the way it was. Since puberty she'd hardly entered a room without most of the male occupants locking on to her bosom. It was tiring.

"My first instrument is violin," he said, without diverting his gaze. "I can help you."

"Okay. Okay. Okay. Ayudame. Help me." She rammed the violin under her chin and played.

McNabb circled her, stroking his chin. He examined every contour of her spectacular form.

It might have been the first time she'd ever played. She scratched and scraped, her fingers missing notes, missing strings, her bowing arm jerking to and fro like she was sawing a plank.

"You just have to relax a little."

She snorted.

"Let me help you." He reached from behind her and cupped her breasts in his hands. She let out a throaty growl, whipped around and brought the bow down on his head with enough force to split the bow and open a gash along the crown of his bald pate. He staggered. The cut widened and gaped like a zipper opening, as if the wound itself had shared his shock before remembering it was supposed to bleed.

Blood bubbled out.

Laura placed her violin carefully in its case.

"I hope you die," she said, and left.

McNabb held his bloody hands in front of him in horror. He could feel the warmth oozing into his ears and down his neck. He fell to his knees and crawled to the door.

Everything went black.

"But I have no bow," she said to Alex, who was holding onto his sides to guard against splittage.

"You're my hero," said Skuggs, eyes as wide as saucers. "You think he's dead?"

"I hope so," said Laura.

"We should go check," said Allan.

"Fuck that," said Elliot, "unless you mean we should go along and finish the fucker off."

"Bows are mui, mui caro."

"They are," said Skuggs in a trance to match McNabb's.

"Expensive," she said. "They cost a lot."

"We could all chip in," said Elliot. "How much are they, fifty quid?"

"Times ten," said Alex.

"Forget it then. Get McNabb to pay for it. And if he's dead we can sell his body parts," said Elliot.

"That's three quid already," said Skuggs without releasing his gaze or his stupid smile.

"We should go check," said Allan. "What if he's dead?"

"They'll dust your boobs for fingerprints," said Skuggs. "How big was the cut?"

Laura shrugged. "Maybe I can borrow a bow?"

"I'm going to check," said Allan.

"Leave the dope," said Skuggs. "We really should celebrate."

Allan got there too late. Students were milling around outside talking in hushed tones and peeking in at the pool of blood that marked the spot where McNabb met his match.

"Is he okay?" asked Allan.

"Lots of blood," said one of the students. "Ambulance came. Looked okay to me. Always a lot of blood with head wounds. Must have fallen."

By the time McNabb came to, his wife had arrived. She sat by the bed knitting something. The click–click–clicking that almost drove him mad every Sunday night when he couldn't find an excuse not to be there felt like pebbles bouncing off his skull.

"What happened?" he asked.

"No idea. Got a call, came here. Saw you. Thought I'd catch up on my knitting." She didn't lift her head for a second. Click-click-click, on she went. McNabb fondled his bandage carefully, and tried to remember what happened.

"Must you?" he said finally.

"Sorry dear," she put her knitting down and paid him the full attention he always demanded when he felt sorry for himself.

McNabb couldn't figure his wife. She was twenty-eight years old but acted like she was older than him. He met her when she was twenty five; an eager young journalist working for the kind of local newspaper that gets delivered free and always comes with a couple of stray dog and cat up a tree stories. She interviewed him for the 'arts' page after he conducted a performance of the local amateur orchestra. She'd played violin as a youngster and, after expressing a half-hearted interest in re-kindling her relationship with the instrument, McNabb persuaded her to take some free lessons. He was married to Betty, his first wife, at the time. They had four children, all girls, two at university and two about to go to university. McNabb loved Betty, and strangely, Betty loved him. But when a twenty-five year old showed interest, that was the story ended for Betty.

Now Betty was married to the local orthodontist. She was happy. She was the kind of woman who just wanted to be married. And now McNabb was married to Shama. She was Pakistani. That was exotic. She was pretty. That was a bonus. She was young. That was unbelievable. He was putty in her hands. She hardly let him touch her until they were married. In the three years since the wedding they'd had sex three times. Mc-Nabb craved sex but Shama wasn't interested. No amount of pawing or persuasion or downright begging moved her on this matter. Now she sat there with her knitting and her bulging belly, and he lay there with a bandage on his head, two mortgages, four girls draining his bank account every month, a brat at home with another on the way.

"What the bloody hell happened to me?" he asked.

"Told you darling. Must have fallen. Not getting any younger are we?"

The pain was like a knife digging out chunks of brain. Why did she have to act like this? Why couldn't she be the way she was when he met her? When he married her? Before the wedding it made sense. She was Muslim after all. It was sweet. She'd never been with a man. It was against her beliefs. But afterwards it was the same. She just wasn't interested in sex at all. It was months before they consummated the marriage, and it wasn't at all what he expected. He'd dreamed of dinner and champagne and magical foreplay. He knew it would hurt her but he'd be gentle, at first, then he'd be able to mould her any way he wanted. She was so naïve, whatever he said would be acceptable to her; she couldn't know any better?

But it hadn't worked like that. She was cold, workmanlike. It didn't seem to hurt her at all. It didn't seem to do anything much to her. She hadn't even closed her eyes. She just lay down on the bed, pulled her knickers down and let him in. Afterwards, she made them both 'a nice cup of tea,' and suggested that he cut bacon rolls from his diet—they made him fat and the smell made her feel sick. He managed to invade her pants on two more occasions, both of which had hit the bull's-eye. She was eight months gone with what would be his sixth daughter.

The thought of another screaming brat about the house made him feel like killing himself. He hadn't enjoyed the first four very much and the fifth was a little bundle of agony. Even when he was young enough to stand such things he hadn't enjoyed them. They got in the way. His daughters brought the end of his true musical aspirations. He'd never have been a world famous soloist, he knew that, but he might have made first chair in a respectable orchestra. But the brats had to be fed. Betty refused birth control point blank. But at least she enjoyed sex.

Allan knocked at the door a couple of times then entered.

"Who the bloody hell are you?" asked McNabb.

"I'm a guitar student sir. At the Academy. You know me."

"What do you want?"

"Wanted to make sure you were okay sir. She didn't mean it."

Shama pretended not to hear. McNabb became edgy.

"She's Latino you see. She's a lovely girl. I think she misinterpreted something."

"Well, it doesn't matter," said McNabb. He had no idea what Allan was talking about but it made sense to shut him up.

"Well, eh, whatever your name is. I'm fine; you can tell the students I'm fine. No need to worry. Just a fall." Shama started in on her click-clicking. Allan was embarrassed, and annoyed that McNabb didn't even know him.

"Please. I need rest now."

Allan left.

"Please. I need rest now."

Shama put her knitting into her bag and opened a novel that had a muscle-bound pirate embracing a raven-haired beauty on the front cover. For a fleeting moment McNabb imagined what the raven-haired beauty would look like naked, then a pain shot from his eye into his nose. He stared at the ceiling and tried not to grieve for the loss of Betty. If she were here she'd know what to do. She'd stroke his head and tell him everything was going to be all right. Somehow he knew that nothing would ever be all right again. He tried to remember the last few hours and how a Latino girl could be involved but all he could remember was Betty and how happy he'd been for the first few years of their marriage, and how happy she'd been until he left her for Shama and a life as cold and empty as a grave.

"I've no idea what he was talking about. Don't know a single Latino."

"Mm," Shama flicked a page.

"What have I done? What have I done?"

"Mm. Just a fall dear. No need to worry."

# SIXTEEN

Elliot dragged Alex to a meeting of the Glasgow Guitar Society. Alex suspected he was still in the doghouse and Laura
needed time to fret about the broken bow, so he agreed to a
couple of hours with what Elliot described as 'a bunch of rank
fucking maniac amateurs'. Elliot wanted to go because he'd
played at their meeting last month and had the idea that they'd
treat him like visiting royalty.

"They've never heard anything like me," he said as he
poured himself a cup of tea. "I've broken a few spirits here, I
can tell you."

The meeting was held in a church basement near the city
centre. A couple of tables were spread with a paper tablecloth; at
least there was free tea and biscuits to fend off the biting cold.
The weather was fine outside, but the church basement was like
a meat locker. The seats had already been arranged in a semi-
circle. Guitar cases were stacked in a corner. In ten minutes the
room was filled with the needy conversation of the enthusiastic
hobbyist, the kind of individuals who might venture out on
freezing November nights to get someone they'd never met
elected, or travel hundreds of miles to glimpse a rare bird or an

unusual stamp. Elliot saw these people as his subjects, his fol-
lowers, his disciples, although they certainly didn't act as if they
thought he was anything special. One or two did come over to
inquire if Elliot would be playing tonight. Elliot hadn't decided
whether he wanted to play or not and it was clear he was disappointed.

A small, elderly man wearing a rather tatty dinner suit arrived. He must have been important because a few of the members milled over to him, shook hands and exchanged
pleasantries the way people do when an acknowledged superior
makes an entrance.

"That's old Farty Frank Simpson. He's the boss, the head
honcho. He's the guy who buys the biscuits and prints the fly-
ers. That's a Fleta he's got there."

"Fleta?" Alex inquired.

"Fleta. A Fleta is to guitarists what a Stradivarius is to fid-
dlers, or a Steinway or a Bozie is to Joannists."

"Expensive?"

"Not compared to Strads. But a good few grand, and a shit-
load more than Farty has a right to." One of the members over-
heard Elliot's insults and threw him a look.

"Know what the fucker did," said Elliot staring straight at
the disapproving society member. "He took the bridge off and
stuck chewing gum under it."

"What for?" asked Alex.

"Cause he's mental. Who knows? He should give me the
bloody guitar and give it a break. It's a crime for such a beautiful
instrument to suffer so. It's not right."

"How you doin?" said Elliot to a man with a head of wiry
copper hair framing a face full of freckles. "How's the gavotte?"
Gary McCallum was a typical society member. He'd taken up
guitar too late in life to pursue it professionally, but every day
after working as an orderly at the Royal Infirmary he practiced

religiously for two to three hours at a stretch. He went for lessons every two weeks where he spent most of the time discussing the finer points of interpretation when he knew deep inside that he should have been trying to find a way to advance his shaky technique. But in the great tradition of hobbyists everywhere he wanted to enjoy the spoils without engaging too seriously in the discipline. Gary wasn't much of a player but he wasn't frightened to take on the most challenging works in the guitar repertoire.

"Coming on. Coming on. A couple more weeks and it'll be ready but I thought I'd get a bit of practice in here tonight. How about you? Playing?"

"Dunno," said Elliot. "Me fingers are frozen tolies in this place. It's so cold."

"I've been toying with the idea of cross string trills," said Gary in effort to engage Elliot.

"Cross string? That'll do I suppose. Why?"

"I think they're more in keeping with the period, don't you? I might even play it in the French style."

"What the fuck's that?" asked Elliot, apparently unaware that his constant swearing might be out of step with tonight's activities.

"I thought you guys knew everything? You can't be serious? Surely you study differing historical styles?" His surprise was genuine enough. He'd often wondered how he'd fare at music college. The thought of having nothing to do all day but play guitar was the most inviting idea in the world to Gary. Surely he'd apply himself to some serious technique studies given such an open expanse in which to develop his skills.

"This is what you get," Elliot said to Alex. "The French style. The guy can hardy play a G major without ramming his tongue halfway up his left nostril and he's lecturing me about stylistic niceties."

Elliot was always more than happy to talk about someone right in front of their faces. Alex got embarrassed for both of them.

"He's having a hard time at the Academy," said Alex.

"Don't apologize for me," snapped Elliot. "Did you actually hear me last week? Correct me if I'm wrong but didn't I play as beautifully as anyone ever played?"

Gary cleared his throat and made a face like either he was amused or constipated. He'd heard Elliot last week all right. When he entered the room this evening his heart almost missed a beat when he saw Elliot sipping his tea. He was filled with admiration wrapped in envy. Elliot had played better than anyone he'd ever heard, but surely it wasn't possible that a guitarist with that kind of ability could be attending their meetings? Elliot was good, but he couldn't be that good? And surely Elliot couldn't be talking about him anyway? He must have been halfway into another conversation when Gary spoke to him. Nobody could be that rude, and anyway, he didn't stick out his tongue when he played. He was sure he didn't stick out his tongue when he played.

"If we might take our seats," came a voice from the tea table.

When everyone was seated in the requisite semi-circle, as if for an intimate bible reading, Frank Simpson stood up and read from a piece of paper ripped from a little notebook. He spoke so quietly and, with Elliot talking in Alex's ear, it was impossible to decipher his messages. After reading what must have been the minutes of last month's proceedings, his voice changed. He shouted as if calling customers to a market stall.

"We have one solo and two duets down for tonight. Any more takers this evening?"

"I'll play if Ginger'll play," said Elliot.

"What would you like to play? Who's Ginger?"

"I'll play whatever Ginger plays. If he doesn't have the music, that's fine. I can pick it up."

"I'll be playing the gavotte," said Ginger. Gary was used to being called Ginger. He'd been called Ginger since he was three years old, along with about a sixth of the population of Scotland. The name was so familiar to him he never took offence. But it was clear that Elliot was throwing down a challenge. He'd worked hard on the gavotte. Three hours a day for four months; it was in pretty good shape and he wasn't afraid to admit it. Maybe Elliot would get a shock when he heard it? "The Bach Gavotte." He might have been a gunslinger in a third-rate cowboy movie challenging the stranger in town. There were even a couple of audible gasps. Alex wondered what the hell was going on. "Can you believe this?" said Elliot.

"Not really." Alex wanted to shoot himself for agreeing to come along in the first place. Elliot had managed to turn the evening into a story about himself. He really should have been helping out a little. Perhaps offering some free lessons or tips instead of challenging people who just wanted to enjoy playing some music. "Elliot, for someone who doesn't believe in guitar competitions…"

"This isn't a competition. You've never felt like this. They can't even hear it. What can I do when people who love the instrument enough to come to this God-forsaken dive, they can't hear it? What hope is there?"

Elliot was smiling. Perhaps if he adopted a few more facial expressions Alex might have been able to work out when he was serious, but certainly he had a glint in his eye that wasn't at all playful. He was digging his nails into the palms of his hands. Elliot was an enigma, but until recently he'd been a happy enigma. Lately his behaviour had gone beyond even the wild limits he'd drawn for himself over the last couple of years. It was plain that guitar society evenings had been gentle affairs, rather befitting the surroundings of a church hall but Elliot had managed to find the place and turn the whole thing into something about him. These people weren't out to get Elliot. Perhaps they might have applauded him with more gusto or greeted him with more enthusiasm but their lack of interest was probably more out of fear than ill manners. Elliot wasn't just a third-year guitarist from the local music college, he was a master of the instrument. These guys—they were all guys—had never been in such close proximity to such a volatile talent. Maybe in the future—had they never met him—they might have paid to see him play and discussed his interpretations with each other over tea and a digestive biscuit? They stared at Elliot with the big doe eyes of feeble creatures about to be torn apart. In their real lives they were doctors and postmen and civil servants and beekeepers, but their presence in this room as guitarists for an evening made them Elliot's prey.

First up was a diminutive middle-aged man and a boy of around twelve. They played a duet Alex had never heard before. The boy was a good player. He had the precise timing of a young talent, although his adherence to the beat was more out of necessity than fancy. The man with him—his uncle, claimed Elliot—was no player at all. He fumbled and tripped along in front then behind the beat, then he lost the beat completely. All the while he made ridiculous faces at the boy as if he was trying to convince the audience that the boy, and not he, was at fault.

"See what I mean," whispered Elliot, "they're all fucking nutzoid. The kid's all right, but Julian's a bucket o' shite."

Alex grabbed his nose to stop himself laughing. He took a few deep breaths and counted until the urge to explode waned. He'd be damned if he'd let Elliot drag him into his little farce. If Elliot made him laugh, then he'd be the bad guy in all this. Elliot always had a huge grin stuck on his puss; he could get away with a public crack-up with hardly any real change in his demeanour.

"Ye can't resist it man," whispered Elliot. "Listen, the bit coming up is hard. Watch the dirty look he gives the kid."

Sure enough, as the young boy soldiered on heroically, his uncle ground to a halt with a huge sigh.

"Watch the kid," said Elliot. "He doesn't give a fuck. He's having a good time. That's me when I was his age—if I played guitar and had a bastard uncle who blamed me for him being crap."

The man grabbed the boy's arm and pulled it. "That's enough," he said. The boy stood up and took a deep bow.

"Good for him," said Elliot offering hearty applause.

The boy went to the corner to get his guitar case, took out a cloth and carefully rubbed down the strings. Frank positioned himself on 'the stage'.

"Next up we have Mike and Lex. They're going to give us some Giuliani." Mike and Lex were good friends. They were both auditors. They were both divorced. They both worked at the same company, and in time they'd realize they were both gay and madly in love with each other. For now, they were both guitarists. Lex had suggested it shortly after Mike's divorce. They started chumming each other to the pub but neither was very interested in pubs or booze. They shared an interest in classical music and the guitar seemed like the perfect way to explore their love of music without too much expense or bother. They took lessons together. They practiced together. They played duets together. In three years neither had advanced very much, but they'd hoped that attending the guitar society meetings would spur them on to greater things. Playing in front of people frightened Lex and terrified Mike but they both felt it might focus their efforts and lead them forward in their studies.

"Man, these clowns are even worse than Uncle Segovia," Elliot was starting to laugh before they sat down. One of them opened his guitar stool with a snap and nicked his finger. Elliot broke down. He tried to ignore Elliot. Alex felt his face heating up, and his stomach gave an involuntary twitch; he was determined not to let Elliot lead him by the nose into his cruel design and closed his eyes to count slowly. Everyone was looking at them; exactly what Elliot wanted. Lex and Mike managed to make the act of setting up a guitar stool as complex as building some flat-pack furniture. They were petrified. When they'd negotiated the stools, the tuning followed. It was cold in the room and damp, the humidity may have been partly to blame but they just couldn't get the things tuned.

"They've both gone out and bought a pack of Augustines yesterday and didn't string the fuckers until an hour ago. Morons. We'll be here all bleedn night. Baaaaaaaaaaaaaaaaa!"

"Look…" It was time for Frank to act.

"A," said Elliot. "That's an open A on the fifth. You want an E? I want some tea." He went to pour himself a cup. "Cuppa anyone?"

There were no takers. The unfortunate pair struggled on for a few minutes until Lex inexplicably started to play the tune; leaving his partner completely stunned. Mike looked at the audience to check he hadn't gone mad. No, it was true; Lex had started the duet without him. He scanned the page furiously, trying to catch up. When he jumped in it wasn't entirely clear that he'd got the right bar, although their guitars were so out of tune with themselves and each other that it was hard to tell. Alex wondered whether it was always like this or was Elliot the reason that the whole evening was falling to pieces? Surely these people didn't enjoy this? Elliot stood in the corner swigging back tea, admiring his creation. Lex got up, almost tripping over his stool, and hurried to put his guitar away. Mike made the kind of gesture normally seen in Italian town squares—huge and redundant. Lex banged around in the corner of the room trying to put his guitar away. When Mike was convinced that the duet had had it for the evening he followed Lex into the corner. In a second they were both laughing. At least Elliot hadn't managed to get under their skin. They took their seats to watch the rest of the evening's entertainment.

Now Gary got up to take his punishment. Elliot was a little fairy tale sprite in the corner, sipping cold tea in lieu of a magic potion. Alex could hardly bear to find out what was in store for the poor guy who'd actually tried to be friendly to Elliot. But he was going to play Bach's Gavotte; the very tune that Laura had played during the most sensational sexual experience of his life. He readied himself to enjoy the music and the associations. He crossed his legs and planted his hands across his lap just in case his enjoyment became visible.

By the end of the fourth bar, or rather the fourth-and-a-half bar—Gary's attempt at what he called a cross-string trill consisted of thumping the notes without regard to their tempo or length—Alex uncrossed his legs; what he was hearing bore no relation whatever to the beauty that sprung from Laura's violin that night; there was no possibility of any baroque snake charming this evening. Elliot smiled broadly and shook his head. Gary soldiered on and on and on. What should have been a delightful diversion became an interminable grind. Even his fellow society members stole themselves as each repeated 'cross-string trill' approached. When he'd finished he stood and gave a great bow; all but Elliot applauded his efforts. Alex wanted to go home. This was a nightmare. He had no idea that such places existed, where enthusiasts would gather to strangle and pummel some of the repertoire's finest works. It made him feel depressed until the idea surfaced that he himself might have been one of these people—obsessed with music but locked into another, more sensible life where time for music had to be stolen; where the proof stood bare that desire does not bring with it the ability to achieve the object of that desire. It didn't seem to make sense that they sounded so bad. Apart from the kid, everyone else had played something that bore such scant resemblance to the music they were trying to play as to make it seem as if it were deliberate. Surely Elliot wouldn't attack these people with all of his musical weapons? What was the point?

But Elliot was on a mission. Gary had hardly vacated the spot that represented the stage when Elliot sat down to play. He made a few tuning adjustments then played the gavotte. By the end of the second measure Alex felt a twitch in his crotch. He tried to ignore it but it started to hurt; the pressure in his jeans grew. Had Laura managed to drag him into a strange world where his sexuality was bound up within music?

Bach gave him the horn?

He crossed his legs. He'd never felt so stupid. When he'd crossed his legs before Gary's performance, it was more a little joke to himself, a reminder of Laura and the greatest evening of his life. Now he was becoming a looney like the rest of them. But maybe this tangible connection between his emotions, his biological functions, and music meant that he might become a proper musician after all? Maybe there was a bright side to his involuntary stiffy?

Elliot became quickly lost in the music, he tossed his head a little to each side when he played the trills, to make sure Gary and the rest of the audience would get it. With his eyes closed and sinking deeper into his musical trance he failed to notice that the audience were deserting him. Apart from the kid— whose eyes were on stalks, his uncle had to physically drag him out—the audience disappeared one by one until Elliot played for Alex alone.

Alex greeted Elliot's emergence from his trance with what he thought he deserved. "Serves you right you arrogant little shit."

"They all left?" Elliot seemed genuinely stunned. "Why?"

"Are you serious? They were just a bunch of people doing nobody any harm and you have to show them up. Elliot the mirror. Elliot the sage. Elliot the maestro. They should have kicked your teeth in while they were at it. Let's go. My arse needs a blood transfusion, it's going to be all pins and needles on the bus, even the left side of my dick has gone numb."

"How did I play?" asked Elliot.

"Christ. Garbage Elliot. Load of shite. Worst thing I ever heard."

"Brilliant wasn't it? I hardly even know that piece, but I completely slaughtered it. If Bach were here he'd be begging for my autograph."

"Bach's not here. Neither is anyone else. Nice job man. You managed to empty a refrigerator full of guitarists."

Alex noticed that the cloth Elliot used to rub down his strings was speckled red, but he was too tired to get into anything deep tonight. And maybe he didn't care much anyway? Elliot was doing some good work on his music. It wasn't what Alex ever planned; he always thought that he was the sole interpreter of his music, but it was plain that Elliot could lead him to a higher place. Perhaps if he went with Elliot, or at least tried to hold onto him, something would stick? Maybe working with Elliot would make him a better musician? All he had to do was suffer Elliot's progressive madness. He had always seemed crazy, but crazy in the way that anyone can be crazy. His frightening intelligence and pasted smile made being with him almost exciting, like a journey, but he was starting to give Alex the willies just as Alex was beginning to believe that his music needed him.

Alex got to the end of his street. It was cold. He was mulling over the evening's entertainment. He felt guilty for not trying to help Elliot. He felt angry that Elliot had burst into his music and revealed so many flaws. He felt jealous because he knew inside that he'd never be able to see music the way Elliot saw music. When Elliot played a phrase or explained to Alex how to play a phrase, it was right, it was so obvious, so easy. He made it seem so easy. But on to the next phrase and the same thing would happen. It was like cooking the greatest meal you ever cooked and having the greatest chef who ever lived taste it and say "Ah, yes, nice, almost… just a little more salt?" It was infuriating. As he turned into his main door a man shot out of the passage and knocked him over. Alex landed on his backside, which was thankfully still a little numb. "Skuggs?" The figure loped around the corner before Alex could confirm his identity, but Skuggs's gait was quite unique.

That was Skuggs.

His spirits lifted when he opened his front door. The flat was warm, the lights were on. Laura was in the living room watching television—something he'd never seen her do. She wasn't practicing.

She was in a good mood. She made coffee. She gave him cuddles. He was in her good books again and it had happened without any silly pleading on his part. He was quite prepared to plead and beg if he'd had an idea it would work, but here she was giving him butterfly kisses and measuring the exact amount of sugar in his coffee. No need to plead. His animal magnetism had done the trick.

"I send your tape to a record company," she switched off the pan before the milk bubbled over, and poured some into Alex's cup. He sipped some coffee. It was perfect.

"No, I don't have anything even near ready for that. Is that what you think I should do? Maybe I should? The stuff I'm working on with Elliot is starting to sound really good though. Maybe in a few weeks." He spread himself on the sofa to enjoy his luscious girlfriend and her luscious coffee. He patted the sofa to indicate she sit by him.

"No," she sat. She laid both hands on his lap. "I send your tape to a record company."

"But why should you send it? What difference would that make?"

She couldn't get through the warmth that had enveloped him. "Alex, I send your tape this evening. It is gone. In the mail. Bye, bye."

He started to choke. She beat his back until his face retreated from purple to crimson. He took deep breaths and planted the coffee cup on the floor in case her asphyxiating brew got him again. He said, "Now, I'm going to stay calm because I know I've misinterpreted what you just said." He took some more breaths. "Now, I thought you said you'd sent my tape off to a record company, but I couldn't have heard that, could I? Because it wasn't your tape to send, and you wouldn't know who to send it to anyway."

"Oh yes Alex. Skuggs, he help me. I tell him what I want to do and he show me all your notes."

He buried his face in his hands and rubbed his eyes until spots changed to colours and the colours became pain.

"Laura. Why? Why?"

"You need," she bit her lip to get the words right. "Kick up arse!" She was pleased to remember all of Skuggs's coaching. "If nobody kick up your arse, you spend your whole life fiddling and fiddling and changing. You never stop. You never say anything is finished."

"So you finished it for me?"

"I finish it for you. Yes."

"I'm gonna smash Skuggs's skull into pieces for this. I knew that was him. He was running away like a dog. Where's his tuba? Did he leave it here?" He rushed around the little flat looking for revenge on Skuggs's prized possession.

"Skuggs, he say you will react badly. He say 'the man will not take this well'."

"No, the man hasn't taken it well. How could you do this Laura? What for?"

"I do it for you."

"You want to humiliate me."

"Your music is lovely. Try to publish. Por que no?"

"Laura, it's not finished. I haven't finished it."

"Skuggs," she said. A vision of Skuggs running off filled him with violent thoughts. He'd drop the tuba from a great height. He'd throw it in front of a bus. "He say you never finish, never. He say your music, it is beautiful. He say maybe the world is ready for computer music. Why not try? He say it is my gift to you."

"So, you do anything Skuggs says?"

"No. I think so too. Skuggs is a good friend. I love you. We want to help."

"I thought Skuggs scared you?"

"He scare me but maybe not too much now. I like him."

"Who did you send it to?"

She handed him a piece of paper. "I write it down. We find so many names on your computer. This one have so many stars beside it. I choose the stars."

He read the name and grabbed the coffee that was now stone cold and threw it back like it was a double Glenfiddich "Quentin Walker". He dug his knuckles into his eyes, not sure what he was feeling. "You picked Quentin Walker. Quentin Walker."

"This is the name on the paper?" she said with enough attitude to remind him that while her English wasn't so great, she had no difficulty grasping sarcasm.

"I suppose it doesn't matter who you sent it to cause they'd all get a laugh at it anyway, but the guy you sent it to is kind of the opposite to what one might want in a producer if one were to ask him to publish computer music."

"What is this 'one'? You are Prince Charles now?"

Her humour and insight shocked the self-pity out of him. "This Walker geezer is Mister Traditional. No, he's Mister whatever existed before there was anything old enough to be called traditional. He uses seventeenth-century recording techniques. He probably thinks a computer is some guy that can add numbers quickly. And…" Alex took the opportunity to stroke her breast with the back of his hand. She smiled. "He only ever worked with the greatest of the great, the real biggies, the giants. I can hardly believe I even wrote his details down. I suppose I thought he'd be the toughest nut of all. Make McNabb look like a pussy. Never mind. You're right. What the hell. He'll bin the tape anyway. I can work on my stuff with Elliot. But you're right. I should send it off. Who knows? Radio is radio. Maybe somebody will play it? Maybe somebody will like it?"

"Your music is beautiful."

"As are you my lovely." Then it just popped out of his head, without a moment's thought. "Do you want to help us with the music?"

Before he had a second to reflect, she flung her arms around him. "Yes my Alex. I have no bow. I will help every minute of the day. I am yours."

"Yes, I know you'll have sex with me but will you help me with my music?"

There was some banging around outside the front door. It was Skuggs; he could never quite negotiate the complexities of a front-door lock. Alex moved away slightly from Laura, he didn't want to plant any images in Skuggs's head that might have repercussions in the bathroom.

The door opened slowly, Skuggs's large head appeared. When he was sure there were no hidden traps in wait, he slunk into the room and closed the door carefully.

"Where's you tuba?" asked Alex.

For a brief moment Skuggs went pale. "In a safe place," he said with an air of mistrust. He knew that Alex could never have got to his tuba, but the possibility nevertheless sent a cold shiver through him. He examined Alex's demeanour and made sure he stood in a place that would give him a clear run out of the door in case of attack. Alex leapt up. Startled, Skuggs fell backwards. Alex put his hands in his pockets and tried not to laugh.

"I hear you've been helping my career? What a good friend you are to me."

Skuggs had the look of a cat not quite sure whether to run or fight. "It's okay then?" He edged towards the door. Alex walked around him to block his escape route and leant against the door.

"Alex, stop teasing him," said Laura.

"Look man," said Skuggs. "You've done some great stuff, but you're so fucked up and full o' shit that you'll never do anything with it."

"Thanks for that Skuggs."

"You spend half the day doing your music and the other half moaning about McNabb as if what he thought matters. It doesn't matter. If you think what you're doing deserves the same place as real music…" Alex raised his eyebrows. "You know what I mean. If you think it's real then get it out there. Test it. If you don't then someone else will come along and do it before you."

"Skuggs, I'll tell you what I want you to do. And if you don't do it I swear I'll find your tuba, no matter what it takes I'll find it, and when I do I'll introduce it to my baseball bat."

"You haven't got a baseball bat," said Skuggs, sure he'd happened upon a flaw in the plan.

"And after I've bludgeoned it and pummelled it into submission I'll find some road works and I'll give the guy a tenner to flatten it with a steamroller… if you don't do what I want you to do."

"What do you want me to do?" Skuggs was sweating; he knew he couldn't keep his tuba under wraps forever, constantly moving it, finding new places. In time he'd run out of hiding places. Whatever it was that Alex wanted, he'd have to do it to protect his tuba. He didn't want his tuba to be a fugitive forever.

"I want you to help me with my music," said Alex. "Elliot is doing wonderful things but I've asked Laura to help as well. I've come to the conclusion that I need help. I always thought that it was just my fingers that got in the way of me being a great musician, but I know that's not true. I can realize any performance that I can define, but I don't have it in me to define a truly great performance."

Skuggs's relief was almost tangible. His shoulders lowered, his head dropped forward slightly, his jaw slackened.

"But I can't have Elliot dictating every note. He's half crazy," he caught himself in the pointlessness of the statement. "I mean really. Much crazier than you. If I leave it to him, the performances I create will be too good. They just won't sound authentic."

"So you want Laura and me in there as well to fuck it up, to make it shite?" Laura leant forward at Skuggs's observation. She didn't much like the idea that her inclusion in Alex's project was purely to diminish it. Alex didn't see it that way, but he could live without another skirmish with Laura.

"I need you to make it human. I need you to make it real. Elliot lives somewhere else. Give him free rein to control a perfect technique and he won't be able to stop himself chasing perfection. In the end it'll all sound false. I know what's in you two. Laura, you've got more music in you than I could ever hope to feel. Skuggs, you bring a directness to your music, a matter-of-factness, a kind of salt of the earth…"

"Christ, I get it Alex. I'm scum."

"Exactly."

"It was a joke," said Skuggs, knowing full well that it wasn't a joke. His training in brass bands gave him workaday skills that orchestral players would kill for. But the nature of his instrument insured that no matter the heady levels his interpretations might reach, they'd never be truly accepted in the way they would if he played one of the more elevated instruments.

"Haven't you ever wondered how you'd sound if you were a pianist?" asked Alex.

"Nah."

"Well you'll get to find out soon enough. Look, Elliot is great but he won't listen to me on music but he respects you, he sees you as an equal. If I work with him alone then I end up being nothing but a programmer. I need you to handle Elliot. I need you to calm him down, to introduce a wee bit self doubt."

"Yer asking the impossible. The wee man never thinks he's wrong." Skuggs took his parka off, revealing a T-shirt that was soaked through. Laura made a face. Skuggs lifted his arm and smelled his armpit. "Whoa! Honkin map of India."

"And maybe we can take it easy with the farting and the honkin armpits?" added Alex.

"Coffee?" asked Laura.

"That would be lovely Laura. I shall retire to the bathroom and wash my stinky pits lest Lord Stone be offended. I shall take my leave m'lady." Skuggs gave a bow that was supposed look gallant. He leant over waving his arm around as if holding a hat. A huge roar shot from his behind. "Sorry."

Laura ran into the kitchen.

"Gotta start working on those farts," he said.

"I'm serious man," said Alex as soon as Laura was out of earshot. "I don't need you salivating over her. I don't need you farting all over the place and getting pissed every day."

"I can't get pissed? Forget it."

"Okay, you can get pissed but you have to control yourself. Seriously, Elliot's starting to lose it."

"He never had it in the first place. He's got too much talent and no life."

"This could be fun."

"No chance. Laura and me'll be sitting around all day waiting for you to get a fucking hemi-demi-semi-wemi-quaver just right while Elliot's screaming it's all crap and his granny could do better. You're asking a lot."

"Where do you live Skuggs?"

Skuggs stuffed his hands deep into his pockets and kicked the carpet.

"I'm gonna build a new library this week. Hopefully Mc-Nabb will be out of action for a while. I can use any piano I want. I was thinking of trying to get Ingles in on the act as well. I can scurry around the place to record the stuff but we really need some freedom when we're putting it all together. Ingles might be the key."

"Ingles?"

"Jeeziz Skuggs, have you arrived on this planet yet? The electronic music teacher?"

Skuggs rubbed his chin.

"The dyke?"

"Oh, aye. Okay. How many people are gonna be working on this?"

"That's it. Four of us. Ingles can let us use the lab. That's what we need." Laura brought Skuggs a large milky coffee. His eyes lit up. "Six sugars? So what are you gonna do when it's finished? What's the point?"

"I'm going to send it off to record companies. Who knows? Maybe you two are right? Maybe it's the right time?"

"What about the tape we sent already? What if the geezer likes it?"

"There's no chance of that."

# SEVENTEEN

Quentin examined the faces around the table, around *his* table. They were tanned and healthy, outdoor types who worked hard and played in boats when they weren't working. They had the lean, muscular tones of the modern executive. Who the hell were these people? One minute they were speaking Japanese, the next they were barking variations on great round American vowels, pumping the decibel level to add weight to an argument.

"Mah gayip analysis suggests an ROI greater than the sixteen percent margins, if we tah-in royalties and projected new business," said the straightforward Texan.

"We gotta lose the fixed costs base here. We gotta re-architect the whole structure," the New York lawyer chimed.

Then the Japanese delegate would quietly put forth his plans, bringing the signal-to-noise ratio back to bearable levels before they were off again.

Each of them had a mantra, a design, an idea for Quentin's business. An idea for *his* business.

On it went, a six-a-side verbal tennis match with Quentin both the ball and the audience, his head batted from side to side, then a little respite from the Japanese umpire then in again for a few lobs and a smash. He had absolutely no idea what they were talking about. He had absolutely no idea what he was doing there. He had no idea what they were doing there, drinking his Perrier, eating his sandwiches, making him feel like a schoolboy who hadn't studied.

"Quentin, whadaya say?" came the Texan to once more humiliate him.

This had gone on for three days. His boardroom invaded by the NARC, the Nippon-American Recording Company, the saviours, the angels, the devourers of art. The NARC was a young company, 'young and dynamic' they said. They'd taken all they knew from the pop music industry and were 'applying' it to 'serious' music. They were having a ball. It was so easy, taking struggling old codger companies and turning them into 'dynamic, young' achievers; just like the people sitting around Quentin's table. Now it was Quentin's turn. Now his beloved company was to be sliced and diced and turned into something 'viable'.

"The music…" said Quentin.

"Yup, you're right. We got a library full of product. We gotta juice it. You are so right," interrupted the Texan.

Juice it? thought Quentin. "Juice it?"

"Yeah, maximize returns on the intellectual property."

Quentin pictured stuffing the Texan's head into a giant juicer. His blood pressure relaxed a notch.

"You got some great stuff," continued the Texan, determined to make Quentin understand. "It's pretty old, but have you heard the crap they use on local TV commercials?"

Quentin didn't know what 'local TV' was, but he knew the Texan had a plan to clean up the market.

"We'll clean up. Re-master those recordings, package them in fifteen- and thirty-second clips, we'll sell thousands of licenses. We got at least a thousand libraries here. I believe you Brits call it a nice little earner?"

The thought of having his beautiful recordings re-mastered and packaged made Quentin feel sick. He had pioneered direct-to-disk recording as a superior alternative to tape. Tape recording offered control where direct-to-disk provided immediacy. Only the very best players could work direct-to-disk, there was no going back, no editing; one pass was all you got. Quentin had made some of the greatest recordings of the greatest works played by the greatest players in the world. The clowns around the table thought he was old-fashioned, quaint, an eccentric old English gentleman who produced quirky recordings using antiquated techniques. They didn't get it. For all their gadgets and their impenetrable language they didn't understand music. But time had caught up with Quentin. There was no longer a supply of concert artists willing to undergo the trials of Quentin's recording process. The process was simple; set up the microphones, press the record button, and play until you get to the end. If you're unhappy, then do it again, the whole thing. Repeat the process until all are satisfied. There was a time when Quentin had to persuade performers to step into his 'torture chamber' but that time quickly turned into his 'golden' period, when artists tested themselves on Quentin's label. He became the acid test for concert performers. They never exactly queued up, but he always had a good supply of willing participants. He wasn't after perfection; the imperfections, the errors and fluffs, the fleeting purple patches, the unique moods of a particular person on a particular day at a particular time created the magic. Quentin believed tape was sterile, like a photograph, pristine and accurate, but lacking integrity; he captured music the way a painter might capture a character or scene. How would they react, he wondered, if he tried to persuade them of his ideas and aspirations? Why had they become valid and he obsolete? Why did everything have to change? Why were they right about everything?

Quentin shuffled over to the drinks cabinet and poured himself a brandy. He cursed himself for trusting his friends. "Just one more," he said to himself. "One more and I'd be happy." He flung the brandy back. "I'm off," he said. "Had enough." He poured another drink and took it with him to his office. He tried not to look at the photographs adorning the walls of his offices; old black and white prints, many autographed with chummy messages to a hard taskmaster. Only the odd silver or gold record, testament to former glories, broke the monochrome monotony. He sipped his drink slowly, listening to voices and music long gone. "Chopped into little pieces," he said. "Forgive me."

He could live with losing his beloved company. He could see the wisdom in introducing new blood. He was willing to take responsibility for the failure, the faltering revenues of the last couple of years. Livelihoods were at stake; the people who worked for him deserved better. His business wasn't just a vehicle to generate profits; it was a labour of love, an experiment, a chance to do what he loved every day, but he had to save his staff, save their jobs. Contacting the NARC was Quentin's own idea, his own fault. He owned a third of his company. There were no majority partners. He'd borrowed from friends then, when success came, he offered stakes in his company as thanks to the friends who supported him; the same friends who sold out to the NARC. When the NARC came to explain their plans Quentin all but threw them out, but they made offers to his partners, who all sold out in a flash. Years of friendship snuffed out with a few bank drafts. Now all those beautiful sounds, all that painstaking, backbreaking work was to be dismembered, surgically re-fashioned in the image of Huxley's

*Brave New World*. What have I done? He asked himself for the hundredth time.

He stared at his desk, as if for the first time. The paper and letters and memos that had littered it, and elicited friendly quips and cracks on his lack of organization, were replaced by a single bottle of brandy and a beautifully-carved championship-sized chess set; a gift from his wife—she had to fill his day with something.

The chessboard beeped. He checked the LCD: *your move* flashed. The idea of a chess computer had filled him with horror, but his wife had the guts of the computer built right into a beautiful classic Staunton set. It was so lovely; he forgot it was a machine—until its infernal beeping mocked him. Nevertheless, the thing had drawn him into many a futile battle—as his wife knew full well it would. Quentin had never beaten his computer, but that didn't stop him trying. When he tired of the beatings, he would set up a grandmaster position to see if it could figure out famous middle or endgame strategies. The way it seemed so human one minute and so mechanical the next amazed him. It would sacrifice pieces without any obvious tactical advantage only to declare its long-term objective when it had him in a crushing positional bind, but then it would play the most ludicrous endgame strategies—providing hope that if he could reach the endgame unscathed he'd have a chance. Today's game held that hope. He'd started the game more than a week before and configured it so that the machine couldn't think while it was Quentin's move. He'd taken days for some moves, even doing a little research, safe in the knowledge that its mechanical brain was asleep and unable to run its dastardly plans against his possible strategies. He couldn't find any way though, to switch off the beeps that came every few hours to remind him to get on with it.

He rested his chin on the table in front of the board; a habit from childhood. The pieces were giant combatants facing off against each other. Quentin was white. Quentin was always white when he played it—the virtually insignificant advantage of a single tempo at least made him feel like he was in charge until it would either throttle his position or offer up a knight or a bishop before cutting his defences to ribbons.

Instead of researching openings or the impenetrable middlegame thickets created by masters, this time he'd decided on a philosophical approach; he'd introduced complications purely for the sake of it. He had little idea what he was doing beyond a weak conviction that his position was solid enough to withstand a tactical assault. If the machine were to finish him before the endgame it would have to open a crack in its own defences. But today he couldn't think. The NARC had invaded his offices again. They could have held these meetings anywhere but insisted on using his offices. They said they wanted to keep him 'in the loop', but Quentin knew it was really just to wear him down, to get him out, make him retire.

He stared through his own armies at the black invaders who were poised to pounce. He'd switched off their brain for now but as soon as he made a move they'd be at it again, a hundred, a million times faster than him. In five to ten seconds they'd make a move, his heart would pound, he'd sweat, he'd try to gather himself, to analyse, to relax. He'd count the pieces; that's always where to start. Start *before* the beginning, each half-move a new game, a new match, a new set of possibilities. Count the pieces. Count the pieces. Slowly. Slowly.

Yes, everything is even, no advantage in numbers. Count them again and again, it can't think unless I let it. Then analyse. Analyse. Pawns first. Where are they? Don't get drawn into tactics. Just look at where they are on the board. White pawns first. My pawns. Where are they? What squares do they hold? Do

they support each other? Are they in touch with the middle of
the board, the high ground? Or are they spread out and unconnected, creeping stealthily along the walls, or stranded yokels on
the battlements? Look at the squares they attack. Just bear it in
mind. No analysis yet. Just bear it in mind. Where are Black's
pawns? Don't think about Black's plans, just look where his
pawns are. Are they defending or attacking, or both? Always
both, always both. Make each as powerful as you can before a
strike. Do Black's pawns defend each other, do they threaten my
position directly, do they defend his pieces, do his pieces defend
the pawns? Is there too much pressure in any spot? Time and
space, time and space. Draw the lines. Draw the lines from the
pieces across the board. Is his queen defending lesser pieces, is it
vulnerable? No, hold back, too much analysis. Not time to
think, time to look, time to feel the position. Look at the
pieces. Where are the bishops? Are they exposed or tucked
away? How many squares does each control? Count them,
count the squares. Are my bishops well-placed? Are they working for the position? Is there any tempo advantage in the bishops and the pawns? Just bear it in mind. Bear it in mind.
Knights? Where are they? Knights are so elusive, their value
changes constantly. Mustn't let them become a liability. Charge
them up, position them well, then strike. Leave it too late and
they're useless. Best to cash in a knight if you can. Blast through
a defence or gain a single tempo or establish a positional advantage. Tal? Yes, Tal, that's what he'd do. But how did he know?
How could he see so far ahead? It's impossible, how did he do
it? Always looking, always searching for the clear ground. Give
him a knight, he'll think he's won; he'll nurse his advantage
until he finds there's none, that he must surrender a knight or a
bishop in turn. Are bishop's best here, or do knights have the
edge? Where are the rooks, at home or is one castled already, if
not, to castle on kingside or queenside? No, never queenside,

forget it, too hard, too aggressive, too exposed, play to your strengths. Defend first.

Where are my pawns?

"Quentin! Quentin, the people from the NARC are here."

He grabbed the wad of fat where his left pectoral used to be. Quentin could always hear his heart beating but he wasn't aware he could hear his heart beating because his brain had long since analysed the sound, without his knowledge, and compensated accordingly. Quentin's brain reckoned that the whoosh-split, whoosh-split of the blood rushing through his veins and arteries with such pressure might distract Quentin from his destiny. Quentin would know that he could hear his heart if he had ever ventured into a doctor's office and offered his ruddy complexion and purple nose as evidence that while he was an alcoholic, the vibrant purplicity beaming from the middle of his face had a stealthier friend, and a heart transplant would expose his brain's efforts to conceal the noisy artefacts of the enlarged and overworked pump that now felt like it was trying to escape its suet-encrusted prison.

Perhaps as a consequence of Quentin's brain's ambition to create and match, in the negative, any sounds that didn't please it, Quentin could hear anything and everything; but not the way a bat might, or an elephant should. It wasn't the frequency or the amplitude that Quentin heard; it was the music. Quentin processed every sound he heard as music. Again, he wasn't entirely aware of this as he'd never had the chance to process sound with anyone else's brain. But over the years, and many lengthy and boring conversations with other members of his species, he'd become aware that he was different. Maybe not different in the way that a circus freak or genius was different, but Quentin's skill, when applied intelligently—and both he and his brain were in close agreement on this point; he was intelligent—had made it easy for him to build a business that was both profitable and personally rewarding. When it came to music, while he couldn't hold a note or play a tune, he could make what a scientist might believe, or even prove, to be subjective; a judgement call, if you will, into a rock solid demonstration of pure, detached objectivity. When it came to sound, Quentin *knew* art. His wife knew this about him and his investors had known this about him.

Quentin was a record producer. Over the years he'd made great recordings, truly great recordings; masterpieces some said. His techniques were simple and, now, obsolete. He'd resisted every new development, every advance in recording techniques; every engineering aid was a gimmick to Quentin. He wanted the listener to experience the music with nothing between the musician and the listener to colour the sound. He recorded only solo performances, and he recorded them with ancient equipment. He had no mixing desk, no facilities to apply equalization or effects. He had nothing to reduce the background noise, no way to eliminate extraneous sounds such as breathing and pedal noise. He'd survived the onslaught of tape. Tape introduced a superfluous layer between performer and audience. Engineers could cut and splice; they could edit an inferior performance, or destroy a great one. Quentin could hear the difference between a tape master and a direct-to-disk master. It was so obvious to him. Direct-to-disk captured everything while tape invited sloppiness. But his company had survived tape, with all of its advantages; he'd managed to keep convincing performers to brave the torture cell that was his studio.

Then came digital. Digital was worse. Digital recordings were broken glass to Quentin. It literally pained him to listen to digital recordings. Physicists proclaimed the limits at which humans could no longer hear the artefacts produced in digital recordings but Quentin was aghast at how awful they sounded. Digital recording brought a new cleanliness to sound engineer-

ing; every offending noise could be edited out, but the warmth
was gone, the life, the vitality of a live performance no longer
had any currency. Digital recording spawned a new generation
of soloists, note-perfect robots who seemed to ape the sound of
the digital recording rather than explore the musical possibilities
of the repertoire. Attrition, death, retirement atrophied his list
of artists. He looked for new, young talent but found none with
the magic he sought. The paradox was that the new young performers had techniques that could take them straight through a
direct recording session with ease, but direct recording somehow put them off. They were used to sitting smugly in a control
booth listening to their triumphs twiddled and tweaked into a
sterile greatness.

Quentin had contacted the NARC in hopes they might
find a place for his approach. Perhaps they could find the talent
for him? But as soon as they arrived it was plain that they had
something else in mind. He threw them out after the first meeting but they came back as owners of most of the company. His
friends had betrayed him. The NARC offered huge sums of
money to his partners; they all sold.

"Tell them to buggar off!" he shouted into the intercom.

He saw a move. Knight to queen's bishop seven! A sacrifice! If he takes it, I own his kingside, his queen is stranded, his
bishop, knight and rook are all locked on the queenside. I can
move my king's rook to king's bishop one and cut off support. If
he doesn't take it, I can move my queen's bishop into support,
then deploy my queen. I've got him.

His hand had hardly left the piece when he felt that familiar
sinking feeling. The LCD flashed: *Mate in five.*

The door swung open and the Texan marched into his office. "Quentin ol' buddy. You gotta come look at our plan."

Quentin picked up a newspaper and rolled it tight. The flashing
LCD was burning him like a branding iron. He couldn't believe he'd
spent weeks analysing, researching, only to take the damned thing

deep into a balanced middlegame, then to just leap into a move without the slightest thought. Quentin moved in on the Texan.

"Chess?" said the Texan.

Quentin smacked him square on the head with as much force as he could muster. The loud crack brought his secretary running into the room.

The Texan was rubbing his head and almost laughing. "This guy has lost it. You've lost it man."

"Not yet," said Quentin. He switched off the computer, reset the pieces then switched it on again. The Texan and Quentin's secretary watched as Quentin rubbed his chin, deep in thought, trying to decide his first move. He moved his king's pawn two squares.

"King's gambit," he said to the Texan. "Didn't I ask you politely to buggar off?"

"You sure he'll be okay?" said the Texan.

"I think so," said the secretary. "Best to leave him be."

The computer indicated king's pawn to king's pawn four. Quentin moved the pawn then noticed the solitary package in his 'in' tray. He played with it in his hands for a while then opened it. There was a letter and a cassette tape. He read the letter.

> Dear Mr. Walker,
>
> This is a recording of the greatest pianist of our generation.
>
> I think you should to listen to it.
>
> Yours truly,
> Alex Stone.

He folded the letter around the cassette and stuck it in his pocket.

Quentin popped the cassette into his hi-fi and went to the kitchen to search for the bottle of Cognac he knew his wife had hidden.

"Who on earth is that? What on earth are you doing?" she asked.

"Where is that bloody Cognac?" He got out from under the sink and brushed down his trousers. "I know you bought a bottle at the weekend."

"I wrapped it, Grumpy. You're not having it till Saturday, so just put it out of your head. Who is that pianist?"

"Eh?" He looked around her as if expecting to see the pianist standing behind her. "Tape? Someone sent it."

"Have you listened to it?"

"No." His brow furrowed. The sound of Chopin's Tristesse Etude #3 drew him. He sat beside the speakers and cocked his head. The Etude finished. Chopin's third prelude in G major poured from the speakers. He gave his wife a pained look.

"That is absolutely magnificent," she said. "Is it a new signing? Who is it? You must record this pianist."

For a full ten minutes after the music had finished Quentin wore the same pained expression. His wife knew better than to interrupt while he was working. She went to the kitchen to heat up dinner. When she came back he was still sitting there. She rewound the tape. The strict meter of Bach's eighth invention seemed to rouse him. He opened his mouth as if to speak, then hung his head down.

"What the bloody hell is going on with that?" he said.

"I think it's magnificent. Now who is it?"

"Rooms."

"Quentin?"

"Rooms. I hear lots of rooms. What the bloody hell is going on?"

"What do you mean you hear rooms?"

"I've never heard a piano like that. It sounds like a Steinway but it's too smooth. I hear rooms. Different rooms with different registers. Even on the same notes."

"Perhaps it's just the way they recorded it?" Marriane had been married to Quentin for almost forty years. He had a suspicious character. His distrust had grown over the years. It was a defence mechanism he'd nurtured to protect him from experts. He liked to find things out for himself. Every time he recorded a new artist or released a new recording his taste, his insight, his business was on the line. She'd never heard this one before. "Well, what do you mean, rooms?"

Quentin jammed his head against the speaker. He might have been Beethoven himself, pressing his ear against the piano to hear something the rest of us never could.

"Quentin!"

He jumped. "Woman, there's no need to give me a heart attack."

"If I want to enjoy a mystery I'll read a book. I have asked you five times what you're talking about. Now put me out of my misery please so that we can sit down and enjoy dinner. I made a lovely chicken casserole."

"Twice."

"Twice?"

"You asked me twice. Not five times."

"I don't care. Let's eat."

"Someone sent this," he handed her the letter. "And this tape. The playing is astonishing, but it's the strangest recording I've ever heard. It seems to be lacking some higher frequencies. That could just be the engineer of course, but he seems to have cleaned up the upper partials while he's at it. I've no idea how one would do that. Or why he'd do it. But the rooms. Can't you hear it?"

In all the years she'd known him he'd never quite grasped the idea that other people couldn't hear what he heard. He could still flatter her when he asked her advice, and she'd been no slouch at the piano herself in her youth. But no matter how many times he'd led her through the strange sonic landscapes that he alone seemed to perceive, she never could complete the journey with him.

"All right," she said, readying herself for a familiar task. "What am I listening for?"

"Let's try the Bach first. It's less opaque, you might be able to catch it there." He started the tape, then jabbed his finger at the speakers repeatedly."

"Quentin, am I supposed to hear something?"

"Every time I point, I'm pointing at a different room. Christ, they're all over the place. Can't you hear it? There… there… there… that's one… another… that sounds like three different rooms across the chord. What the bloody hell is going on?"

"All I can hear is Bach. I don't know rooms but I certainly do know Bach. This is as good a recording as I've heard since Glenn Gould."

"It is like Gould isn't it? The meter, the rubato, so subtle, such command, confidence."

"Do you think it is Gould? Someone trying to play a trick?"

"It's not Gould, it's like him but… there, do you hear, do you hear that room?"

"Oh, for goodness sake darling. No, no, no, I have no idea what you're talking about. Why don't you get in touch with this person and find out who he is? And you can ask about the rooms. Quentin? Quentin?"

She plugged a pair of headphones in and set them on his head. She sat down to eat. He was gone. Lost inside his strange world. This time apparently lost inside his strange world full of rooms. He made little grumbling noises, he was singing. He jabbed his finger into the air; pointing at the rooms he heard. Marriane finished her dinner and went to bed. She knew he'd be up all night listening to this. She wondered whether he might even have all the rooms numbered and measured by the time she came down tomorrow morning to wake him up and massage his neck for the fifty thousandth time. She smiled to herself. He was happy again, searching for his rooms. He'd suffered so much lately. She decided she wouldn't even nag him tomorrow when he complained about his sore neck.

She expected to find him asleep in the chair. She'd wake him. He'd complain about his neck. She'd tell him it was his own fault. But there he was, sitting back in his favourite chair, eyes closed, jabbing his finger into the air like he was popping imaginary balloons. She put the kettle on and made some toast. She almost couldn't bring herself to wake him out of his private world. She watched him for a few minutes more and thoughts of their youth ran through her mind. Her friends, former friends, had been so cruel. He had little money, few prospects, he was small and balding, he was strange; at least that's what they said. But he wasn't strange at all. He was kind. He was thoughtful and gentle. He was intelligent and sometimes, though never intentionally, he was funny. He was everything she could have hoped for in a husband. But there was an intensity about him she had never seen in anyone else. When he concentrated, most especially on music, he seemed to leave this world altogether. He hadn't been this excited by any new music for years. He was the kind of man who simply couldn't retire. He had to work. "Retire and you'll be dead in a year," she used to say. The last few months had changed everything. Now she was trying to make him retire. Work was killing him. Lack of

work was killing him. He hated himself all day for his useless-
ness, his idleness, then he came home at night and hated himself
for making bad decisions. He never was much of a businessman,
but his business managed to survive; a steady trickle of truly
marvellous recordings kept him afloat. The market wasn't huge,
how many people can really differentiate the truly remarkable
performances he could coax from musicians from the more
mundane recordings of the same works by the same musicians?
She kept it to herself, but sometimes she couldn't tell why he
was raving about one thing or another. Perhaps he was the only
one who could tell? Perhaps even the musicians themselves
couldn't tell the difference? His recording methods were hardly
revolutionary. He'd sit the musician down in an environment
where the musician was most at ease, perhaps a concert hall or a
church, or even their own living room; wherever it was that he
felt they would play best. Then he'd spend hours and hours,
sometimes days setting up a series of microphones, testing different combinations, over and over and over, until the musicians
were on the verge of hitting him with his microphones.

He always claimed, to Marriane—he never let his victims
know the truth—that that was part of it, that he could set up
the perfect microphone placement in any environment within a
few minutes. Like a great chef who knows how a combination
of ingredients will taste before cooking the meal; when experi-
mentation becomes a purely mental exercise, he could feel the
acoustics of any room without hearing a single sound. He could
tell instantly how the music might interact with the environment, the structure and shape of the room, the materials, the
density of the walls; it all added up to what he called the sonic
viscosity. His equipment was old, very old. He recorded straight
to acetate. Microphone placement was indeed important, vital,
but the charade was designed to get the best possible performance, to make the musician forget that he had one take to get

it right; to make the music itself an escape from Quentin's interminable quest for the perfect sound.

She gently lifted the earphones off his head. He emerged with a smile she hadn't seen in a long time. "Tea?"

He took the tea, set it down on the side table, then squeezed her hand. "I want to hear this chap."

"Good." She unplugged the earphones. Chopin filled the room. She sat down to listen and allowed herself to dream that this pianist might provide Quentin with the lifeline he needed. That he might produce the one last recording that would let him retire in peace.

# EIGHTEEN

 They didn't speak to each other at all on the way home. McNabb turned the rear-view mirror toward himself to examine the great white cap painted on his skull. Perhaps he could take to wearing a hat until the wound healed? The baby was fast asleep in its car seat; he could see its reflection in the mirror. Shama moved the mirror back, not to see the road behind her but to check on the baby. McNabb closed his eyes and thought about Betty. He thought about their first child, how happy he was. He could remember being happy, he could remember being content, but it was such a long time ago, maybe he was imagining it? Maybe happiness doesn't exist at all? Maybe it's just the mind's reworking of the past? He'd always been passionate, he was a musician after all, but Betty made it seem all right, she made it seem normal and good. Even when he raged she was there to take the edge off his anger. But she got old. She was never a great beauty. She wasn't even pretty. Shama was pretty. He squinted to check that she was pretty. Sure enough, her delicate profile, her golden skin, her thick black hair—now sensibly cropped short, to take care of the baby—her small, pert breasts hidden behind the frumpy camouflage she always wore.

Who was this woman? Why did she torture him so? Why couldn't she have let him alone? What did she want from him? He didn't have money, he believed himself to be handsome and charming—but even if he were, surely that isn't enough?

"You get the door and I'll get Baby," said Shama.

"Is this my life?"

She looked him straight in the eye as if she knew his mind; as if she'd been watching his thoughts all the way back from the hospital.

"This is your life, and we both know it's better than you deserve. Get the door while I get Baby."

McNabb got out to open the front door. He hated that she called the baby 'Baby', as if Baby was the baby's name. Betty used to call him Baby. He watched Shama disappear into the house to clean the baby's bottom or bath the baby or dress the baby or feed the baby. He wished he had someone to call him Baby.

When he was sure that Shama was busy cleaning Baby's arse or hanging it from one of the breasts to which he was forever denied access, he snuck into his study and phoned Betty. The break-up had been rather acrimonious; he did, after all, commit adultery with a girl young enough to be his daughter, but Betty's good nature and her successful second marriage meant he could, from time to time, talk to her as if he hadn't destroyed her life with hardly a thought.

"So," said Betty after McNabb had delivered what he knew of the story of his wound, "you're after sympathy?"

"I just wanted to check on the girls, and let them know I'm fine."

"Considering they didn't know anything was wrong in the first place I expect they'll be happy to know you're alive and kicking." McNabb didn't like the splash of cynicism she always poured on him when he called, but at least now she'd communicate, for the sake of the children.

"I've been thinking about you a lot lately."

"Have you?"

"We were happy weren't we?"

"McNabb," she had always called him McNabb when she wanted to distance herself. "I was happy. God knows why because you were such a pig. But you were never happy. You're just not the happy type. You need more."

"More what?"

"Exactly. More what? Whatever you have. Whatever you've got, you need more of it and you want more of anything you haven't got as well."

"I'm sorry Betty. I am so…"

"I don't want to hear this McNabb. I don't want apologies. My life is wonderful. My life is now the way I always thought it was, except now I'm not deluding myself."

"I'm happy that you're happy. Really, I am."

"Good. The girls and I are fine. I'll tell them that you woke up in hospital with a split head."

"Call me Baby?"

"Pardon?"

"Call me Baby. Please?"

McNabb held the phone until the dead tone was interrupted by a robotic voice telling him to dial again. Tears ran down his face. He pressed the phone into his ear and listened to his Betty call him Baby.

Every day Todd put on his make up, spent a little too much time choosing an outfit, then he'd head to the Academy to take his chair outside the Bursar's office. The students were kind,

mostly, and the staff largely ignored him. He added a little spice
to the place with his cross-dressed protest. He'd already become
something of a talisman. Nobody was quite willing to physically
remove him from the premises, but neither was anyone in the
mood to welcome him back into the fold—at least not until he
started wearing proper trousers. The continuing presence of facial hair was a cause for hope in some—who wanted Todd back
the way children want their divorced parents back—and for
others it was absolute proof of madness. Todd still hadn't quite
managed to get the point about his beard. Cross-dressing was
one thing but wearing a beard made him plain crazy in the eyes
of even a casual observer. He wasn't sure himself why he
couldn't make a complete break with his former gender identity. Perhaps, like ninety percent of the world's counter tenors,
who sport beards to offset the squeaky singing-voices, he felt
that facial hair somehow imparted the truth of his sexuality?
Perhaps he'd look too feminine without the beard? He didn't
want to be mistaken for a female; he just wanted to be himself,
comfortable in the attire of his choosing.

The annual choral concert was almost upon them again. Mc-
Nabb was off with a sore head and Todd was bonkers. It was left
to Ingles to conduct the remaining rehearsals. Ingles was an in-
effectual conductor. She had no interest in conducting and little
interest in the program, which included the usual bit of Bach,
some Beethoven and a couple of tunes that filled the space
where the modern could live without inflicting too much damage on the sensibilities of an audience made up of regular people and a couple of critics. Ingles was entirely obsessed with her
own music and had she not been given free rein to dabble all
day long in her laboratory she would probably have spent most
of her time fighting to get her music into the public domain.
Ingles was an artist. Her belief in her art was unshakable. She

perceived all of the world's repertoire as shoulders upon which she stood. She held no unreasonable ideas about her music. She had no desire for fame, no hankering after acclaim or recognition. She didn't elevate her music above any other music, but she had time only for her own music. She believed she had absorbed quite enough music in her life to fuel her own artistic engine.

When Alex entered the rehearsal and saw Ingles onstage, turning the pages of a score with enough force to transmit her mood but not enough to tear the page, his heart leapt. His new friend was in charge of rehearsals! A return to sanity! The hall was half empty. People were milling around, chatting. The real singers were making little notes in their scores; the others were happily ignoring their scores. The frightened, claustrophobic atmosphere favoured by McNabb was gone. Before Alex had time to choose a place to park himself, Ingles spoke.

"You know," she said. "I don't think I feel like rehearsing today. Anyone who wants to stay and go over anything, feel free to do so. I think we've all practiced this stuff enough, don't you? Someone want to take over?"

As the choir made its way out a voice came from the first row—the row where all the proper singers sat. "What about Principal Todd. He's sitting downstairs. He's still the best conductor in this place. Shall I get him?"

"Why not?" said Ingles. "Go get him. He'll be thrilled." Two or three people left, but the prospect of Todd conducting the rehearsal put bums on seats.

The news that he was wanted in a rehearsal left Todd wide-eyed and breathless. He made a quick visit to the ladies bathroom to freshen up before his entrance. He was greeted with the reception he'd craved the day after his wife died. A solitary slow handclap became a standing ovation from everyone in the hall. Alex applauded heartily. Perhaps, he thought, perhaps things aren't all bad? Perhaps this is a sign that things will get better?

Ingles threw her arms around Todd. She felt she had supported him but had neglected up until that time to provide any physical evidence for her state of mind regarding his recent change in dress sense and subsequent fall from professional grace. His absence, and McNabb's short reign, made her realize how human Todd was, and how easily she might lose everything that defined her. Todd had allowed her to be the musician she was. It was only a matter of time before McNabb would get around to her. When he found out that she received a full salary for teaching a single student—and she didn't even teach him—McNabb would come after her. Looking at this frail figure who once controlled this whole environment, her environment, she knew that she would have to do more to help this poor man. She would have to find out who he was, and help him, somehow, back into the life he built.

Alex was glad that Todd had been offered a little respect, a little love, but not happy enough to endure another choral rehearsal. During a lull in the proceedings he joined the Indian file that was quietly streaming out of the door to catch up on practice, or head to the pub, or to meet boyfriends or girlfriends or whatever it was that music students do when they get to play hooky from choral rehearsals.

# NINETEEN

Alex had to build another library. There were two clear stages in sculpting his music; the first was recording and programming the library, the basic musical building blocks, the second was programming the music. He'd spent a large part of the last three years trying to construct the perfect piano but now he knew that the perfect piano was no good, it was too much; reality and perfection were musically incompatible.

The piano library he'd painstakingly constructed from thirty or forty pianos across more than twenty rooms, twenty different spaces, brought the spaces with them. He knew now that he couldn't build a digital facsimile that captured everything; a general instrument he could apply to all music was simply not feasible. Although Alex had laughed at his comments, he knew that Martin had been spot on about one thing; he hadn't been able to tell which piano was a fake but he was right about the harmonics. There was no way around it. Each note struck on a piano sets off a chain reaction of sympathetic harmonics that interact with the instrument and the room itself.

Alex had to choose a piano; any piano, and make the best job he could recording it, then with every new piece of music he'd have to analyse the complete sound and reproduce that. It meant that from now on he had to use one piano in one space so that he could return to the piano and the space to record the finishing touches, the unique harmonics of a given piece played on a given piano within a given acoustic environment. It was a daunting job to build a brand new library, but at least all the previous work had led him to the conclusion that while he couldn't build a perfect library, he might be able to produce a perfect performance with imperfect tools. Another advantage was that he didn't have to work with the best notes on the best pianos. He wouldn't have to steal a middle C here and low register F# there. Any piano would do and with Laura out of commission (violin-wise) the solution lay in her room, the trombone room. In the trombone room he'd be left alone.

There was still the problem of noise but recording at night would take care of that, in part at least, and he'd written some noise-reduction routines that would eliminate the major part of whatever racket remained without digging too deeply into the music itself. Nobody would notice. He might even be able to leave some equipment in the room to save the trouble of lugging everything around with him. The last thing he needed was too many questions. Nobody had questioned him at all during his previous efforts. Music students and lecturers were a pretty self-involved bunch who couldn't care less about his little experiments. He was a less than mediocre talent floating in a sea of wild ambitions; few students even knew his name, let alone that he engaged in computer high jinx.

He'd set up his equipment in the trombone room. He'd leave it there, under lock and key, until his initial sampling sessions were done. Then he'd move into Ingles' lab to do the programming. The piano in the trombone room was pretty average but it was an average Steinway D—easily good enough. He'd have to get Elliot involved in the later stages of the sampling, after he'd recorded the initial instrument, to help him capture the right harmonics, the right resonances. He'd get Skuggs involved too; Skuggs was a master of the lower register, or at least Alex thought he must be. All three of them had perfect pitch, but he decided not to tune the piano before his sessions; he could fix minor tuning problems in the programming stage and any note out of tune with itself would simply add a little extra authenticity. He could tune pianos but he was no expert, he might make things worse. Anyway, it was another little trick to keep perfection at bay, or at least in check.

Laura had sent his tape to Quentin Walker. Alex had a huge file filled with details of every and any producer he could find. Walker was legendary and the premature sending of the tape had excluded him from potential targets, but Walker was the standard he had to aim at; he had to believe he could fool Walker before he'd try to get published for real. If his music simply sounded like the best piano playing they'd ever heard then maybe they wouldn't hold its counterfeit nature against him? He might have a fight convincing Laura and Elliot and Skuggs that he really did have to make sure it was right before sending it off, but that was a fight for the future. For now, he had to work on the trombone room and his recording plan. He would record with three stereo microphone positions to give him some choice after the fact. Mixing three positions wouldn't interfere with the authenticity of the sound, at worst it would sound like post-processing, at best it would allow him to add room ambience without resorting to artificial processing. The most important thing would be recording as many velocity layers as he could without losing his mind. He'd often imagined a handy machine that he wished someone would build that would play each note with exactly the same velocity across the range of the keyboard; that would make it easier to program the layers, but nobody was about to build a machine that would do that, and he had no idea how to build one himself. He could program computers to do anything that anyone could describe but he could hardly change a light bulb or wire a plug himself; he would have to make do with his fingers and his ears. It wasn't difficult, but it was laborious and repetitive. No matter, with McNabb out of action, Todd recognized as a human again, and with his little band of helpers he felt energized. Maybe he wasn't here just to get a degree? Maybe he really could forge a living for himself sculpting music?

There was no need for Alex to promise kegs of gas; for once Skuggs did everything asked of him without question or bribe. Alex was grateful, he had to ferry twenty blankets, his microphones and stands, leads, pre-amps and his laptop—he'd record straight to hard disk—from his flat to the Academy. He'd need the blankets to fool the piano into thinking it was in another room, balancing the acoustics shouldn't be too hard when perfection wasn't the goal.

The first stage of the process was blanking his mind and listening. The room wasn't completely symmetrical and the piano was pushed back onto a wall. Alex didn't want to spend a lot of time positioning the piano. He got Skuggs—who was no mean pianist himself when the mood took him; piano was a requirement for all students at the Academy—to play piano while Alex stalked around the room with the intensity of a cat sizing its prey. There wouldn't be any ideal position but he had to find the bright spots and the dull spots; he had to map the sonic topography of the environment. He wasn't trying to create the perfect piano so the main concern was simply making a good recording; he would add the sparkle later, in post processing. He knew he didn't really need three sets of microphones, one would do, but three would leave him more options.

Skuggs sat at the piano and played like someone reunited with an old pal. "You're not a bad pianist," said Alex. "Gimme

loud, way over the top, big crunching chords." He was genuinely impressed with Skuggs's little sketches and felt a little sorry
for him; he was really on his best behaviour, sitting at the piano
like a good student, obeying Alex's commands.

"I have many talents," said Skuggs.

"Gimme a scale, slow, one hand."

Alex prowled around the room looking pained, straining to
make sure he neither missed nor superimposed a single sound.
"Another, down from middle C, slower." Skuggs obliged. "This
isn't going to work. Let's move the fucker to the middle of the
room."

They heaved the thing from the wall.

"Does it really matter where we put it," puffed Skuggs.

"Yup."

"Why?"

"If this room was a hundred meters long and we put it
down at one end and I played it with you at the other end, then
we brought it right up to you and played it, would it sound different? If the room was made of metal and I played it, then covered the walls with three feet of cotton wool, would it sound
different?"

"But just a few feet? Are you gonna make me move it
around all day?"

"Nah, we'll move it about a third of the way from that wall
and in the centre here, and that's it."

"Thank fuck for that. I'm hungry."

"What's new? I need you to play stuff. Sit down. Gimme
some Bach."

"What Bach?"

"Anything, I need something clean." Skuggs played a two-
part invention while Alex circled the piano, stopping from time
to time. He pressed his ear against the wall.

"Why're you doing that?"

"No idea. I thought maybe I could hear whether the walls are made from different materials, but I don't hear anything special."

"Man, you must be a Cocker Spaniel. I don't know how you can tell the difference, or how you know that one place sounds different from another."

"You know a good tuba tone don't you?"

"Of course."

"Can't describe it though, can you? It's more like smell than hearing, I think. I think we have all these skills that we don't know we've got, you know, like cavemen had to be able to smell water from miles away, or tell the difference between a deer rustling leaves miles away, or a mouse rustling leaves a few feet away."

"I could tell if it was a mouse."

"That's not the point. The point is that after you do it millions of times you just know sounds without knowing why you know them or exactly what you're after. It's like you go out to buy a suit. You don't know what you want but when you try on the right one, you know it's the right one without knowing why."

"I've never bought a suit."

"What about your dinner suit? The scabby one you wear at concerts?"

"That was my Dad's."

"Gimme something full, something with lotsa notes."

"Like what?"

"What about Brahms? Or kid-on Brahms, something with rich harmonies but moving around a lot." Skuggs cocked his head to one side then smashed great Rachmaninovian chords. "Lots of pedal."

"Pretty fucking brilliant, no?" Skuggs shouted. "Better than you."

"Thanks Skuggs, take a ticket. Gimme something quiet, Satie, something like that?" Skuggs played some extra-wide major seventh inversions. He leant forward into the chords. He was enjoying himself.

"Sometimes I think I am Satie," he said.

"Christ, you're turning into Elliot." Alex grabbed a chair, placed it around twelve feet to the right of the piano and stood on it so that his head met an imaginary line along the trajectory of the piano lid. Skuggs talked like an old lounge lizard while he played.

"I like that about him. It's like, difficult to tell when he's serious and when he's taking the piss, no?"

"The smile."

"Yeah, the wee fucker never stops."

"He has lately." Alex jumped off the chair, moved it a foot to the left then got back on. "Gimme something with a bit of speed." Skuggs speeded up the Satie.

"Come on Skuggs, get real."

"Canny play fast man. Never practice." He tried a Mozart sonata at double speed. His fingers lolled around the keys, unsure of themselves. Still, he talked as if someone else was working his hands. The mess he made of the Mozart hardly interfered with his thoughts. "So, what's up with the wee man?"

"No idea. I think he thinks nobody appreciates him. You know, applause isn't enough for him. He thinks people aren't getting it that he's to music what Christ is to christians."

"He's right, sort of. But he shouldn't dwell on it. He plays the guitar, he's always gonna be on a bit of a beating in this place, but once he gets out there the audience'll find him. He should just take it easy, you know, try to get his end away and relax."

"That's probably the real problem. He prolly needs a good hard shag."

"Don't we all?"

"Really, really quiet now. Not Mozart, jazz, something else. He's so intense. Does he even try to get women?"

"Maybe he's a woofter?"

"Nah. Quieter. Hardly touching the keys. Man, yer okay if yer a woofter, all they do all day is beef each other or talk about beefing each other."

"I used to wish I was a woofter," said Skuggs. He lifted his head and closed his eyes. Alex wondered whether Skuggs was feeling the music or dreaming of lost opportunities.

"It's not like you need a union card, nobody's stopping you."

"I mean, those guys get sex all the time. Trying to get lemons is tough; even for a handsome bastard like me." Alex crawled underneath the piano. "Whoa there! Easy now soldier."

"Right Skuggs," Alex jammed his ear to the underside of the piano. "Lots of pedal. A bit stronger. Chords across the whole range. Even if I was queer I'd kill myself before touching you."

"That's not nice. Got myself a lemon you know, wee viola bird in first year. Lovely biscuits."

"Good for you," he crawled out from under the piano and brushed his trousers down. "By lemon, you mean what?"

"Lemon. Lemon. Lemon curd, lovely bird. Cockney rhyming slang. Apples and pears up the stairs, lemon curd, bird."

"Do I know her?" Alex unpacked his microphones. "Don't stop."

"I hear that all the time… in my dreams. She's wee, first year, viola."

"Am I supposed to recognize her by her viola?"

"She always wears a huge blue coat, too big for her."

"Match made in heaven then?"

"Eh? And boots, she always wears boots all the time."

"Ah, I know who you mean. She's all right, cute."

"Not in the class of your Spanish Mona Lisa."

"I always thought the Mona Lisa was a bit of a dog, like a guy. Nah, she's really cute. Man, she's tiny. You better watch yourself." Alex laid his microphones out on the table by the window.

"How much are those things, you treat them like they're precious."

"Plenty. Plenty. I spent a fortune on these. I don't like to think about how much. I get a sore stomach when I think about it."

"She won't have sex with me," Skuggs played chopsticks and grinned.

"Good. You're too ugly to get sex. I hope she tortures you."

"It's not cause I'm ugly. She's a fucking Christian."

"What is this about Christians man?" Alex unfolded his microphone stands and placed them around the room. "Before I came here I thought, you know, Christians got on with it. This is a Christian country, you don't have to go declaring you're a Christian like it's two thousand years ago and the bastard Romans are on your case. Here it's like they think they're some kind of minority cult and they have to go around telling you they're fucking Christians all the time as if you give a shit."

"Well she's one, and she's slightly mental about it. You know what she does? She goes buskin and then she declares the money she earns to the tax office. You can just see the guy in the tax office looking at this wee thing in her big blue coat with three pound fifty-two in her hand saying she wants the government to know she's been working. It would only be a minor drawback if she'd shag me. I'd go with her to the fucking tax office if she'd shag me. I'd declare the money I filch offa you if she'd shag me."

"Serves you right. What happened to your only ugly women strategy? That's what you get for trying to get sex above your station."

"I'm sicka wankin."

Alex dropped a microphone lead. "Too much information mate. Scales, two hands on the keys right now."

"So what's the deal with Laura then?"

"Deal?" Alex didn't want to discuss his sex life with Skuggs. He didn't want to discuss Laura with Skuggs, but now Laura and Skuggs had become friends and colluded in sending his tape off prematurely. Maybe Laura had already talked to him? He couldn't believe such a thing. It wasn't in her culture to blab about her sex life. He wasn't too comfortable himself talking about his sex life. Skuggs was fishing. He was horny, and his lemon wouldn't comply.

"Come on man. Something weird is going on, isn't it? You guys are hiding something. I heard her playing in that room that night at the party. I heard it man. And then you appear like you've visited nirvana. And you kept the mussed-up hair because you wanted everybody to know you'd been giving it the Roger. You didn't hump her did you?"

"Skuggs man, let's be pals here. If you want to talk about a wee girl in a blue coat who retains at least a vestige of self-respect, go ahead. But it's not some unspoken reciprocal deal. What I do with my tadger is nobody's business but mine. Laura means the world to me. I'm not gonna talk about her like she's a slab of meat on a butcher's board."

Skuggs filled the silence with some modal chords. Alex set up his microphone stands but didn't ask for any more music. He rummaged around in his bag and produced a hammer and nails.

He held the hammer over Skuggs's head. "This is what you need. A sound crack on the nut with my hammer."

"What's it for?"

"Shut up. Play some music."

"Thought you'd finished."

"I have for now." Alex dragged a chair to the wall on the left of Skuggs. He grabbed one of the blankets piled up against the door, stuck a nail in the corner of the blanket and hammered it into the wall. He put in a couple more nails then hung another blanket beside it. "Keep playing Skuggs. I just want to listen. It's nice, you play well."

"I didn't mean to pry."

"Fucking liar."

"Okay. I did mean to pry, but not about your sex life. I heard her playing man. I heard her."

"So?" There wasn't any point in asking him to shut up.

"So? So? She's Doctor Jekyll and Mrs. Paganini. I thought when I saw her in a tight jumper I'd seen the best of her, but I was wrong. Those tits are absolutely…"

"Skuggs, I've still got this hammer here. I *will* hit you on the leg man. I'm serious. Any more drooling and you're getting an atomic dead leg." He jumped off the chair.

"Okay. Okay. Don't tell me what's going on. I'm only yer best mate. Keep me in the dark. Let me work out for myself how come one of the weakest violinists I've ever heard turns into fucking Jascha Heifetz when you get alone with her… with better mams."

Alex worked away at the blankets and the microphone placement until he'd hung too many blankets and moved the stands all the way around the room and back again. Skuggs played piano and waited.

Finally, Alex cracked.

"You've got it the wrong way round man. She's absolutely beyond belief, as a musician. She's got a wee problem that I'm helping her with."

"Mm."

"Mm? You're mm'ing me? Fucking Sigmund."

"So, sex sets her free?"

"No, being with me sets her free. It seems to."

"Sex with you sets her free?" Skuggs's eyes were glazing over and, outside of hitting him with the hammer, there wasn't a thing he could do about it. "Or is it just your presence? Your touch? Your touch? Is that it? You only have to touch her? Is this for real? This is so far out there. You are the luckiest bastard who ever lived. Shit like this never happens to me. Shit like this will never ever happen to me. I'm doomed."

"Well, never let it be said that you can find a subject that you don't find a way to relate it to your own sorry arse." Alex was relieved that Skuggs had shot right past the truth in an effort to get to the point of the story; that this (whatever 'this' was) would never happen to him.

"Is it real?"

"What?"

"You know. Is it chambermaids and cattle prods and that? Is it a kiddon?"

"Skuggs, you reckon she'd jeopardize her career, her sanity for fuck's sake, so that she could keep all her musical magic for me?"

"But she wasn't that crappy to get in the Academy in the first place was she? She must have been pretty good. When you started stalking her, what was she like then? Was she worse than she is now or what?"

He cast his mind back to the first time he saw her. It had taken him weeks to pluck up the courage to speak to her. He was too embarrassed to approach her in public. He'd followed

her up the labyrinthine passages and staircases that led to the
trombone room. Of course, he didn't go in and speak to her
like a regular human being; he'd peer in at her through the little
square window as if he were doing his rounds. She never
seemed to notice him. When he eventually summoned the
courage to enter the room she had simply ignored him and carried on practicing. But now he remembered; the first time he'd
followed her she sounded different, not astonishing, the way she
sounded when they had sex, or dreadful, the way she sounded
when they weren't having sex, just different, like a completely
different person. Now it was clear. He wasn't her salvation, her
hope; he was her tormentor, stripping her of her talent.

He felt sick to his stomach.

"Sup with you?"

"It was me." Alex pinched the bridge of his nose and tried
to hear her playing. He tried to separate all the different times,
the different performances he'd heard. He lifted his hand in a
gesture to make Skuggs stop playing. None of it had quite regis-
tered at the time. At first, he was entranced, transfixed by a
body that radiated sex and drew him like a dog in heat. Then
he'd used her as a sounding board for his bitching and whining.
It was nice to be able to get things off his chest and look up to
see that body in front of him. When it seemed to him that she
would never respond he became even more relaxed, playing
along with her, making silly jokes, admiring her more as an artist might admire his subject; the sexual magnetism was still there
but under cover, held in place, kept at bay. When she responded
it had happened so fast, he was dizzy; in love like a fourteen
year-old given impossible access to his idol. He hadn't met her
until after they had sex. Her performance that evening had
fused with his wildest dreams. But he could hear it now. He
could see himself sitting staring at her; the music like a movie
soundtrack, each cue a clip from a different scene describing her

aggravation, her softening, her yielding, her triumph. He'd thought he was helping her; that she had some weirdo psychological affliction which didn't matter a jot to him because she was in love with him: in love with him! More, her new dependence on him to awaken her virtuosity had given him the security that some codger, part of an old couple together for years, might feel. He knew he was feeding on it and he felt ashamed. He knew now he'd caused it, brought it to life. Was it ready to happen anyway? Was it simple coincidence or was he the catalyst? Skuggs sat silently, expressionless; he knew what Alex was thinking. Alex's history as a programmer, a scientist of sorts, fed his mistaken self-image of a levelheaded, logical, rational man. But Skuggs knew Alex; he knew he was as likely to take a hammer to him as anyone who takes a hammer to anyone when their world is threatened. He kept a poker face; just in case.

"When we have sex, she plays like a goddess," said Alex. Skuggs's upper lip twitched but he kept control of himself. Inside, his heart leapt in glee at the dawning, in Alex, of his insight. "Why am I such a moron?" He thumped his leg.

"We can't all be gifted empaths."

"Don't give me Star Trek man, I used to get enough of that from the geeks at work. This is what I get for surrounding myself with fucking arty types."

"I'm an arty type?" Skuggs rather liked the idea of being described as an arty type. "D'you think you could spend the rest of your life walking in front of me telling everybody that? Kids throw stones at me like I'm an old wino. Arty type? That'll do me. Maybe I'll buy a cravat?"

"Lose the parka and people might mistake you for a member of the human race."

"No way boyo. I love my parka." He wrapped his arms around himself as if someone might try to steal his beloved parka.

"First Elliot, now you? I thought you two were just a couple of dumbo players?"

"Thanks very much."

"I don't need this, man. I need you two to help with the music, I don't need to be analysed by a couple of amateur therapists every time I have a problem."

"So, you do have a problem?" Skuggs puffed an imaginary pipe. "Tell me more. We still have a few minutes left in the session." Alex shot him a look that reminded him of the hammer. "Let's lose the anger shall we?" Skuggs finally injected enough authority in his voice to make Alex remember that he was twice Alex's size and any violence, whatever the provocation, could be met with resistance.

"Sorry Skuggs. It's a bit disconcerting finding out that everybody can read me, that's all."

"Everybody can't read you. Only me. And Elliot." He paused. "That's two? Maybe everybody can read you?"

"I'm so shallow."

"You are." When it looked as if Alex was ready to cry Skuggs took pity. "Look man, what do you care? It's not as if you meant to hurt her, is it? Musicians, musicians are a strange breed."

"You think I'm a musician?"

"I think we funnel everything we've got into our music. We stuff it all in there in the hope that it'll all come out the end of our instruments when we play. Or in your case you stuff what you've got into your computer. We're obsessives. I expect if we meet our soul mates we either don't notice or we pour every little foible into them and expect them to solve all our problems. In your case, you're a shallow bastard who's finally getting a look at himself, finding out he's not so clever, finding out he's not that talented and that he's an emotional vacuum who doesn't deserve even to live. Hee, hee. Couldn't resist that

man. You're acting like such a pussy. And in Laura's case…
Mmm… Laura… Well she has to be completely fucking
bonkers to even look at you in the first place, doesn't she? I
mean, life comes as a package. If she was normal she'd go after
someone gifted, someone dashing and interesting such as myself… would she not? Seriously." Skuggs lifted himself off the
piano stool and let off a giant fart as if to punctuate and add
weight to his thoughts. "Hasn't she met the right guy? Doesn't
the evidence point to you? She's talented, she meets you, her
talents crumble, she throws in the towel and lets you in, her talent returns but only while you're there. Or I should say, only
when you're in there? I have to repeat at this point that you are
one lucky bastard. You need her to make you less of a putz and
she needs you to… eh?" Skuggs suddenly became confused.

"What? What? What does she need me for?" Alex was a
junkie after a fix. Skuggs had all the answers, although the smell
added even more urgency. Alex had to know the answer and get
out quick.

"I forgot what I was talking about."

"I don't need to know. I've had it with your farting and
your mind reading. I'm done here. Let's go get drunk."

Skuggs needed no encouragement. They went and got
drunk. Skuggs had forgotten what he was talking about and
Alex made himself forget; he was tired of all the complications.
He didn't want to take responsibility for another person's
psyche; he wasn't up to it. It wasn't his fault.

They staggered back to his flat. Laura was there, curled up
on the sofa reading a book. A dictionary lay open beside her.
She smiled. Alex smiled. Skuggs smiled.

"I have a wonderful day," she said. "I feel too good."

"Too good?" said Skuggs. "Lucky girl."

"Here," she said to Alex. "Message. You have telephone
call."

Alex read the message and staggered back into a chair.

"Si. Senior Walker, he like."

"What's goin on man?" Skuggs grabbed the paper.

"He want to speak with Alex."

"What did you say? What did he say, exactly?"

"He say he want to speak with musician on tape. I say, not here. He say my number get back to me."

"That's it?"

"That's it. I make coffee for two drunks, yes?"

"Please. Thank you," said Skuggs.

Alex pondered what it meant for one of the most respected producers in the classical music world to even respond to an unfinished tape. He must have seen through it? He must have heard it was a fake and he wants to give the culprit some stick? He must be taking the piss?

"Maybe he liked it?" said Skuggs. "I liked it. We all liked it. See!" he shouted toward the kitchen. "Me and Laura know best." Alex and Skuggs sat in silence until Laura returned with a tray of goodies. Skuggs had a self-satisfied grin plastered onto his face. Alex tried to get past the alcohol and work out what it meant.

"Walker's no mug. It is a good tape but it's full of flaws."

"That's why it sounds convincing," said Skuggs. He thought Alex was suffering his usual plague of self-doubt.

"It's musically convincing, but the music isn't so flawed, it's the piano itself. I built it from, like twenty pianos. I was all over the place recording it. I thought I could create a perfect piano."

"The piano sounds great man. Really clean."

"Too clean. Too sparkly. No mud. No integrity. What's his game?"

"Why's everything always so complicated Sherlock? The guy likes it. Give yourself a break." He sipped some coffee. "This coffee is delightful."

"Tomorrow, you call him? Maybe he want your music?" said Laura. Alex took a long breath and held it. "Maybe he want your music?"

"This guy is such hard work Laura. How do you put up with him? Talk about high maintenance?" Skuggs stuck out his pinkie and drained his cup.

"So, you're saying that the geezer likes your music but he thinks it's shite?" Elliot had a way of getting to the point. Alex had lain awake half the night trying to work out what Walker wanted; what he heard. Maybe this was an opportunity and maybe he was as paranoid as Skuggs believed, but if a crack had opened for him he had to know what was beyond it. Skuggs and Laura were pragmatists, they were happy their decision to unleash his music into a lion's den had worked out. A response was enough; the next step was to contact Walker and find out what he was after, which was surely to publish Alex's music? But Walker didn't know it wasn't real. Laura hadn't explained anything in her letter. Surely the lack of partials, the hundreds of hard-wired ambiences had struck him like a sledgehammer? Elliot didn't trust anyone. Elliot thought people had an ulterior motive for everything. Elliot didn't believe he'd ever met anyone who knew themselves as well as he knew them; he believed people grasped a set of values as quickly as they could and spent the rest of their lives superimposing those values onto their experiences, and the lives around them. Elliot believed he stared life and death in the face every day. He believed he knew the truth and that he could see the heart of matters. He believed composers spoke to him and that he understood their music and their motives. Perhaps Elliot couldn't or wouldn't help? Perhaps he'd slip into 'sage' mode and try to confuse Alex even more? But it was worth a try.

"Okay, tell me about this geezer. Tell me what you know," said Elliot.

"He's an old-timer. He resurrected ancient recording techniques. Techniques that were old even when he started. He records direct-to-disk, one take, with as little technology as possible between the performance and the listener."

"Sounds sensible."

"He's not that well-known, but he's a bit of a legend in the industry. He survived all the technical developments that went on right through his career."

"Why did you send your stuff to, like, the antithesis of what you do?"

"For a genius you are a bit thick, aren't you? Laura sent it. Skuggs found the guy's name in my files and they just sent it off to kick me up the arse."

"All right, let's assume that the guy knows you're a wanker with a computer. Why would he contact you? D'you think he wants to go down that road?"

"No chance. He might just have called back because he was so annoyed."

"All right, in that case none of it matters anyway. You've got no leverage and no future. What if he liked it? What if he thinks it's real?"

"He must have heard all the flaws though. I never wanted to send…"

"Yeah, yeah, right, but how would he know how the flaws were created? If he doesn't know shit about computers, and all he ever did was point a tin can at people, maybe he hears the flaws but doesn't think they're flaws. Maybe he's just curious? Maybe he likes it for fuck's sake? Why is it hard for you to believe that somebody would like your music? You spend half you're time pleading that it's brilliant, then when someone likes it you want a bloody argument."

Alex had cornered Elliot in the cello room. A girl entered. She bashed around, searching for something amongst a stack of cello cases piled three deep. She became a little embarrassed at the silence. They both stared at her until she found whatever it was she was looking for and left.

"Well?" said Elliot, as if something had been decided.

"Well what? That's it? That's what you've got? Maybe he liked it?"

"No, if he didn't then there's no problem. Whatever you do doesn't matter. I thought we agreed that he'd have no idea how you created it? Therefore we have to assume that he likes it. If he heard anomalies but thought it was shit he wouldn't call, would he? Now it's just a matter of how you play it. Say he likes it and he just wants the problems explained to him? What do you do now? You've proved your stupid point then, haven't you? You've got a big-eared Cocker Spaniel panting after your talent, except you haven't got the talent he thinks you've got. But you've won, you can die happy." Elliot took out a tube of Smarties and flung some into his mouth. "Breakfast. What about the new stuff? The stuff I'm doing? Are you gonna send the geezer that? Man, if he likes the shit you sent him, when he hears my stuff he's gonna lose his mind."

It was like a bolt of lightning charging through him. He wanted to smash Elliot's face for claiming ownership over his music. He wanted to find Walker and throttle him into publishing his music. He wanted to have played the music himself. He wanted to have played the music himself?

That was it. That was the key. He'd spent three years trying to convince himself that if he'd had the physical wherewithal he'd be able to do it all at the piano instead of in front of a computer. But he knew he couldn't. Even with all the power of his sample libraries and his computers and his endless hours of programming and tweaking, he still wasn't good enough. Elliot had sat beside him at the computer and everything he said made sense. There was hardly a phrase, hardly a note that Elliot couldn't see there was something wrong with it. His great plan, to produce music on his computer and fool the world into thinking it was really a great pianist sitting at a piano, had failed. He had a huge fish on a hook, but he hadn't the skill to land it.

"Got a letter from Boskov this morning," Elliot pulled a scrunched-up ball of paper from his pocket. "He's offered me a post-grad year at his college."

"What do you have to do to fail in this world?"

"I'm not doing it. Fucking arsehole. I'd rather go on the dole than have that hairy bastard telling me how to play." He tossed the letter into a waste paper basket. "We've still got the choral concert in a couple of days. Fancy getting pissed and having a laugh at it?"

"So why did you keep the letter?"

"Eh?"

"Why not throw it away on the spot? Why bother carrying a big, heavy letter around all day, getting in the way of your Smarties, then come in here and wait until we're talking then throw it away?"

Elliot tilted his head to one side and closed his eyes.

"You need an audience for everything, don't you? You need affirmation. Just like the rest of us you suspect that maybe you're not as great as you think you are."

"That's right." Elliot said it with a little surprise.

"Elliot, I'm this close man," Alex pinched his fingers together. "I'm getting everyone working on this. There has to be a way. Don't you think it would be cool to get our music out there?"

Elliot nodded.

"I don't want to get pissed before the choral concert. I want to finish the music. I want to send it to the guy. I want to do something without any holes, something that he can't turn down. I'm going to have to call him. I'm going to have to call him and talk to him."

"Maybe you can brass it?" said Elliot. "Just tell him you're the greatest player who ever lived and you've been living on a desert island for years but now you want to join the world. These types like that kind of thing. Tell him your recording equipment is all whack but you'll send him another, better."

"Can you speak Chinese? I mean anything, even the odd word?"

"Naw, but I'm fluent in Japanese accent. I've watched a million Kung Fu movies. I talk in Japanese accent to audiences when I can gerraway with it. They think you know what the fuck you're talking about if you pour on a Japanese accent."

"They think you know what you're talking about if you've got a Japanese accent?" He smiled manically. "Elliot. You! He'll believe you."

"You want me to call him?"

"No. But he'll believe you. What's the point of coming clean? He'll only get disappointed that it's not real, then pissed off at me for taking the piss. But he'll believe in a Chinese virtuoso, locked away in a government music school for years. People lap up that shit."

"What, you gonna send him a photo? What do you mean?"

"Let's send him another tape. Let's talk to him. Let's tell him about you. Let's tell him about a guy who's done nothing but study music since he was two. Let's tell him about a guy that can play the piano, the violin, the cello, whatever!" Alex walked up and down the little passageway made by the cellos lining both walls. "This could work." Alex sat down to contemplate his plan. Elliot *was* believable. Alex pictured him in a little Mao Tse Tung outfit. He wouldn't even have to get him a bad haircut. Elliot always cut his own hair, and he cut it so very badly, he even *looked* like a virtuoso. His eternal smile; it wasn't a stupid smile, it was almost always present, but it really was inscrutable. "It doesn't even have to be piano. We could use Skuggs and Laura as well."

"What for?"

"We can send him anything we want. You can be Mozart. No, you can be more than Mozart. You can be anything we want. We can use the piano to reel him in. Your coupon'll do the trick. You look so Chinese."

"Do I?"

"Why not? Are you sure you don't know any Chinese at all?"

"I can swear a bit."

"Doesn't matter. He won't know any Chinese. What's he going to do, bring an interpreter to check you out? He's not looking for any of this. These guys, their ambition is always to find the next big thing, a new genius."

"So, I don't even have to pretend then?"

"Easy, no?"

"You think we'll make money? It would be nice to have some money and not have to bother about anything. I could sit at home all day long watching telly and not even have to get on a bus."

# Twenty

McNabb didn't care that he looked like a mental patient. If he stayed at home one more day he'd have to kill himself. Spending so much time with her reminded him of his life. In the couple of days he'd been recuperating she'd spoken only to let him know that food was ready; bloody curry, always bloody curry. In all the time they'd been married she hadn't once attempted his favourite mince and tatties. Betty made the best mince and tatties in the world and now she made it for an orthodontist with crooked teeth who stole her away after McNabb left her. That he now had a valid excuse for his halitosis failed to make up for the lack of creature comforts that had descended upon him since Shama took over. McNabb hated curry. McNabb hated babies. McNabb hated that he lived with a woman that some might even describe as beauty. He hated when male colleagues nudged him with their elbows or winked their envy at his impossible luck. On the face of it he was the archetypal male menopause success story; married to an exotic woman half his age, out of his league (they'd surely confirm when he was out of earshot), but he knew the truth, that she might as well be an automaton for all the affection she'd shown him. His role was

235

clear. He was to provide for her and her children. If and when she wanted another child, then he'd have sex again. She found sex 'disgusting'. She'd told him as much; that it wasn't him, that it was 'it'. She'd pointed at his groin and made a face. It wasn't him, it wasn't him particularly, anyway, it was the 'thing' that she found so repugnant. Her abhorrence of the male member was his only chance to drag it out, to promise a child then make sure that the delivery system for such a thing never quite presented its package correctly. But the price of a few weeks of relief was another child, another brat, another mouth to feed, another barrier between him and the remote possibility that he might connect with her.

He donned his tweed jacket; the one with the leather patches on the elbows that made him look more like an educator. He slipped on a pair of tan Hush Puppies to match his corduroys—that he believed made him look younger—and grabbed a comb. Like many bald men, McNabb groomed what little hair he had lovingly and often. About to drag the comb around the back of his head he remembered his dome; the white one someone had built on top of his head while he was unconscious. He ambled toward the mirror with the gait of a convict returning to his cell. Betty would have made light of it; she would have rubbed it with a duster to make him laugh, she would have convinced him that he looked distinctive, that he might even start a new fashion, that he was a piece of modern art, that she liked him better with the dome, that she found it quite sexy. He stared at himself and knew that he looked like a mental patient. There was no one to take away the pain anymore, no one to see him for something other than himself, no one to believe that he might be more than himself. There was no one to love him.

"Chicken tonight?" Shama was standing at the bathroom door, holding the baby.

McNabb walked past her like she didn't exist. She kissed the baby's forehead and smiled.

He arrived early; first in, last out, that was the way. He was almost certain the board would have to give him the job permanently, but he couldn't take any chances. There could be spies; there were always spies. Nobody was going to catch him out. Todd was already there when he arrived, sitting outside the bursar's room with his legs crossed and his hands sitting on his lap making one of those little baskets that infant teachers like so much. McNabb folded his arms and watched him. Todd didn't see McNabb; he seemed occupied by a pattern on the floor in front of him. McNabb listened as intently as he could. The Academy foyer was one of those big, reverberant spaces that can turn a mouse into a herd of elephants with ingrown toenails. He wanted to make sure that nobody was around before he approached the pathetic creature sitting in its twin set and pearls; with an immaculately barbered beard to remind the rest of the world that it was completely off its rocker, and no doubt a limp little dick sitting harmlessly underneath a tartan skirt that was too perfectly pressed.

"It won't work. You do know that?" Todd got such a fright he almost toppled off his chair. "Sitting there, you're ridiculous."

Todd got back to staring at the floor.

"You're going to ignore me?" McNabb sauntered over to the stairwell. He squinted and held his hand to his brow as if shading it from a bright light. He walked a few feet down a corridor but nobody was around. "You seriously believe that coming here like that every day is going to embarrass me."

"Something wrong with your head?" Todd kept his gaze fixed on the floor. McNabb brought his hand up and almost touched his dome before he caught himself. He rubbed his nose then folded his arms out of harm's way.

"Nobody cares about you. Everybody thinks you're mad. You are mad. Look at you."

Todd raised his head slowly, his eyes fixed on an imaginary point in front of him until he was staring straight through McNabb. "Don't you have some students to expel? No point standing here wasting valuable time when you could be assaulting children."

McNabb grinned. He took one last trip around the foyer, sticking his head around doors, making a few steps along corridors, then he leant over until his lips almost touched Todd's ear. He whispered, "You're done. You're finished. You're nothing. I've won. You've lost. If only your little wife could see you now."

Todd shot his head around so fast he almost caught him. McNabb pulled back. He stuffed his hands into his pockets and rocked back and forth on his heels. Todd tried to fight it. He locked his jaw tightly, he sucked the roof of his mouth and swallowed but it was no good. The image, the image of a self-satisfied monster grinning arrogantly, swaying to and fro, became blurred. Todd felt he might pass out, his whole body was in a vice, he couldn't pass out in front of this excuse for a human being, he couldn't 'feint like a woman'.

McNabb watched the tears well in Todd's eyes; he watched them melt into the mascara that Todd had applied too heavily; he watched black triangles form under his eyes and waited until they burst forth into sad little lines streaking down Todd's cheeks.

Then he left.

# TWENTY–ONE

The next few days were magical. Laura was on enforced va-cation from her violin. She turned all of her attentions to Alex. She took care of him; she made his life into her life. She took delight in his work, his plans. She was thrilled to sneak into the trombone room every night. He would record, single notes played again and again, over and over and over until each key was mapped across its full dynamic range. They'd make love, on the floor, against the wall, on the piano, at the piano, under the piano. Then he'd record the next note, over and over and over. She had never seen him at work; his patience was endless. Alex loved that she was there. He could hardly believe she could put up with it, and pestered her that she should really have stayed at home, but always she shook her head; it was as if she was enjoying herself. Perhaps the simple freedom from the tyranny of her practice schedule made every moment precious? He'd focus on a note, a single key, entering a state similar to the state in which he'd lived as a software developer. Time had no meaning, it was like floating in space, it wasn't enough to merely listen to the note, he had to feel the note, to enter it, let it envelope him. It wasn't a simple matter of hitting every note with varying attack;

every key responds slightly differently. It was like building a wall of sound; each note split into sixty-four 'bricks'. The bricks of one key had to match the bricks of the next key but there was no real way of quantifying that the layers matched. He could quantify the amplitude, he could measure the frequencies, but experience told him that two measurable dimensions did not tell the whole truth. There was something more, impervious to measurement, something that defined the music within the sound. This is what he had to capture. Laura made it feel easy. She made him feel important.

The work went quickly. The last three years had served as an apprenticeship and he knew exactly what to do and when to do it. Actually sampling the sounds was easy, especially when he could look over at Laura instead of locking himself purely into his obsession. He didn't fret over each sample the way he had in the past. When he got home Laura would go to bed while he forced himself to catalogue each and every sound. First he'd load the sounds into memory then he'd slice them up according to temperament and amplitude. He'd run a little application he'd written to name them. Simply naming so many sounds had taken up so much of his time in the past that he'd forced himself to write something that automated the process, at least in part. When his cataloguing was done he'd slide into bed beside her and thank the gods that his life was good. He never slept for more than four or five hours. He still had to take his new samples to Ingles' lab for processing. He managed to avoid Ingles for four days straight. He was her only student and she apparently never visited her lab in the afternoons. Sleep deprivation was something that he was used to, more than that it was something he expected; a familiar feeling he associated with concentrated effort the way a clerk might associate wearing a tie or a pair of uncomfortable shoes with the office.

Once in the lab he'd transfer his new samples to the simple
network he'd installed. Then, one by one, he'd examine them,
he'd listen to them and simultaneously study the waveforms in
graphic form. He flagged any anomalies, any little bumps or
creases in the waveforms—that looked like ragged pencil draw-
ings of clouds. Then he'd run the waveforms through an imprint he'd made of the room before he started recording. The
imprint was a pristine sonic image of the room without any
sounds whatever; thus it was a 'memory' of the room without
any deliberate sounds; a picture of the background frequencies,
the almost imperceptible rumbles and hisses associated with any
space. He'd use this imprint to eliminate the anomalies, the
noise. By subtracting this imprint from his waveforms he ended
up with the piano and its interaction with the room; the room
itself was gone. All that was left were the dimensions of the
room, the nooks and crannies, the straight edges, the surfaces
dampened by his improvised soundproofing. A digital descrip-
tion of the dimensions was all he needed, he could add or take
away noises if and where he wanted; what was important was
that he had the environment under his complete control.

He'd never felt better, never been happier. But toward the
end of the week the knowledge that he'd soon have to pluck his
plans out of his fantasy and into the real world began to make its
presence felt in the pit of his stomach. He'd have to call Walker.
He'd have to do it all for real. He'd have to flesh out his plan,
perhaps even draw branches the way he used to when he was
programming, to try to pre-empt any potential difficulties. He'd
have to keep working on his new piano but he hoped he could
make time with Walker on that. Walker had responded to the
previous tape. It was that performance that had somehow piqued
his interest and therefore that performance would be enough,
had to be enough, for now.

His almost subterranean existence meant he had no idea of what was going on in the real world; the world where he was a less than mediocre pianist about to get booted out of the Academy. Somewhere, in the back of his mind, he knew that this was another deadline he was fighting against. If he got chucked out of the Academy before he'd managed to build his piano, sculpt new performances, before he'd convinced Walker to release a recording, all would be lost. Doubts scratched at the base of his spinal chord, and while he dismissed them, he could never conquer them. Ultimately, no matter how hard he worked, no matter how clever he thought he was, his fate was in the hands of others. His only chance was to work fast enough that he might get to choose who those others would be.

The phone rang. A bowling ball hit the pit of his stomach, sending waves of nausea reverberating through his body. He shot a glance at Laura, who was spread on the sofa reading a magazine. She put the magazine down and folded her arms.

"Again?" She was tiring of Alex falling to pieces every time the outside world came calling. "It's Elliot. It's Skuggs. Oooooh, it is Walker!" she said with some glee.

"I can't answer. I'm not ready. Will you answer it? If it's him, pretend you're my secretary." Alex kneaded the flesh on his belly around the area where muscles might have formed neat little bumps were he not a programmer turned musician who smoked too much and exercised only during sexual exertions and trips to the shops.

"No," she said, quite mischievously. "Five rings? What to do? Six? Seven? He will hang up and never call you, never."

Alex lifted the phone smartly to his ear. "Halloo?" His voice was pitched a minor sixth higher than usual. Laura covered her mouth with both hands then buried her face into a cushion. Little squeaks of laughter escaped the cushion as he tried to focus his hearing on the earpiece. Nobody was there. Was that someone breathing?

"Yer a fucking wanker Stone, and I want you out of the Academy toot sweet!"

It was Elliot. "And I don't want to hear any more of your shitey computer music either."

"That's funny Elliot. You're a comedian… I think you're about to make Laura piss herself." Laura rolled over and fell onto the floor, still holding the cushion over her face.

"Want me to come over? I'm bored. Where you been all week? What's going on with the music? Did you call that geezer yet? Oh, there's a notice up on the board for you. They're looking for you. The man in the white hat wants to see you."

"Man in the white hat?"

"Mr. Fucking Angry, McNabb, he's after you. You are fucked boyo."

Alex couldn't be bothered worrying about McNabb. It wasn't Walker on the phone, he had the feeling of avoiding a dental appointment; weak and happy but depressed that he still had to face the music.

"Come round. We can talk." He put the phone down. Laura was on the floor, absently playing with the cushion.

"You are so white, you look like Sparky the ghost."

"Sparky eh?" He decided to give her some tickles.

The phone rang. He picked it up.

"Alex Stone?"

Alex grabbed his chest like the heart attack he might have feared if he'd thought more about his unhealthy habits was upon him.

"Hello?"

"This is Alex Stone." He said it the way he might respond in the green room before a concert, all but shitting himself, but somehow exuding an air of steely confidence. The tone in his voice brought Laura out of her hysteria.

"I have a recording of a pianist here. I have a letter with your contact details, and I'd like to know what's going on? I called before and a girl, a foreign girl answered."

"My secretary." This was it. Laura hugged the cushion to herself. He hadn't worked out any master plan. He had avoided dealing with the reality that Walker would surely call again. He'd played endless scenarios somewhere in the back of his mind; they had all tailed off into ludicrous fantasies of wild success and cheering crowds or ended with a swift and crushing blow dealt by the man at the other end of this conversation. "Forgive me for not returning your call…"

"What's going on?" Walker cut him off. Three years as a musician, three years being lectured to and cut off by blowhards had built a kind of switch right inside of him that took him into a Descartesian mind state to withstand pre-emptive attacks against his intelligence. Converting lateral thought processes into literal conclusions was a gift elicited by intellectuals unhindered by the kind of self-doubt scientists or logicians had to aim at themselves to avoid ridicule. There was always something he didn't know about sautille that someone could laugh at; always someone to point out his gross misunderstanding of a few pencil marks on a piece of paper that represented no more than the sin of two notes travelling in tandem or the sacrilege he perpetrated at the piano; always someone to make his own analytical approach inappropriate to art; always someone who knew better and acted like everyone knew they knew better.

"I chose you Mr. Walker. I don't know much about the classical music world and even less about the world of music publishing. But I did some research and decided that you were the only one deserving of the job in hand."

"Job?"

"I need someone to record my man. I need the best. You're the best there is."

"What job?"

"I have a young man here. Came to me through some of my contacts in the Far East. I'm told he's very gifted. I'm a lawyer." At this, Laura pinched her nose to signify some kind of pong was abroad.

"Lawyer?"

"Lawyer, yes, afraid so." Alex had him. He knew it. It was time to enjoy it. Time to spin it out and make it real. He believed himself. If anyone had ever asked him why, on such scant evidence, he believed that Walker was on the hook, he wouldn't know how to answer; it was just a feeling. It might have been something to do with dealing day in, day out, with the type of character who cuts people off? Maybe if you can cut them off and keep them quiet, of their own accord, then you've got them? Maybe there was something in his voice, something almost imperceptible that told Alex of Walker's hunger, his desperation to find a great virtuoso? Whatever it was and however it might appear in the light of day, whether it was happenstance or voodoo or dumb luck, Alex simply knew that Walker needed this.

"I don't understand. I have a recording here…"

Alex cut him off. "Yes. That's right. Yang Li. Piano, I think."

"You think?"

"Not piano? Violin? Tuba?"

"Tuba?"

"No, I'm pretty sure it was piano. Yang Li's staying with me right now, and frankly I don't care how good he is, he's not playing a bloody tuba in my house." He stuck out his tongue at Laura then quickly brought his forefinger to his lips to shush her. She covered her mouth with both hands, her eyes as wide as saucers at Alex's performance. She almost believed him herself.

"Tuba? He plays the tuba?"

"Yes. Brilliantly, I'm told, though please God I'll never get to find out for myself. Yes, tuba, piano, violin." He paused deliberately. He knew this was the key and he wanted to savour it. "And guitar, of course. Never puts the damn thing down. Fine by me. Nice and quiet. Hardly hear him with my earplugs and the telly turned up. Not much of a music lover."

There was a long pause at the other end of the line but Alex not only resisted the urge to fill the silence, he basked in it. He knew Walker was confused but he wasn't stupid; and the confusion wouldn't last long. He had to reel him in, and he had to do it quickly. If he gave him too long to think, then he'd ask too many questions. No point in allowing any suspicion to ferment. He had to drive the hook in deep.

"Look, I have a recording of this chap…"

"Yang Li," interrupted Alex, as much to burn Elliot's new handle into his own brain as inform Walker.

"I need to speak to him."

"Sorry. No can do, I'm afraid."

"No?"

"No English. Not a bloody word. We do have an interpreter on retainer. If you'd like to ask a few questions now, I can get them to him. Those interpreters are bloody expensive I can tell you. I've a mind to get down to the local takeaway and offer a tenner to the kid behind the counter. We've got someone trained at the bloody United Nations, costs a bloody fortune I can tell you."

"I'm sorry. Look, I need to speak with him. I need to know how he recorded the music."

"How he recorded it? No idea."

"I didn't ask if you knew how he recorded it, and I need to ask him where he recorded it. It's very strange."

"Strange?" Of course, this was it. This was the moment he'd dreaded all along. This was the moment he knew he'd have to face. The moment when he'd be found out. When he'd be revealed for the fraud that he was.

"Probably the duff equipment they had at that shitty music school."

"Music school? Which music school?"

"No idea. Big secret, apparently. Very hush hush, my Hong Kong chaps said. All I know is that this young man has been studying music at the school since he was two years old. Two years old! Can you believe that? Of course, I say studying, really the poor chap's been a prisoner there. Actually, I don't believe he's been there since he was two. What say you? Is that possible? Do little tykes play music at that age? No children myself. No idea. Surely he'd have to be at least three or four? What say you?"

"I'm sorry, I'm trying to take all this in. You say he's from Hong Kong?"

"No, no. Well, he came through Hong Kong. Goodness no. He's from China. He's Chinese. Aren't they all these days?" There was a prolonged silence. Maybe it wasn't so long but it felt like too long to Alex. He bit his lip. Maybe he was going too far?

Quentin reached into his pocket and pulled out a freshly ironed handkerchief. He dabbed it on his forehead. Whoever it was he was talking to simply wasn't making any sense at all. He looked at the chess pieces in front of him and wished this conversation could be as simple as the position he'd set up earlier that morning.

"Look, I don't care what equipment was used. I don't care if he comes from Outer Mongolia or Timbuktu…"

"Yes, Outer Mongolia. That's it," said the verbose lawyer at the other end of the line, as if Quentin had won a prize.

"What?" Quentin grabbed the white king and rubbed his thumb against its smoothness.

"He comes from Outer Mongolia, originally, sold into bloody slavery or something. I don't know. When he was a little bod they found out he had talent. I don't know how. They measure them, test them. Whatever it was they did, whatever it was they saw in him, he was sent to the Kung Su music school."

"The Kung Su music school?" Quentin sighed, it all sounded so far-fetched. Perhaps it didn't matter? Whatever they did with the recording, did it really make a difference? He stared at the position and wondered whether the answer might lie in the pawn structure. Maybe it's a simple weakness? he thought. Maybe there isn't any obvious tactical advantage. Maybe it's strategical?

His office door opened slowly. The Huge Texan popped his large head around the door. He held his hand up to his ear as if answering a telephone and nodded. Quentin cupped the mouthpiece in his hand then held the phone up toward the Texan as if to ask him, ironically, if he wanted to make a call. The Texan retreated.

"Who is this young man?"

"I'm told he's he best," said Alex.

"The best what?"

"The best. The best there's ever been, best there ever was, ever will be. I have it on good authority. He put his life at risk to escape. He was smuggled into this country. He's illegal. That's why I need you. Mr. Walker, Yang Li is quite simply the most accomplished musician the human race has ever produced."

"I thought you didn't like music?"

"Well, you know, I don't especially. But I have it on good authority."

"What authority?"

Alex knew this was going nowhere. It was time to end the conversation. Time to reel him in.

"Never mind. I was given your name as the best in the business, that's why we're talking now. I have other... names I use to assess this kid. And I have other names that got him here at great expense to me and my associates. This boy is the real thing. That is all you need to know for now. If you've heard his music and you don't agree there could be any possibility of that being the case then let me know now. I value your opinion because I know you're the best in your field. Is this boy the best pianist you've ever heard?"

"I wouldn't say he was the best but I've only heard a few pieces, and the recording..."

"Never mind the recording. Is he a virtuoso or not?"

"Yes, certainly he's a virtuoso. He has an astonishing technique. Quite astonishing."

"Well, there you are then. Look, take a little time to decide what you want to do. I need to know whether you want to get on board or not. We need to launch his career in the West. He's in danger you know. We absolutely must keep this under wraps until we're ready to unleash him on the world. It may be a matter of life or death."

"Life or death?"

"Yes. Yang Li's life or death. He was being groomed for great things as you might imagine. If they get to him before we provide full exposure, and hopefully provide asylum, he's a goner. This is serious stuff Mr. Walker. I understand if you don't want to get involved."

"I need to hear him play. I need to hear him play, right here in front of me. In my office."

Alex didn't hesitate. At least he could buy some time. They'd just have to think of something. Walker thought he was a virtuoso. That was enough for him. He'd almost forgotten why he was even on the phone. Walker's words danced and danced around in his head. A virtuoso! He was a virtuoso!

"Certainly. Of course. Can I get back to you on this? It may take a little time."

"Yes, call me." Walker heard a pack of NARC executives thundering past his office, their voices vying for position in another inane conversation. "Please," he said, with more desperation than he could manage to mask. "Please, don't take too long."

"No fear. We'll arrange something soon enough. Goodbye Mr. Walker."

"Mm."

"He thinks I'm a virtuoso! He thinks I'm a virtuoso!" Alex punched the air. He knelt beside Laura (who'd spent the whole conversation lying on the floor). She hadn't told him, but she'd been dreading the phone call herself. She had no idea that he could handle it so well. He hugged her so tightly; she had to almost fight to get him off her.

"So, what now?"

"I have to get my new Joanna finished. We have to get some more tunes together."

"What did he say?"

"He wants to hear Yang Li. He wants to hear him in his office."

"He wants to hear him play in his office?"

"Must have a piano in his office. Must be a big office."

"Alex," Laura's smiled disappeared, she looked serious, pained, as if she were trying to talk to someone suffering from amnesia. "Who is Yang Li?"

"Elliot. Elliot's Yang Li."

"Elliot can play piano?"

"No. Well, a little bit I suppose. Doesn't matter. He thinks I'm a virtuoso."

"No, he thinks Yang Li is a virtuoso. There is no Yang Li."

"Elliot's Yang Li. No biggie, he can play guitar instead."

"Guitar?"

"Sure. Why not? Elliot's one of the best guitarists in the world. It'll work."

"He wants to hear Yang Li play piano, so Elliot will play guitar?"

"Yes. It came to me in a flash. Elliot can play guitar instead."

"I am lost."

"As long as the wee shite keeps his gob shut we've got a chance."

"Chance. Alex, I don't…"

"He wants a virtuoso. That's what we'll give him. We'll give him a virtuoso. A real, live virtuoso. It can't not work." Alex planted a large, wet kiss on her forehead. He hugged her again. "This is going to work."

Elliot arrived. It took Alex about thirty seconds to relay the whole conversation with Walker. Elliot looked at Laura after Alex had declared, for the fourth time, that Walker thought he was a virtuoso. Laura could see that Elliot was thinking exactly the same thing as her. Maybe Elliot could bring him back to earth; get some sense out of him? Laura felt no compulsion whatever to pour cold water on Alex. It was good to see him so happy. For the first time in his life his music had received affirmation. His scant piano skills were incapable of attracting much more than the odd lukewarm compliment. Elliot thought it best to let Alex dream a little before inviting him back into reality. "So, he thought you were a virtuoso eh? Maybe this guy hasn't got the ear you think he has. I mean, let's face it, it was a loada shite, no?"

Alex, unusually lost for words, grabbed Elliot's shoulders and gave him a hug.

"This guy really is starved for compliments," said Elliot before pushing Alex off. "So, what now maestro? When we gonna see this guy? Do you think I can learn the complete piano repertoire in time?" He winked at Laura.

Alex was still flying. "Fuck the piano. We don't need the piano. You can play guitar for him. He thinks you can play everything. Guitar, piano, violin, tuba."

"Now that you mention it, did you lose your mind telling him that I can play the tuba? What's that about? Who plays the tuba?"

"Why not? Don't let Skuggs catch you putting the tuba down."

"He's an exception. I make an exception for him. It's all so…" Elliot fought to find the right word. "Ludicrous. I mean, why not just piano?"

"Why not not just piano?" said Alex. He plumped himself down on the sofa then leapt up as if he'd sat on a hotplate. "People never believe me when I'm telling the truth, but when I lie, they do, and when I tell huge, massive, pork pies they seem to swallow it more easily. I think that's a universal truth, no?" He looked to Laura and Elliot for affirmation of his philosophical burp, but none came. They simply stared at him, waiting for the punch line; waiting for him to come down to earth and rediscover the mountain of self-doubt that defined him. "Don't you think? Isn't that why religion is so successful? I mean, if you just go around saying that you like the philosophy of some geezer that lived a couple of thousand years ago, it's really not that exciting, nobody would bother too much about it; it would be a marginal activity. But if you claim the guy is the son of God, or that he got the complete truth of everything dictated to him in a desert, or he sat under a tree for nine years and then knew everything, isn't that better? For following, I mean?"

"I'm not following you, I'm afraid. Got any food?"

Laura took the opportunity to escape Alex's fallout. She loved that he was so happy, but it made her nervous that he was too happy. She was glad Elliot was here to catch him when he fell.

"I make some sandwiches, yes?"

"Oh, Laura, I'm in love. You are as wonderful as you are beautiful," said Elliot. He hadn't eaten a thing in almost two days, and even before that his appetite had waned considerably. Over the years he believed he'd trained his stomach to expect less food, not because of some fad diet or for health reasons, it was more that he couldn't be bothered cooking or going to the shops; he never had much money anyway and preferred to save what he had for his occasional trips to the pub. On cue, his stomach released a groan worthy of a third-rate horror movie.

"He agrees," said Elliot, interpreting for his digestive system. He sat on Alex's big armchair—the one Skuggs always tried to claim—he gripped the arms of the chair tightly and prepared for the world of pain that always followed the ironic little tunes spouted by his gastrointestinal tract. He began to sweat in anticipation of the ten minutes or so of extreme discomfort he was about to suffer. "What you gonna do about Domeboy? You know, you really should get yer arse into the Academy during daylight hours sometime and have a look at the kind of damage your girlfriend is capable of."

"Fuck McNabb." The very sound of his name was a bitter intrusion into Alex's triumph. "I'll deal with McNabb in time." His euphoria deflated ever so slightly. "Maybe I can set Laura on him? Maybe this time with a baseball bat instead of a bow?"

The pain was starting to hit home but Elliot refused to bend. The only clue—if anyone had been looking—to the agony he was suffering, was a hardly perceptible grunt at the start of each utterance. "He is gonna chuck you out. You do know that, don't you? The little fart has already started a clearout. You're never gonna get your precious degree." His legs raised themselves involuntarily a few inches off the floor—he wouldn't give in.

"Fuck the degree," said Alex. "This is better. I lied about the degree. I lied to myself. It was just an excuse I used to cover up my mediocrity."

"Didn't work then. Nobody was fooled." Elliot crossed his legs the way a television interviewer or a supermodel might. It was slow and deliberate; one leg hanging limp over the other, not crossed the way he would normally cross them, with one leg splayed across the other, informal, natural. The foot of the hanging leg made an acute angle as another wave of pain flowed from his midriff; tightening every muscle from the tip of his toes to the base of his neck. His eyes watered, he dug his nails into the arm of the chair the way he'd taken to digging his nails into the palms of his hands, but this time the agony was of an altogether more immediate variety.

Alex remained oblivious. He would have been unaware of Elliot's plight whether he'd been ordained a virtuoso or not; Alex could recognize a voice after years, he could detect the slightest hint of irony, or snobbery, or general smartarsism like they were aural neon signs, flashing and blinding and obvious, but he was completely impervious to the pain of others, whether psychological—as in Elliot's deteriorating grasp on reality—or physical, as suffered at this very moment by the musical genius sat right there on Skuggs's favourite chair.

Laura wasn't so insensitive. "Something wrong?" she asked as she handed him a plate of sandwiches. "You do not look good."

"Haven't eaten in a while. Me stomach wants revenge." Elliot tried to laugh but it came out the way an old lady might titter self-consciously at a semi-registered joke. He reached for the plate but doubled over too far. Laura's worried expression was a giveaway that he wasn't managing to hide the wave of agony that was coursing through him. Alex might as well have been somewhere else; he was deep in thought, his expression changing every few seconds. Rigor mortis would set in before Alex would notice the pain of another; especially when life was treating him so well.

Laura smacked Alex hard around the back of his head. He looked all of nine-years old, rubbing his head, feelings hurt, "What's up?" he pouted.

"Don't you see your friend? He suffers."

"Sup wi' you?" he asked Elliot grudgingly.

"Nothing. Really," croaked Elliot. "Sore belly. Some food and I'll be fine." His reassurance coincided with a waning of the sickly, poisonous messages propagating through his nervous system like Morse code spoken in low frequency pulse. "I'm fine," he said. "Comes and goes." He paused as if mentally searching for the crest of the next pulse that might envelope him. "Really, I think it's gone."

"Could be cancer man. We should get you to hospital."

"Alex!" Laura punched Alex in the chest with such force he landed on the sofa.

"What?"

"You are a cruel boy." Her inability to find the right words in English increased her frustration.

"I'm sorry," Alex said to Laura. She motioned to Elliot. "Sorry Elliot," he said, rubbing his neck with one hand and his chest with the other.

"S'okay guys. Don't fight over me. I just don't take care of meself. Me own fault." His regular smile returned. "We haven't all got screamingly gorgeous girlfriends to look after us you know."

"Maybe we should to take you to hospital? Maybe it is best?"

"Nn, nn, no, no, no, no, no." said Elliot, as if demonstrating some hidden rhythmic guitar technique. "That's not going to happen until I'm dead."

"You might be dead if you don't find out what's wrong." Alex flinched as soon as he said it, realizing he was completely on the wrong tack. "Maybe you should go to the doctor? You really can't go on abusing your system like this," he continued. He darted a glance at Laura, but he was genuine at last, starting to realize that there may be something serious going on in Elliot's neglected physiology. "Make an appointment with the doctor. I'll chum you."

"Let's change the subject shall we? If I ever regress into childhood and need a chum you'll be the first to know."

Sure enough, Elliot was returning to normal. Maybe it was just a stomach-ache? thought Alex, before submerging himself back into his fantasies. Laura jerked a thumb at him and shook her head. Elliot laughed. "Let him dream a bit," he said.

# Twenty-Two

McNabb had it all worked out. He'd even called ahead while he was still in his hospital bed to make sure that little notices were posted on the boards. He wanted to see some people, mostly students but there were a couple of lecturers' names thrown in to add a little drama to the mix. Wags had already christened it 'the roll of the dead'. Nobody spent too long in front of the boards since the names were posted; passers by betrayed insider knowledge in the briskness of their step and even innocents, perhaps searching for an exam schedule or pertinent note from their teacher, took care not to loiter lest they suffered infection from mere proximity to such foreboding.

He sat himself down behind the desk and mentally measured the ratio of the height of the two piles. It seemed about right. Folders on the right were students, maybe ten or so, and on the left were the lecturers. The students would be fun, but the lecturers were the real delicacy. Expelling students meant a few tears, a bit of acrimony, but they could always run back to mummy to get their arses wiped. Firing lecturers was much more satisfying. They'd have to look for another job. They'd have to explain why they were looking for another job. The wonderful thing about people is that they don't trust each other. That means that prospective employers always want references. They can grill a candidate for hours or days but they don't believe a word unless they see pieces of paper written by someone they've never met telling them that the candidate is worthy.

McNabb would never give anyone a bad reference; such an overt display could arouse doubt and even end up with the employer siding with the candidate. No, McNabb would provide references that looked like he was trying his damnedest to look for the best in the candidate. Employers could read between the lines that he was a fair man, too kind to tell the truth. The candidate could suffer without ever knowing why the jobs slipped from their grasp. Even lovelier still; each time the candidate applied for a new job then toughed out the various indignities of the selection processes, McNabb would get to track their progress. Nobody hires anybody without a reference, and they always believe references; it never occurs to anyone that the referee might be anything else than competent and honest. This strange quirk of human nature was yet another sign that the universe was finally responding to him. It was all falling into place.

He lifted the pile of student folders to gauge and enjoy the weight, to feel the weight of their lives in his hands. The first run; the first ten would be students with heavy folders—plenty of reasons, plenty of justification, a few bad grades, maybe some tardiness and, of course, best of all the failure to realize the potential promised on acceptance? Nobody could argue that they were talented when the very individual entrusted with the power to decide such matters had to face the truth; that he had misjudged their latent abilities—not the fault of the student but his own fault? That they would ostensibly suffer for his feigned failure of judgment was hardly likely to be spotted at all, let alone challenged by the very people thus adjudged.

He carefully patted the folders into a neat pile and turned his attention to the two thick folders. He opened the first; Ingles: a post-modern hermaphrodite without a whiff of success to offer in defence. If only these recent wonderful events had happened a few months ago he might have reclaimed the substantial donation inexplicably offered anonymously with instructions to be spent at her behest? He baulked at the six-figure sum she'd spent on God knows what. Perhaps he could recoup a little of the money? Maybe a second-hand dealer, or another institution would give him something? Never mind, the pleasure of telling her he was ridding the place of her damnable contraptions would be priceless in itself. Perhaps he could even start out informing her of his regret that her laboratory would have to be closed? He could listen to her pleading, defending her rights as if the Academy were one of her lesbian causes instead of his very own property? Then, when she reached a state of exhaustion at his kind intransigence, he could point out that without the laboratory to take her time, she would no longer be required? He could ask about her students, in the full knowledge that she had but one, then express his regret that there wasn't a damn thing he could do about it. After all, if she'd taught counterpoint or history or piano, wouldn't he at least have an opportunity to save her bacon? But no, there was nothing he could do; it was out of his hands.

Ingles was a kind of enemy; she represented a musical form for which he had little time and a sexual orientation from which (outside of the impossible possibility of banging a couple of dykes) he recoiled, but Baker was another matter altogether; he wasn't any kind of enemy, he was a real enemy. Baker was the students' pet. Baker was the lecturer they all loved. Baker was the type of teacher who ran around declaring that music was 'fun', as if he was its sole proprietor and final arbiter. He figured that Baker wouldn't put up much of a fight though. Baker was an alcoholic with a conscience; any suggestion that his addiction was harming his students' musical education would probably be enough to send him flopping onto his own sword. McNabb's spies had made it known that Baker's lectures had become sparse and surreal; putting a record on, falling asleep, then a bit of inebriated mumbling, did not, in McNabb's opinion, qualify as education.

McNabb had a feeling that Baker would be the first to take his punishment; and he was. While the rest of the victims sat at home knocking their knees together or pacing up and down, constructing outcomes based on their worst fears and paranoid suspicions, Baker, goody-two-shoes to the last, spotted his name on the board of death and immediately shuffled into McNabb's office, apparently oblivious to the fate that lay in store.

"You wanted to see me Mr. McNabb?" As usual, he looked dishevelled, his hair was greasy—not so rare for an academic— he was clean shaven but his face bore the scars of a razor applied by a man who drinks; tiny pock marks distributed more or less evenly around the cheeks and chin with a fresh red dot here and there, like the surface of the moon viewed from a distance and spattered with flecks of crimson paint. His button-down shirt was not ironed—the mark of the unmarried academic—and his deodorant was pungent enough to suggest he was hiding something about the direction of his life.

"I'll get to the point Baker." McNabb loved to call people by their surnames; it reminded him of boarding school. After enduring years of bullying from older boys (and compounded by the tacit collusion of indifferent parents who refused to hear or believe) he had finally risen to the exalted position of prefect; a position which bestowed altogether too much power upon teenage boys starved of affection and nurtured the ravenous suspicion that developing psychoses were positive and healthy attributes for men-about-to-be. "Your work isn't up to scratch."

McNabb tried not to smile as the barb ripped into Baker's jugular. He let him bleed for a few seconds then absolved himself with a single word.

"Drink."

Already defeated, Baker hung his head in his hands. "I've let them down."

"Yes." It was intoxicating, overwhelming; almost as good as sex. It was like watching one of those naked girls who dance at the peep shows in Soho that he'd creep into when in London. McNabb put another coin in the slot. "They trust you. They hang on to your every word. They look forward…" he corrected himself; best not to let any light into the conversation. "They *looked* forward to your lectures. But you don't give lectures anymore, do you?"

"No." Baker hugged himself like an addict itching for peace.

"I've been told you just play records now?"

Baker lashed out, "There's so much crap… so much shit." McNabb raised an eyebrow; enough to instantaneously send Baker back into a pool of self-pity. He tried to finish his defence but now it would hardly even qualify as an apology. "We frighten them. We teach them that the Greats are gods to be worshipped not artists to be savoured. It's worse than religion; we have the evidence."

"I'm sure it all makes sense to you," McNabb said with the air of a loving family member consigning an unfortunate sibling to bedlam.

"Too much analysis," continued Baker. This was rather entertaining; as if Baker thought he were in some bloody Russian play; the whole world would know he was right, that he was a sane man in an insane world, no matter that he was for the Gulag whatever he said. "We forget about the sound; the joy. We tear it all apart as if any of it could exist without the rest of the universe to complete the meaning." McNabb was lost. Another bloody poet, he thought. "I wanted to be pure. No, not me, I wanted the experience to be pure; the music." Now he was babbling. McNabb watched him the way a mean child might watch an ad hoc dismemberment of a Daddy-Long-Legs. "How could I teach anyone about Bach, Beethoven, Mozart, Mahler?"

"Indeed," offered McNabb.

"Who am I to presume?"

"Indeed."

"I thought I was helping, extracting myself from the equation, the experiment, standing back, letting them hear the whole truth, without editorial."

"You were drunk and too lazy to prepare lectures?" said McNabb. It was almost time to go in for the kill. There is only so much entertainment to be had from wounded prey.

"Yes. I suppose… yes."

"The need to rationalize?"

"Yes."

"You have been a much-valued member of staff here. This really is a tragedy. You will be missed."

"Missed?" Baker was suddenly sober, as if McNabb had thrown cold water over him. He emerged from his introspective musings at the shock of losing his job. "Missed?"

McNabb had already extracted so many varieties of pleasure from this experience he could hardly hope that Baker actually believed he wasn't being thrown out, consigned to the scrap heap; punished for his neglect and incompetence? But it sounded as if this was a shock to him. Could Baker really think he wanted to help him out of his difficulties?

This indeed was a pleasant surprise.

McNabb looked at his watch. He had no pressing appointments. He had no interest in the time of day. He would have been more than happy to sit there watching Baker fall to pieces but there was something gratifying about cutting it short; something like denial, like premature withdrawal, like eating half a bar of chocolate when you craved the lot. Looking at his watch would also remind Baker of his new worthlessness; that there was no point in giving speeches or feeling sorry for himself in this place. Watch checking was a strategy employed by presidents and monarchs and middle managers alike; a simple gesture that sets status in stone. No point in dragging it out until it became a bore.

McNabb sprang from behind his desk and offered Baker the door. "See the bursar. He'll work out all the details." As Baker dragged himself, half dazed, out of the room, McNabb gave his parting shot, "Good luck." Then he closed the door. He took Baker's folder and set it on the desk beside the other two piles of prospective clearoutees in the hope that the sight alone of the three piles might inject a little anguish into the proceedings.

By the time Ingles arrived to take her punishment McNabb had already seen to four students. He imagined the commotion going on outside as one after another of the names on the board emerged from his office with watery eyes and a hangdog deportment.

The students hadn't been much fun at all. A silly little violinist who would jerk then scuttle into the corner every time his hand crept over one of her tiny breasts; she'd jump straight up in the air when he brushed his crotch—usually with a well-tempered erection fighting to free its Y-fronted cage—against her plummy young cheeks. He always said that teaching kept his hand in, but it was too tedious to have to go through all the drama; too many stories to concoct, too many unbelievable excuses for his advances. She was played out. Ejecting her now meant that any ridiculous stories advanced on her part would be obvious attempts at revenge. He'd tried it on with every single one of his female string students but he'd tried to fondle this one every time he was alone with her.

He could hardly remember the first time his silent fantasies had got the better of him. Stuck in a room with nubile young things for hours on end, it was hardly a surprise that a normal, healthy man with a normal, healthy sexual appetite might lose himself from time to time? But he certainly remembered the aftermath of his first advance; he couldn't sleep, he couldn't think, gripped with terror, she would surely spill the beans and he'd be fired, he'd be tried and sentenced and spend the rest of his life in prison getting buggared by ruffians and teaching violin to sissies?

But it never happened. He was free. As far as he knew, she didn't breathe a word. And that was the way it always was; none of them ever reported him. He wasn't even careful to make his advances ambiguous, open to interpretation. And just in case any of them got any ideas then chucking one of them out would send a message to the others as well: This is what you get for being frigid.

The only one who ever responded was his wife, a mature amateur violin student with little talent and irresistible little mammaries. She had resisted and teased; she almost drove him crazy, she was the only one who fell for his theories of diaphragm control (he'd press himself against their backs while fondling an area a clear foot below the diaphragm; like he was dancing a tango but without the dancing); she played the game all the way to the local registry office, then the game was over; for him.

The rest of the students were male. No fun at all. Little shits who'd been rude to him or worse, had elicited a laugh or two at his expense. See how smart they are now without a future, he thought as a cheeky little trombone player burst into tears right in front of him.

But Ingles would be fun. She'd put up a fight. She'd rant and rave and scream on and on about lesbian rights and that he was a monster, a bigot, and he'd pretend he was hurt by her accusations. She'd demand a review in front of the board of governors but she'd turn up in one of her bloody three piece suits with the wide lapels and her cropped hair and her five o' clock shadow and her bloody mixed up chromosomes ranting at a bunch of middle-aged do-gooders who probably hated lesbians more than he did.

But it didn't happen that way. Ingles listened, stony-faced, to McNabb's speech about how the laboratory simply had to go. He waited and waited for a reaction. Ingles just sat and stared at him. Then he thumbed through her file and talked about her only having a single student and how that wasn't enough for him to make a case to the board, and he finished with a flourish about how it was out of his hands and how terribly sorry he was. She didn't flinch for an instant. She didn't even ask if he was finished. She cocked her head a little, taking care not to inject irony into the gesture then, when it was clear he was done, she left.

For the first time since Todd had magically appeared at a choral rehearsal wearing women's clothing he felt doubt worm its way into the back of his mind. He didn't spend a second trying to figure why the dyke had given him the silent treatment, but somewhere something was wrong, something didn't add up. He wasn't about to waste any time trying to divine how the mind of a lesbo might work, but while he would deny it even to himself, her silence had planted something inside of him.

"We need to talk." Todd was deep inside his thoughts when she whispered it into his ear. Todd had watched Baker drag himself into the bursar's office little more than an hour before and it was clear what was going on. McNabb was finally making his mark, showering despair over anyone who dared defy him. That Ingles was a victim was no surprise. She was intelligent and strong and blessed with the soul of an artist. McNabb had to get rid of her in case the board got the idea that she'd be the perfect candidate for the principal's seat.

"We have to talk," she repeated as if he hadn't heard.

"McNabb?" he whispered.

"Who else? This is ridiculous. The little twerp is throwing everyone out. He thinks he's thrown me out. Wanker."

"Later? I don't want to lose my seat. My little vigil, you know. It's enough to annoy him and I won't move unless he gets the police to throw me out."

"Come to my lab." She stood up straight. "Why the hell am I whispering?" she asked (more of herself than Todd). "My lab later," she roared so that anyone within fifty yards could hear. "Look forward to it." She marched up the stairs like a sergeant major on official business. She got to the turn before the first landing and gave Todd a cheeky wink. For the first time since his wife's death Todd felt complete; it was only a moment but it was enough to remind him of life, enough to send hope pumping through his veins. For the rest of the day he smiled at everyone entering and leaving the bursars office; he'd been doing that for days but more in defiance than as an expression of emotion. Now he was beaming, his whole face alight. He had no idea how he and Ingles would shape to do battle with McNabb but it didn't matter. He was up off the ground, out of the gutter and no longer alone.

# Twenty–Three

"I'm not fucking going. He can go fuck himself," said Alex finally, in response to Elliot's taunting, and with a couple of added expletives to let Elliot know that he probably *was* going to go to McNabb to take his punishment. Laura had stuffed Elliot with so much food he was fit to burst. The agony that had torn through his stomach then propagated through his nervous system was long gone. Laura was gripped by the idea that he was suffering from some form of malnutrition; a malady, she suspected, suffered by many more students than people suspected. Elliot made no plea to disabuse her of this theory. Apart from being almost criminally attractive, she was a fine cook; the kind that can 'rustle up' something from whatever is at hand and make it into a feast fit for kings and emperors, she was too much for Alex to enjoy without being reminded of the rest of his life.

"Maybe he won't chuck you out?" said Elliot. "Maybe he wants you to put a computer music course together for him?"

"Stop it Elliot. Little shit."

Elliot sat back to enjoy the feeling of well-being respite from pain (followed by an enormous meal) can bring.

"Let's get down to Quentin Walker's office and see this thing through," said Alex. Both Laura and Elliot seemed surprised at this.

"Thought you were gonna get better samples? Better performance and all that? What about all the stuff I gave you? Been bleedin meself for your music. Gonna pour it all down the shiter?"

"No."

Alex felt like saying "Yes, I am as a matter of fact. He responded to *my* music. *My* music before you got involved. *My* music was enough. We don't need your stinkin genius." But he didn't. "No, you're going to play guitar for him. We're going to go to his office and not play the piano. You're going to play guitar."

"Fine," said Elliot looking at Laura as if Alex had lost his mind. "Maybe he'll get it that he *has* discovered the greatest living musician and he'll hire me instead and kick your arse out of the door like you deserve. When I tell him…"

Alex cut him off violently. "You're not speaking. You say nothing. You agreed to do this. You're not going to make a fool of me in front of this guy. I've worked for this all my life and you're not going to turn it into one of your stupid games. If you're not going to do what I ask on this then tell me now, cause if you blow the gaff deliberately I'll…"

"What? You'll what?" Elliot was still laughing but laughter was never an indication of his mood.

"Just let me know now. Okay. McNabb's going to sling me out. I'm not you. I'm not one of the golden boys. When I fall into a bucket of shit I come out stinking. I don't have anything else. All I have are three-year old programming skills that I can get a crappy low-paid coding job with. I want to work in music. I need music to be my life. I can't go back to that. Do you understand Elliot? I can't go back to that life anymore and I can't do what you do. I won't have a degree, and I'm not a very good musician."

"Don't compare yourself to me. Don't be too hard on yourself." The look Alex threw Elliot told him he'd better at least try to explain himself. "Seriously, you shouldn't compare yourself to me, it's just chance that I'm here and you're here at the same time, and that perhaps we get on a bit better than I normally get on with people. Don't compare yourself with me in the musical talent department. I know you think I'm arrogant beyond anything you could even imagine—and I surely am— but that's only because everyone around me keeps denying the reality in front of them. When... if..." he corrected himself, something new to Alex, and certainly new to Elliot, he pulled a very strange face, as if he'd swallowed something unfamiliar. "You're a good musician Alex." Alex raised an eyebrow and looked to Laura to make sure he wasn't imagining Elliot's compliment. This wasn't what Elliot set out to say. When Elliot spoke it always came out as if he'd already had the idea, written the book, and closed it, it was always as if he were half reading and half improvising along a well-trodden path. Everything, every subject, every utterance somehow came back to him and his talent, it was as if he thought the whole world only existed for him.

"Elliot, if a tree falls down in the forest, does it make a sound if you're not there?" asked Alex.

"Well, I can see that you're becoming in tune with my inner being," said Elliot.

"Fuck you and your inner being. Are you going to do this with me or not? Are you going to do what I want you to do or are you going to go off half-cocked all over the place just to show this guy that you're the new Mozart? Of course, you haven't written a single tune but why bother with evidence when you know what you know? Christ, I just want you to keep your gob shut for a few minutes and play a tune on the guitar. I know you can play and I know that shutting your trap for a few minutes is hard but can you, will you do it?"

"I'll do it. I'll do it. I'll do it."

"Will you follow instructions?" asked Laura.

"Absolutely sir." Elliot saluted, then felt embarrassed.

"Are you a friend or not?" she asked. "In my culture, people die for their friends."

"Steady now," said Elliot. "Let's not go losing our perspective here."

Laura planted her hands on her hips the way she did when she was about to sort someone out. "You think I joke? I am not Alex. There is too much you must know about friends." The tips of her fingers almost met around her tiny waist. "I get tired of listening to who is good and who is bad. It is music. Who cares?" She flung her arms into the air dramatically, giving Elliot a start. Alex felt warm all over. His girlfriend was defending his honour. She was fighting for him, sort of. He hoped she'd give Elliot some of those tungsten rod pokes in the shoulder to make him see sense, but instead she decided to blame the British. "This country. This country is full of jealousy. This place is full of horrible people. Where is your culture?"

"I'm not Scottish," said Elliot. "Chinese Liverpudlian, citizen of the planet earth and all that."

"Bloody hell," said Alex, thinking aloud.

"Are you taking piss from me?" she shrieked. Then she jammed the fingers of her bowing arm onto Elliot's chest. If Elliot had been sitting on a chair equipped with castors he might have had a chance, Newton's laws would have come to the rescue and he'd simply have glided back a couple of feet, but he was in Skuggs's chair, the big chair; his chest bore the full force of her mighty blow. She must have grazed his diaphragm; he let out a breathy exclamation point then sat motionless, his mouth blowing imaginary smoke rings; he had an expression fit for a slab in a fishmonger's shop.

"Jeezis Laura, look what you've done," said Alex trying not to laugh. "Aren't you supposed to nip him in the neck now or something? You know, get his blood flowing again?"

"This country!" she said then rushed into the bedroom to leave Elliot in purple-faced asphyxia. Alex couldn't figure why she had a beef with this country or why Elliot seemed to be its representative here in this room, and while he took some illicit pleasure in Laura's rather extreme strategy to shut Elliot up about himself for a while, Elliot's face was turning black. He looked like he might die. Laura slammed the door hard behind her; it was plain that if Elliot was to die then she wasn't bothered. Alex found himself wondering, almost seriously, whether this is what she meant when she said that friends die for each other in her culture.

He had to do something. He slapped Elliot's back. Nothing happened. Still his mouth opened and closed with the forlorn rubato of a landed fish.

"Bloody hell Laura!" Alex shouted, perhaps more as a confirmation that he was a witness to the murder than any real hope that Laura could pull him back from the brink.

Laura charged out of the bedroom. She headed straight for Elliot and poked him again; just as hard and as seriously as the first time, then she disappeared back into the bedroom. Elliot made a face at Alex that somehow contained all the surprise and anguish in the world. If he had been watching this happen to someone else, Elliot would have been mightily entertained. Now Alex really did believe that she'd meant it. That she really was quite prepared to kill him. Alex slapped him on the back again as if the mere effort itself might be enough to bring him back. It was becoming obvious that Elliot needed the kiss of life, not quite the way a drowning victim might but he certainly needed to get his diaphragm blasted back to its proper shape and function. Alex looked at Elliot's face and the thought of planting his lips over Elliot's made him shudder.

"Laura?" cried Alex with enough real desperation to fire her once again out of the bedroom like a greyhound out of a trap. Elliot's eyes widened with terror as she lunged toward him to administer the third and final deathblow.

She planted her mouth over Elliot's mouth and blew like Skuggs doing a cadenza, then she wiped her mouth and spat the way cowboys spit after they've sucked the poison from the rattlesnake-bitten arse of a saddle buddy.

"This is the last thing I do for you," she said, and wagged her finger at him as if the last three minutes had been a gift; a precious lesson more difficult to administer than to learn.

"Okay," Elliot croaked meekly. Alex could hardly believe his ears. Laura had actually tamed him? Somehow, her violent attack and subsequent good-Samaritanism had propelled Elliot into a state of heretofore unknown acquiescence.

Alex sat on the edge of the sofa to watch Elliot's recovery like he was watching a scientific experiment. Was Elliot simply scared shitless of another attack or had she shown him the light? Had his soul left his body and was it replaced during his black-face period by another, more amiable, soul? Was he taking the piss and if not, would the experience forever scupper his natural tendency to laugh at everything and anything outside of himself? Was he even the same person?

Laura acted as if nothing at all had happened. It was as if the whole episode were wiped from her memory. She fetched him a glass of water and sat on the arm of the sofa and rubbed his neck gently as if she were still treating his prior stomach affliction with a little tenderness. Alex observed them both like he was analysing the output of a non-linear sub-routine; the output bore no correlation whatever to the input. The two of them

might have been a pair of loving siblings, not the smart-arsed
Scouser and the Latino bombshell with the temper of an ornery
camel that he knew them to be.

"I'm made up with this," said Elliot, admiring himself in the
full-length mirror. "Mao Tse fucking Tung." He did a couple
of turns like he thought he was modelling on the catwalk.
"What you gonna wear?"

Alex stepped out of the changing room wearing a heavy,
dark blue pinstripe suit, a white shirt and a yellow tie.

"What's this?" Elliot asked as if he thought Alex would be
wearing the same uniform as himself.

"Armani," said Alex. He fixed the cuffs. "Damn, I'll have
to buy bloody cufflinks as well. If I buy cheapos he'd probably
notice. Damn."

"Armani!" cried Elliot. "You get to wear Armani, and I'm
a fucking soldier in the red army?"

"I'm the lawyer, remember? You're the virtuoso. You're the
Chinese virtuoso smuggled out of China."

"But I'm not in China now, am I? Why wouldn't I get to
the West and develop a taste for expensive designer suits? I look
ridiculous."

"Ten seconds ago you were made up with it."

"I look ridiculous."

"No more than usual."

"You're a lawyer and I'm Chinese?"

"You don't think I'd pass for a lawyer?"

"I'm Chinese but do we have to bludgeon the guy with it?
Is he a bleedn moron?"

"Why don't I play the Chinese virtuoso and you can play
the lawyer then? How's that? That's not too obvious is it?"

"Yer plan's a load of shite. It's full of holes."

"Well, it's all I've got. I'm open to suggestions. Can I remind you that I'm not rich? That I have to pay for all this?" Alex produced two plane tickets.

"We're flying? We're flying to London? We don't have to get the bus? You're such a cheap bastard I thought I was gonna have to pay for me own bus fare."

"We're flying. I want to get down there and back on the same day."

"We're not going to Soho? I fancied a peep show. And I wouldn't mind parading round Chinatown in me new suit."

"So you like the suit again?"

"Snot bad. I can live with it, for a good cause."

When Alex called Walker to arrange the meeting he'd planned to make the call short. Walker was already sold on the idea of meeting with them—hearing Elliot play—he expected more questions, more opportunities to blow the gaff, but Walker simply said he wanted to hear him, that was it; the call lasted less than ten seconds. It was all arranged. Tomorrow they'd be in his office telling the most ridiculous bunch of lies to an intelligent, successful producer. Alex was terrified, but he was always terrified before a performance, and surely this was no different? As soon as he got there, he'd be fine. As soon as the performance started he'd forget himself.

"I look like one of the Beatles," said Elliot. "You think I need a hat?"

Alex didn't think he looked like one of the Beatles and had no idea why Elliot would think such a thing. Elliot looked ridiculous. He looked like a Westerner's idea of a Chinese man living in communist China circa 1965. Maybe Walker did indeed have to be a moron to fall for it? Maybe the plan was full of holes? Maybe Alex just wanted to get in front of Walker to extract more compliments on his music? This was the first time he'd ever got any feedback outside the usual 'sounds good' type of comment from friends aware that he was starved of such things. Walker was a real 'ear'. He was the guy who really could tell the difference. We can all watch a foot race and tell who won but Walker could watch each runner individually, without any reference or benchmark and still tell who won. It had to mean something?

"We're getting a taxi to the airport right?"

"Of course."

"So, the plan is that we go in and I play guitar?"

"Yup."

"I have to keep me gob shut?"

"That's it. Keep yer gob shut and play. That's all you have to do. I'll do the talking."

"What you gonna say?"

"No idea."

"Christ you've got it all worked out then?"

"He wants to hear you play piano. He's not going to. He's going to hear you play guitar."

"This is fucking looney tunes."

"I suppose. In about a month I'll be going to job interviews and telling them I took three years out to do a music degree but I failed so can I please have a job doing something that I've grown to hate. If loony tunes is the best there is then it'll have to do. It's all I've got."

"Ah! Not true. You have me."

"My secret weapon."

"Really, you whiteys are all the same. Deep inside you're shit scared of us chinks cause we're smarter and faster, cause we work harder, we're better at business, our religions aren't dim-witted, we invented pasta and fireworks when you were little more than apes…"

"And you've all got little tiny winkies the size of my pin-kie." Alex crooked his pinkie.

"Exactly. You see what you want to see. You believe what you want to believe. We are all, all two billion of us, exactly the same."

"Two billion?"

"You counted some of us twice cause we look the same to you."

"You mean you think we have a chance with this?"

"No, I mean I'm hung like a bull. But your fido geezer with the supersonic ears, he's probably bought a Chinese meal or two, and maybe he's even thought about visiting the Great Wall. But he'll never know us. We're all Charlie Chan with a stringy moustache and David Carradine doing crap Kung Fu."

"You don't believe any of that."

"Nah, but you better hope he does cause yer plan's a load of shite. Are we going first class?"

Alex paid for the costumes in cash. When he was a programmer he thought he was the type of person who didn't care much about money. He was realizing that the only people who don't care much about money are people who have enough of it. Elliot and Skuggs thought he was a bottomless pit of money but his savings were disappearing fast. What seemed like a great mountain of wealth had diminished into a vanishing nest-egg. This had always been the plan; to use his life savings to cover his costs for three years, but somehow the reality of having blown almost everything, and now with nothing at the end of it, made him feel queasy.

"I'm going to see McNabb later. Take my punishment. Get my arse kicked out the door. Think I should get violent?"

"Nah, take Laura, she'll sort him out for you."

McNabb made him wait outside his office for half an hour. He didn't mind waiting. He knew exactly the course of his life for the next twenty-four hours; then everything would be up for grabs. If McNabb had given him the executioner's call before Laura and Skuggs had sent the tape and Walker had replied, he'd be on the verge of a breakdown. But none of it mattered anymore.

Mrs. Gibb provided enough entertainment to help pass the time. From the moment he sat down she became engaged in a wordless conversation between herself, Alex, and the door, behind which McNabb pretended to be too busy to administer his punishment. In-between deft flourishes at the computer keyboard she'd offer Alex a look of silent condolence, like he'd lost a loved one, then she'd snort at the door, then another pleading smile at Alex. He made sure to acknowledge each and every one of her gestures. He knew that in time McNabb would get around to replacing her and there wouldn't be anyone left to throw imaginary daggers at his door. With her departure the new order would be complete.

"Ah, Mr. Stone." McNabb was happy to see him. "Please, come in. Come in." He offered a seat. He was the perfect host; like one of those Nazi commandants from the movies. Alex half expected him to offer port and brandy snaps with a last request to give up the names of the spies before he faced the firing squad.

But McNabb didn't have the class of a make-believe Nazi commandant. All he had was a hard-on for injecting tiny miseries.

"This isn't working, is it?" The same strangulating phrase used by ten thousand supervisors when they get the chance to fire someone they don't like. Was this the best he could do? He'd been after Alex since the start; surely he had a better speech than this?

"What happened to your bonce?"

"Never mind that."

"Why not? I think it's interesting. You finally felt up someone who wasn't afraid of you. So she split your head open."

McNabb fondled his head the way a blind man might feel the contours of a face. He seemed somewhere else; his fingers traced the lines of the bandages, then he came to and gave him the stare. This was the stare that used to frighten him, but now, with his Egyptian Mummy's headgear, it just made him look ridiculous.

"What you staring at lumpy?"

"I think our business is finished here, don't you?"

"What business?"

"You're out," his face broke into a huge grin. "I'm expelling you."

"Well, maybe."

"No maybe about it. Goodbye."

"Well, you can expel me if you like, but I expect the police might think you expelled me because you sexually assaulted my girlfriend."

Alex leant over the table and gave him a goodbye slap on the head. "Calling you a wanker would be an insult to wankers worldwide. Goodbye." Alex left without leaving any room for a response. He felt quite proud of himself. He thought he was just going to sit there and take it but he'd fought back like Elliot. Well maybe not like Elliot, but at least he'd fought. Maybe spending so much time with him had rubbed off a little?

# Twenty-Four

It took Elliot no time at all to get into character. He hadn't spoken a single word since he donned his Mao Tse Tung outfit. This was a good sign. Alex couldn't be bothered speaking. Everything was a blur then there they were—in Quentin Walker's office—Elliot had made himself a minor attraction at the airport, in his uniform, bowing and smiling at people, he was already Yang Li, Asian virtuoso, without a word of English, spectacularly pleased to engage in an animated greetings ceremony with anyone who paid any attention.

Elliot plumped his guitar case down beside the two chairs parked in the middle of the room. Alex clung on to the ancient leather briefcase his parents had given him when he started work. He'd considered buying a new one but thought better of it; the suit was enough and the old briefcase would have to do.

The office was huge. It was more like a living room than an office. Leather sofas, big, welcoming easy chairs, bookcases that reached the ceiling. It was a strain to even tell what colour the walls were; so dense was the carpet of framed photographs that covered them. Elliot immediately went for a tour. There was a baby grand at the far end of the room, behind the rather modest desk that must have been Walker's. The desk was bare but for an expensive looking chess set with a little LCD that flashed. Alex's heart was almost beating out of his chest. Elliot went to the piano, opened the lid and played a couple of notes. Alex didn't react; too immersed in his own trepidation to notice. Elliot started to play chopsticks. He danced around to try to wake Alex from his trance.

Alex pinched the bridge of his nose in despair. He couldn't be bothered arguing with Elliot anymore. His energy was draining from him like water from a tap. If Elliot wanted to spoil it all with high jinx then he could go ahead and do it. Alex was dizzy with tension and almost too tired to complete the final lap.

Elliot took pity. He closed the piano lid and got drawn to the chessboard. Alex took out a handkerchief and tried to dry his hands for the inevitable handshake to come. He dabbed his forehead then regretted it; perhaps dabbing his forehead would remind his forehead to sweat? That was the way it was for musicians in front of an audience. Singers get shaky legs. Pianists and string players get shaky hands. Wind players get convulsive diaphragms. Alex resisted the urge to try to get hold of himself. He knew it would pass as soon as the performance started. Anyway, he thought, what's new about a sweaty lawyer? Maybe it would help?

Elliot stood like a statue, examining the chessboard for five minutes or so before the door opened and Walker entered.

"Apologies. Last-minute business." He grabbed Alex's hand and gave it a stiff jerk. Walker stared into his eyes. Alex stared back. He wasn't sure whether he was supposed to match the serious torque of Walker's grip. Handshake etiquette was one of the many subjects of which Alex had managed to remain completely ignorant in his lives as a software developer and half-baked musician.

"This is he?" said Walker cupping his elbow in his hand to provide a suitable leaning post for his cocked head.

"This is he," said Alex. Elliot was completely transfixed by something on the chessboard.

"I was very impressed by the tape you sent." Walker made toward Elliot. He seemed content to look for now, to size him up.

"It was a very bad recording. But it contained enough... I'm told." Alex reminded himself that he knew nothing whatever about music. He'd been so intent on making sure that Elliot didn't do anything stupid, he'd forgotten to eliminate the musician in himself.

Walker turned on him. "You look a little young to be a lawyer?"

"Thank you. I can see we're going to get on like a house on fire."

"I mean young to be so successful."

"Thanks again."

"Couldn't find your name anywhere. Practice in Glasgow?"

Of course he was going to check. Alex had considered going the full hog. Renting an office. Planting Laura on the end of a telephone line but, apart from the expense, it would only have provided more opportunities to get found out.

"Don't have an office. Don't need one. Gad about a lot."

"Mm."

This was fine. This was what he expected. "I'm not very well known you see. I tend to represent other lawyers. Dirty work."

"Dirty?"

"That's what my parents call it. I don't really specialize in anything. I make myself available when the law is, how can I put it? Fuzzy?"

"Fuzzy."

"Yes. My client," he gestured at the statue in the red army uniform. "Not entirely legal here."

"Mm. You already told me that."

Alex couldn't remember telling him anything. Damn, he'd gotten so carried away that Walker liked his tape he'd let the whole conversation get engulfed in his excitement.

"Early Alzheimer's?" As soon as he said it he wanted to kick himself. Alex spent all day every day with a bunch of foul-mouthed music students who spent as much time farting, and getting drunk and stoned as they did expressing themselves through their instruments. He was so used to feeling like the prissy one, but compared to a normal member of the human race he spoke and acted like an animal. "Bad joke. Bad taste. So many cultures. So many different mores. I forget conversations and my manners. Profuse apologies."

"None required. Does he move, or is this it?"

Alex wondered whether he'd been too quick off the mark with the apology; this guy was rude. "Mr. Walker, this is Mr. Yang Li." Elliot moved his weight to the other foot. Maybe he was putting it on? Maybe he was immersed in some stupid chess calculation? Either way, it was time for Elliot to do his stuff. "Li? Li?" Alex grabbed Elliot's shoulder and turned him around.

"Aah! Aah!" said Elliot. Walker extended his hand to administer a bit of a crushing. Elliot held his hands in front of him as if praying then he bowed so deeply he had to turn his head around to maintain eye contact. "Ah!" he repeated.

"I'm happy to meet you," said Walker without much of a sign that any happiness was about. Elliot looked back and forth between Alex and Walker as if expecting a translation. This would have been a nice touch if Alex knew Chinese.

"Anyway," said Walker, enough pleasantries, what's that?" he asked, pointing at the guitar case.

"It's a guitar," said Alex.

"Geetah," confirmed Elliot. "Good."

Alex rolled his eyes to try to get Elliot to cool it with the talking.

"Mm. Anyway, down to business. Let's hear this young man, shall we?" He gestured toward the piano.

"Ehm, I'm afraid not," said Alex, pulling a face like he'd eaten some bad oysters.

"I beg your pardon?"

"I tried. Believe me I tried, but he refuses to play piano right now."

"What do you mean, he refuses to play piano?"

"I mean he won't play."

"So why are you here? What is this?"

"He… he says he'll play guitar… sort of."

Elliot was still engrossed with something on the chessboard. Quentin leant on his desk. He looked down at the pieces, then at Elliot. His face was too close to Elliot's. This was dangerous. Elliot was liable to come out of his trance and instruct Walker on the exact nature of his halitosis.

"Sort of?"

"Yes. He says he doesn't mind practicing guitar in your presence."

"Practicing in my presence?"

Elliot looked straight into Walker's eyes. Alex experienced the kind of feeling people have when they say someone walked on their grave. Before Alex had a chance to intervene, Elliot threw out all the promises and assurances that he would not speak under any circumstances. "Dlaw. Fischah, Keles, nine-teenah-sicksety one… ah, brack a foss pehpetual checko."

It was as if Elliot had reached around and smacked Walker on the back of his head. It took a few moments to register; he had to decipher Elliot's thick accent. Walker looked down at the chessboard rather quizzically. "Really?"

"Weewee," confirmed Elliot.

"I took this out of a chess problem book. I didn't even bother to check. I like to solve problems." He became animated, as if he were engaged in a conversation with a chess buddy. "If I know the game it eats away at me. I'm the type of person who reads the end of a novel in the shop before I buy it. So I cover up the details and set up the pieces."

"Velly difficult. Many comprications," said Elliot.

Alex put his hand on Elliot's shoulder in hopes that he'd shut up. "He's played guitar for three months. He won't play piano again until he's mastered guitar."

Walker went to one of the bookcases and scanned the titles with his finger. "Play. Play then," he said without looking around. Alex opened the guitar case and handed Elliot the guitar. Elliot took one of the chairs. He was going to plant it right in front of Walker's desk when Alex grabbed him and walked him to the other end of the room, then pushed him into the seat, he whispered, "Come on now Elliot. We're doing fine. Just shut the fuck up and play like a god."

"Have a little faith," said Elliot. He pointed at the guitar case then at his foot. Alex took out the footstool and handed it to him. Walker found the book he was looking for; he flicked through it. He stopped at a page and checked back and forth between the book and the chessboard, pointing and mumbling to himself. Elliot did a rumba with his eyebrows then cupped a hand to his ear.

"By God, he's right!" exclaimed Walker. He read aloud from the book, "'Both grandmasters accept the futility of any continuation. After defeating Tal, Petrosian and Geller, the eighteen year-old Fischer lets Keres off the hook. Draw.' Impressive."

Walker sat. "He's only played guitar for three months?"

"Flee mumfs," said Elliot. Alex wanted to smash him in the face. His arrogance would spoil everything.

"I still need to hear him play piano."

"Pray!" said Elliot, then he launched into the opening of the first movement of Rodrigo's Concierto de Aranjuez. Alex had heard Elliot play this tune, and justify his performance, many times. As usual, he'd decided that while the Rodrigo was wonderful music, the composer had gotten the opening wrong. The original, written music demands a quick, strummed chord then a sort of triplet chord motif. Elliot had corrected Joachim Rodrigo's classic concerto by inserting some stolen flamenco in the shape of a four finger downward rasgueado followed by a quadruplet played with an upwards brush of the thumb, then a downwards strum of the pinkie and forefinger, with a final upwards forefinger strum—the bit that Rodrigo managed to miss. Much as Alex hated to admit it, it did sound better than the original. "It's more Spanish," Elliot had shouted at Martin one day in the cafeteria. "Naw, it's more Moorish. Rodrigo gets the Spanish thing but he doesn't get the guitar. This is what he meant!" The last statement was his favourite—it always had an effect; that time it sent Martin's head wobbling into a bad mood.

Alex could see it in Walker's eyes. Surprise. Surprise that this strange little man in his strange little suit had recognized an obscure chess grandmaster position played decades before, and now he was rewriting one of the most popular classical tunes ever written.

About a nanosecond before Elliot got to the orchestral intro, Alex remembered that it was a concerto and therefore required an orchestra. Panic shot through his system like someone had injected ice directly into his veins, but it was too late to do anything. Walker was entranced.

"Eeyum bala bum bum bala bum bum, det, det, eeyum bala bum bum det det, yum bala bum bum bala bum bum det, det, yum bala bum bum det det..."

Walker's mouth widened into a gape. Elliot was singing the orchestral part as if this were the only way to perform the piece. He finished the string 'echo' of the guitar theme then dived back into the guitar part, bringing in vocal woodwind statements against the quasi-ostinato like he was stuttering to find the right word then bawling out the brass to accompany his intricate guitar work.

Walker looked at Alex and back at Elliot like he was completely sold. Elliot cowered over his guitar then leant back, crooking his neck so that—had his eyes been open—he would have been looking at the ceiling. But his playing was immense, the music was sublime. His voice was awful but his imitation of the orchestra was a flawless caricature. He captured the essence of each sound, making throaty drawls when the bass came forward, pulling a vinegar face to introduce the French horn section.

Walker smiled. He was beaming.

This was the performance Harpo Marx might have given if he'd had a voice in his movies. He whistled flutes. He went 'chang chunga chung, chang chunga chung, chang, chick, chick,' in lieu of string spiccatos. His tongue darted in and out of his mouth to form perfect clarinet trills. His trumpets went wah, like a jazzman opening and closing a mute. He made a serious face and a Donald Duck quack to suggest a bassoon. His cello solo sounded exactly like his imitation of Dame Janet Baker—which he'd inflicted on Alex on a few inebriated occasions. His vocal orchestra was completely and utterly ridiculous, in stark contrast to the sheer beauty and control of his guitar work. Alex wondered whether Elliot had gone too far—not with his impromptu orchestra, but with his guitar playing. Maybe they shouldn't have said he'd only played for three months? Maybe they'd... maybe Alex had overcooked it?

Then something wonderful happened. First, just a finger, wagging about a little then, an involuntary wave of the hand. He punched the air. He was trying to lead the beat.

Walker was conducting.

He closed his eyes. He brought in both hands; he implored the music to swell then bid it diminish. He drew figures of eight with his right hand whilst gripping an imaginary handle with his left. He was completely gone. Out of it. Lost in the music.

Elliot winked at Alex.

Alex worried. He worried that they'd gone too far. He worried that Walker was playing a game with them. He worried that perhaps they'd done it? Perhaps they'd pulled it off? He watched Walker and Elliot. They looked like two heavy metal fans who'd climbed onto the stage with their heroes; in place of all the head-banging they were teasing and caressing the sounds, it was Imaginary Maestro conducting air orchestra. Was this really the country's greatest classical record producer pulled willingly into Elliot's weird world? There were huge sections of the piece where Alex was sure Walker would come to and chase them from his office, but Elliot sang it like Jolsen; Walker conducting him every step of the way.

Elliot finished with a smile that almost broke into hysterics. Walker clapped his hands and rubbed them together greedily, like a man fresh in from the cold.

Alex couldn't resist it. He went in for the kill. "Do you want to record him?"

The question seemed to surprise Walker. He thought for a moment, "That was... that was... very strange."

The euphoria Alex sensed within himself began to bloom. Like someone whose life passes before them in a flash before death, Alex watched their triumph. They were going to conquer the world.

"I need to hear him play piano. That was delightful. But we must get this business done."

"Hung jzin zeeh bah ho. Jzee bah ho shen szen ho. Hing jzang," Elliot motioned to Walker then to Alex—as if paying Walker a compliment, "Wang fuck, shin ba hang sing seck tah fah." Elliot smiled broadly at Alex, then motioned to him with a nod.

This was it. Elliot had lost his mind. He waved his arms around in the air until Alex got drawn in; he had to say something, anything.

"He says you are a fine conductor," said Alex. This would have to do.

"Velly fine. Velly fine," added Elliot.

"Him zjang bing fin wah zjoo win chang zjin ah… platafohm," said Elliot.

"He says he would be honoured to share a platform with you," said Alex.

"Thank you. Thank you indeed Mr. Li. And if we could hear some piano now…" He gestured to the baby grand. "Then we might even arrange such a surreal event some time."

Walker wouldn't be moved. All of Elliot's efforts had bought some good will and a little more time. It was time to beg. "Mr. Walker…"

"Quentin. Please." Offering his first name at least let Alex know that, while the imaginary platform offered by Elliot could never materialize, he still might have a shot.

"I have no idea why Li won't play piano. I suspect he's worried that somehow if he plays then someone somewhere will get wind of it and that'll be the end for him. Mr. Walker, this is China's son. He has it all. He can play piano, violin, tuba…"

"Tuba? He can play tuba?" Walker seemed entertained by Li's brass aspirations.

"And you can judge for yourself whether you think he has a future as a guitarist."

"The guitar playing was really quite lovely. The vocalizations were the most fun I've had in ages. But I have a business to run." His expression changed at that. He became sullen, as if he'd remembered something. Alex was desperate.

"He's a genius. No, I'm not sure, even though the word has been cheapened with overuse, I'm not sure it encapsulates his abilities." Alex was perched on the edge of his seat. Walker was all the way over on the other side of the room. Alex wondered whether the seating arrangement was one of those deliberate psychological ploys that businessmen use to gain the upper hand during negotiations. "He can do it all. Mathematics. Physics. Anything. You've seen his chess abilities."

"No. He knew about an old game. Impressive? Yes. But plenty of people who can't play that well study old games. I'm one of them."

"Ever beaten your computer?" asked Alex.

"Mm. Not yet. But I keep trying, blasted thing."

"Excuse me. I need to talk with Li."

"Certainly."

Walker was smiling but not as heartily as before. It would all wear off soon. Alex leant over to Elliot's ear and whispered. "Look man, you can beat his computer right?

Elliot adopted the conspiratorial position, hiding his mouth with his hand. "Are you trying to insult me? There isn't a computer born that I can't beat."

"Seriously? I mean really, seriously? You're sure?"

"Unless he has that thing linked up to a Cray supercomputer then no way. The programs are good but they have to run really, really fast. His'll have a piddling little processor in it. Man, I'll burn out its fucking circuits. Challenge it."

"Mr. Walker, what say you that Li challenges your computer... blindfold."

"Blindfold!" exclaimed Elliot. "Brindah fohda," he corrected himself.

"Blindfold?" Walker was interested. "This machine has an ELO rating of two thousand four hundred." Elliot made a sickening sound, as if someone had punched him in the belly. He whispered but didn't even try to cover his mouth now. "You stupid fuck. I didn't say I could beat it blindfold. Two thousand four hundred. Jeezis Christ."

"You said you could burn out its circuits? This is what you said about Allan."

"Allan is a dimwit. This computer is an international master. I can't beat an international master blindfold."

"How do you know?" Alex was sick of this. It was probably all gone now anyway. Walker was looking at them like he was at the zoo watching a couple of monkeys. He was enjoying himself for all the wrong reasons.

"He says he'll play it blindfold," said Alex, giving Elliot a dirty look.

"Right. Let's get down to it." Walker rubbed his hands together then set up the pieces. Elliot turned his chair around. "No need for that. You're pretty far away over there." Elliot ignored him and sat with his back toward Walker.

"Brindah fohda!" shouted Elliot. He was clearly in a bad mood. Alex was already exhausted. He had no idea they'd be there this long. Each second they sat in Walker's room was another second laying themselves open to discovery. He felt like going over to the piano himself and battering out some Bach to get the whole bloody thing over with.

"Pawn to king four," whispered Elliot.

"Pawn to king four," said Alex.

There was an almost inaudible beep. "Black plays pawn to king four," shouted Walker.

"Let's go at the fucker gung ho. If I'm going down, then I'm going down in flames. Let's get at its jugular. This'll tickle him. Pawn to queen four."

"Pawn to queen four," said Alex.

"King's Gambit? I say!" said Walker, impressed with Li's cheek.

"Are you sure Elliot?" Alex asked. Elliot had told him that the King's Gambit was the riskiest strategy in the book.

"Do you want a punch in the mouth?" whispered Elliot. "No. You're right. The way to play computers is to hold a line of pawns. To play positionally. To eek out a tiny advantage and try to nurture it into the endgame. Offering open aggression is basically... loony," he whispered with enough force to make Alex clean his ear with a handkerchief. "Relay the moves. That's your job. Shut the fuck up and let me play."

The next two hours were the longest two hours of Alex's life. Elliot was a pool of sweat. His eyes were two beetroots. Alex had never seen him in such a state. He always found things easy. This game looked like it was killing him. Alex took some hope from the length of the game. At least he didn't get wiped out from the start. Alex had fought off the urge to ask Elliot how he was doing, if he annoyed him too much Elliot was sure to start ranting at him, but two hours seemed enough; he must be doing okay? "How you doing?" he asked.

Elliot lifted his head up and gave Alex a look like someone who'd been mugged then left for days in the desert without water or food. "How am I doing? How am I doing? I'm trouncing him. I've got him by the throat but he doesn't know it cause he's a moron computer and doesn't know any better."

Alex's heart leapt. "Really?"

"No. He's got me by the throat. I'm completely fucked. It looks like Zugzwang."

"Zugzwang?"

"Every, any move I make is bad, bad news, let's play some blues, buckle my shoes. Me mind is jelly I want to watch telly. I'm sick of this, I need to piss." Elliot said it all from so far away. It was hard to tell whether this was part of the mental deterioration Alex had observed over the past few weeks or whether the game was melting his sanity.

"Get a grip Elliot,"

"That helped," said Elliot with as much irony as a whisper would allow. "Yer right that's all I need to…" He stopped mid-sentence like a rabbit caught in headlights.

"You okay? What's up?"

Elliot grabbed his hand. This was getting weirder by the minute. He'd never seen Elliot engage in any physical contact with anyone.

"I've got a draw," he said. "I've gorra fookeen draw!"

Walker checked his watch. This had been quite an entertaining day. Whoever this little man was, he was certainly different. But this game was over. Li had overreached himself right from the opening. There was no way that he could win blindfold with a King's Gambit. The theory was well established. Li had taken the game out of the book at the first opportunity. Walker had analysed a few King's Gambits but it wasn't an opening for amateurs. Spassky had specialized in the King's Gambit and Fischer, and even Kasparov had had a bit of fun with it, but nobody could beat a two thousand four hundred rating blindfold with it. It simply wasn't possible. Li had survived well enough, but then it was more like a chase than a game; Black had maintained a clear advantage from the point where Li departed from the theory.

"You sure?" asked Alex. Elliot offered him a look of disdain.

"He says he has a draw," he said to Quentin.

Quentin was amused. "You're offering a draw? Mm, afraid not. Time is pressing. This has been quite a day. Perhaps he might offer his king?

"Fucking moron," whispered Elliot. "He'll be laughing on the other side of his face in a minute. Offer me king? I'll offer him a smack in the chops."

"Steady Elliot. Just gimme the moves."

"Man, I could go over there and show him the moves but he's too thick to see the strongest lines. This is a work of art. This is the best game I've ever played. It's beautiful."

"You're not finished yet. Gimme the moves."

"Not finished yet? Now I actually have to go through the motions cause I'm dealing with a couple of head trauma patients. The computer should see it after the second sacrifice. It's got no choice. Its best line is a draw. Bishop to queen's rook seven."

"Bishop to Queen's rook seven," said Alex.

Walker sighed. He moved the piece. The LCD flashed *Thinking*. He stretched his arms out. "Sacrifice? Aggressive to the last, eh?"

It was probably less than ten minutes before the computer indicated a move; it felt like ten hours to Alex. Elliot was coming to life. He was more than confident that he had a draw. Now Alex had to try to keep him quiet again.

"Rook takes," said Walker.

"Knight to king six," said Elliot. "Tell him. Tell him quick. Watch this." If Alex could see anything but a couple of red slits he might have seen the glint in Elliot's eye.

"Knight to king six," said Alex.

Walker was bored. This had taken too bloody long. The kid was clever, but so what? He picked up the knight and plonked it down hard on the board to indicate that Li should let them all go home. He leant back against the headrest of his easy chair, closed his eyes and started to drift off. A tiny beeping sound startled him. He'd never heard this particular beep before. He looked at the LCD. *Draw* it flashed in red. "Draw?"

"See," said Elliot. "I've converted him."

"Draw? I don't understand?" said Walker.

"He can't see it but the computer can. Its best line is a draw. All it can do is get kicked up the arse for the next fifty moves. Perpetual fucking checko!"

"Perpetual check, I believe," said Alex, praying that the computer wouldn't change its mind.

"You reckon a draw is enough?" asked Alex. "Can't you win?"

"If I chopped your head off would you grow another one?"

"That's impossible," said Quentin. "You were beaten. From the off you were beaten. A double sacrifice? Who plays a double sacrifice? Who sees a double sacrifice? How did you do that? What's going on?"

"There seems no end to his talents," said Alex. "Quentin, you're the best. The best there is. We're asking a lot, I know. Li is breaking the law and if you record him you may be putting yourself in front of a charge. Maybe we're asking too much. I want you because you're the best, but we can go elsewhere." Alex played his final hand. If Walker didn't go for this now, then at least they wouldn't miss their flight.

Walker took a deep breath and started to nod.

Elliot was folding his footstool. "Fucking hell man, if I don't get out of here I'm gonna piss meself." He said it out loud then became suddenly aware he'd blown the gaff. "Christ." Then he started laughing.

Alex jumped out of his seat. "You moron! You stinking dimwit! You spend two hours beating a computer blindfold then you forget to whisper?"

Walker was smiling.

"It could happen to anyone," said Elliot.

"Thanks for today chaps. It was fun. How did you do it?"

"What? How did we do what?" asked Alex as if ready for a fight.

"The music? The piano? How did you do it?"

"He does it all on his computer," said Elliot. "Not bad eh? You should hear the new stuff. I've been giving him a hand. The new stuff makes the stuff you heard sound like it was played by a guy in a bicycle helmet."

"A computer? Very clever. I knew there was something wrong but I couldn't put my finger on it. I thought I was going to expose you both right away but I must say, with the guitar and the chess you almost had me."

Alex didn't want to hear how clever they were. He didn't want to hear how they'd almost done it. He wanted to go home. Again, someone had exposed him as a cheat, not because he'd heard it in the music, the music was fine, the music had done the trick. It was Elliot's inability to keep his eye on someone else's ball. Elliot stood up and shifted around uneasily. He seemed happy enough to hold back a visit to the bathroom long enough to extract a few more compliments from Walker. Elliot didn't care that they were exposed. He didn't care that he'd performed magnificently on guitar and at the chessboard—perhaps enough to snare Walker? He wanted immediate gratification. He craved acknowledgement. Perhaps he couldn't help himself? Maybe it was impossible for Elliot to give the credit to Yang Li? None of it mattered anymore. Alex was tired of trying to fathom Elliot's motives. He wanted to go home.

The door swung open so forcefully the hinges creaked like they might snap off. A huge man wearing an expensive looking suit and a cowboy hat marched into the room. Walker jumped.

"Quentin," he boomed. "You gotta get with the program,"

Elliot was holding his crotch like he was about to pee himself. The Texan looked at Elliot, his eyes widened.

"What the hell is going on here?"

Walker leapt to his desk, opened a drawer, took out a copy of the Financial Times, rolled it up into a little club then held it in front of him with both hands.

"Hey man, not the newspaper?"

"It's Obi Wan fucking Kenobe!" said Elliot, trying not to wet himself.

The Texan beat a retreat.

"Rooms," Walker said.

"Rooms?" Alex was baffled.

"Rooms… Can you get rid of the rooms?"

"I don't understand," said Alex. "You're all crazy. I don't know why I bother."

"The recording. It's full of rooms. Can you get rid of them? Can you do it all in a single room?"

Finally Alex twigged. "You could hear that? Jeez. The samples were recorded in lots of different rooms. Different pianos."

"We've already done it," said Elliot. His voice was strained. He was about to burst but he couldn't drag himself away from the action. "We did a whole new piano in a single room. Sounds fantastic."

"Give a me a recording like the last one but with a better soundstage and I'll do it."

"You'll do it?" they both said.

"I'll do it. I'll record Yang Li. I'll market him. You can play guitar on it as well if you like," he laughed. "Throw in some tuba. I like the tuba."

"Toilet?" pleaded Elliot.

"Down the hall. First right."

Elliot sped out of the room.

"Are you serious? You're really going to release a recording? Really? Even though we tried to fool you?"

"You didn't fool me. I knew something was up but I didn't know what. I'm a curious person, you see. It nagged at me. I had to know."

"It doesn't bother you, really?"

"The music is wonderful. If you'd come to me a year ago, you would've got the newspaper but things have changed. That little chap is quite a musician, and he's not half bad at chess either. Give me the music and I'll publish it."

Alex's thoughts turned to Laura. She'd made all of this possible. "How about violin? We can do that as well."

"Give me whatever you've got. I'm getting out of this business. I've had enough. If you can give me a violin as good as that piano and your friend's guitar, then the more the merrier," he paused. "but… none of that singing, eh?"

All the way back to Glasgow, Elliot stayed in character. He enjoyed being Yang Li. Alex felt high, as if he'd smoked fifty of Allan's joints in one go. He'd worked so hard, spent so much brainpower and energy on this; he'd imagined his triumph a hundred times, but somehow he was surprised that they'd pulled it off. He wasn't used to success, he was used to fighting against—or imagining he was fighting against—a world full of sceptics. He felt like he was floating around in a giant cavern. The people and the voices around him were far off, unreal. Elliot took care of the taxis and the airport and getting to the right seat on the plane, then getting him into his flat. He'd done it all without a single word of English. He had endless energy to devote to Yang Li. Alex let Elliot lead him around like he was a blind man.

He came to in his living room. He could hardly breath. First, Laura had thrown her arms around him and planted wet kisses all over his face, then Skuggs squished him with a great bear hug.

"Is it true man? The wee man says I'm gonny get to play on yer record? Is it true?"

"Sure. Whatever you want. All we have to do is record it. He says he'll publish anything." He looked at his pals. The girl he'd stalked into his life. The giant tuba virtuoso. And Elliot, still in character, almost—he'd allowed himself to talk pidgin English to his friends. He felt like weeping; now he was an old hand at such things.

"What about recording? You got kicked out of the Academy. D'you think McNabb'll let you finish things off?" Skuggs asked.

"We'll see," Alex answered. McNabb didn't concern him anymore. They still needed the room at the Academy, in case they had to record any last-minute corrections. They needed the lab for the processing juice but Ingles was his pal, there was no problem there at all. He hardly thought about the problems that might be ahead of them. He knew there was nothing they couldn't achieve now, as long as Elliot didn't stray too far from reality over the next couple of weeks he was sure they could handle anything.

"How much man?" asked Skuggs.

"Mm?"

"How much? We gonny be rich?"

Alex hadn't considered money. This wasn't about money.

"This isn't about money."

"Is for me man. Nae muckle money nae deal."

"Christ Skuggs, you sound more like Oor Wullie every day. If there is any money we'll share it, if not, tough, you'll still want to do it?"

"Nah."

"Nah? You taking the piss? This is a big deal recording. What if it sells millions?"

"If it sells millions then I want a fat wad."

"You don't want millions of people to hear you?"

"What the fuck do I care about millions of people? Anyway, they're no hearing me, they're hearing wee shitey over there," he jerked a thumb at Elliot. Elliot bowed quickly. "Yang fuckin Li. He's gonny get all the credit, no?"

"Well, not him. Yang Li is, but Yang Li doesn't exist."

"Tell him that," said Skuggs.

"Yangah Ree," said Elliot.

"Skuggs, it's not like we need a tuba player. I only suggested it to the guy as a favour to you."

"No. Walkah, he say, tuba!" said Elliot.

"Cheers Yangboy," said Alex.

"Ach, fuckit okay. I'll do it," said Skuggs.

"Well, you've saved our bacon again Skuggs," said Alex blankly. "Without your tuba we're nothing. Let's get some chips or something then get to the lab. We've got to work out exactly what we need. Maybe I can get hold of Ingles, book the lab?"

# TWENTY–FIVE

Alex tried to turn the key in the laboratory door; it wouldn't budge.

"Bloody hell." Elliot kicked the door open, almost tearing off Alex's thumb. It hadn't taken Elliot very long to return to his old self. Alex was too busy sucking his thumb to notice Ingles and Todd already sat in the room.

"Ola," said Laura quite matter-of-factly, as if they'd entered a pub and spotted old friends.

"It's the delightful Laura and her clever beau," said Ingles before offering Laura a hug. "And my favourite guitarist too." Ingles grabbed Elliot and hugged him.

"Ahem, do we know each other madam?" said Elliot, clearing his throat.

"You!" Ingles pushed Elliot in the chest as if she really were an old friend. Elliot clasped his hands over his chest. He sidled across to the corner of the room and made sure there were enough obstacles between him and the resident females to ensure he had a chance to deflect any incoming artillery. The fingery-pokery administered by Laura was fresh enough in his mind to make him head for cover.

"What's going on?" asked Alex as if he were in charge of Ingles' domain.

"Indeed?" asked Todd.

"You first," said Alex. He knew that one evening he'd find Ingles in his lab—it was her lab after all—but Todd's presence told that this wasn't any normal evening. Alex wanted to catch Ingles but hadn't expected to see her so soon.

"We're scheming. We're trying to find a way to get things back to normal."

"Losing the skirt would be a start," said Elliot.

"Give it up Elliot," said Alex.

"Mr. McNabb has fired Ms. Ingles, and we have decided to fight," said Todd. "Why are you here in the dead of evening?"

"I just need the computers to get some work done."

"All four of you?"

"They wanted to tag along. You've been fired?"

There was one of those pauses that go on for so long that someone usually feels the need to fill the empty space, but no one did. It was more than five minutes before Elliot broke; not because of any self-conscious need to end the impasse, he had an idea and he wasn't one to hold back when he felt a bulb lighting up in his head.

"McNabb's slung him out as well. We should work together. What's your plan?"

Todd indicated to Ingles to take control. She pulled up a trouser leg and crossed her legs like she was about to give a lecture on post-modern serialism and said, "We don't have a plan. That's why we're here."

"I have a plan," Todd interrupted. "I'm going to sit outside the bursar's office until hell freezes over."

"Nice plan," said Elliot.

"I'm open to suggestions?"

"We could kill the bastard," said Elliot looking at Laura. There was another long silence as first they dismissed Elliot's suggestion then ruminated a little over it.

"Do not be crazy people," said Laura, as if reading their collective desires.

"No," said Elliot. He rubbed his chin. "We shouldn't dismiss it outright. The solution has some merit. Not only does it solve all your problems. It solves some of the world's problems as well. I mean, the world would be a better place without him, wouldn't it?"

"This is crazy," said Laura.

"We should fully explore every avenue, every possibility, before dismissing anything," said Elliot.

"Why are you dressed like… dressed like…" said Todd unable to find the right word.

"Same reason you're dressed like Barbra Streisand. I like the idea of killing him. Let's kill him. Who's up for it?"

"We'd get caught. DNA and that," said Skuggs.

"What about the lab?" asked Alex. "If you've been kicked out, what's going to happen to the lab?"

"I expect he'll sell it or burn it down. I don't know. I'm sure he'll change the locks on me as soon as he can," said Ingles.

"We need the lab." Alex could hardly believe that McNabb might stop him at the final hurdle.

"So, you've gotta get unfired," said Skuggs.

"Reinstated," said Todd.

"Yeah, what he said," said Skuggs. "Couldn't we blackmail him? I mean, he tried to feel up yer girlfriend."

"Is this true?" It was as if someone had opened up the top of Ingles' head and poured red ink into the hole; a pulse of visible rage spread across her face.

"Yes. But I…" Laura beat her fist in the air. "Bam… I broke my bow."

"You still haven't told us why all four of you are here? Why do you need the lab?" said Todd.

"We just tried to con this record producer into publishing this wanker's music as if it were real," said Elliot. "He clocked us," Elliot glanced at Alex. "But he's still gonna produce the music. Not bad eh?"

"I don't understand?" said Todd.

Elliot spent the next ten minutes retelling the whole scene, adding some internal angst to his chess battle and playing down the final gaff that led to their visit to the lab. Alex trusted Todd, he knew him to be a man of fine character. He trusted Ingles too; and without her there would be no more Yang Li. He needed Ingles in gainful employment. Asking Walker for thousands of pounds to buy equipment would be too much. He listened to Elliot relay the tale. He watched him imitate himself imitating an orchestra. He listened like he was watching a play in a foreign language as Elliot retold his epic battle with the computer. He didn't interrupt when Elliot reminded his audience for the fourth time that he was playing blindfold.

He was lost in his thoughts, trying to figure a way to make it all work when Elliot got stuck in mock Chinese.

"Ing shee! Ing shee wang shee foh bah!"

"Eh?" Skuggs was enjoying the tale and wanted more. "Come on wee man, get to the punch line. We get it about the kid-on Chinese."

"Ing shee! Ing shee wang shee foh bah!" repeated Elliot. He studied his audience as if trying to work out who they were and why they couldn't understand. "Ing shee! Ing shee wang shee foh bah!" he said, accenting each word sharply.

"He's off again," said Alex. "I think he thinks he is Yang Li."

This seemed to please Elliot. He jerked a thumb at himself.

"Yang Li is going to need publicity," said Todd. "Why don't we offer McNabb the job?"

"What do you mean?" asked Alex.

"Pride. Status. That's where we have to get him. He wants to destroy us all."

"He doesny want to destroy me," Skuggs interjected.

"Give it time, he'll get around to you. He'll catch you in a Spamfart and you're history," said Alex. This was enough to convince Skuggs. His expression told that he didn't trust his bodily functions not to betray him.

"Let him dig his own grave. Let him announce the coming. Let him be seen to believe. Let him be the first to be fooled. Tie him up in the music and own him," said Todd.

"Can you get this past your man Walker?" asked Ingles. "If we can rope him into this, then we can hold it over McNabb. Maybe it'll be enough. If not then I go to plan B."

"Plan B?" asked Alex.

"Never mind. I hope it won't come to that. I'll make a deal with him. I'll offer him Yang Li. That should be enough," said Ingles.

"I'm not quite sure..." started Alex.

"Just make the best music that you lot can make. Leave McNabb to me. You'll have this lab, one way or another."

"Gonny killum?" asked Skuggs. "Zat plan B?"

"Nobody is going to die, my big, oversized tuba fellow." Ingles winked at Skuggs. Skuggs's face filled with heat.

"Ing shee! Ing shee wang shee foh bah!" said Yang Li.

"I'm not here to beg," she said. Ingles had barged into McNabb's office the way he used to barge into everybody else's. "I'm here to deal. I'm here to make a deal."

"Deal? I think not." He waved his hand, dismissively.

"A friend of mine has put a proposition to me. It's very attractive. I'm willing to pass it on to you. But I want my job back."

"I don't think so." He followed a line in the report he was pretending to read with his finger to indicate his indifference.

"It'll make you famous. They'll be coming from all over the world to interview you. You'll be a star."

"Mm, a star. Yes, always wanted to be a star," he said blankly.

"My friend has found a musician. A virtuoso. A great virtuoso. Perhaps the greatest there has ever been."

"Really, so interesting," McNabb was feigning indifference but hadn't thrown her out; he was listening.

"Quentin says he has a young chap. Chinese. From Red China. New Mozart, Paganini, Horowitz rolled into one."

"Mm. I think I've heard that one before."

"Quentin is not given to imagining such things."

"Quentin?"

"Walker. Quentin Walker, the producer."

It was like offering an old dog a bone. McNabb's head snapped up. "*The* Quentin Walker?"

"There's more than one record producer called Quentin Walker?" She was happy to at least get to return one of his lazy volleys. "A young chap. He's been smuggled out of China. Quentin says he's beyond belief. Says he was thinking of retiring but he's going for one last recording before packing it in. Trouble is that he's here illegally. He's in hiding. Quentin wants to release a record. Can't be bothered with the hullabaloo though. Asked me to handle the press, the pre-publicity. Like one of those experts they turn to to authenticate a document or a work of art? He wants someone respected but not too well known. Someone to be the go-between?"

"What do you mean, go-between?"

"This young chap is going to set the world on fire. It's going to involve everything, music, politics, big diplomatic incident I expect. Quentin wants someone beyond reproach to handle the music side of things."

"Handle?"

She felt like jumping onto the table and bashing him right on top of his bandage.

"Is it too complicated for you? You don't understand?"

"And you want your job back?"

"I need my life to continue on course," she said.

"I can confirm this with Walker? Do you have his number?"

"You can call him. But not today. I want a new contract, iron clad. Here, this is a rough draft." She pushed a tape along the table toward him.

He picked up the tape and played with it, turning it around and around in his hands. "Let me listen to it. Then we'll see."

Ingles got up. "Don't take too long. I'd rather have my lab and my music and my quiet life, but if that tape is all there is for me then it'll have to do. I'm sure there are other colleges with other people who'd like a crack at this. I'll be in my lab." She left, knowing she had him.

McNabb's hands shook so much he could hardly get the tape into the deck of Todd's hi-fi. Quentin Walker was the real thing. He was the most respected and admired producer in the business. He was a personal friend of virtually every great musician of the past thirty years. He was famed for his talent-spotting ability. By the time the music appeared McNabb would have accepted Liberace in lieu of the greatest pianist of all time. He sat back and planted himself beyond his wildest dreams and into weighty BBC2 talk shows. He hardly listened to the music; it was already a simple backdrop, a bit of flock wallpaper behind the pronouncements and of-the-cuff witticisms he'd rain upon the nation.

"He's such an idiot, your husband," said Ingles as she folded the pages of her paperback until the spine broke. "Why did you ever marry him?"

Shama shrugged. She seemed entirely disinterested in the question; she carried on with her knitting.

"Move your legs a bit. You're in my half."

Shama edged over. "I have to get this finished." The rate of clicks accelerated then hit a plateau. Ingles watched for a moment, amazed at her lover's dexterity, then rested her head on Shama's shoulder. Shama smiled without missing a click.

The bedroom door flew open. McNabb appeared, all ruddy and excited. He clapped his hands together, ready to inform his wife of the fame into which they were both about to be plunged.

Shama stopped knitting. She deposited her needles and wool onto her bulbous belly calmly, as if readying herself to listen to her husband's news.

Maybe McNabb mistook Ingles, laying there beside his wife with a book in her hand, for a cuddly toy, or even himself? "I'm going to be famous!" he exclaimed, his brain seemingly unable to process the information right there in front of him.

"I know," said Ingles. "I'm going to make sure of it."

His complexion sank from coronary crimson into bloodless grey with the speed of a chameleon chased onto a rock by a hungry predator. He went limp. He stood there in his crumpled tweed jacket, his white dome—worse for wear—now matching both his expression and his pallor.

Shama took up her needles and wool and started to knit as if she'd waited long enough for her husband's story.

"Aren't we supposed to fight now? For the hand of the fair Shama?" said Ingles. Shama smiled to herself.

Ingles leapt out of bed, her naked breasts followed momentarily, like the second segment of an articulated lorry turning a tight corner. She bounced up and down on the spot; fists tucked under her chin, shifting her weight from one side to the other and darting out the occasional jab. McNabb couldn't believe her breasts; it was as if she'd stuck a pair of tights onto her chest and dropped a couple of grapefruit down the legs. Shama carried on knitting, she gave them little more than a cursory glance, as if she were planted in front of an afternoon soap but had to get her knitting finished by the time the show ended.

"Put em up!" said Ingles, testing her left hook.

McNabb grabbed his left arm in anticipation of the heart attack this betrayal would surely bring.

"Come on! Come on!" she panted, firing straight rights at the man across the room. "Don't try to kid me Music Boy. You've wanted this for a long time. Let's mix it!"

McNabb squeezed his bicep and waited for the crushing pain. He squeezed it harder and harder until his arm was numb, but the agony wouldn't manifest itself in his chest. He was going to have to live through this. He pumped the fingers of his left hand until he could feel them bristle then he went downstairs.

"You'd better!" Ingles shouted after him.

"You're so cruel sometimes," said Shama with hardly a shred of interest.

"That's why you love me so much my darling," said Ingles before leaping onto the bed and planting a kiss square on her forehead.

"You'd better get down there and make your peace before he gets any funny ideas."

"There will be no monkey business while I'm about," she said as she pulled her panties on. She slung her breasts into their support mechanism, popped a sweater on, rolled backwards onto the bed to pull her slacks up then slid her feet into her Hush Puppies. "At least now we all know where we are, eh?"

Shama stopped knitting. "Take some care, will you?"

"Always," said Ingles as she headed downstairs for the man-to-man she'd dreamt about.

The tête-à-tête didn't at all live up to her expectations. Apart from the odd involuntary convulsion—inspired by regular gulps of single malt—he was quite placid throughout her solitary discourse. She explained, in the traditional manner of one mature adult to another, cuckolded, adult that it was over for him and Shama, and that she'd be moving out soon but that this incident and course of events was entirely separate from and unconnected to their business arrangement.

She explained that she had contacted Walker and that he'd shown enthusiasm at her suggestion that McNabb take up the public relations mantle. She thought she detected a twitch at that, but it may have been the whisky.

She left without feeling the slightest trace of guilt. If McNabb had shown himself to be anything other than a monster she might have chastised herself over the affair, her pugilistic ridiculing of the discovery, and the consequent disintegration of his loveless marriage. But he'd displayed cruel indifference beyond the call of duty and, in the process, offered her an emotional hedge against not only the theft of his wife but the destruction of his life—the seeds of which had already been planted. Anyway, it was better than Elliot's suggestion to kill him and be done with it.

She caught herself whistling as she walked home. It had been a long time since happiness had bubbled up inside her and out into the world in the shape of a carefree, throwaway composition; something for her and the universe, and the odd passer-by, to enjoy.

Her friends might have congratulated her on 'turning' the perfect partner were it not for the little matter of the sex—or complete lack of it. But Shama was heavy with child and, in time, they would get to it. After all, it was Shama who made the first move.

She shook off all thoughts of sex and wondered whether she'd have to tell the others that plan B had already swung into action and hit the mark? But Ingles knew McNabb well enough to believe that he wouldn't throw away an opportunity to wax lyrical for a broad audience. Plan B would merely soften him up for the kill.

McNabb was free. At last he was free. He finished the bottle but he was unable to shake the image of Ingles' body parts leaping about in rubbery counterpoint. She thought she'd won, but soon she'd have to live with the automaton and the new brat. Even in this deeply inebriated state it was plain that he was in control and, what had seemed like mere happenstance was really the inevitable unfolding of his ambition. He knew what to do. He would milk Walker and his prodigy of everything they had, he'd cement his rightful position in the world of music then he would fire Ingles again. She would sue, but while she waited for reinstatement he'd dismantle her toys; he'd welcome her back with thirty hours a week teaching theory. He'd either break her or watch her wither behind bars wrought from Bach chorales and dainty Mozartian pastiche.

When the nausea from the whisky and the visions of the bouncing dyke threatened to overwhelm him he staggered into the downstairs bathroom and plunged his dome halfway down the toilet bowl. He regurgitated three-quarters of a bottle of eighteen-year old malt then fell back, gasping, onto the floor.

He wiped the saliva and the whisky splashback from his chin and neck with his sleeve. His heart pounded like timpani aping thunder. His dome had finally had enough; it slipped off to reveal a badly stitched Frankenstein scar that ran from the point where his hairline had once lived, up to the crown of his head.

He knew he'd won. He was going to be famous. He was gong to rule the Academy. He could drink as much as he wanted now without the interminable silent nagging, and he could stuff himself with bacon rolls if he had a mind to.

The thought of bacon rolls sent him crawling back into the toilet bowl. He clung onto the toilet seat until it felt like his stomach had turned itself inside out and retired for the day. His thoughts turned to Betty; she would be so proud of him. Perhaps he might even win her back?

# TWENTY-SIX

 The sessions had progressed well. Alex and Elliot worked hard at honing the music, sculpting it until it teetered on the cusp of human capability without falling into an emotionless, digital abyss.

Elliot refused to change his clothes. Alex had to pay the costumiers from whom he'd hired Elliot's red army uniform a sum he felt would probably fund a whole brigade for a year, so that Elliot could continue his foray into method acting. But every day it got a little harder to get sense out of him; he could still get his message across—that a passage should accelerate slowly then pull backwards and forwards, or that the speed was defined by change in tempo and not tempo itself and that an accent had to accompany and signal changes to properly fool the human brain into hearing sentience at the heart of each phrase—but Yang Li was taking over. It was as if he were becoming possessed, as if Yang Li were more real than Elliot. Luckily, Yang Li was a great genius and picked up the English language fast enough to condemn Alex to a perpetual state of annoyance that stopped short of any overwhelming urge to strangle the both of them. Alex was careful not to engage Elliot or Yang Li in superfluous conversation; he figured—at the rate Li was absorbing his environment—that Elliot and Li were bound to meet somewhere in the middle of his madness. Yang Li was even more punctilious than Elliot (a state of affairs that Alex could never have believed had he not experienced it) but both Elliot's and Alex's acquiescence to Yang Li's superior grasp of interpretation led to the betterment of the music; something with which neither of them were likely to argue. Alex worked hard to banish the fear that Elliot and Yang Li would get into a spat over the placement of an attack, or a brawl as to whether the note should be held a millisecond longer or not. Somehow (although when Alex thought about it, it did seem self-evident) Elliot always approved of Yang Li's improvements of Elliot's improvements.

They were ploughing through Chopin's Revolutionary Etude when Yang Li turned into Elliot. "You know," he said matter-of-factly, as if he hadn't spent the last four hours fighting broken English with oversized gestures and jumping around like a Mao fanboy to get his musical ideas across. "The Buddha showed his first disciple the universe in a flower."

"Mm." Alex was trying to decide whether to slow a run down or introduce a slight error at greater velocity. It was dangerous to introduce errors—technique was important to experts and musos, and he didn't want anyone fooled into thinking Yang Li was merely very good. But it was more dangerous to push the pace too hard; people are used to hearing real, live musicians—too fast and warning bells would ring. "Really?" he added in an effort to appease Yang Li and shut Elliot up.

"He transmitted everything. He held up a flower and the disciple understood. Instant enlightenment. Better than a punch in the mouth, No?"

"Absolutely," No, he told himself to forget errors and he wasn't prepared to slow it down. He'd just have to introduce more subtlety into the tempo. He reckoned the tempo in this piece was defined within the great circular phrases, and not to be found within the measures; it was a temporal structure that contained musical ideas and aspirations rather than notes strung together inside little blocks—it was the temporal dimension of the musical blueprint he had to isolate and describe; not by playing a tune, but by revealing a truth. He imagined his hand swinging back and forward underwater. That was the effect he was after; smooth, liquid, accelerating then decelerating like a musical pendulum. He pictured the tempo tied to a massive underwater Foucault Pendulum, imperceptibly tracing the universe against its environment.

"Universe," he mumbled.

"Yeah. It wasn't just knowledge, it wasn't insight; it was everything. Everything in a flower."

"Good."

"I can give you it, if you like."

"Can you help me with this bit? It sounds okay but okay is worse than wrong."

"If I give you it you won't need to ask me anymore. You can do it all yourself."

"That would be dandy, but seeing as Yang Li's gone for a bag of chips maybe you could help me one last time before you give me the willies?"

"I haven't got a flower but this'll do." He held up a ballpoint pen.

Alex looked at the pen and then at Elliot, and tried his best not to say anything that might offend him or bring Li back from the chippy. "You have a pen."

"Do you understand?" Elliot asked.

"I understand," said Alex, unable to resist the temptation to say it the way a medium might answer a friendly spirit.

"Okay then, let's get down to it."

At last Elliot sounded normal. Alex was about to give him a speech about how he thought they could solve a right-hand run when Elliot added. "Let's hurry. I'm needed on another plane of existence soon and I can't hang about here every day holding your hand."

Alex waited for a smile to tell him it was just Elliot being Elliot, acting crazy like he always did, or used to before he became Yang Li. But none came. Well, he did smile but it wasn't the right smile. It wasn't the smile Alex wanted to see. It wasn't the comfortable self-mocking smile that usually accompanied some serious eyebrow aerobics, it was vacant; the kind you see stuck onto the faces of bald people in orange dresses dancing badly at airports.

"Hang zee foh mah?" Elliot asked.

"Bloody hell." It was late, maybe it was time to pack in for the day. Alex couldn't be bothered with Yang Li.

"Just kidding man. Get a sense of humour."

It really was time to pack in. Now Elliot was pretending to be Yang Li while he was Elliot as well as actually being Yang Li most of the time. It was like having to deal with someone who has Alzheimer's disease pretending to have Alzheimer's disease. Elliot was managing to make the almost impossibly difficult task of generating the music seem easy compared to having a normal conversation.

"Let's call it a day. I'm completely knackered," he said, and hoped Elliot wouldn't try to drag him through any more psychological mazes. A better friend might have suggested Elliot seek help, but only someone who didn't know Elliot well could have ventured such a strategy. Elliot had the same disdain for psychiatry and psychology as he had for almost everything else that deigned to claim knowledge of the human mind—his domain. Asking Elliot to talk to a psychiatrist was about as sensible as asking Skuggs to follow a conductor; they were simply too evolved and would find such a suggestion insulting in the extreme. Alex reckoned that keeping him close and challenging his talents was probably as much as he could do, and he needed Elliot now—at least as much as Elliot needed him—he'd become ravenous for Elliot's (or Li's) vision. His own insight was no longer enough.

# TWENTY–SEVEN

Walker acquiesced without question when Alex asked him if he'd mind using McNabb as a press patsy. Walker was used to dealing with the media and had made as many contacts over the years as his business demanded but he'd failed to find a single friend amongst all the PR people, the editors and journalists, the critics, the TV wags and the celebrity blowhards he'd had to hobnob with to get his music out into the world. This was most definitely going to be his last project. If he blew a few professional relationships apart then that would be fine; he wouldn't need them anymore anyway.

Alex asked him to contact McNabb to offer a bit of hand holding. Although he hoped that a by-product of all the hard work would be either public humiliation for McNabb or a return to normalcy, he still had to make sure he didn't alienate anyone who had the power to propel Yang Li into the public eye. McNabb wasn't exactly an easy person to deal with. Alex tried to explain the problems Walker might face but he merely cut him off with, "I know the type." Alex figured he probably did and left him to it.

McNabb was beside himself with joy when Walker called. After years of anonymity he was going to taste fame. And not just any fame either. If the breadth of fame is measured from someone in a football crowd waving at a television camera to a Nobel Prize winner walking backwards after getting his gong then this was certainly closer to a backwards walk than a 'Hello Mum'.

Alex needn't have worried about McNabb being difficult. When Walker spoke, McNabb was a hand-reared budgerigar nodding and puffing itself up for its master. Walker would simply forward any and all enquiries to McNabb. The word was that Yang Li was the real thing; he could play piano, violin, guitar, even tuba and God knows what else to a standard beyond anything Walker had heard before. McNabb had listened to the tape but took it on faith that Walker had heard Yang Li in person and at length. Walker told him he wasn't going to get to meet or hear Li for now. Li was in hiding until the release of the recording. McNabb would have to pretend he'd heard Li in person. Walker told him to imagine any and every historical figure he wished; he told him to assume that Li's stature was the equal of or beyond the best of the best. He told him he was staking his reputation on Li and that McNabb would be wise to do the same. McNabb made a point of taking notes during the conversation but found himself unable to decipher his scribblings after the fact. But what did it matter? He knew enough. Li was Chinese. Li was the greatest musician ever to grace the earth, and McNabb was to be the arbiter, the herald, the prophet, announcing the arrival of the chosen one.

Walker was not slow in getting to work. McNabb had hardly time to order Todd's secretary to fetch tea and Rich Tea biscuits when the phone started ringing. He would have preferred more information; a release date for the recording, more biographical data on Li; hearing him in person would have been best, but the cloak and dagger aspect thrilled him enough to dismiss such details, and it allowed him free rein to move conversations and interviews into the domain of his own profound expertise rather than talk about someone else. Maybe this was the start of a whole new career? Surely, after Li was unleashed upon the world and Walker was safely retired, McNabb would become the expert of choice when someone was needed to inform the unwashed on the intricacies of serious music and its practitioners?

By the end of his first day as media handler he had a diary glowing with exotic promise: 'Interview with The Guardian,' 'Live Beeb segment,' 'Channel 4 documentary filmmaker exploratory chat,' 'Sunday Times feature'. McNabb hadn't even seen the press release Walker had sent but it had certainly hit the spot. It was happening so fast, he was dizzy. He made a mental note, then wrote it in red ink in his diary beside his first engagement: Buy hat!

Over the next two weeks McNabb and his new Ecuadorian Montecristi Panama did the rounds. The hat helped tremendously. Apart from covering up the ragged gash on top of his head it gave him the little edge that television and newspapers demand of their personalities. Without the scar he might have settled for a bow tie and been mistaken for 'Something in the City' or perhaps a fourth division literary pretender. But the Montecristi set him apart from the other talking heads.

The interviews were much easier than he'd imagined they'd be. There was no Yang Li to paw over, no music to listen to as evidence, no trail or trace or history to interpret and analyse, just his word; the word of an acting principal of a backwater music college. It suited the media perfectly. Had the music been available for all to hear then surely experts would line up on both sides to argue the toss over Li's abilities? Any biographical information would have sent nosey journalists out to Hong Kong and beyond to get the 'real dope' on Li. As it was Mc-Nabb represented the only link between the world and the new saviour of serious music. McNabb savoured his new role as music's John the Baptist. The endless questions on a release date for the music were most enjoyable of all; his answers made it sound like he was hiding something, in the centre of it all, parrying inquiry to shield the truth. But those same questions reminded him that it was all going to end. Soon, Li would complete his recording sessions and Walker would unleash him upon the public; a flood of experts might wash McNabb away? The seed of doubt sent him back to the tape. He hadn't listened to it at all but for that first day, and even then he'd been preoccupied by something or other at the time.

He listened to the tape. It sounded fine. It didn't strike him as anything special though. The pianist was very good indeed, incredible technique but then who hasn't got an incredible technique these days?

There was nothing on the tape, no clue as to how he might increase his media longevity, there were no instructions to guide him, nothing with which to concrete his new status into permanency and, worst of all, it contained no map to show him the route back to Betty's heart.

＾　　　♯　　　♮

With the recording of Li almost done, Alex still had three more sessions to complete; one with Skuggs—a reluctant soloist—his tuba playing would add a little humour, a bit of spice to the final album. People wouldn't know the difference between a great tuba player and any other tuba player but it would stand as a conversation piece, something to tack on to the end of reviews; a final affirmation that Li was the real deal perhaps? After all, what pianist could be bothered to learn how to play such an un-gainly instrument but a true musician, a throwback to times when music was enjoyed for its own sake?

But Skuggs could wait. Skuggs would be easy. He'd sit down. He'd play. It would be perfect. Maybe a couple of takes; just to make sure. It would be a joy to simply record someone without all the nitpicking over the minutiae. But Skuggs could wait.

He had to record Elliot playing guitar, or perhaps Li himself if Elliot was unavailable. Either way, it wouldn't be as simple as recording Skuggs. Elliot was bound to want multiple takes and Alex was sure that as soon as Elliot discovered he could cut and paste phrases from various takes together, he'd want to spend an inordinate amount of time perfecting the recording. Then he'd want to mess with the post-processing. Alex had built routines where he could insert the music into virtual spaces. Elliot was sure to want to experiment with the placement of his music in various concert halls built in pure software. But Elliot, or Li—depending on who was at home—could wait.

First, he would record Laura. This would be the trickiest proposition. He could record her straight. He could set her in front of a couple of microphones and ask her to play. But the caterwauling that might follow was more liable to send her into a deep funk than provide anything usable. He would have to en-sure sexual contact during the whole performance. Moreover, he'd have to make a sonic imprint of the room beforehand, re-corded during sex, in order to use it as a 'negative'; a tool with which to extract the noise—which in this case would be the sound of sex. What excited him more than the actual sex (al-most) was the prospect of Laura getting to hear how good she was. He was pretty sure that while she certainly had a model in her head of the music she was trying to produce, she had no idea of just how wonderful a musician she was. He was excited that he'd get to reveal her talents to her, to make her hear that all of those endless hours of labour to which she had consigned herself had not been in vain; somewhere inside her the correct neural pathways had been forged, the music analysed and understood to the point of reproducibility. That she could only perform while aroused was a bonus that he was not yet sure he was willing to forego. He hoped that if she heard herself she might be able to extract her music from her libido—if indeed her music had been welded somehow to her libido—but he reckoned that, even in failure, the effort alone was worth it. She would at least have something to aim for, and while he genuinely wanted to help her extricate herself, he knew he could live, in bliss, with her problem for as long as it took.

When they entered the trombone room in the dead of night for the session, he had envisaged perhaps (if that were possible?) a sexual experience beyond even that which he had already enjoyed. They felt like a couple of teenagers creeping into her Dad's barn for an illicit roll in the hay. She had borrowed her teacher's bow for the occasion.

After he had tested the mics and placed her in the most advantageous position it became clear that a sweaty session would not be required. Merely touching her shoulder was enough to elicit the greatness within her. Creaky scales and stilted arpeggios warmed with a touch into a demonstration of power and control. As usual, she seemed unaware of the change that took place on contact. He was a little disappointed that sex was off the menu but at least it meant he could concentrate fully on the job in hand. Including her performance in the recording meant she was to be a part of Yang Li. Alex knew the piano playing was good enough—Walker had confirmed that. He knew that Skuggs was as fine a musician as any and professional enough to require only a single take. He knew that Elliot's guitar playing—

presented as a facet of Yang Li—would melt any lingering doubts. But he had to make sure that Laura's playing was up to scratch.

He brushed her hair from her shoulders and caressed her neck. From the first note it was clear that her hiatus from violin had done her no harm. This was the first time he'd got to hear her play without the mighty distraction of his own sexual ambition clouding the sound, or without Alex the Logician testing the effect and drawing broad correlations from his senses to her musical outpourings.

She played the prelude from Bach's third partita. It was magnificent; bold, almost mathematical in tempo, courageous in timbre, the phrasing designed to grab attention, to draw and create an audience. He maintained contact throughout the performance. He was tempted to let go, to lift his hand just a few millimeters, to try once again to hear how she'd play in free fall, but this was about Yang Li, it was about creating the violinist in Yang Li, it was about nailing a performance worthy of Yang Li. No matter how good Li's piano or guitar were, Alex knew that even the slightest slip would invite the critics to feast upon any perceived weakness in Li's arsenal. It would be better to leave out the violin altogether than include a performance that was anything less than brilliant. But he simply couldn't do that now. Laura deserved this. She was as much a part of Yang Li as Alex was. Without her none of this would have happened. When she finished she paused for a few seconds then, in silence, she packed the violin away. Alex could see she was nervous. She'd never heard herself play before. A strange quirk of the kind of training in which many music colleges indulge is that students are hardly ever professionally recorded. An outsider might assume that recording students then analysing the result with a view to improvement might be an obvious strategy, but it almost never happens. Most concert soloists get to hear them-

selves properly for the first time when they are well down the path of a professional career.

It almost brought a tear to his eye to watch her expression as he played the music back. He added a little real-time filtering on the high end, a touch of soft-knee compression and a smidgen of reverb to add a little sparkle to the recording. It was clear that Laura had no idea she sounded so good. This was certainly the performance she had in her head when she played; the blueprint, the pristine ideal, like the fully formed shape an artist might see within a block of marble or wood before they chip away the chaff to reveal the work of art inside.

"I can play." She pulled a little white ball from her pocket and worked it until it became something of the paper hankie it had once been, then she blew a great trumpeting blast into it, making Alex laugh.

"I can play."

"You most certainly can." At last he had helped her. He was no psychiatrist, the root of her problem remained as much a mystery as the root of Elliot's or even his own problems, but he had helped her. Maybe, now that she knew who, musically, she was or could be, maybe she would go on to perform to the extent of her abilities without a safety net? Maybe not? Alex had no idea and he didn't care. He couldn't cure anybody, but at least now he had helped somebody, and helped somebody that deserved something good in her life. He'd never met or even heard of any musician who worked as hard as Laura worked. He loved her madly, but that was a bonus; at last he'd done something worthy. He needed that in light of what he was planning. He was about to do exactly what McNabb had always assumed he did anyway. He was about to cheat people, to offer music, real music, under false pretences. The music was real. Four people formed Yang Li, but the public would assume that Yang Li, the virtuoso on the run from nasty old red China, was a living, breathing human being. He knew now they would believe it because the music was true.

Yang Li was alive.

Walker was getting tired of waiting. Every day his phone was ringing off the hook with journalists and media types trying to get a leg up into the Yang Li story. He spun them all the same pitch. He told them he was staking his reputation on this one then he directed them to that half-wit lecturer at Alex's college. Walker wanted it all done and dusted. He wanted it over with, but he wasn't sure what getting it finished would mean. Already the NARC suits had marched into his office one by one—he wondered if they'd had to draw straws to decide who would go first. They all had a crack at him. Suddenly, all their best-laid plans were taking a back seat to Walker's revelation. They believed, without question, everything he had to say about Yang Li. They weren't interested in Yang Li. Well, they were interested but not in testing his veracity or musicality, they were interested in how such a thing might be fully exploited within the context of whatever strategy it was that they had for his business.

This was the best part, although even punishing NARCies was starting to get a little tedious. But at least they finally realized who he was. The old codger with the rolled up newspaper had become a lion. No more bursting into his office unannounced to confuse him with spreadsheets and PERT charts (whatever they hell they were), no more talk of product or maximization, or market segmentation. Suddenly, they were all pretending to be musicians. Suddenly, they all wanted to meet the artist. He loved telling them to buggar off, and when he tired of that he started telling them to bog off. They wanted to see a contract. They wanted to see the paper, the proof that they owned Yang Li and all rights to Yang Li, and perhaps even rights to his offspring and future descendants?

But Walker had nothing. There was no paper. There was no contract and there would never be a contract. He wanted them to see him. He wanted them to see it—his life's work. He'd even instructed a couple of them to listen to his complete catalogue if they wanted to understand what was going on. They were literal business types and were sure to take his instruction as a cryptic clue to his intentions. It would take them weeks to listen to everything; it pleased Walker to imagine them sitting, hour after hour, listening to all of his recordings, poring over cover blurbs to decipher the workings of a strange old man.

But the NARCies had too much energy. Walker was tiring of them. Even worse, he'd watched that McNabb twerp on television with a silly hat and talking out of it. He had no idea why Alex and his friends wanted to discredit the man but listening to him for more than five minutes did make Walker want to beat him with a big stick.

He got on to the phone to Alex. He wanted the music now. He couldn't wait any longer. The media were primed. If he let McNabb go on any longer he was sure to embarrass him. The time was right. They would arrange a concert at the Academy to launch Li.

"Concert? I don't understand? What do you mean?" Alex wondered if he was the only one amongst the lot of them who hadn't lost his mind.

"We'll invite them all. All the journos, all the blowhards. We'll get them all into the same space for the launch," said Walker.

"I don't understand."

"He can mime. We'll put him behind a bloody sheet. We can tease them even more. He's supposed to be illegal isn't he? It's perfect. A concert will concentrate all of the expectations into a single source. It's easier to handle."

"I still have to record Elliot playing guitar and I have to get the tuba track down as well. This is a wonderful idea. We get him onstage under a blanket, like one of those criminals going into court?"

"That's right, then we project his silhouette or something, play the bloody tape while he pretends to play. Simple. How long will it take to get it all finished? I'm running out of patience with your McNabb man. What exactly is his role anyway?"

"Just a couple of sessions. It's almost done. Elliot and my mate Skuggs can do their stuff in a single session. No more than a couple of days, I expect. We just want to get McNabb's balls in a vice. Get something on him. Get him under control."

"I don't like him one single bit."

"How long before you release the record? Will we make money? I'm almost skint."

"Not long. There will be some money. Don't worry. Just get me the music. I'll talk to McNabb; get him to arrange the concert."

"He'll think he's died and gone to heaven. A concert by the greatest musician who ever lived, in his college."

"Well, you can do what you want with him. I just want the recording finished."

"Soon," said Alex.

Skuggs was easy. He sat down, waited until Alex gave him a signal, then he played the piece right to the end without a single fluff. He played his own arrangement of Arden's Carnival of Venice. The tuba doesn't have access to a huge repertoire. When a tuba virtuoso plays, people expect to be dazzled the way they might watch a contortionist or an acrobat, or tickled with a bit of musical humour. Tuba players aren't allowed to have pretensions to depth or profundity; hearing a great lumbering beast of an instrument produce a few fireworks is about as much as most people can take. Skuggs didn't care that he'd never be taken seriously; he saw himself as an entertainer, a player, rather than a musician. He'd played thousands of concerts; he was the consummate performer. Alex considered a second take but asking such a thing might imply that he hadn't heard what Skuggs produced and, it would be rude.

Skuggs packed his tuba away. "Want me to go get the wee man?"

"Could you? That would be great. Beautiful stuff Skuggs. You're a credit to Yang Li."

"Did yer geezer mention any money?"

"He said there'd be money."

"How much?"

Alex shrugged.

"Don't trust him man. Get some cash off him."

Alex didn't want to get into this. "Don't worry."

"He's at it man. He's just like the rest of them."

"Will you go get Elliot… or Li or whoever's at home? Could you bring him here yourself? I'm not sure if Li can read English yet. Might get on the wrong bus."

"Reckon the wee man'll get back to normal after this?"

"What's normal? He was hardly a picture of sanity before this, was he?"

"Too crazy though. He's too crazy. Shame."

"It's up to him. I think he knows what he's doing. I just need a bit of guitar out of him then he can do what he wants."

"Cold."

Skuggs was right, Alex was cold, but he had no idea what to do. Elliot might have been stuck under one of those hair dryers in sci-fi movies that add a couple of hundred points to your IQ, but that was before he turned into Yang Li. Now he was gone, somewhere else, someone else. Alex was hardly equipped to be Elliot's friend, never mind solve problems expressed on a higher plane of consciousness. Elliot could never be swayed on anything; maybe this is what he wanted? Maybe it was all just a laugh? Maybe he wanted to become Yang Li? Who was he to argue? Alex simply couldn't figure out what helping him might mean.

There wasn't much to do to Skuggs's recording. He slung it into a larger room and used a few filters to melt a bit of superfluous noise in the lower register, but that was about it. By the time Elliot arrived he'd already produced a usable master of Skuggs's stuff.

"Elliot!" Alex hoped that a bit of enthusiasm might coax him into staying for a while.

"How about some Lauro to start?" said Elliot. Alex would have given Skuggs a thumbs-up if he were the type of person who ever gave thumbs-ups. Skuggs was standing behind Elliot. He pointed at Elliot then at his own head and wound little circles against his temple with his forefinger, as if dialing a number on a pulse telephone.

"Wee bastard pretended to be Li all the way here so I'd pay his bus fare," said Skuggs. Elliot ignored Skuggs's complaining; he got his guitar out and planted his footstool into position.

It took Alex a few minutes to arrange the microphones. Elliot went through his tuning ritual, pulling the strings so hard it looked like he might be ready to fire an arrow. Alex checked levels while Elliot tuned.

"Ready?" asked Elliot. Alex nodded. Elliot played a South American waltz Alex hadn't heard before. It was in two simultaneous time signatures—three-four-six-eight. It wasn't the type of waltz designed for dancing although its rhythms would charm the stodgiest set of bumcheeks into movement. It was a potpourri of short, sharp melodic figures that dripped and splashed about an offset pulse. Elliot's left hand shot up and down the length of the fretboard with impossible ease, as if physically picking up musical fragments buried inside the instrument. Then a more percussive mode emerged; the bass rapped an offbeat counterpoint to snatched chords descending into a beautiful melody—the waltz. Elliot held the melody aloft with deep apoyando strokes over a skeletal, tirando accompaniment, without drawing undue attention to the careless beauty.

"Brilliant," said Elliot when he'd finished. "How about some death music? A bit of contrast? You can play this at me funeral if you like. Passacaille, Weiss."

From the first chord it was as if he were playing a completely different guitar. In the Lauro, the guitar sounded rough and ready, gritty, almost cheap; the kind of guitar anyone might pick up in a Venezuelan street market. Now the guitar sounded formal, large, majestic, projecting deep, sonorous tones rich in harmonics. The music was both simple and exacting; a theme and variations over a ground bass. He stated the theme without affect or effect, there was no vibrato, no superfluous additions to obscure intention. Where the Lauro had been elastic and pliable and curvy and hot, this music was solid and dense and strict; straight, Cartesian lines defined, right from the start, the foundations upon which layers of variations explored the gravitational possibilities of the incessant ostinato. Elliot's interpretation might have been a fitting tribute to the memory of a king or an emperor; it was a disciplined, almost geometrically conceived performance. He constructed a perfectly crescendoed pathos from beginning to end, a rising of emotion so subtle, it commandeered the listener's nervous system like a benign invading virus. This was Yang Li—Alex's Yang Li, not Elliot's confused concoction—it was masterful and confident and without a hint of editorial; there was no trace of the performer, only the music existed.

It was perfection.

Alex had his guitarist. He had hardly a second to slip into a success-filled fantasy when Elliot dragged him back.

"Ying pow so fah mah?"

"Bloody hell. We still have to finish the bleedn Chopin man, don't go Yang Li on me yet."

"Wee shite did this to me all the way here," said Skuggs. "No bad though. The tunes were nice."

"They were sublime. But I still need Elliot. Are you kidding Elliot? Is this a piss-take? Cause we need another session, man. Walker wants the music. We've got to finish it."

"Hing see pah, seeee pah foh mow shung."

"Take him home Skuggs."

Alex wouldn't allow himself to be torn. Whether Elliot was faking it or not, the music had to be finished. Whether Alex had the ability or not, the music had to be finished. He tried not to get angry at Elliot, and he tried not to get angry at himself for having to control his anger. He watched Skuggs lead Elliot out of the room; it might have been a kindly orderly ushering a bewildered old folks inmate to his next inconsequential appointment. He sat for a few moments, almost hoping that Elliot would barge back in, laughing at his gullibility.

But Elliot didn't come back. Alex packed his equipment. It was all done. All the recording was done. He still had to finish the generated music though, and he'd have to do it on his own. Over the past few weeks he'd become accustomed to Elliot, challenging his programming skills with ludicrous, uninformed demands, and revealing his musical limitations like a child pointing at the obvious. He wrapped a lead around his thumb and worked it from elbow to thumb to elbow until it was a neat black lariat, ready for the next job. He packed everything away until the only evidence that remained of his recording sessions was a corner filled with little aluminium crates and boxes.

He locked the trombone room door and headed straight for the lab. It was time to finish, to finish it all and pass it to Quentin. He dismissed a chill in the pit of his belly; a chill he recognized as self-doubt. Since inviting Elliot—and Li—into the music he'd become used to them, but surely not dependent on them? He listened to the Chopin Third to get him in the mood.

It sounded different. No, not different, it was the same music but he was hearing it differently. It was more poignant, more pointed. It wasn't that he could hear more or that more of the music was suddenly revealed to him, that wasn't it at all, he heard no more or less than he'd heard before; he could always hear every attack, every harmonic, every tonal relationship, there never was a nuance hidden to him but, and he could hardly believe it, he could hear the intention, the purpose of the music, he could hear where it was supposed to lead—he knew what the composer wanted.

He made a couple of tiny adjustments; almost nothing, it took less than five minutes, but he knew it made all the difference in the world. Without the adjustments it was wrong, just plain wrong. How could he have missed that before? How could Elliot have missed it?

He quickly set to work on the Revolutionary Study. It was clear from the moment he loaded it that the intrusion of Elliot into the music had improved it, and it hadn't left him helpless either. His mind felt clear, but it was more than clarity, he could remember the music the way it was in his head before any of Elliot's suggestions or dogma, he could remember the way he wanted it to sound and the memory brought with it embarrassment at his lack of insight. It was all so obvious now, how could have missed all of this?

He loaded the code into an editor; he knew exactly what he wanted. His mind emptied of conscious thought as he hacked into the code to coax the performance he knew existed within the music. Time passed without meaning. He worked faster than he'd ever worked before, but now it was a joy, it was easy, it was liberating. The intention of every tone, every phrase, seemed written into his mind the way a message might be written into stone; it was decided, finished, complete, but also full of possibilities, the slightest variation in attack or sustain leading all of the subsequent sounds down a self-similar, but different, road. There was only one answer, only one interpretation that worked, but that interpretation was held, like Schrödinger's cat—neither dead nor alive, awaiting the observer to provide meaning—in an indeterminate state, a quantum shadow until the waveform collapsed into reality. He finally knew what Elliot knew, saw what Elliot saw, heard what Elliot heard.

The question was there, somewhere in his mind, he could feel it, a cloud of doubt, moving in and out of view, but he dismissed it, he had no need for it. This newfound insight had come with the knowledge that the insight was real, like a piece of software he might have written with self-checking routines; there was no need to know anything else, no need to question the why or the wherefore. He knew the mind of the composer, the hopes and fears of the composer, the errors, the false starts, the trials and the triumphs, he was privy to everything, he didn't care why he knew; with its coming the impulse to check the source had dissolved. He was still himself, still Alex, but he could hear Chopin's voice; not the way he believed Elliot meant when he'd said it before. Elliot sounded mad when he ranted about hearing voices; a prelude to schizophrenia. Alex couldn't hear his voice speaking English or French or even Hungarian, but he could hear his voice as clearly as he'd ever heard any voice in his life.

There were still difficulties, insoluble difficulties, artefacts of the sampling process, limitations inherent within the digital domain but hidden within the choice of music so that the listener might become part of the solution, involuntarily, unconsciously superimposing the seamless infinity of the analog onto crass digital facsimiles. But, this would do. He had eliminated Quentin's rooms by simply recording in a single room. All of the evidence that the music wasn't real was there, but who would even think to look for it? How many people would know what to look for even if they knew to look? This wasn't about Alex and his music anymore. It was about Yang Li. Yang Li was a great pianist, perhaps the best there was or ever was, but he was also a guitarist, a guitarist as talented as any, and the guitar was real. The tuba was real. The violin was real.

⌃ ♯ ♮

The only problem McNabb could see with a concert was the woofter sitting outside the bursar's office. When Walker had telephoned with the news that he wanted a concert at the Academy, and instructions to invite whomever he saw fit, McNabb was beside himself with joy; his success assured, his future guaranteed. Walker would invite the press, television, the media, and he would invite the board of governors, friends, rivals; people to see him being courted by the media. The whole world would see him introduce Yang Li, present him to the world from his own college. But he'd have to get rid of the tranny downstairs. Force wouldn't work, especially in light of all the publicity that was about to descend upon the place. An angry Todd might cause more trouble than he was worth. Who knows what these types are capable of?

After ruminating for more than five minutes but less than ten, McNabb headed down to the bursar's office to offer a truce to Todd, to give him enough, just enough that he might not decide to besmirch McNabb's triumph. Just a week ago, the necessity to make peace with Todd would have induced revulsion, but Todd was inconsequential now, no more important than perhaps an insect crawling across the lens of one of the many cameras that would soon beam McNabb's face into posterity and fame.

"I'll give you a job," said McNabb bluntly. Todd was startled. "Did you hear me?"

"Job? What job?" Perhaps his own strategy of simply sitting outside the bursar's office was working? Maybe there was no need for any elaborate plans after all? What job? Todd wasn't exactly sure that he wanted a job. Getting a job, any job, hadn't really occurred to him; his vigil was designed to get him his old job—the principal's job—back.

"I don't know," said McNabb. He couldn't be bothered with any of this. Perhaps he should have sent his secretary instead? He had bigger and better things on his plate. "Whatever you want. How about a lectureship?"

"Lectureship?"

Students on their way to classes who absolutely could not find any other route saw McNabb talking to Todd and they steered clear. Such conversations would surely instill anger in McNabb, and he was not one to limit his anger to the object of that anger. McNabb was a man happy to spray anger at anything and anyone in sight, and happy to invoke excess and superfluous retribution upon the innocent.

"Lectureship, lectureship. Why not?" McNabb was careful not to be rude. This was no time to alienate her. All he wanted was a tranny-free zone for the concert. She could have a job as lecturer. What difference could it make?

"What's the catch?"

"No catch. Tenure. Real job. Dress how you like. Do what you want. Teach what you want."

"No catch?"

"I'm the boss."

"You're the boss?"

"You have to do as you're told."

Todd squinted at McNabb. What was he up to? What had Alex and Ingles done? He knew that Ingles had already challenged him to a fight; she had already stolen his wife away, but he didn't know what Alex was up to. Should he take this job or not? Would it interfere with anyone's plans? Was it enough? Was a lectureship enough? Was that a victory?

"Do as I'm told?"

"I'm not trying to take advantage. Really. I need to know that you won't sit here if I ask you not to."

"That's all?"

"That's all."

"That's all?"

"There's a concert taking place here. A big concert. I need you not to talk to the press."

"The press?"

"They want to see me and they want to see Yang Li, my protégé."

"Your protégé?"

"Can you do it? I'll give you a life. You can wear anything you want anytime you want, but not at the concert."

"Can I go to work now?"

"Yes. Go to work."

"When is the concert?"

"I'll let you know." He dashed up the stairs, two at a time holding on to his new hat lest wind resistance reveal his scar.

Of course, it wasn't enough for Todd. A lectureship? He was principal and he'd have his life back, somehow. Sitting outside the bursar's office like Gandhi in lipstick had worked, it had done the job. He had the chance now to take it to the students, to show them he hadn't changed, that he was the same man he always was. It didn't matter what McNabb's motivation was. This was the first step to victory, and McNabb had handed it to him without a fight.

# Twenty-Eight

Yang Li could smell the sea as soon as he woke up. He grabbed his guitar case and left. He followed the scent. It was different from the smell he was used to, but it was still the sea. It was far away. A long walk, but it didn't matter. He smiled graciously at passers-by, as was his way, and he walked until he got to the river, then he followed the river, for a long time, until he came to the mouth of the river, the place where it met the sea.

It was cold, but that didn't matter. The beach was dirty, the water was dark, but that didn't matter. Yang Li undressed; he took off his uniform, his socks, his underwear. He stood naked on the deserted beach. He should have shivered, it was cold, but he didn't shiver, he knew it was cold, he could feel it, but it didn't feel uncomfortable at all, it felt right, it felt safe.

He gathered up his guitar case and walked into the sea. After a few slow motion steps the seabed disappeared under him and he climbed half on to the guitar case and he paddled until his arms were numb. The sea reminded him of his childhood, his carefree, happy childhood in Guangdong province, before the bureaucrats came and gave his parents some paper and took him away.

# The Samplist

A pain tore savagely into his midriff; it twisted like a tornado, his body turned instantly into cold steel. The pain overwhelmed, he curled into a ball, his muscles twitched and closed in upon themselves. It was cold, so cold.

He couldn't breath, he saw the coastline, it was so far away. Fuck, thought Elliot, the bastard's trying to kill me. He wrapped his arms around the guitar case, he squeezed with all of his might but he couldn't tell if it was enough; he was too cold, he couldn't feel his arms, all he could feel was the knife gouging into his stomach, deep, and up into his chest.

His head was under the water. He was upside down. *Fuck.*

Walker got the call a few seconds after he picked up the package. The police had found his business card inside the guitar case. There was a witness who said she saw him swimming out to sea but then lost sight of him. They found some strange clothes washed up on the shore and a guitar case with an expensive-looking guitar inside. They wanted to know who he was. When they realized Walker wasn't family they confided that they expected to find the body soon enough. The water was cold, the currents strong. They knew where to look, where to wait. Walker told them it sounded like Yang Li. He said Yang Li because he didn't know Elliot's last name; he'd almost forgotten that he wasn't Yang Li. He'd thought a lot about Elliot since that day. He was a marvellous musician, an astonishing performer with the mind of a grandmaster. It was his talent that powered Yang Li. Alex had built him, constructed him, but Elliot populated him, breathed life into him. When he put the phone down he took some time to decide he'd done the right thing by denying Elliot. He felt guilty denying him, but not so guilty as to come clean; he wasn't supposed to know who he was anyway. It seemed right.

Walker worried about how his new friends would react. They were in the throes of a great adventure and now it would end. Their friend was dead but so was their creation.

Walker opened the package and popped the CD into the player. Yang Li was bold, powerful, confident; piano playing to match the best. The guitar was gorgeous, the violin full of fire and the tuba made him smile. He picked up the phone to tell Alex.

"We'll make the concert a memorial service," Quentin said to Alex. "Are you absolutely certain he has no family?"

"No." Alex was in shock. Elliot was dead? How could Elliot be dead? What the hell was he playing at, being dead instead of driving him crazy?

"As Yang Li we can at least celebrate his life. People will mourn for an idea more easily than they would the reality of a student guitarist. This way he'll get the acknowledgement he craved in life."

"I can't believe he's dead. He really killed himself?"

"They found his clothes. Guitar washed up. No body yet but they say it's just a matter of time. I'm so sorry Alex. I wish I'd got the chance to know him better. He was quite a character and quite a talent. I was so taken by the whole performance that day, I think I underestimated your friend. I just listened to those pieces you sent. Truly gorgeous. I certainly would have recorded him... Did he do the guitar in one take?" Quentin felt guilty as soon as he said it, but he really couldn't help himself.

"One take. Yes. He was a one-take type of guy."

"I'm sorry. I'm being insensitive."

"No. He was very proud of his talent, his intelligence. I think he was a genius. He certainly wouldn't shut up about it. Everybody and his dog seems to be a genius these days but I think he was the real deal. He made everything seem easy.

Maybe he indulged himself too much? He was so sure of himself he never questioned the limits of his behaviour." Alex was talking more to himself now than Quentin. Quentin was old enough to have lost people; he knew the pain. "He was hurting himself. He had cuts on his hands. He tried to speak to me but I was so jealous of him. I was tired of listening to him complain. He had it all. He had everything I thought would make me happy."

"You mustn't blame yourself."

"I don't. There was no way in this world I could have helped him. I might have been a better friend, but really I think he looked on the rest of us as lower life forms. He liked us, as an audience for his wisecracks, but more really the way a child might like a pet hamster. I'm starting to get the feeling that I knew someone who was truly special and I denied it, even though I could see it all in front of me. It's like knowing someone who towered above us all but because he was always just there, you know, sitting beside you laughing at you, you thought maybe he was the same. Maybe if he'd lived longer he might have achieved great things?"

"Perhaps." Quentin didn't mind listening. He'd stay on the line as long as Alex needed him. He knew the drill.

"He might have gone beyond music even…"

There was a knock at the door. Suddenly, Alex realized he'd have to tell Laura; he'd have to tell Skuggs. Skuggs would be fine but Laura would be inconsolable. "That's the door. Can I call you later?" Alex took a deep breath and prepared a face for Laura that would tell her something was amiss. He'd lead her to the sofa and tell her straight.

He opened the door.

"What's up? How about a cuppa? I'm parched." Elliot breezed past him straight into the kitchen.

Alex's brain went into a semi-catatonic state for a few seconds. By the time he'd come to and gone after Elliot into the kitchen, he'd already put the kettle on and was searching for food.

"Any chocolate biscuits?"

"Right in front of you. Cupboard, bottom shelf. Are you going to provide an explanation or do I have to guess why everyone thinks you're dead?"

"Yang Li tried to kill me."

"Yang Li tried to kill you?"

"Tried to drown me. No McVities? Bloody value biscuits? Cheap bastard."

"Have you ever bought any biscuits with your own money in your life? Dead virtuosos need McVities?" Alex didn't want to ask but the little buggar had him again. "Okay, okay, tell me then. How did someone who doesn't exist try to drown you and how come everyone thinks you drowned?"

"No idea." Elliot popped a tea bag into a cup and poured hot water on it. He scooped five spoons of sugar into it then slopped milk all over the worktop in order to get a tiny drop into the cup. "Look at these clothes man. Got them off a washing line. Some old granny wants her husband's shirt and trousers back."

"They don't look any different to the stuff you normally wear."

Elliot looked down at himself then gave Alex a stare like he was crazy. "I'm sitting in me flat minding me own business. Then I'm freezing, lying on a scabby beach. I thought me balls were going to drop off. I dreamt that I'd gone for a swim." He slurped some tea. "Absolutely freezing. I ran about like a madman. Jumped over a fence. Stole these clothes and some wet blankets then I must have fallen asleep again. I woke up, put on the clothes, jumped on a bus."

"You had money?"

"Made looney eyes at the driver then sat down in the clos-est seat to him. Then I got another bus and came here."

"Rather than go home?"

"No keys."

"Everybody thinks you're dead. Quentin's having a memo-rial service."

"Really? Cool."

"For Yang Li."

"Well, I'm Yang Li, that'll do."

"You tried to kill yourself?"

"Yang Li tried to kill me." Elliot looked at Alex like he thought he'd lost it.

"But you killed him instead?"

"Mm." This seemed to entertain Elliot. "I suppose so. I must have murdered him. When's the memorial? Can I come?"

"You don't think that'll be a problem? You know, the dead guy being there?"

"Who cares? Just another dead chink. Nobody'll know the difference anyway even if anyone knew what Yang Li looked like."

"You're such a racist."

"Bet you a fiver… no, let's make it a hundred trillion quid, plus your soul that nobody would know the difference. Did you finish the recording?"

"Yes."

"All on your own?"

"Yes."

"Did you notice anything?"

"No."

"Have you played the piano yet?"

"What do you mean?" Alex was confused but probably no more confused than he ever was with Elliot. He was happy Elliot was alive. No, he was overjoyed, beside himself, on the verge of tears. But he'd never let Elliot know.

"Christ man, I gave you it?"

"You gave me it?"

"The pen? I held up a pen and showed you the universe?"

"Oh, the universe. Yes, sure okay."

"Go play the piano numbskull."

Alex was surprised at himself for not continuing the argument, but he felt compelled. He headed straight for the keyboard. It wasn't plugged in. He crashed some chords silently into the impotent keys.

He felt it immediately.

Elliot was standing beside him, smiling.

"This is impossible," said Alex, but he knew it wasn't.

"Not bad, eh?"

"This is impossible."

"Now you've got nothing to bitch about anymore. That'll teach you."

"This is impossible." Alex kept saying it but he knew it wasn't impossible. He'd known it from the time he sat down to polish the programmed Chopin. He knew exactly what the composer wanted, and more; he knew what the composer wanted and how to improve the composer's vision—which was impossible, just like it was impossible that Elliot had passed some ethereal gift by showing him a pen. But he could feel it. He ran through some scales and arpeggios, the thumpety-thump of the dead keys offered no indication to the world outside their minds that something wonderful was afoot. It welled up inside him, he thought he might explode; his expression was jammed into the kind of smile Elliot always wore. He raced

through the Chopin prelude; it was like the dream a lot of non-musicians claim to have, where they just sit down at a piano and play—no effort, no strain, just music and joy—his technique had become a plaything, a certainty, for the first time in his life he felt like he was the master of himself, his fingers unconsciously performing ordinary miracles with Chopin's most treasured ambitions.

"I'm still fucking starving," Elliot piped. "Buy us a curry?"

Alex felt a little like the way he felt after he'd smoked some of Allan's hash, he was kind of floating. He looked at Elliot with such gratitude that Elliot took a defensive step back.

Elliot had killed Li. Li was an adversary, some competition, so Elliot had snuffed him out; he had managed to extract his own progressive insanity as if it were a decaying tooth threatening to envelope his consciousness the way only pain can. He'd rolled up all of his eccentricities and foibles and his tiny madnesses and injected them into Li before leading him to his death.

And he'd passed something on to Alex; something precious beyond measure. "You're the buddha," Alex said. "You *are* the buddha." It was simple. It had stared him in the face a hundred times, and a hundred times Elliot had told him as much, but now he knew the truth.

Elliot smiled. "Vindaloo?"

Alex called Quentin to tell him Elliot was alive and to ask him to tell McNabb that Li was dead. Li was dead and he was going to stay dead.

Quentin was overjoyed that Elliot had not passed on and that they still had some play left with Li. He took Alex's word that Elliot was fine and braced himself for a chat with McNabb; he'd call him tomorrow, in the morning, and make it short.

Alex took Elliot for a vindaloo. He took him for a vindaloo and he watched him chomp on his chicken tikka with a face spattered with popadom crumbs, and he knew there was no more to say.

Elliot talked incessantly about the memorial. He'd decided, since his partial demise, that there would be no more music, no more guitar. He was done with show business.

Alex knew there was no more to say.

# TWENTY-NINE

 **McNabb** considered killing himself when he heard the news. There would be no more elevating symbiosis, no more attention, his ticket was gone, his bus had left for good. He poured whisky into himself and nurtured a slow rage. Someone would pay for this. He thought of his dyke wife and her peepaw lover. He hacked at them both with a claymore until they floated in their own blood. He slung them into the bath and whisked them into mince with a chainsaw. He swallowed more whisky and wished he could commit the crime. He wished he could kill them all. He'd grab the orthodontist's great swirls of hair and he'd pull his teeth out one by one then he'd toss him into the bath with the dyke tartare.

The high-pitched chirp of the telephone sent him out of his chair. His heart pounded against his rib cage.

"What is it?" he barked into the phone.

"I want to offer my condolences."

McNabb didn't recognize the voice. "Leave me be."

"This is a difficult time, I know. I have to write an obituary for someone we've never even seen. I'm sorry sir. I'm new here… at the paper. They gave me the obits. I don't have a beat yet. I'm sorry."

"Beat?"

"Just a few words. My editor doesn't quite know how to handle this."

"Handle this?"

"You know. The loss to the world?"

"Yes. The loss."

"Was it true? Was he really as good as they say? Am I the first? Has anyone else called? I know this is difficult but the media is going to go into a feeding frenzy. This is going to go to nationals. It's a real story now… you know, a tragedy."

"Feeding frenzy?"

"You have to be brave. It'll be difficult. It's just an obit."

McNabb couldn't hear him. He'd already forgotten about the killings. Maybe this was better? Maybe a dead virtuoso was more valuable than a live one? Surely when they heard Li, he would have been pushed into the background, ushered back to anonymity? This way was better. They had to come to him. He had a recording. He'd heard him play. They still needed him.

"Piss off." He slammed the phone down and waited for it to ring again. He spent the next three hours grunting platitudes at reporters further up the evolutionary scale than eager obituary writers. Again, it was as if fate had simply had a little fun; played a little game with him before revealing his true worth. He was slurping single malt and parrying advances from some of the most important media names in the business, writing down names and dates, building a list of engagements that would take him into the mainstream. Things couldn't have been better if he'd killed the little bastard himself. He was important, he was in demand, and now it was cemented into Yang Li's death.

He was unassailable.

He was in the middle of a radio interview when he passed out; intoxicated as much by himself as the whisky. The interviewer apologized to him and the audience—this was a difficult time and McNabb was very brave to face the press under such crushing grief.

Quentin let McNabb organize the memorial. It would be at the Academy, in the concert hall. There wasn't much point in having it in a church. Li was probably Buddhist or Confucian or some such thing. And why let some Church of Scotland minister get in on the act with one of their depressing speeches when he could stand on stage during the whole thing?

It would be simple, they would play some of Li's music and he would make a speech. Nobody knew Li. Nobody but Walker had met him. Walker refused to talk publicly about Li—adding the 'Garbo' factor to the media mix and simultaneously elevating McNabb to first, the sole arbiter of the music, and after that presumably the sole expert and reference in what might become the lore surrounding Li. As long as he kept students out of the picture and made sure the woofer wasn't in the building then everything should go like clockwork.

When Laura found out that Elliot and Li were dead except that Elliot wasn't dead after all and that he had killed Li in self-defence and that Elliot had given up music she gave Elliot a sharp jab in the shoulder. Elliot hadn't expected the jab this time any more than he'd expected the last one. Luckily, this one lacked the precision and power of the previous attack and it turned out to be more of a substitute for a hug than a serious attempt to poke holes in him. Of course, Laura didn't want him to give up music but she knew that although his talents were easy and deep, music was a means to an end for Elliot; more like a symptom of something benign and wonderful than the source itself, more a shadow or a reflection of something much larger than himself. Music had provided him three years of living without having to work, three years of fun, but a continuation now would mean at least another two years of listening to Boskov or someone like him, then God knows how many years travelling up and down the country playing in sub-zero church halls to the inmates of the local old folks homes.

The time for music was almost done.

# THIRTY

The memorial service was a big disappointment to Elliot. Somehow he'd pictured one of those scenes he'd watched a thousand times on television where thirty or forty people stand around a grave sniffling and crying before a huge coffin is lowered deep into the ground. Elliot didn't have any beautiful young wife to throw herself onto the casket but he figured at least there would be some kind of sign that he'd be missed. Alex explained to him that there was no body, there would be no actual funeral as such due to Yang Li being alive and well, or at least the guy who pretended to be Yang Li in human form was alive and well and sitting right beside him near the back of the hall and driving him half mad with his ridiculous critique of the whole affair.

Elliot wasn't convinced. "I still reckon that none of these bastards gave a damn about Yang Li."

Alex knew he had to be joking but he was more concerned about whether the audience would enjoy the music or not. A few months ago he would have fretted over whether they'd twig but he knew the work was beyond reproach now; it was real, it was as real as he suspected it might become. The music was real and the death of the fiction that fronted the music would metal plate the story; fossilize the fragments into believability and breathe life into the myth. Where once the critics might have cried fraud, soon they'd defend the memory of a dead genius.

Alex scanned the crowd that seemed built three deep up and into the walls. When McNabb had started his speech all was quiet; but that was almost an hour ago. Cameramen were leaning away from their cameras chatting with each other. Presenters were dabbing handkerchiefs on shiny foreheads and rubbing makeup pads into ruddy cheeks.

Walker had managed to gain entry for Alex, Laura and Elliot. Skuggs didn't want to come at all but pled vociferously that Alex not leave the room without a cheque from Walker. Alex was to deposit the cheque as soon as possible and then hand over exactly one fifth to Skuggs. Alex had no idea why Skuggs thought he deserved a fifth and not a tenth or a quarter or a third but he agreed; while harbouring no plans whatever to try to filch money out of Walker during the ceremony.

Todd, Ingles and her lover watched the ceremony on live television in McNabb's living room. It was a happy coincidence that the so-called serious television networks in the UK were now competing with satellite television and had a truckload of channels to fill. Even such a strange and solemn occasion as the presumed death of a possible virtuoso could demand some live air-time, but as the obituary writer had suggested to McNabb; a tragic death had turned Yang Li into mainstream news.

Of course, McNabb cocked up. Without any warning the first few chords from Chopin's revolutionary study ripped through the hall more like a riff from a heavy metal band than a dead virtuoso interpreting a nineteenth century composer. Perhaps McNabb had agreed on a word or a sign for the soundman and he'd miscalculated? Perhaps the guy was just bored like everyone else and wanted to get the thing over with? Perhaps someone had paid him? Whatever the reason McNabb recoiled from the microphone into which he'd droned for almost a full hour about nothing in particular outside his own 'role' in Li's development and unveiling.

"This is more like it," shouted Elliot. "Wait till they hear the guitar, they'll be spontaneously throwing themselves out of the window."

Alex clocked all the little looks people were giving each other. It sounded pretty damn good; the volume added a bit of melodrama missing from acoustic concerts and pushed the possibility of discovery even further away. Alex squeezed Laura's hand; hearing his music blaring into a hundred inquisitive microphones seemed to burn all of the oxygen within his system, he felt like he might float away without Laura to tether him.

Walker made his way onstage. Chopin's third prelude was racing around the hall. He made a cutting gesture across his throat. He did it so quickly and professionally, like he'd done it a million times before. His presence must have impressed the soundman because the music ended abruptly. He moved close in on the microphone. He wasn't used to speaking publicly into a microphone and he kind of hung his head a little and cocked it to one side; probably the way he would when he was in his control booth trying to coax a performance out of someone.

"The first time I met Yang Li I didn't believe him."

There was an almost tangible change in atmosphere, as if the words had actually carried an electric charge. The media types edged forward, en masse, in their chairs. This is what they came for. The piano playing was magnificent, fabulous, beyond belief, but who the hell really cared? They might have played a recording of any one of forty or fifty people and nobody would have, could have, noticed the difference. If they'd played any one of maybe three or four of the greatest pianists ever recorded, they'd have had to ship in experts to tell them who was playing and why it was special, and even then the experts would probably end up offering each other a black eye.

This is what they came for. McNabb had mumbled and muffled his speech, hardly referring at all to Li, he'd droned on about the Academy and his own recent rise to prominence. He'd thrown a few superlatives in but that was about it. In truth, even if Li had been real McNabb wouldn't have known the difference.

"I still don't believe him."

This is what the recording needed. Walker must have seen that. Playing the music wouldn't be enough. They needed the legend. They needed to be told.

"You have never heard, will never hear, better piano playing. As a pianist Li was among the first rank, the very best of the very best." He cupped an elbow in his hand and pressed a forefinger against his lips as if he were thinking, trying to find the right words. "I signed Li without hearing him play piano." At this there was flurry of activity. Reporters of the old school scribbled shorthand in notebooks. There was a rippled explosion of flashlights and the electronic whir of video turning in a hundred cameras as the news people finally sensed the story.

"I've made it my business to seek out the unique, the gifted, artists who don't simply play music, they explore remote regions of the mind, states of being of which we harbour suspicions but have no evidence. Then they bring back the loot, the plunder, they give us their music to feed our sense, our fondest and most desperate hope that there is more to the universe than that which we see and feel and hear. Yang Li was such an artist... but more, he not only visited those places, he was no tourist passing through collecting memorabilia and artefacts to dazzle us, he seemed to live in that place, always, no... more than that, he may have created those places." Walker gathered himself; his lips pressed against the microphone, his breathing was audible. "Another young life is lost to the world for our lack of understanding. Our fear. But he left a trace of himself, an imprint, a benign glimpse of his universe."

The audience was transfixed. They had come to hear Li but the music wasn't enough. Walker knew that; the music is never enough. Just as a composer requires an interpreter, the interpreter must be explained. It was like listening to Yang Li himself talk in pseudo-Pidgin English that Alex had to further refine into a common language. McNabb was standing back from Walker; wearing a stoic expression that told at once of stolen thunder and molten anger—he would have to fight for the scraps after all.

"Li was the finest guitarist I have ever heard." Walker nodded to the soundman.

Elliot made an audible squeak.

If any camera had roamed to the three seats containing the three students who had managed somehow to get themselves entrance to the biggest death bash of the decade they would have seen three faces too happy to mark such a tragic event.

"Let this be tribute to all of the great musicians who walk alone among us," Walker said a moment before the music came.

Elliot was truly in nirvana. The stark introduction to the Weiss Passacaille offered scant evidence of the unfolding of Elliot's dark interpretation. By the time he had exposed the treasure hidden deep within the simple theme and ground its variations toward an end, audible sniffles and a serious nose-blowing accompaniment weighed in to the Weiss as funeral music. Elliot thought this was swell and he imagined a million viewers across the globe bubbling into paper hankies for his music and his loss.

Then it was over.

It was easy to tell why Walker hadn't allowed any tuba into the occasion; the tuba would have to compete with listener-baggage—better to offer it in the record rather than risk any comedic associations staining the fragile structure that Walker and Alex had built.

Laura was a different matter. She had genuinely enjoyed the whole affair but it was plain that her music was not going to make an appearance. She gave no outward indication but Alex could feel her disappointment. He felt angry and resolved to give Walker some hell. It made sense to leave out the tuba; Skuggs would give not a shit either way and had skin thicker than an elephant even if he had borrowed umbrage for the occasion, but she was hurting.

McNabb approached the microphone and mumbled something but nobody paid any notice; bumcheeks had been drilling into hard wooden seats for more than an hour. The end of the Weiss signalled the end of the event. Like passengers on a long-haul flight a moment after landing, the whole audience leaped up and stretched themselves out in a single action. Alex tried to spot Walker to give him a telling off on Laura's account. He also felt like hugging him; but that could wait.

Stretching on tiptoes to try to find Walker there was a tap on his shoulder.

"Alex, Elliot, the beautiful Laura." It was Walker. Laura wrapped her arms around him and planted a kiss on his cheek.

"I feel like kissing you myself," said Elliot. "I'm made up with that. It was lovely. You made them get it. Thank you. Truly. Thank you."

"It was you. You didn't need any help from me."

"We know that's not true," said Elliot. "We all need help from someone. Lerruz buy you a pint?"

Walker gave Elliot a smile then turned to Laura. "You probably hate me right now?"

She was caught between emotions and tried to deny it but while she loved the man for making it all come true, her disappointment had been crushing; she still couldn't play properly without Alex—she had hoped to hear herself playing today.

"I want to record you."

Her mouth opened and closed as she tried to find the words.

"You have everything it takes to make it as a concert soloist in today's market. Your playing is first class and you are as easy on the eye as any musician I've ever seen."

Walker didn't know about Laura's 'problem'. Before she had a chance to answer, Alex leapt in. "She'll do it. You're right. She's wonderful and she's gorgeous. I'll buy her record right now."

"But… please… you no understand."

"You no understand?" said Alex. She had forgotten how to speak English. She was struggling to deal with the offer of a career; the seal of approval, her dreams made real. "Don't you think in today's market that it's possible to launch a career without live performances?" Alex asked Walker deliberately.

"Of course."

"And with the currency you've gained today, you might be able to just use video, like a pop act?"

"Yes," said Walker. "I think we can do it whatever way Laura wants to do it. I feel the way… I feel the way I felt when I started. This is fun."

"One more question. Could I do the recording? I mean, yes, we can use direct-to-disk techniques, like the way you always do but I don't want to use acetates, I want to use digital hard disks."

"But I can hear artefacts in digital recor…" Walker stopped himself. "Hell, who cares? Yes, you do the recordings. Why not?"

"I think maybe I am dead and in heaven." She sat down.

"This is what you deserve," said Alex.

"Listen guys, this is all very touching." Elliot realized that they'd never take this as anything other than irony from him. "Seriously. Seriously. This really is touching. I'm sure you'll do great Laura. But I have to go."

"Go where?"

"I'm outa here man."

Elliot headed straight out of the hall without looking back. They watched him go without a word to each other. Alex found it hard to believe that he was really gone. This was a guy who had actually died and been resurrected. This was someone who'd displayed almost supernatural talents and then demonstrated the supernatural itself when he transferred whatever it was that it was to Alex.

Elliot was real.

And this time he was really gone and in his place came McNabb. He scowled at Alex and Laura; how the hell had they got in? What were they doing talking to Walker?

There was a tap on Alex's shoulder. "Almost forgot. I'll send you a forwarding address for my cash. I'm skint. And can I stay with you until I've got a forwarding address?" Elliot said with a straight face.

"Man, you like to make exits," Alex said, laughing. "What's up with you?" he said to McNabb.

"How did you get in here?"

Walker leant toward McNabb and whispered conspiratorially into his ear. At first McNabb looked serious, important, part of the moment. In a few seconds his expression changed.

"He's pulling a whitey," Elliot said with glee.

McNabb grabbed Walker's arm as if he might fall over. Walker sat him down. Alex sat beside him.

"Meet Yang Li," said Alex motioning to Elliot then himself and Laura. "We're Yang Li. Now, this is what you're going to do. You're going to go on as the Yang Li expert. Nobody's going to take that away from you."

McNabb looked at him like he was a man with a miracle.

"Don't get carried away. We all graduate like normal people. You get Todd re-instated as principal and you give the prof her job back, okay?" Before McNabb had time to answer he interjected. "When you leave this room you may have the urge to fight this but you mustn't do that. You sexually assaulted Laura and God knows how many other girls. You are excrement and I'd rather see you dead but this will do. You can have whatever you can get from your Yang Li associations but if you try to fight us we'll use the photographs."

McNabb's hand shot to his scar, almost knocking off his Panama, betraying his fear.

"Now, beat it."

McNabb stood up with some difficulty.

"Don't give me that," said Alex almost too loudly, there was still a great hubbub in the hall to shield the conversation from inquisitive ears, but he shot a few glances around to make sure. "Don't play the decrepit old nazi. I know who you are. Just leave."

McNabb left quickly. Everything seemed unreal, a blur, like his mind was being stretched in different directions. Betty? Yes. Betty. A purpose returned to him. He barged out of the hall like a man with a place to be.

"Elliot, you can buppy off as well for a couple of hours. Laura and I need to… talk."

"Give us a tenner, I'll buy you that pint Quentin."

"My treat," said Walker.

"That reminds me, how much are we going to make on this? Am I gonna be rich? Wanna see something *really* cool? Gorra a pen on you?"

Walker laughed.

"We should go get Skuggs. Where the hell is he anyway?"

The drivers had formed a circle around him and were passing a hat full of five-pound notes around.

"How much this time guys?" asked Skuggs.

"Clam up and play, otherwise the trumpet gets pawned."

"You know it's not a trumpet Eric," said Skuggs.

"Just play. Shift starts in five minutes."

Skuggs started into *I'm Just a Girl Who Can't Say No*.

Two weeks later Ingles was back in her lab and Todd was sat, crying, in front of a large table populated by twelve board members. These were the same people who had hired him. The same people who had fully backed him at every juncture and turn. They had just offered him his old job and the emotion was too much. He sobbed heavily into a large linen handkerchief.

"You are the same man I hired. The students love you," said the man sitting opposite Todd: the chairman of governors. He placed his hand on a stack of papers. "And Mr. McNabb has written quite the most glowing recommendation I have ever seen. We have statements from media figures, businessmen… I don't quite know how you did it, but I'm happy that you did. Welcome back."

Todd almost screamed into his handkerchief. The tears he had denied bereavement joined the joy in a gushing torrent of thanks.

When it appeared Todd had calmed enough to communicate, the chairman picked up a small bag that had been lying on the table beside the pleadings of students and lecturers and friends. He handed it to Todd.

"One condition. Only one. But it must be observed."

# The Samplist

Todd looked down at his shoes, his dress; he picked up his handbag and knew it was too good to be true. He gathered himself without looking at the chairman and he cleared his throat to thank them and decline their offer.

Before he had formed the words the chairman spoke again. "Please. The beard. You have to lose the beard."

He was holding a shaving kit.

"In there now," he pointed at a door that led to a bathroom. "You look ridiculous in that beard."

Todd went into the bathroom and shaved off his beard. When he came out he was principal of the Academy again.

Betty tore open the garden shed doors the way she had done every day at midday for the last two weeks.

"It's not happening. Never. Not in a thousand lifetimes. Not if I live to be a hundred years old and I suffer brain damage and you're the only man left alive. Here... take this." She handed him a plate of mince and tatties. He grabbed it greedily. She slammed the door. He wolfed down half of the food as if he were starving, then he stopped eating and said, "Call me Baby?"

Music performed by the characters in this novel can be down-
loaded from:

www.ronak-publishing.com